DEAD
(((AIR)))

DEAD
«AIR»

A Jessie Drake Mystery

ROCHELLE KRICH

AVON

TWILIGHT

This is a work of fiction. Names, characters, places and incidents either are the product of the author's imagination or are used fictitiously. Any resemblance to actual events, locales, organizations, or persons, living or dead, is entirely coincidental and beyond the intent of either the author or the publisher.

AVON BOOKS, INC.
An Imprint of HarperCollins*Publishers*
10 East 53rd Street
New York, New York 10022-5299

Library of Congress Cataloging in Publication Data:
Krich, Rochelle Majer.
Dead air : a Jessie Drake mystery / Rochelle Krich.—1st ed.
p. cm.
1. Drake, Jessie (Fictitious character)—Fiction. 2. Policewomen—California—Los Angeles—Fiction. 3. Los Angeles (Calif.)—Fiction. I. Title.
PS3561.R477 D42 2000
813'.54—dc21   99-059575

First Avon Twilight Printing: March 2000

AVON TWILIGHT TRADEMARK REG. U.S. PAT. OFF. AND IN OTHER COUNTRIES, MARCA REGISTRADA, HECHO EN U.S.A.

Printed in the U.S.A.

QPM   10   9   8   7   6   5   4   3   2

www.harpercollins.com

For our new arrivals:
our granddaughter, Gabriella
and our grandsons, Joshua Isaac and Michael Evan.
You brighten our days.

ACKNOWLEDGMENTS

My warm thanks to those who generously provided me with the background information that enriched this novel: Dr. Shirley Lebovics and Dr. Sara Teichman, for helping me navigate the fascinating, uneven terrain of the human mind; Dr. Gerald Whitman, for sharing his medical expertise; Los Angeles District Attorney Scott Gordon, Stalking and Threat Assessment Team, for several excellent ideas and some sobering facts about domestic violence; Rabbi Yitzchok Adlerstein, for guiding Jessie Drake on her quest for spirituality; and Marion Peterson, for illuminating Jessie's journey. Special thanks to Dennis Praeger, for graciously allowing me to view the behind-the-scenes workings of talk radio, and for his daily weekday dose of intelligent and stimulating on-air conversation.

Thanks, too, to my agent, Sandra Dijkstra, and my editor, Jennifer Sawyer Fisher, for their invaluable support and enthusiasm.

I'm indebted to Detective Paul Bishop, West L.A., for his friendship, advice, and invaluable help in mentoring Jessie Drake and teaching her how "to protect and serve" along with L.A.'s finest. Paul has helped Jessie think like a detective and has saved her from making numerous embarrassing mistakes. Any errors in police procedure are mine; the credit for what is right belongs to Paul.

To my daughter Sabina, whose in-progress reading of my work energizes me and keeps me on my toes; and to my daughter Chani, whose Saturday-morning suggestion was truly inspirational—hugs and kisses.

Finally, my boundless gratitude to my friends and family—my husband, Hershie; our children and their spouses; our grandchildren. You ground me and nurture me and make me feel blessed.

DEAD ((·AIR·))

Someone was watching her again.

Renee Altman was in a Century City mall store, fingering the rim of a champagne goblet, when she had the familiar prickly sensation. Lifting the goblet, she turned and pretended to examine the facets so that she could see who was staring at her.

No one. Just nerves.

At the register she waited while the clerk, who seemed to take forever, rang up her purchase. Then she made her way out of the store and strode in the crisp, late morning air toward the escalator. The salty smell of freshly popped corn wafted toward her from a snack cart up ahead, and she was tempted to stop for a bag when she felt eyes on her again.

Fear fluttered in her stomach, and now she was angry. She whirled around—what the *hell* did he . . . ?—and almost stepped on a small leashed dog leading a heavyset, middle-aged couple whose eyes widened with alarm.

The dog yelped. The man and woman scowled at Renee.

Her face was hot with embarrassment. "I'm *so* sorry." Forcing herself to smile, she searched out of the corners of her eyes but saw no one looking at her. Either she'd imagined the whole thing, or whoever was following her had ducked into a shop or been swallowed by the throng of mall visitors strolling past her, mostly in pairs: talking, laughing, swinging their shopping bags with a carefree motion that filled her with envy.

The woman had stopped scowling. She cocked her head and was squinting at Renee.

"You ought to be more careful," the man grumbled. "You could have—"

"You're Dr. *Renee!*" the woman squealed. Beaming, she

poked her companion's arm with a long, sculpted red fingernail that could have drawn blood. "George, this is *Dr. Renee Altman!*" Back to Renee: "I almost didn't recognize you—your hair is blonder than it looks in pictures. You're prettier, too, and younger," she continued without taking a breath. "I listen to your show *every* day. It's just *won*derful. I can't believe . . ."

On and on and on until Renee thought she would scream. Still scanning the crowd, she only half listened as the woman piled compliment upon compliment— ". . . so insightful . . . really change a person's whole life . . . moral courage so lacking these days."

She noticed that the woman had stopped talking and was waiting for a response. "That's very nice of you to say," Renee murmured, hoping her comment would satisfy, and saw the woman's full face dimple with pleasure.

"Well, it's all *true!* I talk about you all the time. Don't I, George?"

"Uh-huh," from George, who seemed unimpressed with Renee's celebrity. So did the dog. He was tugging on his beaded leash and yipping, his tail furiously fanning the air.

"My friends are going to *die* when I tell them I met you!" The woman dug into a large, ugly, black-and-orange patent tote and fished out a notepad and squiggly shaped pen. "Would it be a terrible imposition . . . ?" She smiled shyly.

"I'd be happy to," Renee said, relieved that the woman hadn't asked for advice. *I have a problem, Dr. Renee . . .*

"Make it 'To Irma,' " the woman instructed, shy no more. She thrust pen and pad at Renee. "That's with an *i*, not like Bombeck. It's so sad she died. Now, *she* was bright, *and* funny . . ."

It was a quarter to twelve when Renee arrived at KMST's studio on Sunset, east of Cahuenga. She inserted her ID card into a slot above a call box, silently urging the electronic black iron gate to slide open faster. Moments later, her white Lexus parked on the lot, she hurried toward the two-story gray stucco building, where she inserted her card into another slot and gained entry into the lobby.

She exchanged quick hellos with Roland, the Don-Knotts-skinny guard sitting behind the tall reception module. He nodded when she showed him her ID, a formality she'd sometimes found silly but now welcomed, and though she knew the security was ample, she wished Roland were taller and looked more formidable.

In the recording booth Ted Harkham, who hosted the nine-A.M-to-noon segment, had stretched out his shoeless feet, ankles crossed, on the hexagonal wood-tone table and was eating a tuna sandwich while the station ran a pretaped fifteen-minute soft news capsule. Harkham was short and overweight and practically bald, but this was radio, not television, and he had a great voice and a quick wit, and energy that crackled through the airwaves.

He greeted her arrival with an exaggerated sigh. "And here I was hoping I'd finally get to cover for you. I just lost a dollar to Alicia—she said you'd make it on time." Shoving the rest of the sandwich into his mouth, he swung his stocky legs off the table and stood, brushing crumbs off his shirt and slacks.

She smiled with a warmth she didn't feel. "Thanks anyway. Sorry about the dollar." By Ted's standards she was early. He generally breezed into the recording booth at five to nine—once in a while, a minute or so after—but she liked to arrive at least forty minutes before her show.

"I'll corrupt you yet." He winked and cleared the table, sweeping newspapers and index cards into an overstuffed worn brown briefcase, then slipped his feet into his loafers and picked up a Nestlé chocolate bar.

"See you tomorrow," she said, wishing him gone.

"Talk the talk." Grabbing the briefcase in one hand, he saluted her with the chocolate bar and left.

The room still smelled of tuna. She sat down and was relaxing against the faint indentations Ted had molded into the chair when the door opened and Alicia, the thirty-two-year-old producer who screened the show's callers, entered. She was tall and large-framed and sometimes complained about her size, but Renee thought she moved with a catlike grace. Her eyes were catlike, too, amber agates in almond-shaped seas of white made whiter by the deep mahogany of her skin. Wavy dark brown hair, brushed into a sleek knot, rippled against her skull.

"Cutting it close," Alicia remarked, sounding relieved and surprised. Her eyes flicked over the shopping bag at the side of Renee's desk.

"Don't complain. I heard you made a buck." Renee flashed a quick smile. "I stopped in Century City and lost track of time. Sorry I worried you."

"I *was* worried. I called your house, but Blanca said you left over an hour and a half ago. Pollin's been asking, where are you."

She placed a hand on a shapely hip. "Why didn't you use your car phone, girl?"

She was speaking in the soft South-Central L.A. cadence she sometimes used, playfully, with Renee, the cadence she'd worked hard to erase. Her professional voice was low and throaty ("I could've been a top 900 phone girl," she often said, laughing), and perfectly "white." She'd told Renee when they first met that she loved the stares of people trying to pretend they weren't shocked to see she was black.

"I wasn't thinking. I *should* have called," Renee said, piqued by the screener's persistence. "How's Trey?" she asked, referring to Alicia's seven-year-old son.

"Croup's better, so I got to sleep some last night, but not enough." She yawned as if to prove her point. "I hope Brynn and Tyler don't get it."

Renee nodded. "Tell Pollin I'm here?"

"I already did." She placed a sheaf of papers on Renee's desk.

Newspaper clippings and faxes from Renee's listeners. Renee liked to scan them every day for interesting material or comments to share with her radio audience, but with eight minutes left until air time, she'd be able to skim only one or two. On top of the faxes was a printout with last quarter's Arbitron ratings.

"Point seven percent?" Frowning, Renee kicked off her flats and flexed her toes.

"It'll pick up," Alicia said too brightly. "There's a piece from the *Sun-Sentinel* on deadbeat dads you may want to use."

Ordinarily, they would have talked about this—Alicia's ex-husband had left her stranded two years ago with three young children and no support. But today Renee nodded absent-mindedly.

Point seven percent share of the Los Angeles audience. With ninety-nine radio stations in the greater L.A. area vying for listeners, two percent was considered good. Anything less than one percent was worrisome, even for a small station like KMST. Point seven percent wasn't nearly enough to satisfy the program director, who had called Renee in three months ago to discuss her slipping ratings.

"You have to be a little tougher," Max Pollin had advised, again, in a tone just short of a warning. "Use a little more humor. And a little more warmth when you greet the callers."

Be tough. Be funny. Be warm. What he hadn't repeated, but had clearly meant, was: Be like KFI's Dr. Laura Schlessinger, the number one talk show host who was besting Rush Limbaugh.

Well, she wasn't Dr. Laura. She'd never promised she *would* be. She'd argued strongly six months ago against being switched from the nine-to-twelve slot to the twelve-to-three that Dr. Laura dominated. (Had Ted engineered that? she wondered again.) Argued for more than one reason. Now the ratings were down, and it didn't matter what she'd said. The buck stopped with her.

She crumpled the printout and tossed it into the trash can at her feet. Alicia was looking at her thoughtfully.

"Something else?" Renee asked more brusquely than she'd intended.

"You okay? Aside from the ratings, I mean."

"I'm *fine*." She smiled but knew she wasn't fooling Alicia, who had been her producer ever since Renee had started at the station three years ago, and was expert at culling the interesting callers from the seriously disturbed and the boring and the ones who wanted to rant at Renee.

Alicia returned to the screener's booth. Renee put on her headset. From the shopping bag, she pulled out a small pewter frame (buying it had seemed so important this morning) and slipped in the photo of her blond six-year-old daughter, Molly. Her chest tightened as she gazed at the smiling face. She positioned the frame on her desk, then started to skim the first article but found it hard to concentrate. She glanced again at the photo, then sat, staring into space.

"Two minutes, Renee." Alicia waved through the Plexiglas window.

Renee waved back, startled to learn that five minutes had slipped by. Focus, she told herself sharply. She thumbed quickly through the papers and pulled a promising story, highlighting in yellow the sections she liked.

"Thirty seconds, Renee," the sound engineer's voice squawked through the headset.

"I'm ready."

Looking up, she saw Max Pollin standing behind Alicia. Their eyes made contact; the program director smiled and gave Renee a thumbs up. Jerk, she thought, returning the gesture.

"Twenty seconds."

Pollin disappeared from view.

"Intro music. Ten . . . eight, seven. . . . And you're on."

Renee squared her shoulders. "*Welcome* to *Talking with Dr. Renee.* This is KMST, AM 612. I'm Dr. Renee Altman, and I'll be here with you today, and every weekday, from twelve to three. The toll-free number is 1-800 . . ."

She spoke about teenage pregnancies, read aloud from an article on the subject that had appeared in the *New Yorker*. Then she scanned the small computer screen in front of her which displayed the data Alicia had entered: name, age, and location of the caller; the line the caller was on (there were six lines altogether); a brief description of the nature of the call.

Line Three was Cynthia from Westminster, forty-nine, daughter sleeping with a fiancé. A good call to start the day.

"*Cynthia,* welcome to the show." Renee pressed line three. Lots of warmth there, if Pollin was listening.

"Dr. Renee?" The voice was thin, quavering. "I can't believe I'm really *talking* to you. I listen to your show all the time."

A typical caller's reaction—after three years, Renee still found it gratifying. "What's on your mind, Cynthia?" she asked cheerfully.

"Sorry. I'm a little nervous." The woman laughed with embarrassment. "Our daughter and her fiancé are planning to spend Thanksgiving weekend with us, and she wants him to stay with her in her room. My husband and I aren't comfortable with that."

"*Du-u-u-h.* Cynthia, if you're a regular listener, you *know* I don't approve of unmarried sex. So for me this is a no-brainer. As for your position—it's your house, your rules."

"That's what my husband says. The thing is, our daughter moved out of state two years ago because we weren't getting along, and this is the first time she's coming home. And she's stayed with her fiancé at his parents', so it's kind of hard for me to argue this. They *are* engaged."

"And tomorrow they could get *un*engaged. Don't let his parents' weakness pressure you, Cynthia, and don't sacrifice your principles to fix a relationship with your daughter. It won't work."

"She says she won't come home unless they can stay together in her room, Dr. Renee. She's very stubborn."

"And you want to *encourage* that behavior? It's emotional blackmail, Cynthia. Tell your baby girl you love her, you'll be disappointed if she won't come, and you hope she'll reconsider so you can all share a wonderful weekend. But don't sigh and don't cry, Cynthia. And don't let her smell your fear."

The woman sighed. "You're probably right. It's just hard to say no, 'cause we really want to have a relationship with her. So you don't think we should compromise at all?"

"Cynthia, I've said *ten times* what I think. Am I talking to myself?" How's that for tough? she thought, wondering again if Pollin was listening. "So figure out what *you* want, Cynthia," she said in a kinder voice, "and then you'll know what to tell your daughter. Good luck."

Renee scanned the computer screen and pressed another line.

Gerald, forty-two, calling from his cell phone about a spoiled son. *"Hi,* Gerald. Welcome to the program. . . ."

Three hours later she was drained of energy and advice. After signing off, she phoned home and talked with Molly, whom the housekeeper had picked up from school. She debated going to Pollin's office to discuss today's show, which she thought had gone extremely well.

Better not. No point showing him she was anxious.

She collected the faxes that had come in during the show, said her good-byes, and left the building, her temples throbbing from another tension headache. Inside her car, she was grateful for the quiet and the delicious solitude and the tactile comfort of the butter-soft tan leather that sighed under her. She started the engine, then switched on the radio to drown out her thoughts.

Traffic was light, and she was home in half an hour. Unlocking the door, she heard Molly's "Mommy!" before she saw the six year old bound into the hallway, her blond curls flying.

The housekeeper was right behind her, padding quietly across the marble floor, a feather duster in her hand.

"Hey, sweetheart." Renee swooped Molly up and hugged her tightly. She smiled at the housekeeper. "Hi, Blanca. Everything's okay?"

"Muy bien, Mrs. Renee. Molly is excited for you to come home," the short, heavyset woman said in a lilting Hispanic accent. "Every minute she is running to the door to see if you are here. Is that not right, *chiquita?"* A broad smile lit her round, freckled face and revealed a gap between her small, uneven top front teeth.

"Are you happy to see Mommy?" Renee nuzzled Molly's neck, which was slightly sour with perspiration. "How was school?"

"You got a present! Come see!" The little girl squirmed in Renee's arms, all elbows and knees.

Renee put her down and followed her into the kitchen. An oblong box wrapped in glossy white paper and topped with a white bow was sitting on the granite ledge that separated the kitchen from the breakfast room.

"Open it, Mommy!"

No outer wrapping, so someone must have dropped it off. She'd ask Blanca.

"Who is it *from,* Mommy?"

"Let's find out." Molly's excitement was infectious. Grinning at her daughter, Renee tore at the wrapping, exposing a plain white box. Inside were two crystal goblets, one with a snapped stem . . .

"It's broken, Mommy!"

. . . goblets identical to the one she'd been admiring this morning. Nestled in the bowl of the damaged goblet was a small white card.

HOPE YOU'RE HAPPY, DR. RENEE . . .

2

Saturday morning was gloomy and overcast, with the false promise of rain. False because, from Detective Jessie Drake's experience, it rarely rained in mid-September in L.A.

She'd planned on attending Sabbath services—Ezra, her Judaic studies teacher, had been gently nudging her for some time to try the beginners-friendly Orthodox synagogue a mile from her house. She pulled a conservative two-piece navy outfit from her closet, then put it back, suddenly nervous about taking the step, even though it didn't mean commitment. Maybe next week.

She was bored, restless, a little lonely, too. A good day to clean her house, if not her soul, she decided as she skimmed the *Times* and clipped coupons she'd probably never use and wondered how her ex-husband, whom she was dating again, was enjoying his visit with his parents in Phoenix.

She put on her cleaning outfit—old frayed shorts and a faded T-shirt—and with Celine Dion crooning "Power of Love" in the background, she sang along as she dusted and vacuumed. She was loading the washing machine when she heard the doorbell.

In the front entry she peered through the privacy window and tried not to stare as she opened the door.

"What a nice surprise, Renee." She kept her tone casual, but it was an effort. What do you say to a former close friend you haven't seen in—what was it? A year and a half? Two?

"I hope this isn't a bad time," Renee said. "I'm not interrupting anything?"

"Just laundry. I should thank you." Jessie smiled, but Renee still looked uncomfortable. "Come on in," she said warmly, moving aside to let Renee enter.

She looked as if she'd stepped out of *Town & Country*. Wrinkle-free gray linen slacks, a short-sleeved, crisply ironed white cotton blouse, pewter-colored flats. Diamond studs sparkled discreetly in her ears, and she had on the perfect shade of lipstick and blusher for a weekend morning.

Just like me, Jessie thought, amused by her own appearance, which would have given her mother and sister heart palpitations. Worn clothes, barefoot, no makeup, her chestnut-brown hair pulled into a messy topknot with a scrunchy. Amused and, okay, a little self-conscious, because it had been so long since she and Renee had seen each other. Renee, she'd noticed, had eyed her, too.

"I should have called first," Renee said.

"Don't be silly. I'm glad you're here."

She led the way through the empty living and dining rooms and down a hall to the den, wondering why Renee was so nervous. Her slate-gray eyes, more intense than usual against her chin-length, layered honey-blond hair, gave her away. That and her fingers. The nails were bitten, the pink-beige lacquer chipped, and she was fidgeting with the clasp of her Luis Vuitton purse, opening and shutting it.

Probably just awkwardness, Jessie decided; she felt the same. *"Speech after long silence . . ."* She lowered the volume on the CD player. "Do you want something to drink? Water, soda? I can make fresh lemonade." Renee's favorite.

"No, thanks." She looked around, taking in the room. "You've redone this. I seem to remember a tan leather couch."

"Gary took it when he moved out," Jessie said casually, though the event had been anything but. "I bought this black one to replace it." She felt a twinge of satisfaction when Renee's face colored with embarrassment.

Renee avoided Jessie's eyes. "That must have been a rough time. I'm sorry I wasn't there for you, Jessie, that I didn't call. I was . . ." Her voice trailed off.

Where? Latent hurt prickled within Jessie; she pushed it away. No point now. "It was rough, but I'm okay. Gary and I are actually friends." She sat down and tried to remember who had made the last phone call, she or Renee. Not that it mattered.

"Are you?" Renee raised a brow and was silent a moment, glancing around the room once more, as if searching for something. "Barry and I are divorcing," she said, turning back to Jessie. "I can't imagine we'll *ever* be friends."

Jessie found herself staring again. "I'm so sorry, Renee. I had no idea." Two years ago she would have hugged her friend, and they would have cried together. Now she felt immobilized by the passage of so much time apart, unsure whether Renee would welcome an embrace or find it artificial.

"No one knows, not even my parents," Renee said. "I don't want to upset them."

Jessie nodded, unsure what to say. Not, "The two of you seemed so happy," which they had—gloriously, wrapped-up-in-each-other happy—because it was banal and because "seemed" meant nothing. She and Gary had "seemed" happy, too. She'd heard that from her parents, and his, from her sister. Part lament, part accusation. *Why didn't you tell us . . . ?*

And the truth was, her impression of Renee and Barry as a couple was a collage of years-old events. Their perfect May wedding, ten years ago, in the lush, rose- and lilac-filled garden of Renee's parents' La Jolla home. Evenings playing Boggle or Pictionary in Renee and Barry's first apartment, short on space but filled with laughter and way too much junk food. The arrival of their daughter, Molly.

By then Jessie and Gary had begun dating seriously, and the two couples had gone out together several times. Wouldn't it be grand? Jessie had thought. But there had been no chemistry between the men (strange, since they were both writers), and after a few more attempts, the relationship had returned by tacit mutual assent to what it had been: Jessie and Renee. And then that had ended.

She wondered if Renee had come to commiserate, one divorcée to another, to draw on old friendship. Whatever the reason, Jessie realized she'd missed her.

"I know what you're going through, Renee. If there's anything I can do—" She stopped and shook her head. "God, listen to me. Two platitudes for the price of one."

A half smile flitted across Renee's mouth. "It means a lot to me that you care, Jess." She sat down and arranged her face into a sober expression. "This may sound crazy, but I think someone's stalking me."

So this was business. Jessie felt a flicker of disappointment that immediately gave way to concern. "Define what you mean by 'stalking.' "

"Watching me, following me." Renee waved her hand impatiently. "Yesterday he left two crystal goblets at my house, just like one I was looking at in a Century City mall store. One of the stems was snapped off."

"You're a celebrity, Renee. This can't be your first fan gift."

"It's the first *anonymous* one, the first delivered to my home.

That scares the hell out of me, that he knows where I live." She shuddered and gripped her elbows. "I know this goes with the territory. Letterman had a woman stalking him for years. Madonna was stalked, Spielberg. I never thought it would happen to me."

"Who delivered the goblets?"

"My housekeeper, Blanca, found the package pushed under the outer gate when she brought Molly home from school."

"What about your salesman? Maybe he's a big fan."

Renee shook her head. "He had no idea who I was." Unclasping her purse, she took a clear plastic bag containing a small card and handed it to Jessie. "This came with the goblets. I didn't touch it—I used tweezers to put it in the bag."

"Good." But not good enough. Plastic gathered moisture, which could destroy fingerprints, if there were any. Too late now. " 'Hope you're happy, Dr. Renee,' " Jessie read aloud through the plastic, then looked up. "Does that mean anything to you?"

"Nothing." Both hands were back on the purse.

"Could be he's hoping you're happy with the goblets because he saw you looking at them, or hoping you're happy in general. It doesn't sound necessarily threatening." Jessie placed the note on the coffee table.

Renee frowned. "And the fact that one of the goblets was broken? Maybe he's being sarcastic, Jessie."

"Maybe." In which case the note, and the intent, were nasty. "But only if he broke it on purpose. He could've dropped the box, Renee. For that matter, your housekeeper could have, or Molly."

"I asked both of them. They said they didn't do it."

"Maybe whoever did it is afraid to tell you."

She remembered vividly the electric tension when a trembling housekeeper (there had been so many) would admit to breaking one of her mother's beautiful things. *I understand,* Frances would say with a terrifying politeness that made Jessie and her sister, Helen, quake. Not for the housekeeper—at worst, she'd be fired— but for themselves, because they would certainly suffer their mother's fury. And when Jessie or Helen *did* break something . . .

"Let's say he *didn't* break it on purpose." Renee's tone was grudging. "If he's a fan, why didn't he approach me in the store? Or sign the card?"

"Shy, maybe?" She could see that Renee wasn't satisfied with that answer. "You keep referring to him as 'he.' You're sure it's a male?"

"How the hell can I be *sure* when I've never *seen* him?" Renee took a deep breath, blew it out, ran a hand through the expertly cut layers of hair. "Sorry. I'm so damn tense." Another expelled breath. "I *think* it's a male. But it's just a feeling."

"You may be right, then. That's your job, feelings," Jessie said lightly.

No response from Renee, who was swinging her leg like a metronome gone wild. It was odd and disconcerting, seeing her agitated. Renee was *always* in control. That was what had drawn Jessie to her, that and the haven she'd provided from the turbulence of Jessie's own fractured home life.

"Has he communicated in any other way, Renee? Phone calls? Letters?"

"I've had several phone hang-ups recently at the house. And a number of unsigned notes came to the station. That's besides the signed ones—I get hundreds of letters and faxes a week."

Her smile was modest, her tone aiming for matter-of-fact, but Jessie detected keen pleasure in the telling. "I'm sure," she murmured, a little put off. "Do you have the unsigned ones?"

Renee shook her head. "I thought they were fan letters, if you can call them that. Not everyone loves the advice I give. Denial." She shrugged. "But none of them were threatening."

"What did they say?"

Renee thought for a moment. " 'Stop meddling in people's lives.' That came about a week ago. One referred to God, but I don't remember the message. Another one called me an unflattering name. They either love me or they hate me. I'm sure that doesn't surprise you." There was challenge in her tone and the intent way she was watching Jessie.

Jessie ignored it. "Were there references to a specific caller or issue in either note?"

"No. Sorry." Her leg was swinging madly again.

"What about the phone calls, Renee? Was there heavy breathing? Any noises you could identify?"

"Just silence, then a hang-up. I pressed star 69 each time, to dial the number where the call originated. No one answered."

Maybe the call had originated from a phone booth. Jessie drummed her fingers on the sofa arm. "You said someone's been watching you. How do you know?"

"A week ago on Wednesday, driving home from dinner with friends, I was *positive* a car was following me. It disappeared before I could get a license number. The next Sunday Molly and I were at the park, and I had the *strongest* feeling someone was watching me. It happened again yesterday at the mall. *Twice.*"

Hardly conclusive. "But you couldn't tell who was watching you?" Jessie kept her voice noncommittal.

"No. So I thought it was nerves. Then yesterday the goblets came. . . ."

Which didn't prove anything, either. "What about Barry? Maybe he's been following you because he's upset about the divorce and wants to know if you're involved with someone else."

"He knows I'm not." Renee had stiffened at the mention of his name. "Barry was with Molly and me at the park, but not at dinner that other night. The divorce is *his* decision, by the way." Chin thrust up in proud indifference.

"I'm sorry," Jessie said again.

"Don't be. We've been having problems for some time, but for Molly's sake, I wanted to stay together. Barry's more interested in wallowing in self-pity. My life is crap, though," she said with wry cheeriness. "No husband, no money, and in a few weeks, with my ratings, probably no show." Her smile was brittle, like meringue about to crumble. "Remember you said I'm bitchy to my callers sometimes?"

Jessie sighed. "Renee—"

"You'll be proud of me. The station honchos think my ratings are low 'cause I'm not bitchy enough." Renee shrugged. "I guess I can go back to private practice. I know you thought I sold out when I decided to do radio." The challenge was back in her voice.

"I didn't think you sold out." Not quite the truth. "I was just surprised. You always told me you loved your practice."

"I *did* love it. And I *love* doing the show—communicating with so many people, helping them, even if you don't think so."

"In all of three minutes per." The words slipped out, and she wasn't sorry. She was annoyed by Renee's baiting.

Renee smiled tightly. "Yes, in three minutes. Sometimes longer. I never claimed I was doing therapy, Jessie. Callers with serious emotional problems don't get on. My screener refers them to therapists. But I get people to face their problems, make moral choices."

"Choices à la Dr. Renee." Now wasn't the time, she told herself, and there was no point. They'd had this conversation before, one time too many. . . .

"I call them as I see them, Jessie. That's what they pay me for," she said coolly. Then she laughed. "Funny, isn't it? Here I am, a paid dispenser of advice, and my life is all screwed up. Did I mention I may lose the house?"

She sounded so forlorn. Jessie's irritation dissolved, replaced by fresh sympathy and the uncomfortable feeling that she was being less than charitable. "What happened?"

"Apparently Barry hasn't been doing a good job of managing

14

our money. He lost most of my earnings, plus what we got from refinancing the house a year ago. *His* idea. And he has the *nerve* to ask for alimony and child support!"

"He wants custody?" Jessie didn't know why she was surprised. More and more fathers wanted to raise their kids.

"Full." Renee spat the word. "He's claiming since he writes at home, and I work five days a week and have out-of-state speaking engagements, Molly will be better off with him. Which isn't true! I *always* make Molly my priority."

Career versus family. One of the issues she and Renee had debated, one that she and Gary had constantly argued about, that had contributed to their divorce. They still had no clear answer. . . .

"My lawyer warned me it's going to be tough," Renee continued. "And my afternoon slot isn't helping. That was the program director's idea—he wants me to draw Dr. Laura's audience." She rolled her eyes. "I used to be home in time to pick Molly up from school if Barry couldn't. Now I can't. He's using that against me, of course."

"Maybe you could get back your original slot. You said the new ratings aren't great, anyway."

"I asked. They said no." Renee chipped at the lacquer on her nail. "Barry's doing this to punish me, you know. My career's a success, his writing's going nowhere." She sat up straighter. "Anyway. You're a detective. You can find out who's stalking me."

Jessie shook her head lightly. "First of all, I'm a homicide detective. This isn't my domain, Renee. And to be honest, what you've described isn't considered 'stalking.' "

Renee stared, openmouthed. "You don't think this is serious," she said dully.

Jessie squeezed Renee's hand. "Of *course* I do. I don't blame you for being anxious. I would be, too. But stalking is long-term, abnormal behavior. A guy could leave flowers on your doorstep every day and it wouldn't be considered stalking. Unless you'd told him not to, and obtained a restraining order, and he violated it. *Then* it's stalking."

"That's ridiculous!" Anger blotched her cheeks. "How can I get a restraining order against someone I can't identify?"

"I know you're frustrated, Renee. But you're not even sure someone *is* watching you or following you," she said gently. "The phone hang-ups are interesting, but not conclusive. Neither are the notes—as you said, you're used to getting fan mail."

"This isn't all in my head, Jessie! What about the goblets? You can't ignore that."

"As I said, leaving the goblets isn't considered stalking. And it *could* be an innocuous gift from a fan."

"It's *not*." Renee chewed on her lip. "You can check the card for fingerprints and find out who sent it. You can check the goblets, too. I didn't touch them."

"There are probably countless prints on them, aside from yours. You touched the goblets in the store, right? There could be prints from the person who bought them, prints from other customers, sales staff. And prints are helpful only if we can match them against those of a person whose prints are on file. Someone who's had a prior arrest."

"Maybe this guy *has* a prior arrest." She leaned toward Jessie. "It's worth a *try*, isn't it?"

"Definitely. But I can't have SID raise prints, and I can't run them, unless they're connected with an official investigation I'm working."

"*Un*officially, then."

Jessie sighed. "I can't, Renee. I wish I could."

"There are ways," Renee insisted impatiently. "You could do it without anyone finding out. I'm sure it happens."

"Maybe on TV or in the movies." Jessie shook her head. "To have the technician raise prints, I'd have to give him a case number. To log on to FIN—that's the Fingerprint Identification Network—I'd have to give my serial number and password. And if someone found out—which is highly likely—I could be suspended, or fired." No good deed goes unpunished—her partner, Phil, said that all the time.

Renee didn't answer. Jessie tried to read her face—disappointment, anger. "You could hire a private security firm," she suggested. "They're expensive, but they often get results."

Renee's laugh was hollow. "What would I pay them with, Monopoly money? If my show gets canceled, I don't even know how I'll pay my attorney."

"What about asking your parents?"

She tightened her lips. "I can't ask them. They're on a retirement budget, and I don't want to alarm them."

Both women were silent.

"So that's it?" Renee shook her head. "I can't believe this. There's nothing you can do?"

"Start keeping a log of events. Write down dates, times, specifics. Phone calls, times when you think you're being followed or watched. Color and make of the car, the license plate number if you can get it."

Renee was nodding, her gray eyes somber.

"If you get a suspicious package, don't open it. Call me. And if you get any more anonymous notes, try not to handle them. Use a tweezers to slip them in a paper bag—not plastic."

"And then you'll help me?" Her tone was childlike in its plaintiveness.

"If you collect enough evidence, I'll take you downtown to a detective I know at the Threat Management Unit."

Renee's eyes widened. "Are you *crazy*? I can't go to the police! I can't let any of this get out!"

"TMU guys know how to be discreet. They have to—they often deal with high-profile celebrities."

"And if they're not?" Again she leaned closer. "If the media find out, my listeners will find out. I'll lose my credibility. Why would a person ask advice from someone who's obviously lost control of her own life?"

"I hear you. But if you're really in danger—"

"Losing the show isn't what scares me most, Jessie. What if Barry finds out someone's stalking me? He'll convince the judge that Molly isn't safe with me."

"He'd be right, Renee," Jessie said firmly. "Until you find out who's following you, Molly *should* stay with Barry."

"No! Molly is totally safe with me. My housekeeper, Blanca, watches her like a hawk. And the house is totally secure, especially now that the property is gated."

Jessie placed her hand on Renee's arm. "You're not thinking rationally. What would you tell a caller who faced this dilemma?"

Renee jerked her arm away. "If I let Molly stay with Barry now, I'll *never* get her back."

"This isn't about custody," Jessie began, but Renee was shaking her head.

"I can deal with my marriage being over. And I can get another job. But I *won't lose Molly.*" She emphasized each word. "I *won't.*" She paused and looked at Jessie intently. "You *have* to help me." More of a demand than a request.

You owe me. The words hovered in the air, unspoken.

"I'll see what I can do," Jessie finally said.

3

"We have two children we adore, Dr. Renee, a three-year-old boy and a five-year-old girl. My husband's a real estate broker. I'm an architect, but I gave up my job when our daughter was born so I could stay home with the kids."

"Good for you, Monica! Believe me, if more moms would stay home with their kids, we'd have fewer messed-up kids."

"Right." She sighed. "The thing is, Dr. Renee, the head of the firm I worked for called me and offered me my position back."

"And you said, 'Check with me in a few years, when my kids are in school full-time.' Right, Monica?"

"Actually, I agreed to think about it," the woman said quietly. "The hours would be flexible, and I'd be home by four."

"I don't know why you're calling me, Monica. You know how I feel about this."

"I know. I listen to you all the time. But I really miss my work, Dr. Renee, and now that the kids are older—"

"Excuse me? You call three and five older? They're barely out of the womb! Unless you're in dire financial need, I don't know how you could consider doing this."

"The extra money would help. We need a second car, and the house could use some fixing up, but—"

"Be thankful you have a house and a car. Lots of people do without the niceties of life so that they can provide the love and nurturing their kids need."

"It's not about money, Dr. Renee. I feel stifled sometimes, unfulfilled."

"Poor baby."

"I know that sounds selfish. But I honestly think I'd be a better mother if I felt more satisfied about myself."

"*What you're really telling me is that you're bored with being a mom.*"

"*No, I'm—*"

"*Yes, you are. The novelty's worn off. You probably breast-fed them and bonded with them and dressed them up in Baby Gap clothes. Now it's just a routine.*"

"*I* love *playing with them, Dr. Renee. I read to them all the time. But I want to do something for myself. Is that so wrong?*"

"*I hope you're going to tell me you'll be leaving your kids with a family member.*"

"*I don't have any family I can leave them with. I've been getting recommendations about nannies from friends.*"

"*So you plan to leave these darlings you told me you adore with a stranger while you're indulging your need for self-gratification?*"

"*I won't do it unless I'm positive they'll be fine. A lot of my friends work, Dr. Renee. Their kids are happy, well-adjusted.*"

"*How do you* know *that? Your friends are telling you that to make themselves feel less guilty. Do you want to be like them, Monica, or do you want to live up to the commitment you made when you decided to bring these kids into the world?*"

"*I didn't think I'd feel this way,*" she whispered. She sounded on the verge of tears.

"*Well, you should have thought about it, Monica. If you weren't sure you were signing up for the whole stint, you should have bought a Barbie and Ken and designed a house for them.*"

A car had followed Renee to the radio station Tuesday morning. At least, she thought so.

"I don't know the make," she told Jessie defensively when she phoned her at the West L.A. police station. "But it was a champagne color."

Like thousands of other cars in L.A. "Did you get the license plate number?" Jessie asked, not really hopeful.

"No. The car turned right before I had a chance."

"Okay." Yesterday, Renee had called to report that a *black* car had followed her home from the market. She hadn't been able to get that license plate number, either.

"You think I'm paranoid, don't you?" Renee sighed. "If not for the damn goblets, you'd think I was imagining all this. Did you find out who bought them?"

"I *told* you, Renee. It was a cash sale, and the guy who handled the transaction won't be back till Wednesday."

Saturday afternoon Jessie had met with the store manager, who had ascertained that only two of that particular goblet had been sold Friday between eleven A.M., when Renee had been in the store, and a little after one P.M., when her housekeeper had spotted the package inside the gate.

"So you'll talk to him tomorrow?" Renee asked.

Jessie reminded herself that the woman had a right to be impatient. "I plan to, after work. I'm doing this alone, Renee, on my spare time, and I haven't had much of that lately."

Not even lunch hours. She and her partner, Phil Okum, were investigating two homicides: the stabbing of the Iranian owner of an Oriental rug store on Beverly west of La Cienega, and the shooting of a wealthy Westwood woman in what appeared to be a follow-home burglary. They were putting in overtime, too, which Jessie didn't mind. It enhanced her paycheck significantly, and unlike Phil, she didn't have a household to run or come home to. Phil's wife, Maureen, was giving him a hard time about the late hours. So far Gary hadn't complained. Maybe he was afraid to. . . .

"I really appreciate this, Jessie. If I sound ungrateful or if I'm nagging, I apologize."

"Forget it. Let me know if you receive any more anonymous notes. And remember: Don't open any suspicious packages. Try not to go anywhere alone. Vary your route to work, et cetera." No response. "Renee?"

"I'm scared, Jessie," she whispered.

Jessie felt a rush of pity. "I know. But look, the goblets could be from a secret admirer."

"Like the guy who was in love with Rebecca Schaeffer?"

Not a comforting analogy. Schaeffer, a young actress, had been killed by an obsessive fan years ago when she opened the door to her apartment in a quiet section of L.A. "I don't think you should jump to that conclusion, Renee. But you're right to be cautious."

"You still have the gift card?"

"I put it in a safe place." In a paper bag in her bedroom desk drawer. Out of the corner of her eye, she saw Phil approaching. He was holding an apple, and she nodded approvingly, pleased that he was taking his diet seriously.

"You haven't told anyone about this, have you?" Renee asked, her voice sharp with anxiety.

"No, but I'd like to share this with my partner."

"Jessie—"

"Phil's totally circumspect. And he has good ideas. I'll phone you as soon as I learn something. Try not to worry." She hung up quickly before Renee could continue the conversation.

"Good ideas about what?" Phil asked, settling his large frame into his chair. "And where do you get off, calling me 'circumspect'?"

She smiled. "That was my friend Renee Altman. She thinks someone's stalking her, but she doesn't want to go to the police."

He raised a brow. "The radio talk show host, right? Maureen listens to her all the time. Her and Dr. Laura. After that, it's Oprah or Rosie, depending on who's the guest. I know not to call home between noon and four." He made a face.

"I wasn't into talk shows, but I *was* hooked on soaps. My mom raised us on *All My Children* and *General Hospital.* Helen and I weren't allowed to say a word until the credits rolled." In college, Jessie had cut classes to watch the shows with friends; when she was in the police academy, she'd taped them for later viewing. Helen, still a devoted fan, filled her in periodically.

"I can see how you'd get hooked." Phil nodded. "Six, seven years ago, when I was laid up for a month after I took a hit to my chest? I used to watch *General* and a couple of the others. You get caught up with the story line."

"You watched soaps?" She looked at him, surprised, then smiled mischievously. "I never would've guessed, Phil. I'll bet the guys don't have a clue."

"They don't. This gets out, I'll know who it's from," he warned with mock gruffness, but his face had reddened and he glanced quickly at Marty Simms and Ed Boyd, the two other homicide detectives, sitting ten feet away. "I didn't know you and Dr. Renee were friends. So what's she like?"

"Charming, pretty, smart. Always ready to help. She was two years ahead of me in high school, but took me under her wing." Jessie hesitated. "She helped me through some tough times."

"High school can be hell," Phil said with feeling, and Jessie didn't correct him. "I was the kid no one ever wanted on the team. I hope my boys have an easier time." He sighed. "So now Dr. Renee thinks she's being stalked, and she wants you to return the favor, huh? Why won't she go to the police?"

Jessie repeated what Renee had told her. "So she's afraid if the station finds out, she'll lose her show, and Barry will get custody. I promised I'd try to find out what's going on. If there *is* anything."

"You don't think someone's stalking her?" He frowned at the apple as if it were a foreign object, then took a bite.

Jessie shrugged. "She says people and cars are following her, but she has no proof. Angry notes and phone calls go with the territory if you're a celebrity. Renee said so herself. And the goblets could be a friendly gift."

Phil nodded. "Paranoid?"

Jessie considered. "We've been out of touch, and she's more high-strung than I remember." A little harder and more arrogant, too, she added silently. "Then again, she's upset about the divorce and the custody battle."

Her phone rang. She lifted the receiver, hoping the caller was a snitch she'd been trying to contact who might have information about the knifing of the rug shop owner.

"West L.A., Detective Drake."

"What do you say to dinner, a movie, and a night of passionate sex?"

Gary. She smiled. "And *you* are?"

"That's what happens when I go away for the weekend, huh? You forget I exist."

"You takes your chances."

"I missed you, Jess," he said softly.

Her stomach curled. "I missed you, too, Gary." She was blushing and swiveled away from Phil, who was fluttering his lashes at her and puckering his lips. "When did you get back?"

"Late last night, but this is the first chance I've had to call. I've been knee-deep in this domestic violence piece. Heavy stuff. Before I forget, my parents send their love and a box of mandelbrot my mom baked just for you. I ate half of them on the plane, but don't tell her."

She laughed. "So you had a nice long weekend?"

"Hot as hell, but what do you expect from Phoenix in September? And fattening. I swear, whoever invented the stereotype of the Jewish mother had Martha Drake in mind. What did *you* do? When you weren't pining for me, that is."

"Cleaned house, shopped, spent too much of my paycheck. I visited Hilda on Sunday," she said, referring to an elderly Jewish woman she'd befriended who resided in a board and care facility. "She sends regards. I think she has a crush on you."

"Better grab me while I'm available, Jess. So how did you like services at the synagogue?"

"I didn't end up going."

"Chickened out, huh?"

She heard a tinge of relief in his voice—or maybe that was her own insecurity. He'd been vocally supportive about her decision to try the services, but she wasn't sure how he really felt about her newborn interest in Orthodox Judaism and where it

would lead. It would obviously complicate their already complicated relationship.

"Basically, yeah," she said. "But if I'd gone, I would've missed
Renee Altman. She stopped by Saturday morning." I am *so* good
at rationalizing, she thought.

"Renee, huh? It's been a long time since you've seen her,
hasn't it? So was it weird?"

"A little awkward at first. But then it was fine."

"So what'd you talk about?"

"Stuff." She liked to think she was a woman of her word—
at least she'd picked up *one* noble trait from her mother, who
was difficult in so many ways.

"Girl talk?"

"Mostly." She debated, then said, "She and Barry are getting
a divorce." That much she could reveal.

"No kidding." Gary was silent a moment. "What happened?"

"She's not sure herself."

"So that's why she came over? To tell you?" He sounded
skeptical.

"More or less." She felt almost disloyal not telling him (unlike
in the past, he'd been keeping her confidences lately) and was
glad he couldn't see her face. "About tonight, Gary, I won't be
home until late. I'm meeting Brenda for a late dinner after my
Hebrew class. I haven't seen her in ages." Brenda Royes was a
detective who had gone to the academy with Jessie.

"I'm willing to settle for the passionate sex. Or any sex."

He laughed good-naturedly, but she knew he was frustrated
about the nonintimate nature of their relationship—her decision.
She was frustrated, too. Maybe she'd ask Dr. Renee . . .

"Tomorrow night?" she suggested. "Dinner and a movie and
meaningful looks."

"I have a poker game. I'd bow out, but I was the big winner
last week, and the guys'll kill me. Especially Phil. He lost a
bundle."

They agreed he'd pick her up on Thursday at seven. She said
good-bye and hung up the phone, knowing that Phil, six plus
with a burly physique and a glower that would make the most
macho suspect quake, was basically a romantic softy and was
probably grinning at her, logging the phone call as another hopeful step toward the day she and Gary remarried.

Phil had always liked Gary, had been saddened by the divorce,
delighted when Jessie and Gary had started dating again. Sometimes she felt the heavy burden of not wanting to disappoint him.
And her sister, and lately even her mother, who had envisioned

her daughter marrying a doctor or lawyer but had been charmed by Gary.

Jessie looked at her partner. The smile was there, but he didn't say a word. That was one of the things she liked best about him, aside from the fact that he was smart as hell and treated her as an equal. He was interested when she wanted him to be, offered a hefty shoulder to cry on, which she'd used once or twice. But he never pried, never pushed.

"So did you come up with any good ideas about Renee's stalker?" she asked.

"Just the obvious one. *Cherchez le* spouse." He took a last look at the apple core and tossed it into the trash can. "I figure you came up with the same thing. The husband's jealous, so he follows her around. Wouldn't be the first guy to do it."

"She says no. The divorce was his idea."

"So maybe he's angry and trying to spook her for the hell of it. Or—" He stopped. "Or, if he rattles her enough so she goes to the police, the fact that she's being stalked will get out, and he can convince the judge the kid's better off with him."

Qui bono. Jessie nodded. "That's what I was thinking."

"Clever. But nasty. You'd have to be a mean bastard to do that." Phil tugged gently at his mustache. "What's he like?"

"He never struck me as devious, but how well do I really know him? According to Renee, he's jealous of her success, determined to punish her by getting full custody of Molly."

"Does Renee think he could be trying to rattle her?"

"If she does, she didn't tell me. And I didn't suggest it to her. I don't want her to confront Barry. If he *is* stalking her—hell, who knows what he'd do in the heat of anger? If he *isn't,* he'll know she's being stalked and use it against her in court."

"Catch-22." Phil grunted and swiveled back and forth in his chair. "It may *not* be Barry. You said Renee has tons of fans. Maybe one of them's obsessed with her."

Not exactly a comforting thought.

4

"You just missed Pollin," Alicia said, entering a small office where Renee sat, scanning faxes from her radio audience. "He wants to meet with you after the show."

Renee frowned. "Did he say why?"

The screener shook her head. "He asked me how you are, if you seemed to be under stress lately. I told him no."

"Thanks."

"For lying, you mean?" An arch lift to her brows. "I'm not about to play Big Brother for Pollin."

"Alicia, I *told* you. It's the ratings. How can I *not* be tense, with Pollin breathing down my neck?"

"Hey." She held up her hand. "We're not best buds, Renee, and that's cool. You don't have to tell me what's wrong, just like I don't spill my heart out to you every time one of my kids gives me grief, which is pretty damn often. But a person would have to be blind not to see that something's bothering you."

It would be a relief, sharing the burden with a colleague she trusted. She stared into her coffee mug. "Barry and I are getting divorced," she said finally, looking up. "He wants full custody of Molly."

"Oh, honey." Alicia sighed deeply. "I'm real sorry."

Renee's eyes smarted. She was touched by Alicia's concern, but uncomfortable. She hated feeling vulnerable. "I'm okay about the divorce, and there's no way I'll give up Molly. But I'm worried about the effect on my audience if the news gets out. And I don't want Pollin to find out."

"Getting divorced isn't exactly a crime, Renee."

"The audience may not agree. And Pollin may figure I'm the wrong person to host this show. And with the lower ratings . . ."

"I hear that." Alicia nodded somberly, frowning.

Renee pursed her lips. "This is where you say, 'Don't be silly, Renee. You have nothing to worry about.' "

Alicia flushed. "Well, you probably don't," she said after a brief hesitation. "The publicity will bring new listeners, and it'll make you more human, more accessible. Which is a plus. Everybody roots for the underdog."

"Yeah, but will they turn to the underdog for advice?" No answer from Alicia. "So has anyone else asked about me?"

"You're not the hot topic of conversation at the water cooler, if that's what you mean. Madonna still has you beat. So does *Seinfeld,* and that's in reruns." She smiled.

"Do I sound tense on the show? The truth."

"You sound *fine*—I'd tell you if you didn't. Look, you're worrying prematurely. This whole thing will blow over, and the ratings will pick up."

"Don't sweet-talk me." Renee's turn to smile.

"I *know* they will. Word'll spread. You're an okay host, but I'm the world's best screener." Alicia was grinning now. "Today's show will be great. I have a dozen terrific calls lined up."

"*Genuine* calls?"

They both laughed, breaking the somber mood. When Renee had begun hosting the program and was developing an audience, she and Alicia had enlisted help. Alicia's mother and sister had called in, varying their voices and problems. Renee's parents had done the same. So had Barry. In those days, he'd been eager to help launch Renee's new career, loving. . . .

Well, those days were gone, and so was Barry. *His* loss. She was finished crying about him. She had Molly. That was all that mattered. And she would build up the ratings and make the show a great success.

She drank the rest of the coffee and continued reading. Twenty minutes later she was on the air, giving her opening spiel, and all thoughts of Barry disappeared. The magic of doing something she loved. She took the first four calls, then broke for a commercial.

"We have Giselle on Two, down-and-dirty sibling rivalry," Alicia informed her. "Stan on Four, regret about giving poor advice. He sounds a little off, but interesting."

The break was only minutes, but Renee had learned to use the time well. She phoned her book agent and left a message on his machine, then contacted her publicist to confirm a January speaking engagement in Seattle. When the commercial ended, she reintroduced herself and held her finger over Line Four.

"Hi, Stan. What's on your mind?" She pressed the button. No answer. "Stan?"

"I've been getting up the courage to call you, Dr. Renee. I have to tell you, I almost hung up."

"Well, I'll try not to bite your head off. I've already had lunch." She laughed lightly. "So how can I help you?"

"Like I told your screener, I'm afraid I gave someone the wrong advice, and it's caused a lot of harm."

"Stan, you have your radio on, don't you? You need to turn it off while you're on the air."

"Done."

"That's better. So what kind of wrong advice did you give? Financial?"

He sighed. "I wish it was that simple. No, this person asked me for advice about a family matter, and I gave it. But I see now I was wrong, Dr. Renee. Dead wrong."

Alicia was right about Stan. There was something a little intense about his voice. "What kind of advice was this, Stan?"

"I don't feel comfortable discussing that," he said crisply. "But it doesn't really matter, does it? I was wrong, and I shouldn't have opened my mouth. I shouldn't have mixed into something that wasn't any of my business. Don't you think so?"

She was startled by his anger, flashed Alicia a look. Alicia raised her shoulders.

"I can understand why you're upset, Stan. But don't take all the blame. Your friend approached *you*. He *chose* to follow your advice."

"He *trusted* me." More anger.

"It's kind of hard for me to comment on this, not knowing the particulars. You have to do everything possible to remedy the situation. Have you told your friend you were wrong?"

"Not yet. I know that's what you're going to tell me to do. That's probably why I've been putting off calling you."

She was puzzled and a little impatient. "Stan, you obviously don't need my advice. So what *do* you want from me?"

"I've done a lot of damage, Dr. Renee. He'll hate me."

"Probably. He'll need to blame someone for his choice, and that'll be you. Talk to him in person, if you can. Tell it to him straight, just like you told me. Try to make things right."

"That's what you'd do?" Challenging, almost.

"Absolutely. I'm not saying it's easy. And be prepared for him not to forgive you—not right away. You're not going to come out of this a hero, but you'll be able to live with yourself."

"You're right, of course. So have *you* ever given the wrong advice, Dr. Renee?"

The question took her by surprise. "I'm sure I have. I don't claim to be infallible."

"On the show, I mean?"

"Most of the feedback I get is positive." She didn't like where this was going, hoped Pollin wasn't listening. "Well, good luck, Stan. I hope things work out all right." She disconnected the call, picked up Line Five. "*Sue Ann,* how can I help you?"

"Dr. Renee? I think my mom's stealing stuff from stores, and I don't know what to do. . . ."

Max Pollin ushered Renee into a gray leather armchair and walked to his desk.

He was medium height, with a short neck swallowed by his shoulders, a thick chest and waist, and thin legs made thinner by tight-fitting slacks. He looked as if he were wearing a sandwich board.

"I caught most of the show today," he said, perching himself on the edge of his desk like Humpty Dumpty.

She smiled. "I thought it went well."

"Mnnn." No expression in his smoky blue eyes.

He crossed his arms on his chest, swung his skinny legs. Offered her a lollipop, which she declined, then plopped one in his mouth. She'd heard he was trying to quit smoking.

"How do you feel the show's going, Renee?" he finally asked, lollipop out. "Overall?"

"I think it's doing *great,* Max. Interest is building, we're getting more and more calls." As if he didn't know. She was annoyed with herself for trying to score points with a twenty-eight-year-old *pisher* eight years her junior who was sucking on a lollipop, for God's sake.

"And you, Renee? How's everything?" Waving the lollipop like a wand.

"I'm fine, thanks. Alicia said you were asking about me. Why is that, Max?" She made no attempt to conceal her irritation.

"Just concerned about my talent," he said, sounding genuine. He cocked his head. "To be honest, you seem tense lately, not yourself."

"I *appreciate* your concern, but I'm perfectly fine, thanks."

"It's not just my opinion. Look, your private life is your business, Renee. Everybody has problems, right?" He shrugged. "But if it affects the show, it becomes *my* business."

Who had talked to him? "I'm not tense, Max. I'm not having problems. If someone said otherwise, they're wrong." She met his eyes.

Another "Mnnn."

"I know you're unhappy with the ratings. I am, too. Even though I know they'll improve," she added quickly. "Maybe I should return to my earlier slot."

Pollin shook his head. "You'd be against Limbaugh again. And Praeger, now that he's doing the morning."

"Those shows are different than mine. The format, the tone. My ratings are lower because I'm head to head with Dr. Laura, Max." *Your* decision, she added silently.

"Ted Harkham's doing great in the nine-to-twelve. The right mix of politics, celebs, and hot-button issues. Why mess with success?" Pollin sucked on the lollipop, then crunched it.

She winced at the sound and waited.

"Three-to-seven's a possibility," he finally said. "I could switch you with Caroline. You could be a good alternative to Larry Elder and Stuart Logan."

"You know I can't do that, Max. I have to be home with Molly. As it is, I get home later than I like."

"Lots of moms home then, needing good advice. Teenagers, too." As if she hadn't said anything. "Caroline would love the noon-to-three."

Caroline's idea, or Pollin's? "Max, we've discussed this before."

Just last week Caroline Bemar, the talk-show lawyer who did the three-to-seven, had complimented Renee on her show. Maybe that had been a ruse to keep her off guard. Maybe *Caroline* had told Pollin Renee was tense. Or maybe Pollin *wanted* Renee to think that. . . . She didn't trust him. Or Caroline, or Ted, who had basically usurped her morning show.

"Molly's not a baby anymore," Max said. "How old is she now, five?" he asked with avuncular affection.

"Six." He bought her gifts every birthday. Last time it had been a full play kitchen complete with dishes, pots, pans. His then girlfriend, Sondra, had picked it out. "Molly's not a baby, but she needs me, Max. I advise parents on the air to stay home with their kids unless they absolutely have no choice. I'd be a hypocrite, taking that slot."

"Barry works at home, right?" He raised a brow. "Are you

saying a dad's not as good a caretaker as a mom?" he asked playfully.

She tensed, wondering whether he knew that Barry had left. "I'm not saying that at all, Max. I *encourage* dads to parent their children. You know that. But it's important to me to spend time with Molly."

He nodded. "We could split the slot, give you the first half so you'd be home a little after five, try out George Torres for the other half. He's been pitching me for months. That'd give you enough quality time, wouldn't it?"

Was he patronizing her? "I think a three-hour format is really more effective than two, Max," she said calmly. "For my kind of show." She wasn't about to let him cut her back an hour, not without a fight. "If you're totally set against my doing the morning, I'll stick with the twelve-to-three."

"Even against Dr. Laura?" He smiled.

Hot anger forked through her. He'd probably been playing her all the time, suggesting the late afternoon slot just so she'd beg to keep the noon one. "I can make it work."

"That's why I put you there." He slid off the desk and walked over to her, put his broad hand on her shoulder and squeezed. "I have faith in you, Renee. By the way, we need to get you a catchy close. Something like Dr. Laura's 'Go take on the day.' Give it some thought."

((**5**))

"So my point is, Stuart, that they need to bring back affirmative action to even out the playing field."

Stuart Logan snored loudly into the mike. "I'm sorry, dude. I fell asleep a couple of points back. Were you saying something I'd be *remotely* interested in?"

"Seriously, Stuart, don't you think I'm right?"

"What do I *seriously* think? I think you're a loser, Cal. A *serious* loser. Negative to your affirmative, man. Get a life."

"See, I can't get a life, Stuart, if I can't get a job. That's what I'm trying to tell you."

"Well, you can't get a *jaahaab*"—Logan warbled the word— "if you spend your time calling talk shows, man." He disconnected the caller. "Whine, whine, whine. Ray, how'd you let this jerk on?"

The screener laughed. "You said you wanted to up the intellectual quotient, talk about more serious issues."

"I must've been gone when I said that. Did you see the new ratings, Ray? We're closing in on Larry Elder. I love you, Larry, but watch your butt, man. Are we getting Dr. Laura's numbers?"

"Not even close."

"Ray, Ray." Logan sighed. "Get me some Prozac. Better yet, get me a date with Pamela Anderson Lee. Man, I can't believe she had that boob reduction. We're her fans, right? How come we didn't get to vote on this?"

"We're ahead of Dr. Renee this quarter, Stu. Rumor has it KMST is looking to replace her if her ratings don't pick up."

"It's a dog-eat-dog world, Ray. Ronn Owens dethroned Michael Jackson. A couple of months later, Owens is history. Minyard and Tilden—funny, funny, funny, then *hasta la vista*. One minute you're hot, the next minute you're gone, baby, gone. Walter from Costa Mesa. How're you doing, dude?"

"Hi, Stuart. I don't think you were fair when you criticized Madeleine Albright about the way she's been handling the Mideast peace negotiations. No one could do better."

"One of Hugh Hefner's playmates could do better, Wally. Matter of fact, that's a terrific idea. We take a playmate of the month, send her to the Gaza Strip. Two weeks later, everyone's singing, 'Make love, not war.' "

"I'm sorry I called, Stuart. You have deep-rooted psychological problems, you know that? You have no respect for anyone or anything."

"Wally, you're so uptight, you're scaring me, man. You sound like you need an enema." Logan ended the call. "Ray, I'm telling you, this is a winner. Send notes to Bill Clinton and the Nobel crowd. I could get a peace prize. Where are they, Switzerland?"

"Sweden."

"Same thing. Do you think I have deep-rooted psychological problems, Ray?"

"Only about ten or twelve."

"Thank God. I was worried I was perfect. Which one do you think I should work on first?"

"I'd have to say your insatiable interest in sex and prurience."

"Funny, I thought that was my *best* quality." Logan laughed. "Maybe I should call Dr. Renee and ask her advice."

"Do it fast before she goes off the air."

"You know the problem? They've got way too many of these shrink-a-dink shows. Dr. Renee needs a new angle to up her ratings. A nude shot of her on the Internet, maybe. I'd put one up of me, but I want people to love me for myself, not my buff bod. But I don't have to worry. You know why, Ray?"

Ray chuckled. "Why is that, Stuart?"

"Cream rises to the top, baby. The rest of the stuff becomes low-fat yogurt, date expired. So who do we have next, Ray?"

"Denise from Laverne."

Logan pressed a line. "Denise, what's happening?"

6

"I'm getting married, Dr. Renee. My parents are divorced, and I haven't been close with my dad, but I'd like to have him walk me down the aisle. My mom doesn't even want him at the wedding, especially if he brings his wife. He left my mom for her."

"He sounds like a real prince. How long ago was this?"

"Fourteen years. My mom remarried a year ago, but she's never gotten over it."

"Gee, I don't know why. How old are you, Sandy?"

"Twenty-two."

"Any siblings?"

"A sister. She's nineteen."

"So let's see. Your dad skipped when you were eight and your sister was five. Did he stay involved? Share the parenting?"

The woman hesitated. "Not really. It was difficult, because things were so bad between him and my mom, and his new wife didn't want us coming over."

"And that's an excuse to give up being a father? I don't think so. My question is, why would you want someone who abandoned you fourteen years ago to participate in a meaningful way on your wedding day? Why would you even want him there?"

"He called me when he heard I was getting married. He wants to get closer to me and my sister, to make up for all the years he wasn't in touch. He wants to be a family again."

"Just like that, huh? Wave a magic wand, and presto, fourteen years of absence and neglect disappear."

"I want to give him a chance, Dr. Renee. And I'd like to be a family again, too. Is that so wrong?"

"It's a fantasy you've been indulging for fourteen years, Sandy. You and your sister and your mom are a family. A real family. Your *mom's the one who raised you. She's the one who did the carpools, made the lunches and dinners, took you to doctors' appointments, talked to your teachers. Your dad hasn't earned the right to walk you down that aisle."*

"He's offering to pay for the whole wedding, Dr. Renee. He really wants to make amends."

"What he *really wants* to do is bribe his way back and buy your love. And maybe stick it to your mom. Don't let him."

"So I shouldn't invite him at all?"

"If you talk to your mom, explain that this is important to you, and if it's okay with her, he can be a guest. If *it's* okay *with her,*" Renee repeated sternly. "And if you want to reestablish a relationship with your dad, that's your choice. But don't do anything that would hurt your mom. She deserves better."

"You're right." She sighed. "I'll have to tell him. It'll be hard. He was practically in tears when he talked about walking me down the aisle."

"Get him some Kleenex."

The twenty-something-year-old sales clerk, whose name was Austin, sat on a chair in the store manager's small, windowless office and listened solemnly while Jessie talked. He was nervously stroking the beginnings of a light brown goatee, as if he were coaxing the stubble to grow more quickly.

When she was done, he shook his head. The action sent a curtain of straight, white-blond dyed hair over one eye, obscuring it completely.

"Sorry, I don't remember who bought the goblets."

"But you *do* remember selling them last Friday?"

"Not really. We were crazy busy that day, and we sold a lot of crystal stemware. Stemware's a popular item," he added, with a salesman's perky enthusiasm.

"Your manager said only two of *those* goblets were sold that Friday, and you made the sale." She kept her tone conversational, not wanting to intimidate.

"I must've, then." Austin sounded unhappy. "But I don't remember who bought them. Is it like really important?"

"It could be." Or it could be nothing. "Can you remember if it was a man or a woman?" She wished he'd move the hair off his face. She found it disconcerting having him look at her with only one eye visible, like a cyclops.

He scrunched his face up in a pained expression and raked

his upper lip with his teeth. "A man?" he finally ventured. Then, "Yeah, it was a *man*. I remember him saying he thought his friend would like the goblets, 'cause of the design." He sounded happily surprised by his accomplishment.

Way to go, Austin. Jessie nodded to show her satisfaction. "Can you describe the man?"

He gazed at her balefully, like a dog asked to perform a too-difficult trick after having just pleased.

"You can probably recall a lot more than you realize, Austin. Picture his motions."

He sighed a skeptical "Okay" and pushed the hair off his face. His eyes narrowed and took on a faraway look, but after a minute or so, he shook his head again. "Sorry. Nothing stands out."

Jessie suppressed a sigh. It had been a long day. Acting on a tip about the homicide of the owner of the rug shop, she and Phil had spent three hours in his Cutlass on a stakeout that had yielded nothing but cramped muscles and strained bladders. After that they'd spent more fruitless hours talking to pawnshop owners in the hope of tracing one of the pieces of jewelry stolen from the murdered Westwood woman.

Jessie was weary with frustration and, not for the first time since she'd stepped into the store, wondered if she was wasting her time trying to identify the person who'd sent crystal goblets to Renee and scared her to death. Maybe Renee was paranoid.

Maybe not. In any case, Jessie had promised to do her best. "Austin, let's try this. Take a deep breath, close your eyes and relax. C'mon, close them. I won't tie you up." She smiled.

He looked dubious, but obeyed, inhaling deeply and resting his stubby fingers on the arms of his chair.

"Okay. You're standing at the cash register. You ring up the stemware and tell our man what he owes. Are you with me, Austin? Don't open your eyes," she added quickly.

He nodded.

"He takes out his wallet and hands you the cash. So now you're looking right at him." She paused. "Can you see him?"

Ten long seconds of silence. Then, *"Yeah."* His voice was filled with wonder.

All right! "Is his hair dark or fair?"

Austin considered, then opened his eyes and said, "Dark brown," in that same surprised tone. "Kind of like yours, a little wavy. A regular haircut. Nothing special."

"That's very good, Austin." Jessie smiled encouragement. "What about his eyes? What color are they?"

Austin frowned. "He was wearing tinted glasses, so I couldn't tell."

Tinted glasses inside a store, on a cloudy day? "Is he tall or short?"

He shut his eyes again. "Mmnn . . . about my eye level, maybe a little taller. I'm five nine and a half."

It was amazing, she'd learned through her fifteen years of police work, how specific questions and the right mood could prompt a lagging memory. "Fat or thin?"

His brow creased in concentration. "Average. Not skinny, but not built." He opened his eyes. "Hey, you're good at this!"

"I try." She smiled. "Did he have a beard or mustache?"

Austin closed his eyes again, then shook his head. "Nope." His eyes flew open. "He had me clean them. The goblets, I mean. I just remembered that. He said they looked spotted."

Spotted, or bearing his fingerprints? Maybe Renee's fears were warranted, Jessie thought. Or maybe the goblets *were* spotted, and she was being overly suspicious. The pitfalls of being a cop. "Did he fill out a gift card?"

Austin thought for a moment. "Nope. But he asked me to drop a couple in the box."

Nothing sinister about that, unless he'd wanted to fill out the card at home, where he could be careful not to leave his prints. "What about rings? A wedding band, maybe."

Silence. "I can't remember."

"Anything else you can recall about him? Earrings? A tattoo? A scar? Take your time," she said again.

But there was nothing else.

Last night she'd searched through a stack of loose photos but had found no clear pictures of Barry. She showed Austin a photo of Renee, one she'd taken three years ago when they'd driven to Laguna, just the two of them, for the art festival. The day had been balmy. They'd strolled from booth to booth, admiring the artworks and jewelry and crafts, then walked to the beach and sat on the warm sand, talking about things that mattered and things that didn't as they watched the waves roll in.

Austin gazed at the photo. "I definitely saw *her*. She was kind of spaced. Just standing around, looking at stuff but not really seeing anything, you know? And then all of a sudden, she's wanting me to ring up this frame she bought, and she's in a real hurry." He sounded peeved.

"Did you notice anyone around her?"

"*With* her, you mean?" He shook his head, and his eye was covered again.

"*Watching* her?"

"I wouldn't—" He stopped abruptly. "This guy, you mean, right?" He looked at Jessie thoughtfully. "She's the lady who got the stemware?"

"I didn't say that."

"But she *is*, right?" He was enjoying this now. "So this guy sent the crystal to her, and that's why you want to know all about him, huh?" Suddenly he frowned. "Is she dead?" He sounded alarmed and excited at the same time.

"No, she's not. Thanks a lot, Austin. You've been very helpful. If you think of anything else, call me right away." She handed him her card.

He looked at it before he pocketed it. "You're a homicide detective. If she's not dead, how come you're so interested in this guy?" He cocked his head. "So is she *somebody*?"

"Everybody's somebody," Jessie told him.

7

From Century City she drove toward Santa Monica and found the address she wanted: a mocha stucco, three-story apartment house on Prosser, north of Olympic, with flaking cream-colored trim and rust stains dribbling from the gutters. The narrow ribbon of lawn, parched and yellowed, cried out for seed and fertilizer. Much like her own lawn. Sighing, she parked her Honda and made a mental note to nag her gardener, who always needed reminding.

This wasn't a security building; it didn't even have a lobby. She checked the bank of mailboxes on the side of the building. There it was. Barry Altman.

Number Nine was a second-floor apartment at the rear of the building. After climbing a steep, narrow flight of stairs to a tiny landing, she pressed the bell and waited, assailed by the unmistakably pungent smell of cauliflower emanating from the apartment to her left.

Half a minute later she rang again. He might not be home, she realized, but then she heard, "Coming!" and a few seconds later the door squeaked open.

He was staring at her, and she wondered whether she'd changed so much in two years that he didn't recognize her. Except for a few strands of gray in his medium brown hair, he hadn't changed at all. He had the same casual, professorial good looks, wore the same kind of Land's End clothes. Today it was a button-down-collared pale blue twill shirt, camel Dockers, brown moccasins. A day's growth of stubble darkened the bottom of his face, making him look more rugged.

"It's Jessie," she said.

"I know." He sounded contemplative, his hazel eyes evaluating her from behind fashionably small metal-framed glasses softened by a faint brownish tint.

She was evaluating him, too, trying to see him through Austin's eyes: Five ten, brown hair, medium build. So were countless other L.A. men, many of whom wore tinted glasses.

"Can I come in?"

"Sure." He moved aside and made a sweeping gesture with his hand. "Welcome to my palace."

She stepped into a small room furnished with a computer desk and an armless secretary's chair, a brown bean bag chair, a card table, and two metal folding chairs. Stacks of books, magazines, and newspapers lay on the natty olive-green carpet, along with a few scattered Lego blocks and a doll whose heavily mascaraed blue eyes were staring at the ceiling. The place was a far cry from the spacious, professionally decorated Brentwood home Barry and Renee had bought three years ago.

"I take it you're not here collecting for the policeman's fund." He stuffed his hands in his pockets. "Renee sent you?"

"She told me about the divorce, but she doesn't know I'm here."

He nodded, then narrowed his eyes. "So how'd you know where I live? My new address is unlisted."

She shrugged.

He thought for a moment, nodded again. "Perks of being a detective, huh?" A brief, tight smile. "So why *are* you here?" More accusing now. "Are you planning to browbeat me into accepting her demands?"

She remembered his sarcasm—it wasn't a quality she'd particularly liked—but there was a nastier edge to it now. Then again, things had changed, and he probably perceived her as the enemy. Which she supposed she was.

"Can we sit down?"

"I'm not being a good host, am I? Out of practice." He strolled to the card table and pulled out one of the chairs for her. "Something to drink?" He picked up an empty beer bottle and a paper plate bearing the remains of a frozen dinner.

"That would be nice." She sat down.

"Beer okay? Or are you on duty?" He was clearly mocking her now.

"Diet Coke, if you have it. Room temperature would be great."

He took the paper plate into the tiny kitchen area and was back a moment later with a bottle of Heineken, a can of Dr Pepper, and a plastic cup.

"No Coke." He placed the can and cup in front of her.

She didn't love Dr Pepper. "This is fine." She felt like telling him he didn't need another beer, but she wasn't his mother, or his conscience.

He sat down and, uncapping the Heineken, leaned back with his legs crossed and took a sip of the beer. *Your move.*

"Renee told me you're insisting on full custody of Molly," Jessie said. "I figured I'd talk to you about it."

"Since when did this become your business?" he asked casually, but his lips had thinned into an angry line.

"Renee and I go back a long time, Barry. You know that." Holding the soda can by the rim, she snapped off the tab and filled the cup.

"I *also* know that the two of you haven't been in touch for almost two years." Very snide.

She nodded. "But now we are. Renee's extremely upset about this whole situation, and I'd like to help, if I can."

"I forgot. You're the expert on divorce, right?" He smiled. "But you had a miscarriage, if I remember, so you're not an expert on custody, are you?"

She didn't answer. Inside, she winced and liked him a little less, felt a little better about what she was doing.

"I'm sorry. That was mean." He took a swig of the beer. "You know why she stopped talking to you? You criticized her. About giving up her practice, about the way she talked to callers. Renee doesn't like criticism."

"Very few people do," Jessie remarked.

"She said you were jealous because she was becoming a celebrity. 'After everything I've done for her'—meaning you, Jessie— 'this is how she repays me.' That's what Renee said." He drank some more, watching her.

She couldn't decide if he was nervous, or suspicious. Which he had a right to be. Or a little drunk. She wondered, too, if he was telling the truth about Renee. "Let's talk about Molly."

"She's a terrific kid," he said, his voice suddenly husky. He sat up straight and put down the beer bottle. "She's the best thing in my life."

She was moved, in spite of herself, by his raw emotion. "Renee feels the same way. She doesn't want to lose her."

"She doesn't have to *lose* her. She can visit Molly all she wants." He sounded sincere. "But Molly should live with me. It makes more sense. Renee's busy with her career. I'm home all day, all night."

"Molly's in school when Renee's at work," Jessie pointed out.

He shook his head. "Only till one. Now that I've moved out, Blanca picks her up from school. She's a nice woman, very capable, and she loves Molly. But Molly needs to be with a parent, not a live-in housekeeper with passable English. I guess I'm overprotective since the accident."

Jessie looked at him blankly.

"Renee didn't tell you?" He raised his brows in surprise. "Molly ran into the street and was hit by a car. It's a miracle she wasn't killed."

"My God!" she exclaimed, her hand at her mouth. "When?"

"A year and a half ago. It was rough going, but she's okay." His eyes took on a distant, pained look. "She had some broken ribs and a fractured ankle. And she lost her spleen, which isn't a big deal as long as we're on top of things."

A year and a half ago. That was when she and Gary had separated. Was that why Renee hadn't called? Because she'd been preoccupied with her own pain?

"We let go the housekeeper who was with her at the time," Barry continued. "I'm not saying it couldn't have happened if I'd been in charge, but I didn't feel secure leaving Molly with her. And now we have Blanca. She watches Molly like a hawk, but you can see why I'm cautious."

Jessie nodded.

"And Renee's not always home on time, you know. Once in a while she has meetings after the show. There are evening appearances, out-of-town engagements. The more famous she gets, the more she'll have to be away."

Jessie heard a touch of envy along with the concern for Molly. And resentment? "I'm sure Renee would be happy to have Molly stay with you when she's away."

He snorted. "Why should Molly have to go back and forth like a yo-yo? She should be with a parent who can care for her full-time, and that's me. *This* is my workplace." He waved toward his computer desk.

She was reluctant to admit that his arguments were sound. Because she was Renee's friend? Because, like most people, she automatically assumed the child should live with the mother? She wondered what would have happened if she hadn't miscarried.

Would Gary have fought for custody? *She's a detective, Your Honor. She places herself in danger every day. I'm a journalist, I can write at home. . . .* Then again, if she hadn't miscarried, they might still be married. . . .

"What about Renee?" she asked, pushing out the thoughts that kept returning, like unwelcome visitors. "She needs Molly, and Molly needs a mother."

He looked at her evenly. "Molly needs *both* her parents, but that isn't the reality. I wish it were. I'm not the villain here, you know. Did Renee tell you I left her?"

Jessie nodded.

"Because I couldn't handle her success, right? You know what? I couldn't. Overactive male ego, low self-esteem. Whatever." He shrugged. "I'll tell you, she didn't make it easy. Constantly throwing it in my face that I haven't earned much with my writing, that we're living on *her* money. I don't need to hear that all day." He lifted the bottle and, tilting his head back, finished the beer.

"Renee told me she may lose the house."

"And that's my fault, too, huh?" He grunted. "I begged her to get a financial adviser—what do I know about investing? But she insisted I take care of the money. We refinanced, spent a lot remodeling the house, invested the rest in stocks and mutual funds that didn't do so well. And *I'm* to blame?" He shook his head. "Ask her why she bought the Lexus. Ask her how much she spent in the past two years on clothing and jewelry."

She didn't want to hear the intimate details of the breakup of their marriage, marveled that she and Gary had escaped this ugliness. Not that they hadn't had their share of pain.

"The two of you might benefit from counseling," she said, though counseling hadn't helped her and Gary.

"I'm willing," he said simply. "She doesn't think she needs it. She's changed, you know." He twirled the empty bottle. "Ever since she started doing the show. She's still a good person, inside. And a good mom—I'll give her that. But she believes her own hype. She thinks she's an effing Greek oracle dispensing wisdom and morality." He paused. "I feel sorry for her."

"Wouldn't it make more sense for the two of you to work this out? For Molly's sake?"

"There's nothing to work out." He stopped the bottle. "I want what's best for Molly."

"So does Renee. You said she's a terrific mother."

"When she's home. And I said 'good,' not 'terrific.' She used to be terrific," he said sadly. "A terrific mom, a terrific wife. Now she's driven about her career, about her audience share, about the goddamn ratings."

"You can't blame her for being ambitious," Jessie said, unsure whether she was defending Renee or herself.

"You know something? I really believe she made me feel like crap because, consciously or unconsciously, she *wanted* me to leave. I'm not a big success. I speak my mind about the way she does her show. But she couldn't *initiate* the divorce. Bad publicity for a woman who preaches family above everything."

Jessie shook her head. This wasn't the Renee she knew.

"Why do you think she begged me not to tell anyone about the divorce?"

"She told me her parents don't know. I guess she wants to figure out a way to tell them first."

He snorted. "She hasn't talked to them in months. Like I said, Renee doesn't like criticism. The truth? She's afraid her ratings will drop if this gets out and the station will ax her."

"People get divorced," Jessie said. "It's not a crime."

"It is if you set yourself up as Miss Perfect. Sometimes . . ." He stopped, played with the bottle. "Sometimes I think the only reason she's fighting me over Molly is 'cause it won't look good to her public if she gives up custody."

She gazed at him steadily. "You don't believe that."

He shrugged and tipped the bottle over his open mouth until a few lingering drops fell in. She made no move to fill the silence, which was broken by the thumping of footsteps from the apartment above them.

"You talked to Renee recently," he finally said. "Did you notice how stressed out she is?"

Jessie's interest quickened. This was why she was here. "She's stressed out because of the divorce, because you want to take Molly. That's understandable."

He shook his head. "It's more than that." He leaned closer. "I'm worried about her," he said, his voice intimately low. "I asked her what's bothering her, but she wouldn't say. Maybe she told you." More of a question than a statement.

Someone's stalking me, Jessie. She feigned puzzlement. "What could be bothering her?" She was watching him carefully, assessing him as she'd done from the minute she'd stepped into the apartment.

"*Something's* definitely wrong. She's jittery, jumpy. I can't help worrying how that's impacting on Molly. It can't be good for her, that's for sure." He frowned. "Whatever's wrong, I hope it doesn't send Renee over the edge."

Maybe you do, Jessie thought. "Renee's made of sturdy stuff. You know, the courts usually grant custody to the mother, unless she's unfit. And Renee's hardly unfit. You might get more generous visitation rights if you cooperate."

He smiled. "I'm not worried. My lawyer says I'll probably win."

"Your lawyer gets paid whether or not you get Molly. Why make him rich?"

"I'll take my chances."

"*Somebody's* going to lose," Jessie said quietly.

"Not me." Stubborn, now.

"What makes you so sure?" she asked, deliberately goading him.

"I *won't lose Molly.*" A muscle twitched in his cheek. "Whatever it takes, I'll do it. You can tell that to Renee." His hand tightened around the neck of the bottle.

Renee's words, spoken with the same angry intensity. "If I didn't know you better, Barry, I'd say that sounded like a threat."

He frowned, then smiled wryly. "Oh, yeah, I forgot. You're a cop. You gonna cuff me now, Detective?" He extended his hands.

She couldn't decide about him. "I thought I could help. I guess not." She stood and slung her purse strap over her shoulder.

He sighed, then pushed back his chair and stood. "That wasn't a threat."

"Good. Because I wouldn't want you to do anything stupid, Barry." She looked at him hard. "I've seen too many tragedies that started out as stupidity."

"I'd never hurt Renee!" He sounded appalled at the thought. "Even if I hated her, which I don't. I'd never do that to Molly."

"You're hurting Renee now."

He tightened his lips. "All I want is what's best for Molly."

"So you've said. We're all pretty good at convincing ourselves that we know what's best. Maybe part of you wants to beat Renee, take her off her pedestal." She paused. "Just something to think about."

He didn't answer.

"Thanks for your time, and the soda."

He glanced at the can and full cup. "You didn't even taste it."

"I'll take it with me. One for the road."

8

She was tempted to pour the Dr Pepper onto the thirsty lawn but waited until she was on the sidewalk, out of view of Barry's apartment window. Carefully holding the can by its top and bottom ridges, she emptied its contents into the gutter. Inside her car she slipped the can into a paper bag.

She was pleased with herself, but felt a surprising twinge of guilt at having deceived. After fifteen years of police work she'd mastered the art of lying convincingly, lying without qualms, because cops were allowed to lie to get the bad guys. But this was Barry, her friend's husband, a guy she'd laughed with, had Thanksgiving dinner with. Pass the cranberry jelly, please.

Maybe Barry *was* a bad guy. If he was stalking Renee, Jessie was justified in coming to his apartment under false pretenses. (She'd sincerely tried to persuade him to reconsider about Molly, even if the marriage was dead. That hadn't been false.)

If he wasn't, it was just a soda can.

At home she slipped on latex gloves and, dusting the can with white powder, nodded in satisfaction when the whorls of Barry's fingerprints emerged. All five. With a strip of wide transparent tape, she lifted the prints, placed the tape onto an unlined index card, and labeled the card.

From her bedroom desk she took the bag in which she'd placed the gift card and brought it into the kitchen. She went to the garage, where she rummaged through dusty piles of cobweb-laced things she'd accumulated over the years and was always meaning to get rid of. She found the goldfish bowl behind a stack of old suitcases.

Back in the kitchen, she used tweezers to remove the gift card from the bag and lay it inside the bowl. She squirted Super Glue onto the bottom of the bowl, careful to avoid the card, and covered the bowl tightly. If there were any fingerprints on the card, the fumes from the glue would raise them.

She phoned her sister, Helen, and commiserated with her about the morning sickness that was extending into her second trimester and the dearth of fashionable maternity clothing.

"Mom's coming in Saturday," Helen said, "so keep the day free. We'll have brunch here, then go shopping or something. I *desperately* need a few pairs of shoes."

Preferably "or something." Jessie didn't share her sister's and mother's intense love of shopping or clothes, and shopping with her mother, who tended to criticize everything Jessie liked, was generally a harrowing experience.

"I can't do the morning, Helen, but the afternoon is fine."

"You put in *way* too much time on your job, Jess. You need to relax more."

"You're probably right."

She had no intention of telling Helen she was contemplating attending synagogue services Saturday morning. Her sister was uncomfortable discussing their mother's recently revealed past: Frances Claypool, née Freide Kochinsky, had been six when the Germans invaded Poland; she'd been hidden by a Polish family and had been the only one of her family to survive the war.

And Helen bristled with defensiveness bordering on hostility whenever Jessie referred to her newly discovered Jewish identity.

Jessie understood her sister. Helen was comfortable with her life; more importantly, she craved stability and control. That was why, as a teenager, she'd run away several times to escape Frances's physical abuse; why she'd married a man fourteen years her senior; why her closets and linens and spices were impeccably organized and her house always spotless. Her emotions weren't as neat or controlled. She'd carried the legacy of abuse with her, but seeing a therapist was helping, and her life was finally approaching normalcy.

So why would she accept a heritage that would complicate everything? Her husband, Neil, was a nonpracticing Protestant. Helen considered herself Christian, too. But according to the laws of matrilineal descent, she was Jewish, her nine-year-old son, Matthew, was Jewish, and so was her unborn child.

The real question, Jessie knew, was not why Helen *didn't* want to embrace Judaism, but why she herself did. Until recently, she'd never thought much about God, though she'd always believed in His existence. Her family had rarely attended church—probably, she suspected, because Frances's past had made her ambivalent toward the Episcopalian faith into which she'd married but never converted. And Jessie's father, Arthur, had undoubtedly ceded to his wife's wishes, as he did in most matters. Peace, or the semblance of it, above all.

Initially, Jessie had been curious about Judaism, and a homicide investigation had brought her into contact with a number of Jews, including Ezra Nathanson, now her mentor and teacher. But it wasn't only curiosity that had fueled her desire to learn more about her heritage, to read books on Judaism that resonated with her and led her to contemplate religious observance.

In many ways she was like Helen—she needed stability, order. That was why she'd become a detective. But it wasn't enough, somehow, and her life five months ago had been anything but stable.

A failed marriage. Enduring grief over her miscarriage. Another aborted romantic relationship. Pain and sadness and the embers of anger about her tortured relationship with her mother. The realization that, while her career was challenging and gratifying, something was missing.

Maybe that something was Judaism. It had certainly struck a chord. So here she was, embarking on a journey she found exciting and intimidating. And she couldn't share it with her family.

She said good night to Helen, then warmed up macaroni and cheese in the microwave and turned on the TV. From spirituality to sitcom, she thought, noting again the glut of shows about single career women seeking significant others. She missed Gary, wished he were here.

During commercials, she raided the pantry for snacks she knew she'd regret eating and checked the fish bowl. No prints yet. *A watched pot . . .*

Law and Order was on, one of her favorites. She enjoyed watching the crime show, liked the fact that the captain was a black woman. A new female prosecutor, dark-haired and pretty and model-thin, had replaced last season's attorney, who, according to the story line, had given up her career when the alternative had been to lose custody of her daughter to her ruthless ex-husband.

Barry had never struck Jessie as ruthless, but he was determined to win Molly. She wondered what Renee would do if faced with the choice of giving up her show or losing custody.

In the morning she found partial prints of both thumbs and what she decided must be both index fingers. She was disappointed with the meager results and still unsure whether someone had tried hard not to leave his prints on a gift card, or whether this was a benign secret admirer, too shy to make himself known.

She compared the whorls with those of Barry's thumbprint and index finger. Similar, but she couldn't tell if the patterns were identical. Even an expert needed eight prints to identify someone, sixteen to go into court.

And she was hardly an expert.

9

In the middle of the night Renee heard the crying. Soft, catlike whimpers, they pulled her out of a restless sleep and pinched her heart.

Molly lay huddled on her side, her blond curls splayed against the pillow. Her thumb was in her mouth, her index finger rubbing the tip of her nose. Tear streaks glistened on her cheeks.

"What's wrong, baby?" Renee brought her lips to Molly's forehead. Cool. She breathed a sigh of relief. "Does something hurt?"

She nodded quickly.

"Show me where."

Molly rolled onto her back. She took Renee's hand and placed it on her chest. "Feel."

The rapid pumping beat against Renee's palm. For a second she was back in the labor/delivery room, watching the incredibly fast flickering of the heart-shaped icon on the fetal monitor. Normal, the nurse had reassured.

"Your heart hurts?"

"It doesn't really *hurt*. But it's beating too *hard*, Mommy."

"It's beating just fine. Here. Feel mine." She took Molly's hand and pressed it against her own chest. "See?"

"A boy in my class said if your heart beats too fast, it could push right out of you."

Renee laughed. "That's the silliest thing I ever heard, Molly. Your heart can't push out of your chest. Your chest is very, very strong."

"He said it could."

"He's trying to scare you, sweetheart. You have nothing to worry about. I promise. Try to sleep." She smoothed the light coverlet, then leaned forward to kiss her daughter's cheek and saw her frown. "Don't you believe me, Molly?"

"I *do* believe you." Molly's eyes filled with fresh tears. "But I'm afraid to sleep, Mommy." Her voice trembled. "If I'm asleep, the monster will chase me again."

The nightmare. It had haunted Molly for months after the accident, and then, blessedly, had stopped. The thought that it was back filled Renee with anguish.

"The monster isn't real, Molly. He *seems* real, but he's only in your dream." She stroked the child's forehead, but the frown remained.

"He *is* real, Mommy." She propped herself to a half sitting position. "He was chasing me so fast. He was running faster and faster, and this time he almost *got* me."

"Oh, Molly." She drew her daughter close and cradled her.

Molly rested her head against Renee's breast. "He *scares* me, Mommy. Daddy said he won't let the monster get me, but Daddy isn't here."

Renee's chest tightened. "*I'm* here, Molly. I won't let anybody hurt you."

"Is Daddy coming back? You said maybe he'll come back."

"I don't know, angel." Coward, she thought, angry with Barry, with herself. "But I'm here with you, and I promise I'll take care of you. I'll leave the night-light on if you like."

Molly pulled away. "What if he comes in the daytime, when you're at work?"

"He's only in your dreams, Molly. He's not real."

"What if there's a *real* monster? Can you ask Daddy to come home? Please, can you?"

Renee felt a surge of prickly annoyance; then sudden, heavy sadness. "Daddy will always be here if you need him, angel. He loves you and would never let anybody hurt you. And the monster—"

"He's so *big*!" Locking her hands tightly around Renee's neck, she sobbed quietly against her mother's chest.

Renee rocked the child and stroked her hair until her cries subsided into sniffles. "It's okay to be scared, Molly. Dreams can be very scary, even for grown-ups."

"Did you ever dream about monsters?"

"Sometimes."

"What if he catches me, Mommy?"

"He won't."

"But what if he *does*?"

"Monsters are just like bullies, Molly. The more you're afraid of them, the bigger they seem. They swallow your fear and it fills them up, like a balloon." Inhaling, she puffed out her cheeks and was rewarded by a timid smile from Molly.

"So if I'm not afraid, he can't hurt me?"

"That's right." Renee eased her onto the bed and adjusted the light blanket. "You're a smart, strong girl, smarter than any stupid old monster." She kissed Molly's forehead. "Okay?"

"Okay." Dubious. The thumb back in her mouth.

"Good night, angel."

"Can I sleep with you, Mommy? Just tonight?"

Not a good idea, Renee knew. But she couldn't say no.

Molly brought her pillow and comforter and favorite doll and snuggled against Renee in the king-size bed. Within minutes her face was slack with sleep, her breathing shallow.

Renee lay watching her awhile longer, then edged slowly away and adjusted the comforter across her shoulders.

Sleep eluded her. After a few minutes, she gave up and slipped off the bed, careful not to wake Molly. She walked to the window and stood, arms hugging each other in loneliness and angry despair, while she stared through the sheer curtains into the blank darkness.

10

He had been standing on the pavement, watching the house, washed a pale gray by the reflection of the three-quarter moon, when the lights came on in the second-floor master bedroom.

A slim shadow streaked across the yellow of the thinly veiled, mullioned window.

Renee.

Light blinked on in another bedroom.

The shadow appeared briefly, then bent down and disappeared from his view as it blended with another, smaller gray shape.

Madonna and child.

How sweet, he thought, his chest ballooning with rage. How very sweet. How very, very wonderful that the two of you are happy, that you're happy with yourself, your all-knowing-never-makes-a-mistake self.

He heard a thrumming sound. A car coming up the street. He disappeared behind the thick trunk of a cinnamon tree and waited until it passed.

The silence was louder now, echoing in his ears. He wanted to roar it down, wanted to roar out with the smoldering fury bubbling inside him like lava, but of course he couldn't.

And she could still make things right, he reminded himself. If she wanted to.

Figures moving together across the room.

The light went out.

They were in the master bedroom now. Another minute, and she would darken this room, too.

Out, out, brief candle.

Not that it mattered. He could see her through the darkness.

52

The light stayed on.

A few minutes later she appeared at the window and looked at him. *Right at him!*

He felt a thrill of excitement. "Do you see me, Renee?" he whispered. "Do you?"

But of course she didn't. She hadn't seen him the other times, either.

11

"I want to read you something that really touched me," Renee said after she began the program Thursday afternoon. "This letter is from Sally, and it made my day. Here goes:

" 'Dear Dr. Renee, several months ago I was listening to your show, which I do every day.' Bless you, Sally!" Renee smiled. " 'I heard you advising a woman who'd had a fight with her brother to try to patch things up. Family was more important than pride, you said.

" 'Dr. Renee, my sister and I hadn't spoken since we quarreled eight years ago about an inheritance. I thought about phoning her so many times, but I was too stubborn. After listening to your show that day, I phoned her, and I thank Heaven I did. She'd lost her husband and was terminally ill, with only a few months to live. She hadn't called me because, like me, she'd been too proud.

" 'I flew to Omaha, where my sister lived. My children are grown, so I stayed, with my husband's blessing, until she died. It was painful seeing her getting weaker and weaker, but it was a comfort for me to be able to take care of her, and not leave her to strangers. We couldn't make up for the years we'd lost, but the time we spent together and the talks we had were special.

" 'I want to thank you, Dr. Renee. If not for you, I wouldn't have called my sister, and I would have regretted that for the rest of my life. You were my guardian angel. God bless you.'

"Well." Renee sighed. "Thank you, Sally, but I can't take credit for this. You know, we all look for signs at some points in our lives, to push us into doing something we wanted to do all along, what we know is right. So I'm humbled that Sally found a sign in my show, but the credit goes to her, for swallowing her pride and listening to her heart. That's a lesson for all of us."

Renee cleared her throat. "Okay. Let me just wipe my eyes before my mascara drips onto my blouse, and we'll go on." Dabbing at her eyes with a tissue, she scanned the computer screen. Line Three, Mark from Mar Vista, forty-six, being sued by former business partner. Line Five, Celia, from Alhambra, thirty-eight, doesn't know if she should repay a years-old debt.

"Mark, you're talking with Dr. Renee." She pressed Line Three. "How can I help you today?"

"Well, I hope you can be *my* guardian angel, too, Dr. Renee," he said in a low, rumbling voice.

"Gosh, I'm no angel. Alicia, my screener, will tell you that." She winked at Alicia, who formed devil's horns with her fingers. "So, tell me your problem."

"Okay. Here goes. My former business partner is suing me, Dr. Renee. He and I started out . . ."

Something about the voice, she thought, something . . .

". . . and he claims he owns an equal share in a piece of property we bought together years ago."

Barry! You son of a bitch, Renee mouthed, helpless to do anything but listen. Clenching her hands, she turned aside so that the sound engineer couldn't see her reddening face, wondered whether by now Alicia had recognized Barry's voice, too.

". . . fact is, my former partner has a lot of valuable properties. This is the *only* property I have, and *I'm* the one who developed it. We were supposed to share responsibility, but he's been busy with his other interests. Now that we've split up, he wants fifty percent of the current value of the property."

"So what's your question for me, Mark?" she asked, struggling to speak calmly. His voice sounded a little slurred, and she wondered if he'd been drinking.

"Well, legally I suppose he's entitled to his share. I don't deny it. But morally?"

She wanted to strangle him. "Morally, he's entitled to the property, too," she said, knowing that the "property" was Molly. "You may regret your choice of partners, Mark, but that doesn't give you the right to renege on your agreement."

"Right. But here's the thing. I have knowledge about my ex-partner that—"

"That *what*, Mark? That would force your ex-partner into relinquishing his claim on the shared property?"

"That's not what I mean."

"Isn't it? Aren't you asking me to sanction blackmail?" she demanded, venting her anger into the hapless mike.

"Blackmail? No way. But my ex-partner's planning to manage

several properties for an investment group. He gave my name as a reference—this was before the lawsuit—and now he asked me not to say anything negative about him. He offered to give me a cut on the deal if I make nice."

Bastard, she fumed. He was such a clever bastard. He'd agreed not to tell Pollin—*I don't want to hurt you, Renee.*

"So my moral dilemma, Dr. Renee, is, do I have an obligation to tell them the truth? That he neglected the property? That he doesn't have what it takes to be a manager, to make sound business judgments?"

"You'd just love to do that, wouldn't you, Mark?" she snapped. "You'd love to ruin him."

"They're placing their faith and trust in him, Dr. Renee. They have a right to know the facts."

She gripped the edges of the table. "That sounds vindictive and self-serving, Mark. Don't fool yourself into thinking you'd be revealing this for the benefit of these investors."

"But that's—"

"You're not noble, Mark. You're mean and petty."

"So let's say I don't call them. What if they call me?"

"I don't think you can be objective about your ex-partner."

"So you think I should lie? Is that what you're telling me, Dr. Renee?"

Go to hell, she thought. "You should reexamine why you're doing this, Mark. Deal with your anger and your jealousy and your need to take revenge. Thanks for your call." She disconnected the line, her hands shaking with anger, and took a calming breath before she scanned the computer screen.

She spoke to a teenage girl who was worried about her alcoholic mother ("Get out of there, fast"); to a woman who was sure her father-in-law had molested her six-year-old boy and didn't know whether she should allow him in the house ("Are you *nuts?*"); to a ten-year-old boy who felt bad about having joined in with some other boys who'd keyed a teacher's car ("Fess up and take your punishment like a man").

She wasn't surprised when she heard Alicia's voice on the IN STUDIO line the minute she broke for a commercial.

"I am *so* sorry." Alicia sighed. "I didn't recognize his voice when he was talking to me." She sounded embarrassed, angry. "That *was* Barry, wasn't it?"

"Or his clone. I didn't recognize him at first, either. How did I sound?" she asked, suddenly anxious.

"Terrific, professional. What the *hell* was he trying to do?"

"Boost the ratings? He *is* asking for alimony and child support."

"Seriously."

"Just giving me grief." She hesitated. "I think that was a threat: either I give up Molly, or he tells Pollin about the divorce."

"And kill the goose that lays the golden eggs?"

"What can I tell you? He's that determined."

"Stay cool, girlfriend. Don't play his game."

Renee glanced at the smiling photo of Molly, felt her stomach muscles tighten. She debated, then picked up the private phone and punched Barry's number.

Three rings, and still no answer. Either he'd called from somewhere else or, more likely, he was home but wasn't answering.

The machine picked up on the fourth ring. She tapped her fingers impatiently on the table until she heard the beep.

"Listen, you vermin," she said quietly into the phone. "You want to tell Pollin, tell him. I don't care anymore. But I'm going to make sure you *never* get Molly. As of now, I don't want you picking up Molly from the park or coming to the house unless you call me first to make arrangements. And I want you to drop off the remote gate opener." She paused. "You want to get nasty, Barry, I can get nasty, too. You want war, I'm ready for war."

She slammed down the receiver and had a moment of intense satisfaction, which quickly gave way to apprehension.

She shouldn't have called.

Another set of calls, more commercials, then a news break.

Renee was finding it harder to focus on the callers, which wasn't fair to them. During the next break she fixed herself a cup of coffee—regular, not decaf—and did better with the following group of callers.

Suzanne, forty-two, had a problem with a co-worker; Hank didn't know if he should reconcile with his wife. Luanne was struggling with a parent with Alzheimer's. . . .

She took Luanne's call first, then Suzanne's. She wasn't in the mood to deal with marital problems, hers or someone else's, but Alicia had accepted the caller.

"Hank, welcome to the program." She pressed Line Four.

"Thank you, Dr. Renee. I'm glad you're taking my call."

"You need to speak up. You sound a little unclear."

"Cell phone. I'll try my best. Anyway, I'll get right to it. My wife left me a week ago, and I don't know what to do to get her to come back."

Renee frowned. "I'm confused, Hank. You told my screener *you're* unsure about reconciling with your wife."

"Yeah, well, I was afraid if I told her my wife left *me,* she wouldn't put me on." He laughed nervously.

"And why is that?"

"You *know* why." He laughed again, more confident now. "The guy's always to blame, isn't that right?"

His tone was light, but Renee discerned anger. She glanced at Alicia, who was usually infallible about weeding out the crazies. The screener raised her hands, palms up, and shrugged.

"Why did your wife leave, Hank?" Renee asked.

"That's what's driving me crazy. I thought everything was

fine, and I came home ten days ago, and she's gone. Just like that. She took our five-year-old son with her."

"I don't buy it, Hank. A spouse doesn't leave if everything's 'just fine,' " Renee said, fully aware of the irony of her situation. "If you're calling for my advice, you have to be honest with me, and yourself."

"I'm *being* honest. Vicky and me, we have a good marriage. It's not perfect, but what is?"

Uh-huh. "Describe what you call 'not perfect.' "

"We fight sometimes. Who doesn't?"

"What do you fight about?"

"Stuff. I want her to stay home with our son, but she wants to go back to work. Her friends put ideas in her head. They make her want stuff we can't afford on my salary. I tell her I don't want her hanging out with them, and then she gets mad and tells me I don't control her."

"You don't, Hank. You can't dictate who she can be friends with. She's not your little girl."

"We can work all that out. But that's not the point. The point is, Dr. Renee, I want her back. Her and the boy."

No "I miss her." No "I love her." Just, "I want them back." As if he owned them. "Has she contacted you?"

"Nope. She called her folks so they'd know she and the boy are okay, but she wouldn't tell them where she was."

Maybe they knew, Renee thought, but were protecting their daughter. She wasn't about to suggest that to Hank.

"The last time Vicky left, and she went to them? They sent her right back, told her straight off her place was with her husband. They like me just fine, Dr. Renee."

No wonder Vicky hadn't gone to her parents. Renee was beginning to have a bad feeling about Hank. "So this isn't the first time Vicky has left, huh?"

"Like I said, every couple has problems," he said brusquely. "Anyway, Vicky wouldn't have left if someone hadn't put ideas in her head."

"One of her friends, you mean?"

"People shouldn't meddle in other folks' lives, don't you think? People shouldn't butt into stuff that isn't any of their business."

"As a rule, you're probably right, Hank." Trouble, she thought. This guy is trouble. "So your wife has left, and you want to get her back. Why are you calling *me*?"

"She's a big fan of yours, Dr. Renee. She listens to you all the time. Hell, I'm sure she's listening to you right now. So I need you to tell her to come home. She'll do it. She thinks you're the smartest."

Renee exchanged worried glances with Alicia. "Hank, I appreciate your concern, and I'm flattered that you think I can help. I wish I could. My advice is, wait until Vicky contacts you and see if she'll go with you for family counseling."

"We don't need counseling, Dr. Renee. I'm right as rain. So's Vicky, when she thinks for herself. All we need is to talk, then everything will be back to the way it was."

"I'm sorry, but I don't think it's that simple. I can hear how upset you are, Hank, and I know you want to make your marriage work. I'm going to put you on hold, and Alicia will give you the names of some professionals who can advise you."

"I told you, I don't need advice! I need you to talk to her, Dr. Renee," he said, calmer now. "She'll do what you tell her."

She wanted to end this call. "I can't do that, Hank."

"Listen—"

"Thank you for calling. I hope you'll get help so that you can try and work things out with your wife. Wait for Alicia."

She put him on hold and pressed Line Two, troubled by the call, grateful for the discipline she'd developed that enabled her to clear her mind of Hank and poor Vicky, who had probably been smart to leave him. By the third call she'd almost forgotten all about him.

"A creepy guy, Hank," Alicia said, entering the recording room during the longer news break.

"Thanks for reminding me." Renee grimaced and took a sip of coffee. "Did you give him the names of some therapists?"

"He hung up before I could. He sounded so *normal* when I screened him. I must be losing my touch. First Barry, then Hank." Her tone was casual, but she looked embarrassed. "I guess it's not my day."

"Not mine, either. I should've listened to your advice. I called Barry. He wasn't home, but I left a nasty message."

Alicia shook her head. "I thought you were smarter than that. Did it make you feel better, at least?"

"For all of one second." She drained the remains of the coffee. "It was a dumb move."

"Yeah, but it's done, so there's no point beating yourself up about it."

"This Hank person wants his son. Barry wants Molly. What happened to the good old days, Alicia, when fathers split and left the kids with their moms?"

"Gee, thanks."

"Oh, God, I'm sorry," Renee said quickly, her face coloring. "That was stupid and insensitive."

Alicia sighed. "When Joe skipped out on us two years ago, I didn't think I'd manage, raising three kids by myself. And I've cursed him plenty for not sending so much as a dime to help out. But I guess there are worse things than being a single mom and making do on a shoestring budget." She paused. "So what now?"

"Barry will call Pollin. Then he'll leak it to the media."

"If he does, he does. You can't allow that to be hanging over your head all the time."

"Thirty seconds, Renee," the engineer announced.

Alicia returned to her booth. Renee adjusted her headset and waited for the engineer's cue, thinking.

"Three, two, one. And you're on."

She reintroduced herself, then took a call from a man who didn't know how to deal with a critical mother-in-law. She listened attentively and gave him her best advice. ("Try not to react to every comment, Roger, and decide whether she's critical or you're defensive. And if that doesn't work, tell her how you feel— in a nice way.") But part of her mind was still on Barry, wondering when he'd make his move.

Enough, she decided. Alicia was right. She looked again at Molly's photo and faced the mike. "Before I take the next call, there's something I need to say." She had a moment's hesitation—she could still turn back. Then she thought about Barry's call and cleared her throat. "I feel strongly about keeping my personal life private, but I suspect that in the very near future, that choice will be taken out of my hands."

She glanced quickly at Alicia. Her eyes had widened, and she shook her head in bemused disbelief. Renee wondered what Pollin was thinking if he was listening.

"My husband and I have separated." Her face was tingling now, her palms were clammy, but she felt enormous relief at the burden that had been lifted. "I'm saddened and pained by what is a very private matter. At the same time, I feel an obligation to my listeners, who trust me to guide them, to set the record straight before rumors spread."

"You go, girl," Alicia said through the IN STUDIO line.

"If you listen to my program, you know how deeply committed I am to the sanctity of the marriage vows and the preservation of family. I want to assure you that my commitment isn't just talk, that I would do anything in my power to change the unhappy circumstances I find myself in, and that I'm determined to provide my daughter with a loving, secure environment.

"This is the only time I'm going to discuss my situation on the air, because it *is* a private matter. This is a difficult time for me, but I take comfort knowing that you, my radio family, are interested in truth and that you won't allow sensationalism to undermine your trust in me."

She glanced at the computer screen and pressed Line Five. "*Janice,* welcome to the program. . . ."

((•13•))

"I have a dilemma, Dr. Renee. My best friend, Tara, is headed for serious trouble, and I don't know what to do."

"What kind of trouble are we talking about, Samantha?"

"Drugs."

"That is serious. How do you know she's doing drugs?"

"She's been hanging out with some kids that everyone in school knows do drugs, and—"

"Hold on, Samantha," Renee said sharply. "That's not the same thing as knowing for a fact that your friend does drugs. It's dangerous and wrong to jump to a conclusion like that."

"Well, another person who was at this party with Tara? She told me she saw Tara doing coke, and when I confronted her about it, she admitted it to me."

"What exactly did she say?"

"That it's no big deal, that she knows what she's doing. She said I'm ragging on her 'cause I'm jealous that she's popular with the cool kids and I'm not."

"Could that be true, Samantha?" Renee asked gently. "Take a few seconds to think before you answer."

"I'm a little jealous," the girl finally said, her voice low and uncertain. "Tara doesn't have much time for me anymore."

"That must be painful, Samantha. And I'm sure it's not easy for you to admit this."

"Yeah." She sighed. "But I'm really worried about Tara, Dr. Renee. I don't think she knows what she's getting into."

"I think you're right. So what's your question for me?"

"Should I tell her parents?"

"Of course you should. They need to know this."

"But she'll hate me. She'll know I told them."

63

"Probably. But being a good friend, Samantha, means doing what's in your friend's best interest. It's not always easy, and you don't always get a reward for it."

"What if her parents don't believe me?"

"They may not believe you, Samantha. A lot of parents are in denial when it comes to facing the fact that their kids have a drug problem. But that's out of your hands. You're doing your part—giving them information vital to their daughter's welfare. The rest is up to them."

"I hope I'm doing the right thing."

"What does your heart tell you, Samantha?"

"That I should tell her parents," she whispered after a few seconds of silence. "Thank you, Dr. Renee."

"You don't have to thank me—you knew before you called what was right. You're doing a brave thing, sweetheart. God bless you."

"This is my fault," Jessie said after Renee, sitting taut as a coil in Jessie's breakfast nook, told her about Barry's call to the station. "I went to see him last night."

"You went to see *Barry*? Why?" Renee looked startled, then narrowed her eyes. "You think he's the stalker." A statement.

"It's a possibility. As you said, if the judge hearing your case finds out someone's stalking you, he'd be more likely to award Barry custody."

"So Barry makes it happen." Renee played with the napkin Jessie had put in front of her, next to a glass of still untouched lemonade. "I considered that."

Jessie regarded her with interest. "You didn't tell me."

"I guess I figured if I didn't say it, it wouldn't be true," she said softly, her fingers working the napkin. "You live with a man for ten years—you sleep with him, share your dreams with him, bear his child—you don't want to believe he could hate you so much."

She'd never heard Renee sound so vulnerable. "I talked to him, Renee. He doesn't hate you."

"No, he's just trying to scare me to death and ruin my career. What a comfort," she said dryly.

"We don't know that." Jessie explained about the fingerprints she'd taken from the soda can. "So nothing's conclusive either way."

"But what do you *think*? Is it *him*?" Her gray eyes were intense.

"I don't know."

Renee was silent a moment. "Well, you tried."

"I told him you didn't know anything about my coming to see him. He thinks I was there to talk about Molly. He didn't seem angry when I left, but I guess he was."

The napkin was in shreds. Renee balled up the remains. "What did he say?"

"He's adamant about wanting sole custody." *I'll do whatever it takes.* "I'm sorry, Renee. I thought it was worth a try."

"Don't be. I think part of me was hoping you'd do that. Scare some sense into him. What's a cop friend for?" She smiled wanly. "So what else did he say?"

"He told me Molly was hit by a car, but that she's okay. You must have been terrified."

Renee shut her eyes briefly. "I thought I'd die when I saw her," she said, her voice low. "But she *is* okay, thank God." She rapped her knuckles against the oak edge of the Formica table.

"I wish I'd known."

"You couldn't have done anything. Barry won't admit it, but he blames me for what happened. I was delayed at the station, so Molly was with the housekeeper. I'm sure he blames me for our breakup, too."

"We didn't really discuss it." Jessie was uncomfortable with the lie but didn't want to play referee. "Did anyone else at the station recognize his voice?" she asked, changing the subject.

"My screener. *After* he got on the air. But it doesn't matter anymore. I told my listeners Barry and I separated."

Jessie raised a brow. "I thought you were worried about people finding out."

"I was, but Barry was threatening to tell the world anyway. Now I don't have to wait for the shoe to drop. God, the relief!" She sighed. "I was sure the program director was going to fire me, but Max was totally supportive. He said he wished I'd felt comfortable confiding in him before."

Jessie nodded. "So you worried for nothing."

"Maybe. I'm not sure how sympathetic Max would've been without all the supportive faxes and calls that came in right after my announcement." She laughed.

"I'm not surprised. You have a loyal following, Renee. I've heard how they talk to you. They adore you. They hang on your every word like it was gospel."

Renee smiled thinly. "And as I recall, you disapprove."

Not this again. Jessie suppressed a groan. "That wasn't meant as a criticism."

"But you *do* disapprove."

Why was Renee doing this? Jessie debated, then said, "Sometimes that kind of blind dependence makes me nervous. I sure as hell wouldn't want the responsibility."

"Well, sometimes it makes *me* nervous, too. A guy called the show today. His wife left him, but he's sure that if I tell her to go back to him, she will."

Jessie took a sip of lemonade. "What'd you say?"

"I told him I couldn't do that and advised him to get help. He probably won't. And all the time I'm thinking, who am I to give marital advice?"

"Have you told your parents yet?"

Renee looked at her sharply. "No. Why?"

"Don't you think you should, now that the news is public?"

Renee unballed the strips of napkin and took her time laying them out on the table. "To be honest, I'm not sure they'd care. We haven't talked in a while."

So Barry had been telling the truth about that. "Of course, they'd care. They're your parents. You're their only child."

"They'll blame me for the divorce, even though Barry walked out."

"You don't know that. They've always been supportive of you, Renee." Not like her own mother. Frances had faulted Jessie when she and Gary had separated, had regarded her failed marriage as another blow against her. Jessie's father had been tacitly sympathetic, as always, had offered to help her financially. Not what she'd needed. Not then, not before. Not now.

Renee pursed her lips. "Ever since I've become a success, they've become very critical of me, Jessie. I can't afford to surround myself with negativity."

"They love you, Renee. I'm sure they want what's best for you."

Renee tilted her head. "Correct me if I'm wrong," she said in a quiet, flinty voice, "but when you came to me all those times, hysterical because your mother beat you or called you a failure or a slut or a disgusting, ungrateful daughter, I don't remember telling you she wanted what was *best* for you."

Jessie felt her face flooding with color—where had this come from, this venomous, irrational anger? She wondered how much Renee had changed.

"The point is, I supported you, Jessie. I validated your feelings. And I would really appreciate your doing the same for me right now. Is that so much to ask?"

They looked at each other without speaking. The doorbell

rang. Saved, Jessie thought wryly, glancing at the kitchen clock. Ten to seven. Gary was early.

"Excuse me a minute," she said, getting up.

"I'm sorry I overreacted," Renee said stiffly. "I know you're trying to help."

"Forget about it. I'll be right back."

Her face was still tingling as she walked to the entry hall. She peered through the peephole, then opened the door.

"I'm impressed," she said, thinking how much she'd missed him. "You're early."

"Couldn't stay away."

He stepped inside. Slipping his arm around her waist, he drew her toward him. She was about to tell him about Renee, but then he was kissing her and she felt flushed and pleasantly achy. God, she loved his touch. Reluctantly she pulled away.

"Something wrong?" he asked.

"Renee's here," she whispered. "In the kitchen."

"Please say she's not coming with us," he whispered back.

"She's leaving in a minute. Come say hi." She noticed the cardboard box he was holding. "What's in the box?"

"The mandelbrot. What's left of it."

He followed her to the kitchen. Renee looked surprised to see him, and a little flustered, but she smiled warmly as they exchanged hellos and how-are-yous.

She turned to Jessie. "Can I talk to you in private?"

What now? Jessie thought wearily, still bruised from their earlier exchange.

Gary excused himself and left the room. Renee took a brown lunch bag from her satchel and handed it to Jessie.

"I almost forgot to give you this. It's one of the notes I told you about. I found it in the trash. I used tweezers to handle it, but my prints are on it from before."

At least she'd remembered not to put the note in plastic. Jessie gave her points. "What does it say?"

" 'What God hath done . . .' I couldn't find that quote in my *Bartlett's*. Maybe he meant 'wrought.' "

Jessie frowned. "Samuel Morse's first telephone message?"

Renee nodded. "I have no idea what that's supposed to mean to me. But if Barry wrote it, he would've looked up the quote and gotten it right. Can you check the note for prints, like you did with the gift card?"

"I'll try." I should open a lab, Jessie thought, then chastised herself for being ungenerous. "I'll need your prints for purposes of elimination."

Renee looked surprised, but nodded. Minutes later she watched without speaking as Jessie, wearing latex gloves and using the kit she always kept at home, carefully rolled her prints onto cards.

"This feels so strange," Renee said, wiping the ink from her fingers with a treated towelette when Jessie was done. She tried a smile. "Now I know how criminals feel."

Hardly. Jessie slipped the cards she'd labeled into a fresh paper bag, then removed her gloves and tossed them into the trash. "I'll let you know if I find anything. Oh, and get me a recent photo of Barry. I'll take it to the Century City store and show it to the clerk."

At the front door Renee hesitated, then leaned forward and pecked Jessie's cheek. "I'm sorry about before. You're trying to help me, and I pay you back by biting your head off."

"I know you're under a lot of tension."

"That doesn't excuse bad behavior. Friends?"

"Friends," she echoed, her annoyance seeping away.

Renee sighed. "I don't know what I'd do without you, Jess."

"I haven't done much, except piss Barry off."

"That in itself isn't totally without merit." She chuckled. "Say good night to Gary for me."

Jessie found him in the den, watching *Jeopardy*. "Ready to go?" she asked from the doorway.

He didn't even look up. "What is Trail of Tears?" he yelled at Alex Trebek and exclaimed, "Yes!" when Trebek stated the question.

Gary was a master of trivia, like her dad. She let him watch a few minutes, amused by his boyish enjoyment of the show, then said, "I'm starving." He sighed, but shut off the TV.

On the way to the restaurant, she asked about his visit with his parents. They'd relaxed in the pool, he told her, watched family videos, dropped hints about wanting a grandchild.

"Hmnn," Jessie said, ignoring his pointed look.

"They want me to come back for Rosh Hashanah. Did I tell you they've joined a Conservative temple? They're getting more religious in their old age."

"Fifty-eight isn't old." Her parents were in their early sixties, and she didn't like to think they were aging. "Are you going?"

"Only if you come. They asked me to invite you."

"Ezra's sister, Dafna, invited me to spend the holiday with her family. I said yes." She was pleased to be wanted, grateful to have the excuse. She wasn't ready to spend the Jewish holidays with her former in-laws, even though she really liked them and they'd always treated her with affection, even after the divorce.

"Oh."

She couldn't tell whether he was hurt or disappointed. "Strange, isn't it? Five months ago I didn't even know I was Jewish."

"Ezra will be there, too, huh?"

"You have nothing to be jealous about. He knows I'm smitten with you." She rested her hand on his thigh.

He drove awhile in silence. "They're very Orthodox, right?" he finally said. "You think you'll fit in?"

"I guess I'll find out." She was nervous about this herself, even after five months of reading texts on Jewish philosophy and taking classes during which she'd learned the basic rules of Jewish observance. But books and classrooms were a nonthreatening environment. . . . "I could ask Dafna to invite you. I'm sure she wouldn't mind."

"No, that's okay." More silence. Then, "So what's with Renee? She looked pretty stressed."

"She is." She was surprised he'd waited so long to ask. Even for a reporter, he was incurably nosy, sometimes annoyingly so.

"It's more than the divorce, right?"

Again, she was tempted to tell him. . . . *Do not put a stumbling block in front of a blind person.* The maxim popped into her head. It was a metaphor, Ezra had explained, for not setting temptation in front of someone. "I can't talk about it, Gary. I promised her."

"Okay." He nodded. "But is she asking you for help as a cop, or a friend? You can tell me that much."

She turned the radio to an oldies station and listened to Marvin Gay sing about sexual healing.

"Is she in danger?" Gary asked a minute later. To his credit he sounded concerned, not curious.

She thought for a moment. "I don't know," she finally said, troubled by her answer.

((14))

Molly dreamed about the monster again.

Renee was awakened by her cries at three in the morning. She calmed the little girl and lulled her to sleep, reading to her from *Tell Me a Trudy,* one of her favorites. Once awake, Renee found it difficult to fall back asleep, and in the morning she was exhausted after a restless night.

Several cups of regular coffee helped, and though she was a little wired from the caffeine when she arrived at the station, by the time the show started she was feeling fine.

Very fine. All six lines had callers holding, and Alicia had reported that the phones and faxes had been busy all morning with supportive messages for Renee. A few fans had sent flowers. Gratifying news for Renee and for Pollin, who came into the recording booth and wished her an effusive hello. She wasn't as pleased by the news, reluctantly relayed by Alicia, that she'd been the subject of several talk shows. There was nothing she could do about it, and she wasn't about to dignify their comments with a response, on or off air.

During the first segment of the show she spoke to a woman who thought her daughter and son-in-law were too permissive with their children ("Butt out," Renee told her), to a fifteen-year-old girl whose friend was spreading rumors about her ("Ignore the rumors, dump the friend"). The caller on Line Four sounded interesting: He'd stolen something and wanted to return it to the owner, but didn't know how to go about it.

"Hi, Larry, welcome to the program." Renee pressed the line and relaxed against the back of her chair. "What can I do for you today?"

"You have to help me get my wife and son back, Dr. Renee."

There was static on the line, but she recognized the voice immediately. She threw an impatient look at Alicia, who was scowling.

The screener made a cutting gesture with her hand. End the call.

Renee shook her head. Maybe she could persuade the man to get help. "You called yesterday, didn't you? But you gave me another name." She kept her voice nonconfrontational.

"What's in a name, right, Doc? Yeah, I called yesterday. Sorry I lied about the name, but I *had* to talk to you again."

"What *is* your name? Your real name?"

"Hank. The thing is, I'm real worried about Vicky, how she's doing. I hate that she's alone with our son like this. It's a lot of pressure."

Renee frowned. "You think your wife could be abusing your son?"

"No, nothing like that. Vicky's a terrific mom. It's just that I know she's sorry she left, but she's probably too ashamed to come back."

"Has she called you?"

"No. But I just *know* it. So I wanted to tell her I'm not mad. I totally understand why she left. I love her, and all I want is for her to come back. We'll take it from there."

"Well, Hank, if Vicky is listening, she hears your message, and she can decide what to do."

"That's the thing, Dr. Renee. She can't decide, not on her own. She's been brainwashed by her friends. So I need you to tell her to come back."

Back to square one. Renee sighed. "Hank, you know I can't do that."

"You're supposed to be helping people, isn't that right? That's what you do on this show!"

She flinched at his anger and silently commended Vicky for leaving. "I'd like very *much* to help you, Hank. I gave you the best advice I could. I told you to get counseling. But you hung up before my screener could give you the names of some therapists."

"Like I said, I don't need a shrink telling me there's something wrong with me, 'cause there isn't. All I need is for you to tell Vicky, right now on this show, that she should come back. She'll listen to you."

"Hank, I can hear how unhappy you are, but I can't do that. I don't know you, I don't know Vicky."

"You knew her enough to tell her to leave, didn't you?"

She stiffened. "Excuse me?"

"You heard me." Belligerent now. "She called in a couple of weeks ago. You told her to take my boy and leave me. So now I'm giving you the chance to make it right."

The SCREENER button flashed. Renee felt stirrings of unease but ignored it and shook her head again at Alicia, who was gesturing more emphatically now, running her hand across her throat. *Kill the call, kill the call.*

"I have a lot of callers, Hank. They call about a lot of different problems." She didn't recall a Vicky, but not long ago there had been a woman with an abusive husband. . . .

"You said so yourself, Dr. Renee. A couple of days ago you told a caller who'd caused trouble by mixing in somebody else's business that he should do everything he could to make it right. Do you remember *that* conversation?"

"That was you?" she said softly. Her chest tightened, and now she felt alarm.

"Vicky trusted you, Dr. Renee. You don't know squat about me or our marriage, but you told her to leave me. So now you have to tell her you were wrong."

Her headache was back, pounding at her forehead. "I can't do that, Hank."

"So what's the deal, Dr. Renee? You tell people how to lead their lives, but you don't practice what you preach? Is that it?"

"Hank, I want to discuss this with you at greater length. I have to break for a commercial right now," she said, nodding at Alicia to make sure she got the message. "So don't go away."

"Don't cut me off!"

She pushed the headset off her ears and quickly picked up the receiver to a phone that allowed her to speak to callers off the air. "I'm not cutting you off, Hank."

"Yeah, but I'm not on the air anymore. I have my radio on— I can hear the commercial."

"I'd like to discuss this with you, Hank. I'd like—"

"What's the matter, Doc? Are you ashamed to have your listeners hear how you messed up a family?"

"Hank, you're angry and hurt that your wife left you, and if you want to blame me for that, I can't stop you. But in your heart you know she didn't leave because of something I said. You need help, Hank."

"I want you to go on the air and say, 'Vicky, I was wrong. Go back to your husband.' And she'll do it."

"I can't do that, Hank."

"You can, but you don't want to. You don't want to admit

you screwed up. You said a person has do whatever it takes to make things right. You *said* that, didn't you?"

"That's true, Hank. But—"

"You'll be hearing from me, Doc."

The line was dead.

She was still troubled when she went back on the air, and had to struggle to put Hank, or whatever his real name was, out of her mind and focus on the other callers.

An hour and a half later she signed off. She threw down her headset and was collecting her things when Alicia entered the room.

She handed Renee a stack of faxes. "Why'd you keep that jerk on, Renee?" she demanded, clearly annoyed. "You should've ended the call right away."

"*You're* the one who let him on. *Again.*"

Alicia flushed. "The son of bitch changed his voice," she snapped. "You think I'm *happy* about this?"

She couldn't afford to alienate Alicia. "Of course not." She sighed and touched her arm. "I'm sorry. I know you didn't recognize his voice. I'm just tense."

"I *should've* recognized his voice."

"And I should have ended the call. I thought I could help him." Renee shrugged.

She slipped the faxes into her tote and had slung the bag over her shoulder, prepared to leave, when Pollin walked in.

"What the hell was *that* all about?" he asked, shutting the door behind him. "Did you tell this guy's wife to leave him?" An unlit cigarette in his hand, instead of the lollipop.

She refused to buy in to his anxiety. "I don't recall the specifics of the call, Max," she said with a calm she didn't feel. "A few weeks ago a woman *did* tell me her husband was abusing her. And yes, I urged her to seek help."

"But did you advise her to *leave?*"

"I may have."

Pollin leaned against the table. "We could be open to a lawsuit. I have to check with our attorneys."

Alicia rolled her eyes at him.

"This is the show's format, Max," Renee said. "It's what you pay me to do, give advice." An hour ago you were *thrilled* with the show, she added silently.

"There's advice, and there's advice. What did he say to you when you took him off air?"

"Basically, what he said before. That I should tell his wife to come back to him. I told him I couldn't do that."

"How'd you end the conversation?"

"He hung up on me." She hesitated. "He told me I'd be hearing from him."

Pollin snorted. "What do you think he meant by that if not a lawsuit?" He rubbed his chin with his free hand. "Let's find out exactly what you said to his wife."

"It may not be the same woman. I don't recall anyone named Vicky calling the show recently."

"Her husband's sure. Maybe she used another name."

"Seems to run in the family," Alicia remarked.

"Our tapes go back six months, right?" Pollin said. "Alicia, check the ones starting from a week ago and work backward."

She looked at him coolly. "I'm a producer, Max, not a detective."

Pollin frowned.

"I'll do it over the weekend," Renee offered. "I have my own set of tapes at home." She told herself she was curious, not anxious, but her stomach was in knots.

Pollin nodded. "If he calls back on Monday, Alicia, make sure you don't let him on with Renee."

"*Thanks* for telling me that, Max." Alicia smiled tightly. "Like I couldn't figure that out for myself."

"Don't get defensive."

She glared at him. "Don't tell me how to do my job."

"You let him on today, didn't you? Apparently, it's the second time he's been on with Renee. Maybe the third."

"He changes his voice, Max," Renee said, before Alicia could retort. "Not just his name."

He scowled. "I don't like this. I think this guy is trouble."

She wished she could disagree.

Stuart Logan leaned into the mike.

"So you know what I say? I say, enough with Hillary and Bill for this Friday P.M. We have more important stuff to talk about. Did you guys hear that Dr. Renee, KMST's combo of Joyce Brothers and Don Rickles, is splitting with her husband?" He swiveled toward his screener. "Ray, did *you* hear that?"

"I'm the one who told you about it, Stuart."

"Come on, Ray. You're supposed to make me look good on the show." He laughed. "So, guys, what do you think about that, huh? Here's this woman who's mouthing off all the time about how divorce is such a no-no, and she ups and leaves her husband! How do you spell 'hypocrisy'?"

"We don't know who left who," the screener said.

"*Whom*, wise guy. Who left *whom*. This is a classy show, remember that. Anybody have the skinny on this breakup, call in. Okay, we have Louise from Beverly Hills. Talk to me, sweetheart."

"Hi, Stuart."

"Hey, Louise. What's on your mind?"

"Well, I heard your comments about affirmative action, and I—"

Logan disconnected the call. "Boooorrring! Go buy a fur coat and don't bother me, okay? Fred, from La Puente. What's happening, Fred?"

"Stu, one more point about Bill Clinton. With all the evidence that he lied, why don't you think there's going to be another trial after he's out of office?"

"Don't you listen to the show? 'Cause it's a waste of the taxpayers' money, my friend, and in the end, the jury's not going to convict. In the famous words of Johnny Cochran, 'If he won't admit, you must acquit.' Forget Billy boy. What about this Dr. Renee thing? Any info?"

"I don't listen to her show, Stu."

"More power to you, my man." He ended the call, chose another line. "Alice from Monrovia. What's up, Alice?"

"Thanks for taking my call, Stuart. I'm a fan of Dr. Renee's, and I'm sure if she and her husband are divorcing, it must be his idea. Either that or she had a very good reason for leaving him."

"Are you her friend, Alice?"

"No, but—"

"Her hairdresser? See, I don't know how you can assume anything about Dr. Renee's motives. You know what they say about 'assume,' right? It makes an ass out of you and me."

"Dr. Renee believes in making marriage work, Stuart. She talks about it all the time."

"And I talk about trying to stop lusting after women. You married, Alice?"

"I *am* married, happily married."

"That's an oxymoron, sweetheart. You have a sexy voice. Are you wearing a thong?"

"You're disgusting, Stuart."

"I try." He laughed. "Thanks for your call, Alice." He chose another line. "Ray from Pasadena. How're you doing, my man?"

"I'm cool, Stuart. How about you? You cool?"

"Cool as Ice T. So what's on your mind?"

"I'll bet her husband had about enough of her smarty-pants, I-know-better'n-everybody attitude."

"So you think *he* left *her*, huh? You listen to her show?"

"Nope. But I know what she's all about. I seen lots of women like her."

"Uh-huh. Well, thanks for calling, man." Logan ended the call. "Come on, people. There must be info about the doc on the Internet. Find out. Call in or fax. Ray, do we have something to give to a caller who gives us the inside scoop?"

"A station T-shirt."

"I hate those dumb T-shirts."

"Dinner for two at the Eclipse."

"Now we're talking. Donna, all the way from San Diego. Are you going to win dinner for two?"

"Hi, Stuart. I don't think it's right that you're talking about Dr. Renee's personal life on your show."

"And why is that, sweetcakes? It affronts your sensibilities?"

"I heard her yesterday, Stuart, and you could tell it was painful for her to talk about this."

"Well, why'd she do it, then?"

"She said there were going to be rumors, and she wanted to set the record straight."

"Well, Donna, lemme clue you in. A, she's a celebrity, and celebrities know they have no right to privacy. B, she opened up on the air, so she's fair game."

"Well, I think it's mean-spirited and nasty, Stuart. So is your whole show. You have no respect for anyone."

"I am crying, Donna. Boo-hoo. Do me a favor, will you? Get a life. And if you don't like the show, tell your friends, so they'll listen, too." He chuckled. "Andy, from Woodland Hills. What's up, Andy?"

"You know what I think, Stuart? I think she did it for the ratings."

Logan nodded. "Interesting point, Andy."

"I mean, she's opposite Dr. Laura, right? She can't be getting the listeners Dr. Laura gets. So she figures, hey, she's gotta do something."

"I think you're on to something, Andy. Too bad I'm not married, or I'd try the same thing."

"So do I get dinner for two?"

"Sorry, man. That's for someone who has real info. But thanks for the call." Another line. "Joanne, you're on with Stuart Logan."

"Hey, Stuart. I don't agree with the caller who said Dr. Renee's doing this for the ratings. But I think it was inappropriate of Dr. Renee to do this on the air. She should have more dignity."

"Like me, you mean?" Another laugh.

"Well, I don't think she should subject her audience to the War of the Roses. And she has a young daughter. What does *she* think about all this?"

"Thanks for the call, Joanne." He disconnected the line and faced the screener. "Hey, Ray. You heard Joanne. What'd Dr. Renee say when she went public?"

"Not much. Just that she was going to make a good home for the daughter, protect her."

"Oh-oh, Ray. Gimme some ominous music. Do I hear round one of a custody battle?"

"Maybe."

"Hillary and Bill, you're over. What does Mr. Renee do for a living, do we know?"

"I checked. He's a writer."

"A shrink and a writer. What are the odds this kid's gonna come out normal? Hey, people. Who should get custody, the shrink-mom or the writer-dad? Don't be sexist, now. Ray, can we get Mr. Renee on the show? Maybe he wants to tell his side."

"I'll give it a try."

"They don't pay you to *try*, Ray. They pay you to *do*. Doo-wa, doo-wa, doo-wa." He chuckled. "Craig, from Hawthorne . . ."

((•16•))

"Our seventeen-year-old daughter, Katie, is pregnant and unmarried, Dr. Renee. We're just heartbroken."

"That is heartbreaking, Vincent," Renee said quietly. "How old is the father?"

"The same age. They go to the same high school."

"So much for sex education classes, right? Has your daughter told you what she plans to do about the baby?"

He sighed. "She won't have an abortion, which is our first choice. And she won't marry the baby's father, even though he's willing. She says she doesn't love him. She intends to have the baby and give it up for adoption."

"That sounds like an excellent plan, Vincent. Why are you and your wife opposed to it?"

"We don't want a stranger raising what's basically our flesh and blood. It doesn't seem right."

"But you're okay with aborting that same flesh and blood? Come on, Vincent. Level with me."

"I guess I don't consider a two-month fetus a baby."

"Try again, Vincent, because I'm not buying. What's your real objection?"

A few seconds of silence. Then, "We don't think she'll do it. Give it up, I mean. And then where will she be?"

"I see. So you think it's better if Katie and this high-school stud marry just because they happened to make a baby? Does that make any sense to you?"

"At least she'll be able to hold her head up. We're willing to help with the bills until they get on their feet.

"That could be a long-term commitment, Vincent."

"It's worth every penny if it keeps Katie from ruining her life.

We live in a small community, Dr. Renee. There's no way she can hide this."

"And what about you and your wife, Vincent? Are you worried about holding your heads up, too?"

Another silence. "I won't lie, Dr. Renee. We're shamed by what she did. Who wouldn't be?"

"You're entitled to feel angry and embarrassed, Vincent, but what's important is the welfare of that innocent baby. Your daughter's smart enough to realize that marrying a boy she doesn't love isn't the answer."

"She should've thought about that before she got pregnant!"

"Absolutely. But she didn't. So now what? You can't force her to marry this boy."

"Well, that's our question. We're the ones taking care of her. We pay for her food and clothing and doctor bills. We bought her a car. Is it wrong to tell her that unless she marries this boy, she has to move out?"

"Which means you'd be punishing the baby."

"We're hoping it won't come to that. You're always saying how important it is for a child to have two parents. That's what we want for our grandchild, too."

"No, what you want is to pretend your daughter didn't get pregnant out of wedlock. This baby can have two loving parents if he or she's adopted, Vincent."

"So Katie doesn't have to take responsibility for her actions?"

"Katie's taking responsibility for her actions. To tell you the truth, she sounds a hell of a lot more mature than you and your wife. If you force her to marry this boy, odds are the marriage won't last. That's what the statistics show. And then she'll be right back in your house with the baby, and you and your wife will have something else to embarrass you and keep you from holding your heads up high."

At three-thirty Jessie was ready to call it a day. She made a halfhearted attempt at organizing the loose papers on her desk, then gave up and covered them with two "blue books" filled with crime scene photos.

She was pleased with the day's events. She and Phil had finally located one of the items stolen during the course of the Westwood home shooting—a woman's gold watch, the face circled with diamonds, the back inscribed with the initials N.G. As in Noreen Gelbart, the woman who'd been killed.

Dumb of the killer. A lucky break for the police. The nervous pawnshop owner, who had produced the watch only after Phil, his eyes mean and cold, threatened to book him as an accessory, reluctantly identified the man who'd given him the watch. Simon LeRoux. They hadn't found Simon, but they had his rap sheet (his street name was Silo)—mostly burglary, no violence—and a list of known acquaintances, whom they would start questioning on Monday.

She picked up her purse. "Have a nice weekend," she told Phil.

He looked up. "I thought you were putting in overtime tonight."

"I'm bushed. I'm going to make it an early evening. Any plans this weekend?"

"A barbecue with Maureen's family on Saturday at their house. I get to listen to my father-in-law, the lawyer, tell me about the killing he's making in the market. But there's good news. Maureen said I can have a whole inch of steak."

"She loves you, Phil. She wants to grow old with you. She wants Brian and Chris to have their dad around."

He sighed. "I know. It's just damn hard to watch everybody around you stuffing their faces when you can't. I've been on this diet for three months and I've lost five lousy pounds."

"You cheat, Phil," she said kindly. "I see you do it."

"Whatever." He grunted. "I don't want to discuss this anymore, okay?"

She knew he was anxious about lowering his cholesterol, especially since a West L.A. detective in Burglary had suffered a serious heart attack two weeks ago. She'd put on a few pounds herself, lately—way too much pizza and junk food—and hadn't had a complete physical in ages. She made a mental note to call her doctor for an appointment.

"What about *your* plans?" Phil asked.

"I'm spending tomorrow afternoon with my sister and mom. And Gary's taking me to Maple Drive for dinner. I've been dying to go there."

Phil grunted. "He won enough off me this week to afford it. Think of me when you're ordering dessert. I'm basically paying for it."

She smiled. "I will."

"What's with your shrink friend? Maureen heard her say on the radio that she and her husband were separated."

"Renee figured she'd beat her husband to the punch. She hasn't phoned today, so maybe things have calmed down."

Phil nodded. "No news is good news. See you Monday."

Almost everyone was gone. She said good-bye to Simms and Boyd and the civilian receptionist downstairs. From the station she drove to a Ralph's supermarket, feeling at once awkward and eager with anticipation as she looked for and found a bag of packaged braided challahs with a kosher certification and a small bottle of Kedem grape juice. She'd intended this morning to buy the challahs at a kosher bakery, and wine at a kosher market, both on Pico, not far from the school where she was taking Judaic studies. But in the end she'd opted for the anonymity of a large, general market where no one would look at her with curiosity.

She'd felt shy about telling Phil she was planning to observe the Sabbath tonight. She'd pleaded exhaustion with Gary, and with Helen. She hadn't told Ezra, either. In a way it was like going on a blind date with someone you hoped would be the man of your dreams. She wanted this to be a special, intimate experience, unencumbered by the knowledge that she might have to report about it to others. And what if she was disappointed in the experience, or in herself?

At home she put away the groceries, placed in the oven the pan of chicken and potatoes she'd seasoned this morning, then stood in front of the refrigerator and scanned the magnetic Jewish calendar that she'd picked up a while ago.

Candle-lighting was 6:53. She'd been lighting Sabbath candles for over a month, ever since Ezra had given her a pair of ceramic candlesticks, but not every week, and not always on time. Last night she'd decided she would light the candles on time tonight and observe the Sabbath laws until the flames died out.

Over the past few months she'd read several books on the beauty of the Sabbath. Last night she'd made a list, using notes from her Judaic classes as reference, of what she could and couldn't do once the Sabbath began.

No writing. No cooking. No tearing of anything—paper, plastic, foil, fabric, threads, leaves, et cetera—except to avail oneself of readibly edible foods. No sewing. No carrying of items outside of one's property. No switching on or off of lights. No driving or phoning or watching TV or listening to the radio. No activity that initiates or enhances the usage of electricity or fire or gas.

"So many no's," she'd commented to Ezra months ago, after one of her earlier classes. "I don't understand why God would want us to observe a day that's so restrictive."

"Actually, the Sabbath is His gift, and the no's are liberating."

She raised a brow. "Liberating in what way? It's easier to use a vacuum than a broom, to drive somewhere than walk. Faster, too."

"Yeah, but why the rush, and what's your destination? Another sale at Loehmann's? A board meeting? A movie? The no's strip the day of worldly clutter, Jessie, of the mundane and superficial. They help us focus on what's important."

" 'The world is too much with us,' " she murmured.

" 'Getting and spending, we lay waste its powers.' Senior lit in high school. My teacher was a dragon, but I remember a lot." Ezra smiled. "Wordsworth's talking about nature, not God, but at least he sees the problem."

"And keeping the Sabbath is the solution?"

"While the rest of the world goes on conducting business as usual—phoning, faxing, e-mailing, shopping, driving, making mergers—to a person who keeps the Sabbath, all that's irrelevant. He uses the day to reconnect with his essence, with his family, with God."

She thought for a moment, then shook her head. "Sounds idyllic, Ezra, but not very realistic. The world *is* doing business as usual. What if you miss out on something really important?"

"Like what? Closing another million-dollar deal, or bidding on that huge ad campaign?" He paused. "Is that what we're all about—money, success? Or are we interested in the quality of life, in family?"

"What about life itself, Ezra? What if someone's sick? You don't drive him to the hospital?"

"To save a life, Jessie, you're *obligated* to violate the Sabbath."

"And to investigate a death?" She seldom worked weekends, but couldn't rule out the possibility. She could just imagine her lieutenant's face if she told him she had to stop an important interrogation because of the Sabbath.

Ezra nodded. "Not a problem. Since the purpose of investigating a murder is to identify and apprehend someone who might very well kill again, in essence you're trying to prevent the taking of another life."

"So what you're saying is, I have no excuse, huh?"

Ezra had smiled.

It would be wonderfully healing, Jessie had thought, to strip herself of the grit and ugliness of her job and immerse herself in the spiritual for twenty-five hours every week. Wonderful, but daunting. She'd been overwhelmed by the number of rules there were to learn and practice, unsure whether she was willing to make all those changes in habit, in lifestyle, in thought.

"Small steps," Ezra had counseled when she'd voiced her concerns. "Anything that's deep and profound can't come overnight."

The timer buzzed. She removed the chicken from the oven and shut the gas. She switched on the light in the kitchen. She did the same in the breakfast nook and den, and in the bathroom off her bedroom. Again she felt as though she were preparing for a special date. Which she supposed she was.

She placed the candlesticks on the breakfast room table, which she'd covered with an ivory linen cloth, and lit the candles, pleased that she knew the blessing—the *bracha*—by heart. Before, she'd enjoyed lighting the candles, making the blessing, but this time she was shy and excited, just as she'd been in the supermarket, as though she were about to cross a threshold. Using a prayerbook with English translation, she recited the blessing for the grape juice, which she'd poured into a crystal goblet. Then she recited the blessing over the challah.

The grape juice was overly sweet, the challahs adequate—inferior, she was certain, to the freshly baked ones she could have bought at the bakery. But she felt something spiritual tug at her core.

Maybe it was the candles. They softened the light from the overhead fixture, and she'd always been drawn to their dangerous beauty. But she'd had candlelight dinners and hadn't felt this enveloping serenity.

The stillness, then? Not a lonely stillness, which usually led her to turn on the radio or television while she ate, more often than not, in the den, or pick up the phone and call someone. This was a stillness that encouraged contemplation, introspection. "Delicious solitude," Thoreau had called it, but it wasn't exactly that, either, because although she was alone in her apartment, she was connecting on some level with all the other families and individuals—some novices, like herself—who were celebrating the Sabbath.

Maybe, she decided, she was feeling this emotional pull because she'd opened herself up to the spiritual, because she'd invited the candles and the wine and the challah and the lovely stillness to be her guides.

She was suddenly struck by the incongruity that the meal she was eating by the light of the steady Sabbath flames wasn't kosher. What did God make of that? she wondered.

Small steps, Ezra had said.

She cleared the table, did the dishes, then went to her den bookcase, where she'd arranged various Jewish philosophy books, most of which she'd read at least once. She brought two of the books to the breakfast room table—Heschel's *The Sabbath* and Soloveitchik's *The Lonely Man of Faith*—and began rereading.

The phone rang. She looked up, startled, and was tempted to answer it. But the moment passed, and her answering machine picked up on the fourth ring.

It was Gary. "I thought maybe I could get you to change your mind about tonight, but I guess you made a *really* early night of it," he said. "See you tomorrow night."

She felt a flash of guilt that she hadn't told him. But what was the point, really, since she didn't know where this would lead? And it mattered only if she decided to marry him again. She didn't know whether she planned to do that, either.

She sat at the table, reading, long after the candles' flames sputtered and died.

((•**17**•))

"... do you think, Dr. LaCrosse, that it's Dr. Renee's responsibility to explain the reasons for the breakup of her marriage to her listeners? If not, don't you think she's leaving herself wide open for criticism?"

"Well, the fact is, Joan, that this is a complicated issue, and one has to use caution before—"

He shut off the radio with an angry twist of the dial and uncapped a bottle of beer.

More talk.

That was all that was on, talk about Renee. She probably loved it, every minute, even though she was pretending not to. "This is personal, so I won't discuss it. This is causing me deep pain."

Bullshit.

He knew her so well.

He was coming very close to hating her. He'd given her every chance to make things right—had basically warned her, on the air, that he wouldn't sit by and let her ruin his life. Gave her a choice.

But she didn't care. Not Renee.

And she was more popular than ever. That really burned in his gut, the fact that more and more people would be listening to her spew her garbage because she'd made a mockery of him in front of the whole world, while he was left with what?

Nothing, that's what.

No wife, no career, his own child taken away from him. Permanently, if she had any say about it.

A man could take just so much.

He nodded and downed the beer, wiped his mouth.

Whatever happened, it would be her fault, not his.

((18))

"I'm glad you decided not to work." Helen shut the door behind Jessie. "It'll be fun, spending the day together."

"Absolutely." She'd changed her mind about attending synagogue, not because she'd "chickened out" again, but because she didn't want to rush into what could be an infatuation. "I saw the Cadillac across the street," she said, walking with Helen along the wide center hall. "Is Dad here, too?"

"In the family room, playing checkers with Matthew. They look so sweet together." Helen smiled and unconsciously ran her hand across the slight swelling below the waistband of her skirt, a gesture that had become habit. "Dad and Neil are going to baby-sit Matthew while you and I are out with Mom."

Her sister looked a little pale but lovely, Jessie thought, like a delicate Victorian beauty. "How's Mom?" So much depended on Frances's mood, which was mercurial.

"Fine. She's freshening up. I'll tell her you're here."

"Freshening up" for Frances meant reapplying her makeup and making certain every strand of her blond hair was in place. Helen always took pains with her appearance, too.

To please her mother, Jessie had dressed with care—freshly laundered beige slacks, a white short-sleeved silk sweater, white sandals with heels she'd made sure were unscuffed. She'd put on clear nail polish, applied a little more makeup than she normally did, had brushed her wavy hair into a neat ponytail and worn the half-carat diamond studs, a recent gift from her parents.

She walked to the family room and stood in the entrance, watching her father, who was sitting at a game table across from Matthew. He *did* look sweet, engrossed in play with his nine-year-old grandson. He'd played games with Jessie and Helen when they were young, too, had taken them on pony rides and to amusement parks and to the beach, had taught them how to ride a bike and play tennis. But she'd realized when she'd left home that she and her father had never really talked much. Not about things that mattered, anyway.

Matthew glanced up suddenly and noticed her. He grinned, revealing another missing tooth. "I'm beating Grandpa, Aunt Jessie! Right, Grandpa?"

"You certainly are." Arthur Claypool stood and, leaning over, ruffled the boy's coal-black hair. He smiled at Jessie, who had moved and was standing next to the game table. "You look beautiful. You always do." He kissed her.

"Thank you."

She flushed, touched by the love and pride in her father's eyes, and returned his embrace. She tried to imagine what he would say if she told him how she'd spent last night. Probably nothing. Just as he'd said nothing all those years when he'd pretended not to know what Frances was doing to his daughters. She felt stirrings of hurt but supposed that he'd probably paid a price for his silence.

Matthew squeezed her tightly and suffered her kisses. "We're going to watch *Godzilla*!" he exclaimed just as Frances and Helen entered the room. "Daddy went to Blockbuster to rent it."

Frances wrinkled her nose. So did Helen, and Jessie had to smile, because they looked almost identical with their short blond hair, green eyes, and expressions of disdain.

Frances kissed Jessie, then drew back and studied her, eyes narrowed. My turn, Jessie thought, standing taller and bracing herself, but her mother said, "Very lovely, dear." So she'd passed.

They waited for Neil to return with the videotape, then took Helen's car to the Century City mall. Jessie sat in the back, Frances up front next to Helen, who was driving because she was less nauseated if she was behind the wheel.

Helen switched on the radio to an oldies station. That much, at least, we have in common, Jessie thought, but Frances reached over and pressed the search button until she found a classical music station. Which Jessie liked, too, so why did she find her mother's action annoying?

She wasn't surprised when, a moment later, Helen pressed a series of buttons. Jessie heard blips of conversation: Tips on how to play the stock market, how to make a fool-proof soufflé, how to fertilize a garden. A talk show host interviewing a psychologist.

". . . my question is, Dr. Lewis, what effect does a therapist's admission that her marriage is over have on her devoted listeners? Will they question the advice she gives them?"

"There's no easy answer, Sharon. The truth is . . ."

They were referring to Renee. Jessie was about to ask Helen to switch the channel when Frances said, "Do we *have* to listen to this?" and Helen returned to the classical music her mother had chosen. But she'd made her point: It was her car, her radio.

"They're talking about Dr. Renee, Mom," Helen said. "I was listening to John and Ken when they said she and her husband separated. That's all Stuart Logan's talking about. He's really ripping into her."

"The Moran girl is getting divorced?" Frances asked, turning around to Jessie.

"Her married name is Altman, Mom." Frances always referred to Jessie's and Helen's friends, no matter how old, as "girls," and always by their maiden names.

"I'll bet he's having an affair," Helen said. "That's what Stuart Logan's been saying."

"Stuart Logan is the worst of shlock radio." Jessie hoped Renee wasn't tuning in to the guy's late afternoon show. "Barry's not having an affair. They're just unhappy living together."

"Who could be happy living with *her?*" Helen snorted.

Frances said, "I remember her as a very nice girl, Helen."

"Do you listen to her program, Mom? She's so mean, she makes people cry sometimes."

"We don't get her show in La Jolla. We get Dr. Laura, though. I assume these callers know what she's like, so maybe they want to be reprimanded."

A good point, Jessie thought. But why did they?

"In any case, it's refreshing to know there are people on the air who don't coddle their callers. You're too close to that car, Helen," she warned sharply.

"No, I'm not."

"If he stops short, you'll crash right into him."

"I know how to drive, Mom."

"You can't be too careful. If you're not worried about yourself or your mother and sister, think about that baby."

Helen tightened her hands on the steering wheel but pulled the car back. Jessie couldn't see her face, but assumed that had tightened, too.

"Are you still as friendly with Renee, Jessica?" Frances asked after a moment of uncomfortable silence. "You used to be at her house more than at your own. I never understood why."

Yes, you did, Jessie thought. You just don't want to remember. "We weren't for a while, but we've reconnected."

"That's nice." Another silence. Then, "I hope things work out for her."

So did Jessie. Renee hadn't phoned all day yesterday, or today. A good sign.

Helen parked in the underground structure, and they took the escalator to the outdoor court. The day was warm and only a little humid, with a mild breeze. Jessie would have preferred strolling outdoors, window-shopping, but she accompanied her mother and sister to store after store. Bloomingdale's first—Helen picked up two pairs of shoes and her mother, a purse—then Anne Klein, then a maternity shop.

"You're sure you're okay with this?" Helen asked before they entered, solicitous but hopeful, too, and how could Jessie say she found watching her sister model outfits that looked ridiculously large on her tiny frame and the plum-size mound she continually caressed a painful reminder of her own miscarriage? It wasn't fair to Helen, who had every right to revel in her pregnancy, and it made Jessie feel small and selfish.

After three more stores she felt she'd paid her dues, and when they neared the theater complex, she suggested seeing a movie. They decided on *One True Thing*. A bonding experience, Jessie had thought as they'd carried their popcorn bags into the theater. A mother and her two daughters seeing a film about a mother and daughter.

"I love Meryl Streep, don't you?" Helen whispered while they sat through a coming attraction. "She's wonderful."

"She's *always* wonderful," Frances said. "Fabulous cheekbones. I don't think she's had anything done."

Jessie suppressed a smile. Her mother, who had had a facelift several years ago, was always evaluating other women for evidence of plastic surgery.

The movie began. Jessie had known that the story, about a young journalist who comes home to care for her dying mother, would be a two-hanky affair, but she hadn't been prepared for the wrenching pain of watching the relationship between the mother, a warm, nurturing woman who took pleasure in her family, and the contemptuous daughter, who dismissed her as an insignificant housewife doing insignificant things. Sitting in the darkened theater next to Frances, Jessie cried for Meryl Streep's character, who was dying of cancer, and for the daughter, who realized almost too late how narrowly and wrongly she had viewed her mother and was overwhelmed by the enormity of losing her.

She cried, too, for the closeness she'd never had with her father or with Frances and wondered if she'd been looking narrowly at her mother, eyes hooded by anger and grievances nourished by her stubborn unwillingness to let go of the past, wondered how many years she'd wasted.

She felt a hand covering hers, and turned toward her mother. Throughout the movie Jessie had stolen glances at Frances, who had watched soundlessly, her face inscrutable.

"A beautiful, painful film," Frances said, her voice soft and shaky. She squeezed Jessie's hand, and Helen's.

Small steps.

((·19·))

Monday morning Renee awoke with a blinding headache to the ringing of her alarm. With her eyes shut, she groped for the button on her radio and cut off the blaring sound, then turned and rolled into Molly. She was momentarily startled, having forgotten that the little girl had fallen asleep in Renee's bed after another visit from the "monster."

She loved watching her daughter sleeping, loved watching the rise and fall of her small chest. But her head hurt too much. "Time to get up, sweetie," she whispered. Leaning over her, she blew warm breaths on Molly's cheek.

The little girl stirred and slipped her thumb into her mouth.

"Mommy doesn't feel good, sweetie. Can you get up now? I want to rest awhile."

Molly's eyes flew open. "Are you sick?" More curious than worried.

"I have a bad headache." She pointed to her right brow. "Can you ask Blanca to help you dress? And fix you some breakfast?"

"What should I wear?"

"Whatever you want. Blanca will help you choose."

"Can I wear one of the new things Daddy bought me?"

"That's fine."

" 'Kay." She wrapped her arms around Renee and planted a kiss on her brow. "Is that better, Mommy?"

Renee smiled weakly. "It's magic. It's *so* good I'll be up soon."

Her head throbbed. Shutting her eyes, she took deep breaths and felt the jostling of the mattress as Molly moved off the bed. A while later she heard footsteps approaching.

"The *señora* would like something for her headache?" Blanca asked softly.

Blanca was such a dear. "Please. Two aspirin. They're in my medicine chest, top shelf."

The housekeeper was back in a moment with the tablets and a wet washcloth, which she placed on Renee's forehead. The cool darkness was soothing.

"You try to sleep, *señora*. I will take Molly to school."

"I'll get up in a few minutes, as soon as the pills work."

"*Señora*, there is no need. You should rest."

Renee sighed. "You're so sweet, Blanca. Let me see how I feel when Molly's ready to leave. And please remember what I told you. If Mr. Altman comes to the park or house, I don't want Molly to go with him. If he's angry, don't be afraid. Tell him to call me." She repeated this in Spanish.

The housekeeper nodded solemnly. *"Bien, señora."*

Thirty-five minutes later, her head still pounding, she gratefully accepted Blanca's offer and Molly's good-bye kiss and drifted off to sleep. When she came home from work today, she told herself, she would have to do something about the "monster." Maybe she could get Molly to talk about it, or draw it. That had helped last time.

"Who died?" Ted Harkham said.

Renee stared at the baskets of flowers that filled the recording room. "It's a bit much," she agreed, feigning embarrassment though inwardly pleased by the effusive display. She walked over to one of the arrangements and read the attached note: WE'RE WITH YOU, DR. RENEE!

Ted cleared his things off the table. "Sorry to hear about you and your husband. That was pretty gutsy, by the way, going public with it."

She tensed and turned to look at him. "You think it was a mistake?" She'd been having second thoughts all weekend.

He laughed. "Hell, no. You're the topic of conversation on most of the other talk shows. Stuart Logan did a whole hour on you on Friday."

She grimaced. "That wasn't exactly my goal. He's so obnoxious."

"So what? He's giving you free advertising. You're *hot*, Renee. All this will die down, but you'll have tons of new listeners. Most of them will stick with you. This is the best thing that could've happened."

She supposed he was right. She didn't like the fact that her popularity and ratings would rise at the expense of her privacy— she would never have done that intentionally. But there was no going back now, so why not reap the benefits?

Ted left. Renee settled herself at the table, put on her headset, and began the program. Several callers prefaced their questions with supportive comments—she thanked them and made it clear she wasn't going to discuss her private life.

During the next three hours she was half expecting Barry to call. That would be just like him, wanting to have his say. But he didn't phone, and she was relieved.

She was even more relieved that there had been no more nasty notes, no hang-ups, no cars following her. She wondered whether Barry had been her stalker, whether a visit from Jessie had scared him off.

Renee arrived home after three-thirty and was disappointed to find the house empty. Blanca had probably taken Molly to the park. Renee didn't begrudge Molly her fun, and she'd talked to her during the two o'clock station break. But she'd been looking forward to seeing her, to feeling the small arms tight around her neck.

She emptied the mailbox and entered the kitchen, which was filled with soft Spanish music emanating from an under-the-cabinet radio. Packages of cellophane-wrapped frozen lamb chops—Molly's favorite—lay on the counter next to a wooden bowl with the beginnings of a salad. Dark green romaine leaves were draining in a wire basket in the sink.

Fixing herself a cup of coffee, she flipped through the envelopes and magazines, tensing in anticipation of more anonymous notes. But there were none. In her office she checked her phone messages and gritted her teeth when she heard Barry's terse, "Call me." When hell freezes, she thought, and erased the message, pleased by the speed with which the machine sent him into oblivion. She wished she could do the same.

Her coffee cup drained, she went upstairs to her bedroom, where she changed into sweats and read the new issue of *Time* while she exercised on the treadmill, one ear straining for the sound of Molly's small feet, which would be pounding up the staircase any minute now.

A half hour later they still weren't home. It was only a little after four, still broad daylight, but Renee began to worry. What if something had happened to Molly in the park? What if Blanca had taken her to a hospital? What if . . .

Stop it, she told herself. Molly was at the park, playing with other children her age. Blanca frequently brought her back later than this.

Renee stopped the treadmill and stepped off, her forehead glistening with sweat, her heart hammering with exertion and unease. She checked the entire house, upstairs and downstairs—it was possible she hadn't heard them return—then opened the French doors and walked into the backyard. It was a hot day. Maybe Molly had persuaded Blanca to let her swim. But the pool was empty, a smooth sheet of blue.

Back in the house, she stood in the kitchen for a few moments, telling herself she was being silly, then grabbed her purse and car keys and drove the eight blocks to the park, half expecting to see Molly and Blanca at any moment.

The park's jogging path was practically empty, but even from a distance she could see that the playground was filled with strollers and young children of varying ages and the women, sitting on benches, who tended them. She scanned the playground and suddenly saw Molly, her long blond curls dancing as she climbed up the stairs to a landing that led to a slide.

Renee's heart swelled. "Molly!"

The little girl turned around and positioned herself at the top of the slide. Someone else's blue-eyed child, screaming with delight as her little body skimmed down the smooth, shiny slope.

They weren't here. She tried to absorb the information calmly, reasonably. Maybe they'd left the park and stopped for ice cream. The weather was warm, and Molly loved ice cream, and Blanca tended to spoil her. Renee would have to talk to the housekeeper about that.

She approached the women on the benches. Most, she soon learned, were Hispanic; with them she used the faltering, make-do Spanish she'd practiced on a series of housekeepers. Some were Russian and knew more than a little English. Several of the women knew Blanca and Molly—*"Que linda, la pequeñita!"*—but no one had seen either of them, not today.

She felt stirrings of anger. Blanca had no right to take Molly somewhere other than the park without leaving a note. Renee returned to her car and drove home, prepared to berate the housekeeper, who by now, of course, was no doubt back in the kitchen, finishing the salad she'd started or seasoning the lamb chops she shouldn't have left on the counter to defrost, everyone knew that wasn't safe, while she listened to the music from the radio she'd carelessly forgotten to shut off.

The house was as Renee had left it, deafening in its solitude.

It occurred to her, as she bit her lips to keep from crying out her panic, that in spite of her instructions, the housekeeper hadn't been able to stop Barry from taking Molly. Blanca had probably been afraid to call Renee at the station and tell her what had happened. That made sense, Renee thought, irritated with the housekeeper, who had no doubt decided to go to the market to avoid being here when Renee arrived. That was probably why Barry had called, to tell Renee he had Molly.

Using the portable phone, Renee punched in his number and was gratified when he answered on the second ring.

"It's Renee," she said coldly. "I got your message. Listen, I told you—"

"I wasn't sure you'd call back. Look, I know you went public about us. I wanted to say I'm sorry about calling your show the other day. It was dumb and mean."

"It was." She was about to lash into him for taking Molly, but what if Molly wasn't there? She strained to hear the child's voice.

"I don't blame you for being pissed. I think we've both behaved rashly, but I'd like to think we could be civil to each other, Renee, if for no other reason than for Molly's sake."

"*You're* the one who started all this."

"Yeah, I know." He sounded sheepish. "I wasn't planning to say anything to Pollin. I was just angry that you sent Jessie to grill me."

"I didn't send her. That was her own idea. Anyway, it doesn't matter. All I'm concerned about is Molly's welfare."

"She says she's having nightmares about the monster again."

"When did she say that?" Renee asked—too sharply, she realized.

"Why are you upset? Did you ask her not to tell me?"

"No. I'm just curious. When did she tell you?" She held her breath, hoping he'd say, *Just now*.

"Yesterday, the day before that? I can't be sure. I talk to her every day, you know. Why didn't you tell me?"

So Molly wasn't there. Renee didn't dare let on that she didn't know where their daughter was. Barry would just love that. So would his attorney. "I was hoping they'd stop."

"What are you doing about it?"

She bristled from habit, but decided he sounded concerned, not accusing. "What we did last time. I'm giving her baths before bed to relax her, leaving on a night light. I've been reading her funny stories."

"What about getting her to playact? That helped last time."

"I'll try that, too. If nothing works, I'll take her to see the therapist again." She walked toward the front entry.

"It's my fault that the nightmares are back, right?"

You're the one who moved out. She bit back the words. Opening the door, she stepped outside and looked up and down the block. "It's not about *fault*, Barry. She's obviously confused and alarmed by what's happening. We have to tell her the truth, together."

"I think you're right. When?"

"Soon." She scanned the block again. Where *were* they?

"Before we do, you and I should talk. I've been thinking about the custody, Renee."

Her heart skipped a beat. "What about it?"

"I'm thinking maybe we can try to work something out."

She couldn't believe what she was hearing. "What changed your mind?" Jessie, she thought.

"I'm tired of the war, Renee. More importantly, I guess I finally realized I'm not being fair to you. Or to Molly."

She wasn't sure she believed him, but wasn't about to look a gift horse in the mouth. "When do you want to get together?"

"Soon. I'll give you a call."

She disconnected the line, gave a last look up and down the block, then shut the door and returned to the kitchen. Maybe they'd gone for ice cream first, *then* to the park. She was about to drive there again when she remembered Molly's new bike. Silly that she hadn't thought of it before. Molly was crazy about the bike. Blanca had obviously taken her riding.

She passed through the laundry room to the attached two-car garage and frowned, surprised to find the door unlocked. Opening it, she stepped into the garage and flipped on the light switch to her right.

There was the pink-and-white bicycle, still shiny in its newness. She was filled with disappointment—she'd been so sure!—and was about to leave when she noticed, several feet ahead, a still figure lying face up on the cold concrete floor. Blood was pooling near the head.

She heard herself screaming and swayed for a moment, overcome with dizziness and nausea as bile rose in her throat. Then she ran to Blanca's side.

The woman's eyes were open, staring at the ceiling. Renee knelt and took her hand, warm but heavy. She couldn't detect a pulse, and when she placed her ear over Blanca's chest, she heard no heartbeat. Still she raced back into the house to phone 911. Maybe, please God, Blanca was alive after all.

Where was Molly?

The phone was ringing. She lunged for the receiver, which she'd left on the kitchen counter. A telemarketing call.

She hung up and phoned 911, explaining what little she knew, that her housekeeper had apparently been injured and showed no signs of life. That her daughter—she sobbed the words— was missing.

Hurrying back to the garage, she crouched again at Blanca's still form, felt again for some small sign of life. But there was nothing.

She couldn't bear seeing Blanca like this. She went into her office to wait and noticed that the answering machine light was blinking. She pressed the playback button and waited for the tape to rewind.

"I have Molly, Renee."

She stopped the machine and moaned with relief, almost sank to her knees—thank you, God! Her hand shaking, she phoned Barry and wept when he answered the phone.

"Renee? Is that you?"

"Something's happened to Blanca! I think she's dead!"

"What do you mean, *dead?* How can she be dead?"

"I found her in the garage. There's no pulse, Barry! And her head is bleeding. She must have fallen and hit the concrete. And her eyes . . ." She couldn't stop shivering.

"Did you call the paramedics?"

"They're on the way."

"I'll be right over."

"Thank you!" she whispered.

"Poor Blanca. Is Molly okay?"

She froze. "Molly's with you."

"What are you talking about?"

"You left a message on my machine, Barry. You said you had Molly. I don't know why you didn't tell me when we spoke before." She was nauseated with fear.

"You don't know where she is?" he asked in a deadly quiet voice.

"You said you had her!" she insisted, as if that would make it true. A noise was beginning to blare in her ears. "You said—"

She realized that Barry had hung up, that the noise she heard was the sirens.

((**20**))

"My problem is, Dr. Renee, that my fiancé isn't happy about having my ex-husband in my life."

"Why is he in your life if he's your ex-husband, Carol?"

"Because of our kids. We have a seven-year-old son and a five-year-old daughter. He spends a lot of time with them."

"Can't fault him for that. And why is that a problem for your fiancé?"

She laughed, embarrassed. "He's kind of a jerk. My ex-husband, I mean. We weren't getting along for some time, and I finally realized it's because we have such different values."

"Different in what way?"

"I didn't call to talk about my divorce, Dr. Renee. That's behind me. But I don't know what to do about my ex-husband. I know he wants to spend time with the kids, but—"

"It isn't behind you, Carol, because you had children with a person who you now decided is a jerk. I don't know, but that doesn't seem like a good reason to break up a home. Maybe you should have thought twice before you married this jerk and made babies with him."

"He wasn't like that when I married him, Dr. Renee."

"So he changed? I don't think so, honey. Maybe you're a bad judge of character. Or maybe you get tired of people. Five years from now you may decide to divorce this wonderful fiancé."

"It's not like that, Dr. Renee. I'm more mature now. I know what's important. About my ex-husband. I've been taking the kids to his place so he won't have to come to the house, but next month is our son's birthday, and my fiancé doesn't want my ex at the party."

"Is he worried your ex is going to make a scene?"

"No. He's just real uncomfortable, because the kids kind of ignore him when my ex is around. So he suggested that my ex have a separate party for our son."

"Well, you can do that, Carol. And you can plan on having separate birthday parties for the next umpteen years, and separate holiday gatherings and graduation parties, but I don't think it's fair to the kids. And what happens when it comes to weddings and christenings?"

"I know." The woman sighed.

"The truth is that your ex-husband is always going to be a part of your life. And if your fiancé has a problem with that, maybe you ought to sit down and figure out who's the real jerk."

They still had no leads on the slain shop owner. They'd interviewed relatives, friends, and all the merchants on either side of the Oriental rug shop and had come up empty. Jessie found it hard to believe no one knew anything about the murder. More likely, they knew but were afraid to tell. She started rereading her notes from an interview with the dead man's cousin.

"Here comes the judge," Detective Marty Simms muttered.

She looked at Simms, then at Lieutenant Karl Espes, who was striding toward the Homicide tables with a military air.

"Lambert called in a new one," Espes announced crisply. He was five feet ten inches, had square shoulders and a husky build. Jessie had never seen him slouch.

Phil pointed to the "blue books" cluttering his desk. "Love to help out, Lieutenant, but Jessie and I are working two right now."

Espes swiveled his thick neck and fixed beady brown eyes on Simms, who was picking at his lower lip.

The fingers dropped to his side. "Boyd and I are trying to get a lead on the Sumac murder," Simms said. "We don't have enough hours as it is, Lieutenant."

"You're making me cry, Simms." No smile. "It's yours and Boyd's."

"Yes, sir." Ed Boyd quickly pushed back his chair and stood.

Even when sitting, the six-foot Arkansas native gave a lanky appearance. Freckles and strawberry-blond hair made him look younger than his twenty-eight years, Jessie thought. More naïve, too, which helped put suspects off guard.

Simms rose and hitched his pants. "What's the deal?"

"Thirty-something female, DOA." Espes paused. "Plus a kid is missing," he added somberly.

For a second no one spoke. "Son of a bitch," Phil said, his voice heavy with anger and pain.

He was probably thinking about his two young sons, Jessie thought. "There but for the grace of God . . ." She flashed to Matthew, mentally knocking wood that her nephew was safe, but it didn't really matter if you had a child or nephew or niece you worried about. Simms, a bachelor who prided himself on being unattached and uninvolved with family, looked equally grim.

"What's the address?" Simms asked quietly.

Espes read the address from a slip of paper. "That's in Brentwood."

Jessie felt as if the air had been sucked out of her chest. "What's that address again, Lieutenant?"

Espes repeated the address. "What's your interest, Drake?" He was looking at her curiously.

"That's my friend's house. Renee Altman." Her voice sounded strangled to her ears. "Do you have anything more on the DOA.?" Renee is dead, she thought, and Molly's been kidnapped. My fault.

"Apparently she's the housekeeper."

Not Renee. Jessie was almost dizzy with relief, though she felt a pang of sadness for the woman whose life, no less valuable, had come to a violent end.

"Can I have this, sir?"

"Your partner just said you're swamped."

"I need to be on this, Lieutenant." She hoped she didn't sound stubborn. Espes didn't like stubborn.

"You said it's a friend. You're too close, Drake."

"He's right, Jess," Phil said kindly.

She threw him an angry look, then faced Espes again. "Dr. Altman came to me last week, Lieutenant. She told me someone was stalking her."

"Why does her name sound familiar?" Simms asked.

"She's the radio shrink," Phil told him.

"No kidding!" Boyd looked impressed. "My mom listens to her show."

"Junk," Simms muttered. He picked at his lip.

"So now we'll have an effing media circus." Espes grunted. "Tell me about the stalker."

"Renee doesn't know who he or she is." Jessie repeated, in brief, what she knew. "I promised her if she gathered evidence, I'd take it to TMU."

Espes nodded. "You went by the book, Drake."

"I should have taken this more seriously."

"You did what you could. Legally, no one was stalking her. No way I would've authorized police protection."

"The housekeeper's dead and Dr. Altman's daughter has been kidnapped."

Espes frowned. "I said the kid was *missing*, Drake, not snatched. Not even a rookie detective would make an assumption like that without knowing the facts."

He was right. Jessie felt herself flushing and wondered if that was a smirk on Simms's fatuous face. "Why would someone kill the housekeeper?"

"A jealous boyfriend or girlfriend? Or maybe she interrupted a burglar. Lots of possibilities. The kid could've witnessed the whole thing and run away."

"I still think it's too much of a coincidence, Lieutenant. What about the stalker?"

"*Alleged* stalker," Simms said. "We don't know that there is one."

Espes scowled at him, then faced Jessie again. "Does your friend have any idea who this stalker could be?"

"Not really." Jessie hesitated, then said, "I liked the husband for it, but I wasn't sure." She explained why she suspected Barry, why she had her doubts.

"So maybe the husband got tired of playing the game and snatched the kid," Simms said. "Cheaper than paying the lawyers to drag it out in court."

"Then why kill the housekeeper?" Jessie shook her head. "She wouldn't have stopped him from taking Molly. Renee said he often picked her up from school."

"So he hired someone to snatch her."

"Enough speculation," Espes snapped. "Simms, you and Boyd set up a perimeter. I'll have twelve uniforms do a door-to-door for the missing kid. And get everything you can about the housekeeper."

"Lieutenant." Jessie cleared her throat. "I really want this case, sir."

"So you can do your *mea culpas*?" Espes shook his head. "Suppose it turns out your friend's the killer, Drake? Suppose she had her little girl kidnapped and has her stashed somewhere 'cause she doesn't want her ex to get his hands on her?"

"Renee wouldn't do that to Molly."

"See? That's the problem." Espes's smile was snide. "You're not going there with an open mind."

She'd stepped into that. "I can have an open mind, sir."

"I don't think so." His eyes were like granite.

"If the husband's involved, I'll get the evidence against him. If Renee is, I'll do the same."

He frowned, and she thought he was about to end it. "You have too much on your plate as it is."

She took that as a sign that he was weakening. "I'll do the paperwork for all my cases after hours and forgo the overtime." She could see that he found that appealing.

"What about your partner? Maybe he's not keen on putting more on his plate."

She glanced at Phil. Please.

"I'm game." He sighed. "Maureen'll probably kill me."

"Simms and I can pick up the slack, if necessary, Lieutenant," Boyd offered.

"Speak for yourself, D'Artagnan." Simms scowled.

Espes ran a hand over the top of his closely shorn head. "We try it," he finally said. "You cross the line, Drake, you forget for one second you're a cop, I pull you." He looked at Phil. "I'm holding you responsible for your partner."

Phil nodded. "No problem."

("**21**")

"So what do we have?" Phil asked Henry Futaki.

"Major trauma to the head. A concrete floor isn't very forgiving." The medical examiner peeled off latex gloves and discarded them. "The back of her skull looks like a cracked eggshell."

"Anything else?" Jessie asked, pushing the image out of her mind.

They were standing in the garage, about ten feet away from the body of the dead housekeeper. Jessie had taken photographs of the scene. Phil had charted the position of the body. The paramedics had left. Technicians from SID, some of them in the house, others here in the garage and in the back yard, were dusting for prints and looking for other evidence. One of the patrol officers who had responded to the 911 call was securing the house. His partner, along with twelve other uniformed police, each supplied with a xerox copy of a photo of Molly, were canvassing the neighborhood, searching for the missing child.

Routine procedure, Jessie thought, but so different now that her personal world had been invaded.

"Definite signs of a struggle," Futaki said, his eyes black balls hooded by black, bushy brows. "Tissue under her nails, a broken wrist that I don't think was from the fall. Bruises on her upper arms." He spoke in his usual monotone.

"Was she pushed, or did she fall?" Jessie asked.

"From the severity of the injuries to the head, I'd say she was pushed. Hard," he added, pursing his lips.

"How long has she been dead?" Phil shifted his weight to his other foot.

"What am I, a magician?" Futaki pierced him with an irritated look. "Body's still warm, no rigor. Sometime within the past few hours. That's the best I can do."

Phil smiled. "Quincy could do better than that, Doc."

"So call *him*. They haven't renewed his series—he's probably available. Television." He snorted. "I'll let you know when I have the autopsy results, so don't call to nag."

"Like that would help."

A few minutes later Jessie left the garage with Phil and entered the house. "Something of a prima donna, isn't he?"

"No one likes to be bugged, Jess."

She supposed not. "I can never joke around with him the way you do."

"Henry's okay. He takes a little while to warm up."

Three years? That's how long she'd known him. Phil had known him longer—maybe that was why the two of them were chummier. And because they were both men.

"You're sure you want me to talk to Renee?" she asked.

They'd discussed this on the way here. "You're her friend, not his. You said he wasn't thrilled when you went to see him last time. You talk to her. I'll talk to him."

Jessie nodded. "Makes sense, but Espes won't like it."

Phil smiled. "Espes isn't here."

One of the patrol officers, Roger Lambert, was in the spacious, air-conditioned family room where Renee and Barry were sitting on opposite ends of a long, L-shaped taupe chenille sectional sofa. Barry was hunched forward, his head in his hands. Renee, her face rendered clownlike by mascara streaks on her cheeks, was gripping her arms tightly, as if trying to keep her body from falling to pieces.

They looked up when Phil and Jessie entered the room.

Renee cleared her throat, but her voice was still hoarse when she spoke. "Did they . . ."

"They're taking the body away soon." Did it make it easier or worse, Jessie wondered, to hear "the body" instead of a name?

"How long—" Renee swallowed hard. "How long was she dead when I found her?"

"The medical examiner is estimating a few hours. He'll know more after the autopsy, but without other evidence it's pretty much impossible to pinpoint an exact time of death." Jessie sat down on an upholstered chair next to Phil.

"So she was dead when I came home from the studio?"

The pleading in her voice and eyes reminded Jessie of a supplicant seeking absolution. Barry was looking at Jessie intently, too. "Probably." It was almost six o'clock now. A "few hours," she decided, could be three. She didn't look at Phil. "We'll have to contact her next of kin." She took a spiral notepad from her purse. "Who would that be?"

"Her parents, in Guatemala," Renee said. "Blanca shared an apartment with a friend near downtown. That's where she spent her days off. I have the woman's phone number and address."

"We'll need to question all her friends and relatives."

"Why?"

Renee had told them about the message on her answering machine. *I have Molly.* So odds were, unless the phone call was a cruel hoax, they were dealing with a kidnapping, not a missing child. "Maybe Blanca knew the kidnapper. Could be he killed her because she could identify him."

"What would Blanca have to do with a kidnapper?"

Phil said, "Your housekeeper may have talked to a friend about her rich and famous employer, and the friend could've told a friend. That's how it goes."

Renee shook her head. "Not Blanca."

"You're probably right, but we have to check it out."

"I understand." She stood up shakily, as if coming out of a daze, and left the room.

"Barry, you told Officer Lambert you saw a man loitering in front of the house a few days ago," Jessie said. "When was this?"

"Wednesday, I think. Or maybe Thursday. I can't be sure."

"Did he do anything that made you suspicious?"

"Not really. But I didn't like the fact that he was just standing in front of the house. I thought maybe he was a fan of Renee's. She's had fans come to the house before. That's one of the reasons we put up the gate."

"Did you talk to him?"

"I was going to, but when I approached him, he left."

"Can you describe him?"

"He was more or less average-looking. Tall, well built. Dark blond hair. He had a little scar at the corner of his right eye."

"Good thing you're observant." Phil smiled. "Then again, you're a writer. Did you mention this to your wife?"

"No. I didn't think he was dangerous or anything."

Renee returned and handed Jessie a slip of paper. "I don't know who Blanca's other friends are, aside from a housekeeper down the block. Her name is Lupita."

Jessie copied down the information and the dead woman's full name. Blanca Gutierrez. "What about her family? You said they're in Guatemala?"

Renee nodded. "Her mom and dad, a sister and a brother, three kids. She sends them most of her paycheck."

"She was planning on going home next month for a visit," Barry said. "The first time in six years. She was so excited."

It was terribly sad, Jessie thought, unimaginably painful, really, to feel compelled to leave your country and live and toil among strangers so that you could make life a little better for those you left behind. She would get the family's name from the friend, maybe a phone number, and have someone contact the authorities in Guatemala, who would have the unenviable task of informing them why there would be no much-anticipated visit.

Lambert said, "I took Mrs. Altman through the rooms. She didn't find anything missing."

Except her daughter. "What about Molly's room, Renee? Did you notice whether any clothes were taken? Any toys that could help someone recognize her?"

It was hard to be professional, to talk dispassionately about Molly as though she were any other missing child, not a little girl whom Jessie had cooed at and bought gifts for, had even helped bathe.

Renee shook her head. "But she has a lot of clothes, so I might not have. Why doesn't he *call?*" she wailed suddenly. "If he wants money, why doesn't he call and *tell* us, damn him!"

"He'll call when he's ready, Renee. This is his way of assuming control."

"I want to know that Molly's all right!" she whimpered. "I can't bear to think how terrified she is."

Jessie had nothing to say to that. "I know you told the officers you weren't sure what Molly was wearing this morning. Shock can do that. Can you tell us now?"

Renee turned white, as though someone had bleached her face. She licked her lips. "I don't know," she finally whispered, clearly aware of the enormity of her admission.

"You don't *know?*" Barry's eyes were rimmed in red, and he looked as if he'd aged a decade. "She's your daughter, and you don't know what she was *wearing?*" His voice shook with fury.

Renee flinched but faced him. "I woke up with a terrible headache. Blanca helped Molly dress and offered to take her to school. I was resting when they left the house."

Barry looked at her with disgust and turned away. Renee lowered her head and tore at the mutilated skin around her thumb.

It was a fallacy, Jessie knew from years of experience, that a tragedy or crisis brought people together. More often than not, it intensified the grievances and strained the relationship to the breaking point. She'd been a witness to many such bitter exchanges, some of which she'd welcomed as the source of leads for her investigation. Now she was acutely uncomfortable, and she wondered if Espes hadn't been right.

"If you look through Molly's closet and drawers, Renee, you could probably figure out—"

"It was a new outfit!" Renee exclaimed. "The one you bought her, Barry. I just remembered."

"Give yourself a medal."

"This isn't helping," Jessie told him firmly.

"She didn't even know she was *missing!*" He turned to Renee. "Blanca was lying there for God knows how many hours while you were toning your thighs."

"I thought they were at the park, Barry. Blanca often takes Molly to the park. I *told* you this."

"Describe the outfit you bought Molly, Barry," Jessie said.

He gave Renee a withering look, then faced Jessie. "I bought her a *few* outfits a couple of weeks ago. I'm the one who usually takes her shopping." Another glance at Renee. "I don't know which one Molly picked today."

"Let's have a look," Phil said, rising from his chair.

((22))

Jessie moved next to Renee, who made no attempt to follow Phil and Barry and Officer Lambert upstairs—self-protection, no doubt, so she wouldn't be reminded again of her dereliction as a mother. Convenient for Phil, who would use the opportunity to question Barry alone while Jessie did the same with Renee.

"He blames me for what happened," Renee said with half-hearted defiance when they were gone.

"He's frightened, Renee. He has to blame someone. We all do that."

The muscles in her face twisted. "Oh, God, I want her back!" she whispered, gripping Jessie's arm. "Help me get her back!"

Jessie felt her eyes tearing. "We're doing everything we can, Renee. I promise." Small comfort. She loosened Renee's hand and patted her back.

"You're thinking I should have listened to you and had her stay with Barry." She wiped her eyes and nose with her fingers. "But I really thought she'd be safe, especially after you told me Barry might be the stalker."

Your fault. The words stung, but Jessie made no attempt to defend herself. She probably *had* given Renee a false sense of security, even though she'd urged her to take Molly to Barry's. Maybe she hadn't taken Renee's fears seriously enough.

And now she had to be a cop, masquerading as friend. "I know how worried you were that if the judge found out someone was stalking you, he'd give Barry custody."

"That was a stupid reason. Stupid and reckless. You were right, but it's too late now, isn't it?"

"It's easy to give advice when your child's not involved. I don't know what I would have done in your situation." Not really a lie. "Barry was so adamant about demanding sole custody. I don't blame you for being anxious."

Renee sighed. "You can't even imagine."

"You didn't want to lose Molly. Any mother could understand that, but the judges nowadays?" Jessie shook her head and sighed. "Sometimes I don't know what they're thinking, taking kids away from their mothers."

Renee picked at her thumb. Jessie hated this, lulling her friend into confessing that she'd engineered Molly's abduction. She didn't believe for one minute that Renee had done it, but Espes was right. She had to keep an open mind.

She wondered how Phil was doing. Probably having the same conversation with Barry, with a twist. She could imagine what Phil was saying: *Judges nowadays, they're supposed to give the father a fair shake, but most of the time they're still giving custody to the mother.*

"You hear about mothers who run away with their kids to protect them," Jessie said. "That doctor, Elizabeth something? She sent her kid out of the country. She sat in a cell for years because she wouldn't tell the judge where her daughter was."

Renee nodded. "I remember that."

Like what, women make better parents or something? Sometimes they're the worst parents. Especially career women. You tell me, how can you be a good mom if half the time you're not home with your kids?

"I admire her," Jessie said. "I think she did the right thing, don't you?"

"I guess. But the father was a molester. Barry's a good father. I can't say he isn't."

"But he was being so *unreasonable,* and he was so angry at you. What if he decided later on not to let you see Molly? I'm sure that's what you were worried about."

I have kids, too, Mr. Altman. Two boys. So I know what you were going through. I'd never let my wife keep them from me. No way.

"If my husband threatened to keep my child from me . . ." Jessie let her voice trail off. "I really understand how a mother could take her children and disappear, even if it *is* against the law."

Sometimes a man's gotta do what a man's gotta do, right? To hell with everything else.

"He was reconsidering asking for sole custody," Renee said.

Jessie eyes narrowed. "You didn't tell me, Renee."

"He just told *me* when I called him today, the *first* time."

"Did he say why?" She kept her voice casual.

Renee shook her head. "He apologized for calling the show. Then he said he'd been rethinking the custody issue and promised we'd meet soon to talk about it. I think I rattled him when I told him he couldn't just come by and take Molly whenever he wanted. But now he'll never trust me." Her eyes teared again.

Interesting that Barry had a change of heart just before he learned that his daughter had been kidnapped. Coincidence, Jessie wondered, or an attempt to divest himself of motive?

She was pondering the possibilities when two men from GTE security arrived. Renee showed them the various phone jacks in the room, then resumed her seat on the sofa and watched as they set up the phone trap.

They were done a short while later and were leaving just as Barry followed Phil into the room. He looked more haggard, if possible, than before—the aftermath, Jessie supposed, of searching through his daughter's clothes. Unless, of course, he wasn't really worried about his daughter. . . .

Renee glanced in his direction, then quickly away.

"Talk to you a minute?" Phil motioned to Jessie and stepped into the hall.

"How'd it go?" she asked when she joined him.

"The little girl was wearing a denim jumper and a yellow T-shirt, both from Old Navy. Her favorite store, Altman said. And blue Nikes. Lambert's passing that on to headquarters, and to the uniforms talking to the neighbors."

"Missing child or kidnapping?" The information would be out on all the police department bulletins. If the call *was* a hoax, and Molly was missing, they would alert the media, hold a press conference. If it was a kidnapping, they'd try to keep things as quiet as possible.

"My guess?" Phil pursed his lips. "Kidnapping."

"Mine, too." They'd have to alert airport security and train and bus stations, provide them with a photo of Molly, although the kidnapper probably had his own car. And if he took Molly out of California, the FBI would be called in. More complications.

"How'd the father seem?" she asked.

"Terrified. Lost it when he started looking in her closet. Started shaking."

"Real?"

Phil considered. "Real enough. But if he had someone snatch her, and didn't bargain on the housekeeper getting offed, he'd have good reason to shake."

She looked over her shoulder at Barry, then back at Phil. "Something he said makes you think he arranged this?"

"Nothing he said, nothing he didn't say. My gut says something's bothering him, though. But he didn't bite. You?"

Jessie shook her head. "I don't think she has a clue about what happened to Molly. And I'm keeping an open mind," she said, though Phil hadn't made any comment or raised a brow. "Did he tell you he was rethinking the custody?"

"Nope." Phil cocked his head. "Was he?"

"He *told* her he was. A couple of hours ago, when she phoned him the first time." She repeated what Renee had said.

Phil stroked his mustache. "Interesting timing."

"Isn't it? So is the fact that he didn't tell you."

Phil nodded. "If he planned the snatch, it looks better if we learn about his change of heart from her. Less obvious."

They returned to the family room and found Barry and Renee sitting exactly as they had before, frozen in a tableau.

"We'll need another photo of your daughter," Phil told them.

"Are you going to use dogs to track her?" Barry asked. "I can get you something she wore."

"We don't have track dogs. Just dogs that hunt drugs."

"They *always* use dogs," he said stubbornly.

"That's mostly in the movies," Phil said in his kindest voice. "We're going to do everything we can to find her, Mr. Altman. That's a promise."

"She could be dead by now!"

"We can't guarantee she isn't, but why would the kidnapper let your wife know he has your daughter if he killed her?"

"Because he's playing some game. Because he's some crazy sadist." His hands were clenched into fists.

"He *wants* something from you and Renee, Barry," Jessie said. "Probably money—that's what they usually want. He needs Molly alive so that he can get it."

"We don't *have* much," Renee said, looking at her husband.

"He doesn't know that," Jessie told her.

"Maybe Renee told him I blew her millions, like she's been telling the rest of the world." Barry glared at his wife. "I may not be a financial genius, but I know what our daughter was wearing this morning."

"I'll need that photo," Phil said.

The room was filled with pictures of the golden-haired, golden-smiled child. Some on the ledge of the tiled fireplace, some hanging on the wall, others on the shelves of the built-in bleached wood bookcases. She was much bigger than Jessie remembered, but the sweetness in the face was the same. Her heart ached for the little girl—God only knew what she must be going through—and she said a silent prayer for her safety.

Renee picked up a framed photo from the bookcase, then set it down. "We have loose photos of Molly in the other room. That's easier than removing one from a frame."

Not easier, Jessie thought as Renee left the room, but with her world falling apart, she was probably trying to preserve a semblance of order and normalcy.

"She didn't even know what Molly was wearing," Barry said, addressing Phil. "Can you believe it?"

"Barry."

"What?" He turned abruptly toward Jessie and drew in his breath, preparing for battle.

"Even if Renee had found Blanca the minute she came home from the station," she said quietly, "Blanca probably wouldn't be alive. And Molly would be gone, and we'd still have to wait to hear from her kidnapper."

He didn't answer.

"It doesn't help that you're at each other's throats."

"No," he agreed, and stared at his knees.

Jessie leaned against the sofa. Phil tapped his fingers on his knee.

"She needs her amoxicillin," Barry said suddenly, his head jerking up. "I told you she had her spleen removed? It makes her more susceptible to infection. That's why she needs her amoxicillin, every day."

"You'll tell him that when he calls," Phil said. Not needing to specify the "him."

"He won't care. Why would he care?" Almost a groan.

"He left a message. He's going to call again and tell you what he wants. So he needs her to be in good shape."

"Where will he get it? He needs a prescription, and he sure as hell won't go to a doctor to get one. He knows they'll be looking for him." He buried his head in his hands.

Phil exchanged a look with Jessie. "Let's worry about that later," he said. "First, let him call."

23

Renee returned with photos of Molly, then resumed her seat on the sofa, miles away from her estranged husband.

Phil said, "Dr. Altman, I noticed that your entire property is gated."

"We did that about a year ago, after Molly ran into the street and was hit by a car. We didn't want to risk that happening again. And because of my show, I have a rather high profile. So we thought all around it was a good idea."

"Was that gate open or locked when you came home today?"

"Locked. We *always* keep it locked. There's a keypad, and you punch the code to open and shut it. If I'm in my car, I use a remote."

"Can it be opened from the inside without a key or remote?"

Renee shook her head.

"It's a high gate," Jessie said. "The assailant could have climbed over it to get inside your property, but I don't see how he could have left that way with Molly. Does she know the combination, Renee?"

"I don't—"

"She does," Barry interrupted. "She's a smart girl. She showed me one time but promised she'd never use it unless I said it was okay. So she could've told the kidnapper."

Phil said, "Dr. Altman, you told Officer Lambert the front and back doors were locked when you came home, and so was the outside gate. But the inside house door to the garage wasn't?"

"Right. Blanca probably took Molly to the garage to get her bike. Barry bought it for her a week ago. She loves riding it," Renee added mournfully.

"The reason I'm asking, I'm trying to establish whether the

kidnapping took place when your housekeeper was *leaving* the garage with your daughter or returning."

"What difference does that make?" Barry demanded.

"Maybe none. We just want to establish a clear picture of the events. Would the housekeeper have left the door unlocked?"

"Blanca *always* locks the door to the laundry room," Renee said. "She's been careful lately about locking *all* the doors."

"Why is that?"

"Molly's been having nightmares about a monster." Renee's eyes welled. "She's afraid to be left alone, even for a minute. And she watches Blanca lock the doors, so she won't worry that the monster will be waiting in the house."

The poor kid, Jessie thought. Plagued by imaginary monsters, and now caught by one that was all too real.

"Would she have opened the garage door before she locked the door to the laundry room?"

Renee considered for a moment. "She might have."

So the kidnapper could have been waiting on the premises and entered the garage at that point, Jessie thought. Or he could have followed Molly and Blanca *into* the garage when they came home. Which made more sense.

"There's a key to the laundry room," Phil said. "What about the garage door itself?"

"There's a different key, and a remote for the car. The same remote that operates the outside gate. We have two sets."

Phil said, "I'm assuming we'll find one set of keys on your housekeeper or somewhere in the garage. Can you check to make sure you have the other set?"

Renee looked puzzled, but once again left the room. A moment later she was back. "Barry's keys aren't on the hook, where they should be." She turned to her husband.

"I don't have them," he said, his voice curt.

"How do you *know?* They could be in a pants pocket. It wouldn't be the first time you didn't put them back."

"I *said* I don't have them."

"Maybe you could check when you go home," Jessie suggested. "What about the remotes?"

"Mine is in my car," Renee said. "Barry still has his. You were supposed to drop it off," she said coldly.

"I did, when I brought over the bike for Molly. I gave the remote to Blanca."

Renee frowned. "She would have told me."

"Maybe she forgot. We can't ask her now, can we?"

"We'll look for it," Jessie said. "Did you—"

"What if the kidnapper took it!" Barry exclaimed. "If he has the remote, he can open the gate and garage whenever he wants to. You should change the combination, Renee."

"How would he have known where it was?"

"Maybe he searched for it. I know I returned it. You're not safe, Renee."

"What a surprise, Barry. I didn't know you cared."

He pursed his lips and looked at the wall.

Jessie felt a surge of sympathy for Barry, whose concern sounded genuine, but found his thinking illogical. She couldn't imagine the kidnapper searching for a remote after he'd assaulted the housekeeper and had a terrified child on his hands.

Still . . . "Did you notice anything out of order in the house, Renee?"

"No."

"You have an alarm system?" Phil said.

"Yes. There's a button in the garage that sets the alarm. You press it just before you use the key or remote to shut the garage doors. I don't understand how the kidnapper just happened to be around when Blanca took Molly riding."

"He was probably watching the house for some time," Jessie said. "When did Blanca *usually* take Molly out?"

"Between two and three. And they'd usually be back around three-thirty, when I come home."

"And when was the last time you talked to Molly or Blanca today?" Phil asked.

"I already *told* the officers." Renee bristled with impatience. "I spoke to Molly at two, during a station break."

"Maybe Blanca *did* know the kidnapper," Barry said. "Detective Okum is right, Renee. She could've mentioned you to someone. One of the women in the park, maybe. And this person could have visited Blanca last week and taken the remote and given it to a boyfriend or a nephew."

Renee sighed. "If you lost the remote, Barry, just say so."

"What if you're wrong? If this person knew Blanca, she'd also know her routine. You really should change the combination."

The phone rang. Renee clutched the edge of the sofa cushion. Barry jumped up and headed for the desk that held the phone.

"You answer it, Renee," Jessie said. "The kidnapper addressed you in his message. The phone trap is set. Speak as naturally as you can."

Barry hesitated, then sat back down while Renee hurried to the desk and brought the receiver to her ear with a shaking hand.

"Hello?" Only a small quiver in her voice. "No. No, thank

you." She hung up the phone. "MCI, wanting to know if I'd like to switch long-distance carriers." She returned to the sofa and slumped down onto the cushion.

Phil said, "Let's go over the sequence of events, Mrs. Altman. You unlocked the front door and found no one home. You drove to the park to see if your daughter and housekeeper were there. You returned home and called your husband—"

"And lied to him," Barry interrupted. "She pretended everything was just fine."

Jessie quieted him with a look.

"Then you went to the garage," Phil said. "What made you do that?"

"I remembered the bike. I thought Blanca had taken her riding." She turned to Jessie. "I told you all this! Molly's missing. Why are you wasting time about all these stupid details instead of trying to find her?"

"We're not wasting time, Renee. We're waiting for the kidnapper to call. In the meantime we need to get a clear idea of exactly what happened." And see if you change any details. . . .

Phil said, "When you found your housekeeper, you phoned 911?"

Renee sighed. "Right. And then I noticed that I had a new message on my answering machine. I thought it was my husband's voice, telling me he had Molly, so I called him."

"But it wasn't your husband's voice."

"No."

"Why did you think it was?"

"I guess I assumed it was, from the first part of the message."

"What did the entire message say, exactly?" Jessie asked.

"I *told* the police officers what it said." Renee sounded exasperated. " 'I have Molly, Renee. I'll be in touch.' Something like that." She frowned. "There was something—" She stopped and shook her head. "I can't remember."

"Try, Renee. It might be important."

Renee nodded and narrowed her eyes in concentration. A moment later she shook her head again.

"Let's get back to the message," Phil said. "Why would you think your husband left it?"

"I hadn't heard the whole message when I called him. I only heard the first part, that he had Molly. Barry often takes Molly to his apartment, and he lets me know."

"But you don't have the message."

"Somehow it got erased."

"You erased it?" Jessie asked casually.

117

She gave Jessie a weary look. "I didn't think so, but I guess I must have."

"Did *you* hear the message?" Jessie asked Barry.

He shook his head. "When Renee tried to play it for me, it had already been erased."

"You tried to play it first," Renee said. "Right when you got here."

"No, I didn't." Calm.

"You *did*. I remember. Then you told me to try it."

"Is that correct?" Phil asked.

Barry scowled. "Are you suggesting I intentionally erased the message? Why the hell would I get rid of evidence that could lead to my daughter's kidnapper?"

"Nobody's saying you did it intentionally," Jessie said.

"What is this, a Jonbenet Ramsey thing? You think I'm involved in my daughter's kidnapping?" His face was red.

"We don't think that at all, Barry," Jessie said in a soothing tone. "We're just trying to establish what we know. Let's talk about the kidnapper's motive. Did he mention anything about money, Renee? Take a second to think before you answer."

"He didn't say anything about money. I would have remembered. He just said he'd get in touch." Again she frowned.

"Did you remember something?" Jessie asked.

"Something about what he said is bothering me. I only heard it the one time. But it's . . ." She shook her head.

"Try not to focus on it. It'll come back to you."

Renee nodded.

"Mrs. Altman, you told Detective Drake you believed you were being stalked," Phil said.

Jessie was studying Barry's face, which had turned white. Genuine shock, or feigned? She couldn't tell.

He stared at Renee. "What's he talking about?" he demanded.

"Apparently your wife thinks someone's been following her," Phil said when Renee didn't answer. "He left a couple of notes and made some hang-up calls. He dropped off a gift at the house."

"Someone was stalking you, and you didn't *tell* me?" Barry's voice rattled like a radiator about to explode.

"I wasn't sure."

"You were sure enough to tell the police!"

Renee glanced at Jessie, then back at her husband. "I thought if you knew, you'd use it against me in court. You'd tell the judge that Molly isn't safe with me."

Barry's laugh was terrible.

"I never for a *moment* believed she could be in danger! I thought—" She stopped and looked at Jessie.

"You thought what?"

"It doesn't matter," she said dully.

"You thought *what*? Look at *me,* damn it!"

"I thought maybe you were doing it," she finally said.

"Why in hell would I— Oh, I get it." He nodded, then sat silent for a moment. "Well, that's great. That's *just* great. My wife thinks I'm some kind of evil sadist." He turned to Jessie. "You think so, too, right? That's why you came over the other night, to check me out. So what'd you decide, Detective?"

"I haven't, yet," she said evenly, and met his eyes.

"Oh, my God!" Renee covered her mouth with her hand. Her eyes were wide with fear. "I remember what he *said*! Pollin thought he was going to sue the station, but that's not what he meant."

"You're not making sense, Renee," Jessie said gently.

She twisted toward Jessie. "The man I told you about? The one who wanted me to persuade his wife to go back to him? He phoned Friday and said it was my fault she left."

"Your fault?" Jessie frowned. "Why?"

"He said I advised her to leave him. When I said I couldn't tell her what to do, he threatened me."

"What did he say?"

" 'You'll be hearing from me.' That's what he said on the answering machine, too. 'You'll be hearing from me.' "

"It's not unusual wording," Phil said.

"It's him! He wants his wife and son back, and I wouldn't help him. Don't you see?" She grabbed Jessie's hands. "That's why he took Molly."

24

"When did this man's wife supposedly call you?" Jessie asked.

"He told me, but I don't remember. He sounded intense the first time he phoned the show—he used a different name. The second and third times, he was angry with me. But I never in a million years thought he'd harm Molly! I didn't think he was the stalker. If I had, I would have called you, Jessie."

Crying softly, she turned to Barry, but he didn't so much as nod. Jessie wasn't sure whether he was ignoring his wife, or whether he hadn't heard her. He was staring at the wall, as if in a trance, clenching and unclenching his hands.

"When did he first call you, Renee?" Jessie asked.

Renee faced her again. "Monday. He said he'd given someone wrong advice and didn't know what to do about it. Thursday he called as Hank. Friday he called again and told me he'd been referring to *me* on Monday, to the fact that I'd advised his wife to leave him. My God, he's crazy! And he has Molly!"

Jessie put her hand on Renee's arm. "I know this is terribly difficult for you, but you have to pull yourself together. Do you have the tapes of your shows?"

She nodded quickly. "All of them." She wiped her eyes. "I keep them in my office here in the house. I'd planned to listen to them over the weekend, to see if I could find the call from Vicky. But Molly was so anxious, so clinging. . . . The tapes didn't seem all that urgent."

"I want you to get all the tapes of his calls, Renee, and find the one when his wife phoned in. She might not have used her real name—maybe she was afraid he'd find out. Do it now, Renee," she said when Renee made no move to get off the sofa.

Renee glanced anxiously across the room at the phone. "What if he calls?"

"Barry will answer." Jessie looked at him out of the corner of her eye—still no response. "Detective Okum will help you, Renee," she said, and saw Phil's comprehending nod.

"All right." Renee sounded uncertain and looked over her shoulder several times as she left the room with Phil.

Jessie waited a moment. "I'm glad we can talk alone, Barry. You may be in some trouble," she said in a low, sad voice. "I'd like to help, if I can."

"Can you get Molly back?" he asked softly without turning around. "Because that's the only help I need."

"My partner wants to take you in for questioning."

He turned and stared at her. "What in hell for?"

"He's convinced you know something about the kidnapping."

"That's crazy!" His face was blotched with color.

"I told him I don't think you had anything to do with that." She paused. "But you *were* stalking her."

A muscle twitched in his cheek. "I didn't stalk Renee."

"You wanted total custody of Molly. You told me yourself you'd do anything to get her."

"That's not what I meant!" He licked his lips, ran a hand through his hair. "Jesus, you twisted everything, didn't you! No wonder—" He stopped.

"No wonder what?"

"I didn't stalk her. You're barking up the wrong tree."

"You dropped off two crystal goblets with an anonymous note. 'Hope you're happy.' " She thought, but wasn't sure, that she saw something flicker in his eyes.

He shook his head. "That's crazy. For all I know, Renee bought the stuff herself and wrote the note, just to set me up."

"I don't think so."

"I don't care what you think. Molly's been kidnapped by some maniac, and I don't have to deal with this garbage!" Jumping up, he walked to the bookcase and took down the photo of Molly that Renee had been looking at before.

"The salesman who sold you the goblets identified you from a photo Renee gave me," Jessie lied. "Renee doesn't know—I was going to tell her today, but then all this happened. I haven't told my partner yet, either."

"The salesman's mistaken." Barry's voice was terse, clipped. "I didn't buy Renee anything."

"You tried not to leave fingerprints on the gift note you included with the goblets, but you *did* leave some. I matched them to your prints on the Dr Pepper can."

He returned the framed photo to the shelf and faced Jessie.

"A, you're lying, because I didn't leave that note. B, even if they *were* my prints, stolen evidence is inadmissible."

His smile was smug, but she could sense his nervousness. "You *gave* me the soda, Barry. So the prints are admissible." She softened her voice. "You'd make it a lot easier on yourself if you told me the truth. I can explain to my partner that you were worried about losing Molly, worried that she wasn't getting the supervision you thought she should have. Today proves it, right?" She saw again that she'd touched a nerve.

"I didn't stalk her."

"You're not giving me much of a choice here, Barry. I'm going to have to tell my partner, and my lieutenant. And then it'll be out of my hands. I won't be able to help you."

"Like you helped me when you came to my apartment?"

Jessie sighed. "Suit yourself, Barry." She rose and headed toward the doorway.

"It was a spur-of-the-moment thing," Barry mumbled.

She turned around. "Following her?"

"I *told* you. I never stalked her." He hesitated. "I saw her in that Century City store, holding the goblet. I followed her out of the store, figuring I'd talk to her. But I chickened out. I went back to the store and bought the goblets and dropped them off at the house."

"Why didn't you sign the note?"

"I figured she'd know they were from me."

He sounded truthful. Which meant nothing. She'd interrogated killers who sounded and looked like altar boys. "And the note?"

He shrugged. "It was a dig. 'Look what you've done to us, to what we had.'"

She cocked her head. "You're the one who walked out."

"I told you, she made it impossible for me to stay."

"So you broke the stem on one of the goblets."

Another, sheepish shrug. "A little symbolism from the writer. Shattered dreams . . . I was sure she'd get it."

"And call you up, asking for a reconciliation?"

"Something like that." His face had reddened again.

Jessie shook her head. "Not a very romantic gesture, unless you're Stephen King."

"I was trying to make a point. Anyway, that was it. But I never followed her."

"Come on, Barry." She smiled in a friendly way. "Even if you followed her, that doesn't mean you were trying to spook her. You were curious to see if she hooked up with some other guy. Anyone would understand that."

"Who's the writer here? You've got an overactive imagination."

"You didn't send her any other notes? Call the house and hang up when you heard her voice? We can trace the records."

"Go ahead. You won't find anything."

He sounded more confident now. Which meant either someone else had followed Renee or Barry hadn't called from his home.

He stood and walked over to the phone. "Why doesn't he call? Why the *hell* doesn't he call?"

Renee had located a tape with a call made two and a half weeks ago from a woman named Linda who was considering leaving her husband.

"I'm not sure that's Vicky," Renee told Jessie, "but it's the only call that fits."

Phil was holding a small tape recorder and four cassettes. "On his last call, Hank told Dr. Altman that his wife had phoned in a couple of weeks ago. We checked the tapes from the past four weeks. This is the one. She fits."

He set the recorder on the travertine coffee table, slipped in one of the tapes, and pressed PLAY.

"*. . . and I wish you the best of luck with your new job. Well, that's not easy, is it? Giving up a great-paying job for one that pays less but gives you more time at home with your kids? All right. Let's see who Alicia has next for me.*"

"Here we go." Phil pointed to the tape machine.

"*Linda, welcome to the program.*"

"*Dr. Renee? I'm so glad you took my call. I've been trying to get through for a long time.*" She had a sweet voice, heavy with sorrow.

"*Well, I'm glad, too, Linda. How can I help you?*"

"*I've been married for seven years, Dr. Renee. We have a five-year-old son who's the best boy in the whole world, and—*"

"*Linda, I don't have time to listen to your whole life story. Why are you calling today?*"

"All heart, aren't you?" Barry sneered.

"*. . . know if I should take my son and leave my husband.*"

"*Is your husband abusing you or your son?*" Silence. "*Linda, I can't hear you.*"

"*This is so hard,*" the woman whispered.

"It's a simple question, Linda," Renee said, not unkindly.

"He hits me," she said with obvious reluctance. "At first it was just a slap once in a while? But things are bad now, real bad, and I don't know where to turn." She was sobbing now, the words coming out between cries.

"Linda, honey, listen to me carefully. It doesn't matter whether he gives you a little slap or chokes you. If my husband laid a finger on me in anger, I'd be out of there in a flash."

"I want to leave, Dr. Renee. But I'm afraid of what he'll do to me when he finds me."

"That's not a reason to stay, Linda. But it's a damn good reason to leave."

"I know." She sighed. "He's sorry afterward, Dr. Renee. And he promises he won't do it again. And what about our son? He needs his daddy."

"He doesn't need a daddy who beats up Mommy. And what happens when Daddy starts slapping his son around, too? 'Sorry' doesn't cut it, Linda. Unless your husband gets help, he'll never change."

"He says he doesn't need help. He says lots of couples go through stuff like this, and they handle it on their own."

Renee sighed. "Why are you calling me, Linda?"

"I want to leave, but I'm afraid. I don't know what to do."

"You have to do whatever it takes to protect yourself and your son. I think you know that."

"I don't have anywhere to go, Dr. Renee." She wasn't whining, just stating a fact.

"There are shelters, Linda, where you can be safe."

"I can't go to a shelter. He'll find me."

"There are agencies and hot lines that can help you. Stay on the line, and I'll have Alicia give you some numbers to call."

"He'll find me, Dr. Renee, wherever I go. You don't understand. He—" She stopped.

"He's what?"

"He has ways."

"You can contact the police and get protection."

"Maybe I should stay and make the best of it."

"I can't tell you what to do, Linda. But why don't you get those numbers from Alicia and think about it?"

"Thank you, Dr. Renee."

"I wish I could do more to help, Linda. Be good to yourself."

Phil leaned over and switched off the machine. "That's it. Looks like she took your advice, Dr. Altman."

"She *wanted* to leave," Renee said. "She said so."

Jessie wasn't sure whether Renee was justifying herself to Barry, who wasn't even looking at her, or to herself. Not that it mattered. Vicky's husband had heard what he'd wanted to hear and had chosen to blame Renee for his wife's defection. And the irony was that while Jessie faulted Renee sometimes for her caustic or too-pat advice, this time she agreed with her. Vicky had been smart to leave.

"Renee, do you know if Alicia gave her the phone numbers of some shelters?" Jessie asked.

She shook her head. "I can ask. But Alicia wouldn't know how to contact this woman."

But if Vicky had fled to one of the shelters Alicia had referred her to, maybe Jessie could find her and track down her husband. "What about the Hank phone calls?" she asked Phil.

"What Dr. Altman said. He blames her, wants her to go on the air and tell Vicky to come home."

"I'll take them to Manny Freiberg, let him listen to them." Manny was a police psychologist at Parker Center who had helped Jessie over the years with some of her cases, and with personal issues as well.

"Can I listen to them?" Barry asked. "I want to hear the son of a bitch's voice."

"No problem." Phil removed the cassette, inserted another one, and pressed PLAY.

Barry's face tightened when he heard Hank's voice, then went blank as a mask and remained that way until the third taped phone call was over. Jessie wished she knew what he was thinking.

"Why doesn't he *call?*" Renee asked again, more weary than angry.

Jessie was beginning to wonder the same thing. "I'll stay a while longer," she told Phil. "You go on home. Maureen's probably mad as it is."

No argument from Phil. She left the room with him, feeling acutely sorry for Renee and Barry, alone with each other with nothing to say.

"Barry sent the goblets," she told Phil when they were out of earshot. She repeated what he'd told her. "He still denies stalking her. Maybe Hank is the stalker."

"Maybe."

The sky was darkening, the air cooler. She felt chilly in her short-sleeved cotton blouse. "What are you thinking?"

"He's one defensive guy, Barry. He's hot under the collar when his wife suggests maybe he has the missing keys and remote."

125

"Maybe he's embarrassed that he forgot to return them. Gary's like that—can't admit when he goofs. For that matter, all you men are like that." She tried a smile to camouflage the uneasiness she felt.

"And the custody? He calls her up out of the blue and tells her maybe he'll be nice?"

"It *could* be a coincidence."

He looked at her with interest. "You're the one who thought it was odd, Jess."

"That was before we knew about Hank."

"What about the tape? He erased that by accident? Or is that something else all men do?"

"He says he didn't even hear the message, Phil."

"She says he *did*." They were at Phil's Cutlass. He leaned against the driver's door. "Maybe she thought it was Barry because it *was*. He erased the tape so we couldn't listen to it."

Goose bumps dotted her skin. She hugged her arms. "You really think he kidnapped his own daughter?"

"I'm bothered by that gate. How'd the kidnapper get out with the little girl if it was locked?"

"Barry said Molly knows the combination."

"So he says. We don't know that's true. *He* knows the combination, doesn't he?" Phil paused. "I'm not saying he kidnapped her, Jess. I just think we should keep our minds open to the possibility."

She nodded agreement. "If he wanted to take Molly and leave town, all he had to do was pick her up from the house like he often did. He didn't have to kill the housekeeper."

"You said Renee changed the rules. She told him he couldn't just come by anytime he wanted, right? She would've instructed the housekeeper not to let Molly go with him. Maybe the woman tried to stop him. He got angry, pushed her too hard. She fell."

"Why leave a tape at all, Phil? Why not take the kid and run?"

"To throw us off. With a kidnapping, he figures it's his kid, how hard are the police going to look for them? But now he's killed a woman. The police are going to call in the FBI and pull out all the stops to find him. With the tape, he makes it look like someone else snatched her. And he tells us this bogus story about a guy he saw loitering in front of the house."

Jessie thought that over. "So where's Molly? If you're right, he can't keep her at his apartment. Too risky."

"Probably at a motel somewhere."

"Indefinitely?"

"I don't think he's thought this through, Jess. It's not what he planned."

"You're serious about this? You want to put a tail on Barry?"

"Right now it's just a theory, Jess. Maybe there's nothing to it. Maybe Hank is the kidnapper."

She tried to read him. "But you don't think so?"

"Maybe. Or could be a coincidence. This Hank may be angry, but that doesn't mean he's going to kidnap Dr. Renee's kid."

Jessie considered, then shook her head. "Why would Barry do something so risky? It's not as though he's desperate. He told me his lawyer was confident that he'd get custody. He's the stay-at-home dad. Renee's away a lot."

"Who knows what was going through his head?"

Jessie sighed. "I just don't see him doing something like this, Phil."

He looked at her kindly. "Espes was right. You're too close."

Maybe she was. "What happens to your theory if this Hank calls?"

"He hasn't yet, and it's been hours since the little girl disappeared. Interesting, don't you think?"

((**25**))

"I found out my sister-in-law had an affair a year ago, Dr. Renee, and I don't know if I should tell my brother."

"Why on earth would you do that, Margo? Is the affair over?"

"Yes. But he should know, shouldn't he?"

"You're assuming he doesn't know."

"He would have told me, Dr. Renee."

"You sound clairvoyant, Margo. Do you have a crystal ball?"

"We're close, Dr. Renee. We tell each other everything."

"Believe me, sweetheart, nobody tells another person everything. I see several possibilities. One, your brother knows what happened and has decided to forgive your sister-in-law and move on. So hearing from you would only dig up old wounds. Two, he suspected but didn't want to know, in which case he certainly doesn't want anything confirmed for him now. You'd make him feel stupid on top of everything else."

"If I were in his shoes, I'd want to know."

"Would you? I don't think so. And if he had no idea at all, why tell him now? The affair's over with."

"I don't know. It doesn't feel right."

"You know, Margo, this isn't about you and your feelings. Telling your brother something that would only hurt him is a pretty selfish thing to do. Now why would you want to do that?"

"I don't want to hurt him. I want what's best for him."

"I don't know, Margo. I sense that you're just dying to tell your brother that the wife stepped out on him. Could there be some jealousy here? Maybe you think your sister-in-law's coming between you and your brother."

"That's not it, Dr. Renee. I like my sister-in-law—at least I did, until all this. What if my brother finds out about his wife from someone else? I did."

"There's something you're not telling me, Margo."

"No, there isn't."

"Well, you think about it, Margo. And when you're ready to be honest with yourself, call again."

Claudia Newman scrutinized Jessie's badge through the privacy window before she opened the door.

"You can't be too careful, especially after what happened." The tall, reedy blonde shook her head. "Have they learned anything about the little girl?"

"I'm afraid not." A door-to-door search in an eight-block perimeter had turned up nothing. No one had seen Molly by herself, or with a stranger. No one had seen a suspicious person or car near Renee's home today or anytime within the past few weeks. "Your housekeeper and Dr. Altman's were friendly. I'd like to ask her a few questions. What's her full name?"

"Lupita Morales." Claudia looked uncomfortable. "She'll be nervous about talking to a police detective."

"I don't care if she's an illegal, Mrs. Newman." Jessie smiled pleasantly. "She may know something that could help us find the child."

Claudia grimaced. "I hope we're not going to be invaded by the press, like last time."

By "last time," Jessie knew, she was referring to the brutal murders several years ago of Nicole Simpson and Ron Goldman, found just blocks from here. The quiet Brentwood neighborhood had been besieged by reporters and hundreds of curious thrill-seekers who had flocked to the sight as though it were a shrine.

Jessie remained in the entry while Claudia went to find the housekeeper. A few minutes later the woman returned and led Jessie to the living room, where the housekeeper was waiting.

She was a slender, short woman, probably in her late twenties. She held her tightly folded hands on her lap and darted anxious looks alternately at Jessie and at her employer, who was translating. Jessie had a high-school knowledge of Spanish, but she wanted to make sure she understood accurately what the housekeeper was saying, and she assumed the woman would feel less intimidated with her employer there lending moral support.

"She says she doesn't know much about Blanca's personal life, except that her entire family is in Guatemala," Claudia told Jessie. "They used to go to the park together—that's where they became friendly."

"Ask her if Mrs. Gutierrez mentioned seeing a man hanging around Dr. Altman's property during the past few weeks." Jessie watched Lupita's face while Claudia translated.

The housekeeper shook her head. *"Solamente el esposo. El visita todo el tiempo."*

Only the husband. He visits all the time. "Ask her if she saw Mrs. Gutierrez today, and if so, when."

Another shake of the head. Lupita said she hadn't seen Blanca at all today.

"Was Mrs. Gutierrez nervous about anything lately?" If Renee was right, and her angry caller had kidnapped Molly, then Blanca wasn't involved. But what if Renee was wrong?

Claudia translated Jessie's question. The housekeeper quickly shook her head no.

Too quickly. And she was avoiding Jessie's eyes. "Tell her not to be afraid," Jessie said. "Tell her it's important for me to know everything so that we can find the Altmans' little girl."

Again Claudia translated. The housekeeper looked uncertain. She began hesitantly, then erupted into rapid-fire Spanish and gesticulated excitedly with her hands. Jessie heard "Molly" and *"immigracion"* several times, and *"miedo."* Fear.

Claudia turned to Jessie. "She says Blanca was very nervous. A few days ago, a person from social services came to the house to speak to her about Molly. She told him to come back in the late afternoon, when Mrs. Altman would be home, but he insisted on talking to Blanca right then. He threatened that if she didn't cooperate, he'd turn her in to Immigration and she'd be in serious trouble, possibly deported."

Lupita's eyes were riveted on Jessie.

Had the family court judge sent someone to investigate Renee and Barry? She wondered if this was the man Barry had seen loitering in front of the house. "Did she let him in?"

"She was afraid not to. He asked her about the Altmans— what they were like as parents, who took care of their daughter. He asked more questions about Mr. Altman."

To see if he should be awarded custody? "Anything specific?"

Claudia spoke again to the housekeeper. More rapid-fire Spanish from Lupita, who was wringing her hands.

"He wanted to know if Mr. Altman had a drinking or drug problem," Claudia told Jessie. "Blanca was afraid to lie. She told him Mr. Altman had started drinking more heavily a while ago, but that he was a nice man and a devoted father. Then he asked her who Molly would be happier with. Blanca told him she couldn't answer that."

Curious. Jessie wondered when Renee had mentioned the drinking to her attorney—before or after Barry's harassing phone call to the station. Maybe this was her way of retaliating.

"Did Blanca tell Mrs. Altman about this man?" She waited while Claudia translated and Lupita answered.

Claudia faced Jessie. "He warned her not to say anything to either of the Altmans, that he would know if she did."

"Did he talk to the little girl?"

More translation. Lupita shook her head. *"La niña estuve con su papa."*

Molly had been with her father. "What day was this? *Que día?"* Jessie asked, addressing the housekeeper.

"Viernes, en la tarde."

Friday afternoon. The same day Hank had made his angry second call to the show. Coincidence? She wondered uneasily if the man had pretended to be from social services to gain access to Molly. But Molly had been with Barry, so he'd returned today.

"What did he look like?"

Claudia translated. The housekeeper shook her head again: Blanca hadn't said much about him.

"Please tell her that if she remembers anything else, she should call me right away." Jessie handed a card to Claudia, another to Lupita, then stood and started to leave the room.

Lupita spoke again in Spanish.

Jessie turned around.

"She remembers one thing Blanca told her," Claudia said.

"Un hombre grande. Beeg." Lupita accented this pronouncement with both hands and widened, somber brown eyes.

The lamb chops, defrosted, were on the counter where Renee stood, wiping the blood that had seeped from the cellophane wrapping and turned the white grout pink.

"Have you eaten anything?" Jessie asked.

"I'm not hungry. This is hard to get out." From the cabinet under the sink, she took a can of cleanser and sprinkled the powder onto the counter. She turned to face Jessie. "Should I offer the officers something?"

Lambert and O'Reilly would be here until two officers relieved them. In the morning, other officers would arrive. "Coffee would be nice. Sandwiches, if you're up to it." Keeping busy might take Renee's mind off things. "Where's Barry?"

"He went to his apartment. He's coming back, but plans to go home to sleep in case the kidnapper calls his place."

Phil would find this interesting. "I don't think he's going to call tonight, Renee."

"He *has* to." She nodded stubbornly, her hand squeezing the scouring pad. "He has to know about the amoxicillin."

"I think he'll call tomorrow, during your show." Unless he didn't call at all. Jessie wasn't sure how serious Phil had been earlier, speculating about Barry. In any case, she had to consider all the possibilities.

"Of course." Renee smiled tightly. "It's a game, isn't it? Well, I'm not playing. How can I do the show when my baby's been kidnapped? I don't even know if she's alive."

"He's not giving you a choice, Renee. We can use this to our advantage. Someone may recognize his voice and call us."

"This is obscene." Renee sighed, tired, defeated. "You think Molly's alive, don't you? There's no reason to think he'll hurt her?" Her gray eyes were anxious.

"No reason," Jessie agreed and had an urge to cross her fingers. "What happens if Molly doesn't get amoxicillin?"

"An infection could become very serious, very quickly."

"Was she okay this morning?"

Renee nodded. "But without a spleen, she's highly susceptible to pick up something that wouldn't affect you or me. Bacterial or viral. And if she didn't get immediate medical attention—" She stopped. "I can't even think about it."

"I may be wrong, Renee. Maybe he *will* call here. Someone will stay with you in case he does."

"You're leaving?" Her face paled, and she looked stricken.

"The officer in charge will page me if he *does* call, no matter what time. There's nothing more I can do now." She'd tried contacting Alicia at home on the chance that she had the phone numbers of the shelters to which she generally referred abused women. But the screener hadn't been in.

Renee was silent a moment. "There's no way I could have known he'd do something like this."

"Don't blame yourself, Renee," Jessie said gently.

"I've been going over and over that poor woman's call. I couldn't have said anything different."

"No," Jessie agreed.

"He was controlling, abusive. She was in danger. How could I tell her to stay?"

"You couldn't."

"You told me to leave Molly with Barry. I should have listened."

Jessie didn't answer.

Renee turned and scrubbed at the grout.

26

Jessie arrived after class started and found a seat in the back of the room. She'd felt guilty leaving Renee, but there really *was* nothing more she could do until the kidnapper called. And the truth was, she'd felt a need for a dose of spiritual uplifting to dispel the oppressive mood in the house. She supposed she could have stayed to be a buffer between Renee and Barry, but at some point they would have to face each other.

Ten minutes later she wasn't sure why she'd come here. She found it difficult to follow Ezra's lecture. She'd missed much of what he'd said earlier and her mind kept going to Molly, a little girl plagued by nightmares about monsters.

She remained in her seat after class ended, lost in thought, then glanced toward the front of the room where Ezra was talking to a smiling young woman whose body language said she was definitely flirting. Why not? Jessie thought, with a twinge of something that wasn't exactly jealousy. He was a catch—an intelligent, sensitive, good-looking widower, tall and lanky with curly dark brown hair. And nice. So very nice. She'd been flattered a while ago when he'd expressed interest in getting to know her, had found telling him about Gary awkward. If she weren't involved with Gary, who knows? . . . It occurred to her suddenly that she hadn't talked to Gary all day. She didn't know if he'd called her at home; she hadn't checked her messages.

The woman left. Jessie studied Ezra as he ambled toward her and tried to figure out why he looked different. A gray tweed jacket, she realized, instead of his usual camel.

"I know I was late," she said. "Sorry."

His brown eyes were thoughtful. "You okay? You seemed preoccupied during class."

She sighed. "My friend's daughter is missing, probably kidnapped. Her housekeeper was murdered. I can't stop thinking about the little girl, feeling her fright."

He nodded somberly but said nothing.

"I've been a homicide detective for over five years, Ezra. I've seen my share of evil, and I'm not really surprised by the horrible things people do. But I'm having a hard time figuring out how the God I lit candles for on Friday night could let some monster kill an innocent woman and kidnap a six-year-old child."

"The big question." He sat down next to her. "I don't have an answer for you that isn't going to sound pat."

"Try me."

"I can tell you that the world we live in is a temporary place, that there's an afterlife where evil is punished and good is rewarded, that we believe in the reincarnation of souls."

She shook her head. "That doesn't cut it for me, Ezra. What about *this* world? What about the terror this child is experiencing, and her parents' anguish?"

"You want a God who's going to swoop down like Superman and rescue the innocent. I'd like that, too. Evil exists. So does goodness. And each of us has the free will to choose a path."

"This little girl didn't *choose* to be kidnapped, Ezra."

"No. No, she didn't." He sounded terribly sad. "We don't understand God's plan, Jessie. It's like looking at a jigsaw puzzle and seeing only one piece. By itself, it's senseless, pointless. With the other pieces, it forms a complete, perfect whole. God sees the whole puzzle, and we trust that God is good."

"*Why?*" she pressed.

"Because we recognize the preponderance of good over evil in the world. Because we believe in His ability to right wrongs."

She sighed. "I don't know."

"Why do *you* believe in God, Jessie?"

She considered. "Because it's too scary *not* to."

He nodded. "Not a bad answer."

She hesitated. "Can I ask you a personal question, Ezra?"

He didn't answer immediately. "You want to know how I felt about God when I lost my wife and unborn child," he said softly.

"If it's too painful to talk about . . ."

"I didn't blame God, if that's what you want to know. I wasn't angry at Him. I was angry at the sick people who committed this vile act of hate, and I tried to accept what happened."

"You didn't question Him?"

"I always ask Him questions. That's not the same thing. And I accept that I'm not always going to get answers, that I don't understand. Just as I believe He hears my prayers, but may decide to say no."

"I don't think I could react the way you did. I don't have your faith."

"Years ago I didn't think I could react that way, either," he said quietly. "And just because I accept God's will doesn't mean I don't grieve, Jessie. I grieve every day." He paused. "The Talmud tells about Bruriah, the wife of Rabbi Meir. She was a renowned scholar in her own right, and used to learn three hundred new laws from three hundred rabbis every day.

"Two of her sons died one Shabbos. She didn't want to tell her husband until Shabbos was over, as there was nothing to be done and she didn't want to ruin the tranquillity of the day or disrupt his Torah studies. When Shabbos was over, she went to him. 'I must ask you a question of *halacha*,' she said. 'Someone lent me a precious object to watch over and asked for its return today. Must I return it now?' Her husband answered, 'You must return it, of course.' She took him to the room where their two sons lay dead. 'God gave us these precious gifts to watch over,' she told him, 'and today He has asked for their return.' "

"It's an amazing story," Jessie said after a moment. "She sounds like an amazing woman. But I don't think I could ever be like Bruriah, Ezra."

"I don't think I could, either. What's the little girl's name?"

"Molly. Molly Altman."

He sighed. "I'll pray for her."

27

"Absolutely not, Detective Drake." Max Pollin shook his head. "There's no way this station can allow you to put a phone trap on our lines. It's a First Amendment issue."

"I understand your reluctance," Jessie said politely. "But I believe that the kidnapper is going to call Renee while she's on the air. And with the trap, if we're lucky, we can locate him and find Molly." They could probably get a judge to issue a warrant, but that could take time, especially if the station resisted.

Pollin leaned back in his chair. "You don't know that he's going to call during the program."

"Max, he didn't call yesterday," Renee said with barely restrained impatience. "He didn't call last night or this morning. Why do you think that's so?" She'd been up all night, waiting for a call that never came. Her eyes were red-rimmed, the lids puffy; blusher only intensified her pallor and sunken cheeks and gave her a cadaverous look.

Jessie ached for her. She'd barely slept all night, either. Twice, half asleep, she'd jumped up in her bed, shaking at the gruesome images of Molly that flashed in front of her. At five A.M. Tuesday morning, she'd brought in the *Times* and been startled by the Metro section's headlines:

**RADIO TALK SHOW SHRINK'S DAUGHTER KIDNAPPED,
HOUSEKEEPER MURDERED.**

Gary's byline.

It had taken a moment for that to register. She'd dressed hurriedly, furious with Gary for not having had the decency and courage to phone. Goddamn it, he owed her that much! She'd tried him at home—she didn't care if she woke him up—but he didn't answer, and she didn't leave a message. Then she drove to Renee's to prepare her, but Renee had already been bombarded by television and newspaper reporters. She hadn't mentioned Gary's name, and Jessie hadn't asked, but wondered uneasily whether she'd seen the byline.

"This guy may *never* call." Pollin sighed deeply. "I'm sorry, Renee, but you have to face the possibility, painful as it is." He glanced at Jessie.

Renee flinched. "You're wrong, Max," she said firmly. "He doesn't want Molly. He wants his wife and son back. He said so."

"I agree with Dr. Altman," Jessie said. "I'm sure he'll call." She felt like throttling Pollin and marveled at Renee's control. This was not the same woman she'd seen yesterday, on the verge of falling apart.

Pollin picked up a cigarette and held it between his fingers. "You don't even know for a fact that the kidnapper is this Hank person."

Renee clenched her hands. "The kidnapper said, 'You'll be hearing from me.' That was a clear reference to Hank's words."

"You can't be sure. You told me someone erased the tape, so there's no way to compare the voices. What if you're wrong?"

Renee glared at him.

What if it's Barry? Jessie thought. "Mr. Pollin, I don't think you want to be the person responsible for preventing us from finding Molly. If you're right, and the kidnapper isn't Hank, or he doesn't call the station, then no one's hurt. And if he *does* call, then we can catch him."

Pollin put down the cigarette and leaned forward. "Do you think for *one minute* I'm happy about refusing to cooperate? I'd do anything to save a child, *any* child. And Molly's not any child. I love that little girl. But there are constitutional issues here. Callers have the right to privacy. We could be shut down for violating that right and face massive lawsuits. Unfortunately, that's the bottom line."

A small price to pay for saving a life, Jessie thought.

Renee said, "Max, here's *my* bottom line. I'm not doing the show unless you agree to the phone trap." Very calm now.

He raised a brow. "Is that an ultimatum?"

"That's a fact."

"This is a terrible time for you, Renee. I totally understand that you're not up to doing the show."

Weasel. Jessie glanced at Renee.

"I'll quit, Max."

He swiveled in his chair. "I'd hate to lose you, Renee. And I'd hate to see you sabotage your career in a moment of anger, especially since your show has really picked up momentum in the last few days."

"I'm not doing the show to boost the ratings, Max. I want to catch this creep. I want Molly."

"I wish I could help you, Renee. In your heart you know that's true. But my hands are tied." He held them, palms up, in a gesture of helplessness.

"Apparently not everyone feels the way you do, Max. I spoke to a rival station early this morning, after the news about Molly broke. They've agreed to allow a phone trap on their lines if I take my show to them."

He frowned. "Which station?"

Renee smiled.

He cocked his head. "There is no station. You're bluffing."

"Then call my bluff, Max. Let me walk out this door. But once I do, I'm never coming back." She placed a finger on her lips. "Gee, how many listeners do you suppose I'll have while this is going on?"

"You'd let a station use your daughter's kidnapping to boost its ratings?" His voice was filled with disdain.

"You're hoping to do exactly that, so don't sound so sanctimonious."

Pollin pursed his lips. Color crept halfway up his neck.

"They talked about doing the right thing, but I'm not fooling myself." Renee pushed her chair back and stood. "You know what, Max? I don't care what they get out of it, as long as they agree to the trap."

"Let me think about this, Renee."

She checked her watch. "It's nine-fifteen. You have till nine-thirty. That's when I told the other station I'd give them my answer. And Detective Drake has to let phone security know where to show up to install the trap before the show."

"I can't make that kind of decision without talking to our attorneys, Renee." He was frowning and had picked up the cigarette again.

"Yes, you can, Max." Renee nodded. "And if we catch this monster, you'll be a hero, the station will be a hero. And you'll have terrific ratings."

He scowled. "This isn't about ratings."

She looked at him evenly. "It's *always* about ratings, Max. We both know that."

He twirled the cigarette and studied it as though it held an answer. "Okay. You win."

"Thank you."

No gushing, no gloating. Just smooth as silk. Jessie was impressed.

"So which station is it, Renee? You can tell me now."

She shook her head. "That would be inappropriate, Max."

"But there *is* a station?"

"Absolutely." She met his eyes. "Which phone can Detective Drake use?"

Fifteen minutes later she accompanied Jessie down the hall and out of the building. "Thanks for coming, Jessie."

"You're the one who convinced him. I'll check out these shelters your screener told me about. Are you going home?"

She shook her head. "Barry's there, waiting in case Hank calls. I'm staying here until the phone trap is installed. I want to make sure Pollin doesn't change his mind before the men from phone security arrive."

"He was gracious about letting me use his phone to call GTE."

"He's not a bad guy. Just wants to keep his job, like the rest of us."

"There is no other station, is there?"

"Nope." A quick, wry smile. "I was good, wasn't I?"

"*Very* good. What would you have done if he'd called your bluff?"

"Done the show anyway. If Hank calls, maybe he'll let me talk to Molly." She bit her lips. "You don't think Pollin is right, do you? That the kidnapper may never call?"

Jessie thought about the children whose faces were copied on milk cartons and leaflets, children who were never heard from again; and others—like Polly Klaas, snatched from her bedroom during a slumber party—whose bodies were eventually found.

She squeezed Renee's hand. "He'll call."

She sat in her parked car and, using her cell phone, spoke to Phil at the station and told him what Renee had done.

"Gutsy lady." Phil grunted with admiration. "How's she holding up?"

"Better. I don't know how Barry's doing. I thought I'd go talk to his attorney, see if she'll verify that he thought getting custody was a sure thing." And rule out one motive. She'd obtained the name and phone number from Renee, who had probably wondered why Jessie needed the information but hadn't asked.

Phil snorted. "She won't talk to you."

"Probably not. But it's worth a try. Anything new?"

"We have a lead on Silo, a.k.a. Simon LeRoux."

The man who'd pawned the gold watch. Finally.

"According to his girlfriend, Rowena, Silo came by her place two weeks ago and gave their three-year-old daughter a load of expensive toys. Like Christmas in September. Which was funny, Rowena said, because Silo's always crying poverty."

"And all of a sudden he's flush." Jessie nodded. "What's with that name, by the way?"

Phil laughed. "Rowena showed me a picture. He looks like a storehouse for food. *Big* guy, bigger'n me, ever since Maureen's had me on this diet."

"Be glad she did. Why'd the girlfriend tell you this?" From her purse she took out a granola bar and tore at the wrapper.

"*Ex*-girlfriend. She's mad. Said she needs money for rent and food, which Silo never gives her, not for toys. Plus he stepped out on her with another honey. Anyway, she told us a couple of places where Silo hangs out."

"I'll be at the station in twenty minutes. I can talk to the attorney later."

"No need. Harris from CAPS is my date," Phil said, referring to Crimes Against Persons. "He's got time to kill, and he offered to help out. Espes is thrilled."

"As long as you don't get too attached to him." She was disappointed not following up with her partner, but wanted to talk to the attorney. And she wasn't wild about Lou Harris. Harris was from the old guard that had resented women joining the force. Supposedly, he'd mended his ways. It takes time, Phil had said. "Anyone call for me?"

"Your sister, three times. She heard about the Altman girl."

Helen had probably left messages on Jessie's answering machine at home, too. "Did Gary call?" Very casual.

"Nope."

She felt another surge of anger. "Anything else?"

"We got an anonymous call from a guy who said the Iranian had shady stuff going on."

"Drugs?" Jessie bit off a chunk of granola.

"Or smuggled goods. He wouldn't say. I figure Lou and I will visit the wife, put some pressure on her." Phil grunted. "Talk about sweeping stuff under the rug."

She groaned. "Ha, ha."

★   ★   ★

Barry's attorney, Margaret Lisbon, looked like a Betty Crocker mom who baked her own bread and sewed curtains and made sure the lunch boxes had healthful snacks. She was short and plump with a thickening middle, chin-length, softly waved salt-and-pepper hair framing a round, lined face, and bifocals. Hardly the thirty-something, ultra-thin, miniskirted woman Jessie had expected (she was watching too much *Ally McBeal*, she decided), but a great choice when you were fighting for custody. A family court judge would look at her and say, "This woman knows what's best for kids."

"Please have a seat, Detective Drake." The attorney pointed to one of the upholstered armchairs in front of her cherrywood desk. "I'm sorry I kept you waiting. I've just returned from Cleveland, and my morning has been swamped with appointments and calls." She smiled at Jessie. "You told my receptionist this was related to a police investigation?"

"That's correct. I wanted to ask you about Barry Altman."

"Detective." She shook her head slowly, as if chiding a youngster who'd stuck his finger into the cookie dough. "You know I can't discuss my conversations with Mr. Altman. That would be unprofessional, a violation of attorney-client privilege."

Jessie nodded. "Under normal circumstances, I'd agree with you. But a little girl's safety is involved."

"Unfortunately, Detective, these days divorce and custody battles *are* normal circumstances. That's just a fact of life. As to Molly Altman's safety in her father's care, there's no reason to think otherwise, no matter what Dr. Altman is suggesting."

The woman didn't know. Jessie kept her face expressionless. "Mr. Altman told me you were confident he'd win custody. But I assume that's changed."

"As I said, I can't discuss this with you."

"He harassed her on the air and threatened in veiled language to inform the station of the divorce unless Dr. Altman gave up custody of Molly." She saw a flicker of concern cross the attorney's face. "Dr. Altman has the tape of that conversation. The judge will be more sympathetic to her when he hears it."

"The judge will view Dr. Altman's actions as a desperate attempt to cast aspersions on my client."

"You're referring to the fact that she felt forced to expose her private life to her public or be blackmailed?"

"I thought—" She frowned, then narrowed her eyes. "Why

exactly are you here, Detective Drake? Is Dr. Altman charging my client with extortion?"

"Not as far as I know."

The attorney paused. "May I see a business card, please?" She glanced at the card Jessie handed her. "You're a homicide detective." She sounded angry, surprised. "What's going on here?"

"Dr. Altman's housekeeper is dead, and Molly is missing, probably kidnapped."

Her face registered shock. She was silent, absorbing the information. "You suspect my client of kidnapping his own child?"

"We're not ruling anyone out at this time. I'd appreciate your cooperation with our investigation."

"At the risk of sounding redundant, Detective, I can't reveal what my client told me."

"I'm not asking you to reveal what Mr. Altman told you. I'm asking whether *you* told *him* you were less certain about the outcome of the custody battle."

"You want me to give him a motive to kidnap his daughter? I don't think so." She smiled thinly, but the blue eyes were steely. "You took advantage of the fact that I was unaware of what's happened."

"I'm doing my job.

"And I'm doing mine."

Interview over.

In the elevator Jessie contemplated what she'd learned. Margaret Lisbon hadn't confirmed that Barry was anxious about his chances of getting custody, but Jessie had sensed her concern.

She wondered what the attorney had meant when she'd talked about Renee's "desperate" attempt. It wasn't Renee's going public about the divorce—Margaret Lisbon had seemed surprised by Jessie's assumption.

Barry's drinking?

Jessie nodded. That was probably it. The court was hardly likely to give custody to someone with a drinking problem. Maybe that's why Barry had told Renee he was willing to rethink the custody. He was backing down, anxious that he might not win.

How anxious?

28

He was the seventh caller.

It had been hellish, trying to concentrate on what people were saying when all the while she was waiting for his call. Renee had been talking to a man upset because his parents liked his wife more than they liked him ("Grow up and give them a reason to like you," she'd counseled) when Alicia whispered, "It's him, Line Five," on the IN STUDIO line.

For the first time Renee understood what people meant when they talked about the blood rushing from their head. Her chest pounding, she turned to Jessie, who was at the table in front of another mike, earphones in place. A plainclothes policeman was sitting on a chair nearby.

Renee pressed the orange COUGH button, which allowed her to keep her comments off air. "He's calling on Line Five," she said, her voice little more than a hoarse whisper.

So Phil was wrong. There *was* a Hank. Jessie hadn't liked thinking Barry was involved, but Molly was far safer with a desperate father than with a stranger bent on revenge. She signaled with her hand to the officer to contact GTE security. They could trace the call instantly.

"Finish your call, Renee," she instructed calmly. "Try to sound as normal as possible."

Renee nodded. Clearing her throat, she released the COUGH button and interrupted the caller, who was still discussing his parents, with a quick but polite good-bye. She turned to Jessie, eyes stricken, and pressed the COUGH button again. "I can't do this."

"Yes, you can." Smiling encouragement, Jessie reached over and squeezed Renee's hand. "Remember, don't lose your cool or make him angry. You don't want him to hang up."

"Okay." She released the COUGH button, licked her lips, and pressed Line Five. "Hank, you're on the air." The words echoed in her ears.

"Well, golly gee. Thanks for taking my call, Dr. Renee, and not making me wait an hour," he simpered. Light static crackled in the background. "Don't take me off the air," he warned, his voice lower. "If you do, it's adios."

"You'll stay on the air, Hank."

With thousands of people listening—in their homes, in their offices, in their cars. And maybe, Jessie thought, just maybe, one of them would recognize his voice and identify him. Earlier in the day, she'd leaked to several radio and TV stations the probability that Hank would be calling during Dr. Renee's show. Less than an hour later her "news" had been broadcast as a special bulletin on the networks and local radio and TV channels. She'd seen Pollin just before the program began, trying to look appropriately serious and concerned. She wondered what he was really thinking.

"So what's up, Doc? Long time no speak. How's the advice business lately?"

Renee seethed at his banal cruelty. "Is Molly all right, Hank?"

"She's fine. A real sweetheart, your daughter. Pretty little thing. Good thing for you I'm not into stuff like that."

Jessie had told her he'd try to goad her, but it didn't stop the fear and revulsion that swept through her. She dug her fingernails into her palms. "I'd like to talk to her, Hank."

"No can do."

Don't beg, Jessie had told her. Be reasonable but firm. "I need to be sure she's okay. You can understand that. Let me talk to her, or I'll end this call."

"You're not exactly in a position to call the shots, Dr. Renee."

"Give me a reason to trust you, Hank."

A moment of silence. Then, "Half a minute, no more. No questions. Just enough so you know she's okay. "

"That's fine." Her heart was thumping wildly in her chest.

"Mommy?"

The voice was tinier than she remembered. She shut her eyes and bit her lips to fight back tears. "You're going to be okay, Molly. I promise you."

"I'm scared!" she whispered. "I want to come home now."

"Of course you're scared. But you're going to be okay. He doesn't want to hurt you, Molly. Remember your dreams? Remember what we talked about, sweetheart? If you don't show him you're scared—"

"That's enough." Hank was back on the line. "First things first. I know L.A.'s finest are listening, and that's cool. I could've told you, 'Don't bring in the cops, or else,' but folks always call them in anyway." He snickered.

"I explained to the police how distraught you are, Hank. They know you acted in desperation. If you bring Molly back and give yourself up, they'll take that into consideration."

He laughed. "Is that the best you can do, Dr. Renee? With advice like that, your show won't last the week. Last I heard, cops don't treat kidnappers kindly. And the housekeeper's dead."

Jessie felt a fresh wave of resentment at the media (at Gary!). By revealing the housekeeper's death, they'd reduced the odds that Hank would turn himself in. Too late now.

"They know you didn't intend to harm her, Hank," Renee said.

Good, Jessie thought. She nodded at Renee.

"Damn right I didn't! It's her own fault for trying to stop me. It didn't have to go down like that."

"I understand. But you know, Hank, keeping Molly won't bring your wife and son back. It'll just frighten Vicky. If you bring Molly back, Vicky will respect you for doing the right thing."

"Cut the psychology crap! Vicky respects me fine. Like I said, it's her friends that put wrong ideas in her head."

The officer approached Jessie. "He's on a cell phone," he whispered in her ear.

"Damn," Jessie muttered under her breath. They'd have to a search warrant to get the cellular service subscribing company to release the identity of the owner of the cell phone line. That could take three to four hours.

"Tell me what you want, Hank," Renee said.

"You *know* what I want. My wife and my boy. It would've been real simple, but you wouldn't do the right thing. You know what they say—'What God hath done, let no man split asunder.' You messed in my marriage, Doc. You've got only yourself to blame for all this."

So Hank had written at least one of the notes, Jessie thought. Maybe Barry was telling the truth, or part of it.

"I want to help you, Hank," Renee said.

"You think I'm an idiot?" He snorted. "You don't care about me. You want your little girl. That's just fine. We can help each other. You convince Vicky to come talk to me, face-to-face, and bring the boy. Let her decide if she wants to go with me where we can start over. And then you get your little girl back."

"What if Vicky doesn't want to go with you, Hank? Will you bring Molly back?"

"Vicky will go with me," he said stubbornly. "She's crazy in love with me, always has been. She knows I'm the only one's going to take care of her right. She knows I did all this because I love her and the boy. First get her to agree, then I'll spell out the details of where and when."

Jessie scribbled on a piece of paper and handed it to Renee: ASK HIM WIFE'S LAST NAME.

Renee nodded. "If you want me to persuade Vicky to come back to you, I have to know her last name so that I can find her."

"Hey, Doc, if I knew where to find her, I'd do it myself. I figure she's in one of those shelters where they brainwash women into hating their men."

Jessie had struck out with the shelters Alicia had told her about. Could be the people she'd talked to really didn't know anything about a woman who fit Vicky's description. Could be they knew and weren't saying.

"There are so many shelters, Hank," Renee said. "Tell me her last name so I can locate her."

"You mean, so you can locate *me*. I'm invisible, Doc. No one can find me. But Vicky's probably listening right now, Dr. Renee. Tell her to call in and get her to see me."

"What if she doesn't call in, Hank? What if she's scared?"

"She'll call."

"What if she doesn't?"

"Hell, you've got the entire police force ready to help you. Let *them* find her." He laughed.

Renee gripped the edges of the table. "If no one can find you, Hank, you have nothing to lose by telling me her last name. Or her maiden name. Tell me her maiden name. Maybe her parents know something they didn't tell you."

"You don't need to talk to her parents." He sounded impatient now. "Vicky will call you. I know she will. She wants to be with me as much as I want to be with her."

"Hank, there's something you need to know. Molly's resistance to infections is very low. Because of that, she needs to take amoxicillin every day."

"She looks fine to me, Doc."

"She may *look* fine, but if she picks up a virus or bacteria, she'll get very sick, very quickly. I know you don't want that to happen."

"Good try, Doc, but I'm not buying. The cops'll have every

pharmacist in the city waiting for me. I'll call you tomorrow, same time. I hope by then you have some good news for me."

"I'm not making this up, Hank. Molly needs the amoxicillin. If she gets sick, she could die without it."

"Well, then, I guess you'd better hope Vicky calls in soon."

"Hank—"

She heard a click and realized he'd hung up. A second passed, then another, and another.

"Dead air," Alicia said on the IN STUDIO line. "Renee, we have dead air. Should I go to commercial?" More urgent now.

Renee's head was pounding. She felt paralyzed with fear, her tongue thick and unwieldy, like a block of wood. Through the headset she heard music, then a taped advertisement, and said a silent thank-you to Alicia.

"You don't have to go on, Renee," Alicia said. "Ted Hark-ham offered to sub for you, right? He's still in the building. I'll run a pretaped news segment while I get him, and—"

"I have to make an appeal to Vicky."

"Ted can do it."

"No, I have to do it."

The commerical ended. Renee cleared her throat, waited for the engineer's signal, then began. "This is Dr. Renee Altman. Vicky, if you're listening to the show . . ."

29

Phil swiveled back and forth in his chair. "So he called, huh?"

"He let Renee talk to Molly for a few seconds." Jessie set a cup of hot water on a cork coaster. She pulled out her chair and sat down. "So at least we know she's alive, thank God." She rapped her knuckles against her desk.

During the station break after Renee's on-air appeal to Vicky, Renee had collapsed in Jessie's arms. The break over, she'd pulled herself together and taken the next call. Again she'd turned down Ted Harkham's offer to fill in for her. The show must go on, Jessie had initially thought as she watched Renee slip into her professional role, but she realized that listening to others and counseling them was probably taking her mind off her own help- lessness and giving her back a measure of control. And maybe Vicky would call.

"What else did Hank say?" Phil asked.

"Not much. If Renee convinces his wife to come back, he'll return Molly. He's calling again tomorrow, same time." She dunked a tea bag into the cup of water.

"What's the wife's last name?"

"He wouldn't say. Renee pressed, but he told her his wife would call. If not, he said the police would have to figure it out. Playing games," she said disgustedly. "Anyway, there goes your theory about Barry."

"Maybe." Stroking his mustache.

She frowned. "Give it up, Phil. Hank is *real*. He has Molly. I heard her voice." Forlorn, terrified. Jessie tried to block it from her mind.

She added two packets of artificial sweetener to the tea and was stirring absentmindedly when Lou Harris walked over. He was older than Phil, probably in his mid-fifties. He had a thin face with leathery skin and heavily lined eyes. He'd let his sideburns grow long, and today he was wearing jeans and boots with spurs.

"Hey, Jessica. Okay with you that I cut in on your dance partner?" He was smiling at her, exposing tobacco-stained teeth.

She did her best to look friendly. "No problem. How'd it go with Silo?" she asked, embarrassed she'd forgotten to ask Phil.

"Nothing yet. But we're hopeful, right, pardner?"

A conspiratorial wink elicited a grunt from Phil but managed to make her feel excluded. "I appreciate your helping out, Lou," she told him.

"Hey, why not? I got the time, and I understand you're friends with this Dr. Renee. I hear the guy called in to her show. Any idea who he is?"

"Nope."

"Damn." He sighed. "It's tough when a kid's involved." He turned to Phil. "I'm thinking we should pay another visit to the bar where Silo hangs out. Maybe he'll show."

"Too soon. We don't want to be conspicuous. Maybe tomorrow."

"Say when. Good luck finding the little girl, Jessie."

"Thanks." She waited until he was out of earshot. "Did you see his getup? He thinks he's Clint Eastwood."

Phil smiled. "Who's he hurting?"

"He's just so damn affected. 'Howdy, *pardner*,' " she mimicked. "I was waiting for him to pull out a wad of tobacco."

"He's going through a rough time, Jess. Most of his former partners have retired. He's getting there, but doesn't like it. And it's hard for him, being partnered with the young turks. They're not keen on him, either."

"Maybe he's got his eye on you."

Phil cocked his head, a bemused smile spreading on his face. "You're jealous."

"No, I'm not." She felt herself flushing.

"Yeah, you are." He sounded pleased. "Hey, I'm not looking to change partners, Jess. I'm just happy to give Lou something to work. He's a good guy once you get to know him, has a heart as big as Texas. He would've made a great dad, but he never married. I guess that's why he works with underprivileged kids. To fill the void."

"I'll try to be more patient."

She pulled over a pad with lined paper and began writing up the notes of the case while the tea cooled. Out of the corner of her eye she noted that Phil was swiveling back and forth, his hands locked behind his head. His usual thinking position.

"Try this," he said a few minutes later.

She looked at him.

"The dad's afraid he's going to lose Molly, but he knows if he snatches her himself, we'll be on to him in a flash. So he gives this guy Hank the remote to the gate and has him do the deed, the idea being he'll stick around a few weeks, play the terrified dad, then meet up with Hank and Molly and disappear."

Jessie shook her head. "He looked genuinely terrified to me, Phil. I don't think that was an act."

"He *is* terrified. He didn't count on Hank's killing the housekeeper. Now he's an accessory to murder."

She thought that over. "There's one major problem with your story, Phil. Barry just *happened* to find a guy whose wife skipped because Renee advised her to?"

"It's a setup, Jess. There *is* no missing wife."

"You heard Vicky—or Linda, or whatever her real name is. You heard Hank. That was *real*, Phil."

"We don't know that. Barry's a writer. Writers have good imaginations. He wants to divert suspicion from himself, so he pays this guy Hank, or whatever his real name is, to make those calls, pretend he's angry at Renee."

"What about Linda?"

"She could be part of the setup. Or . . ." He pulled gently at his mustache. "She could be for real. Barry heard her call and used it to his advantage. So now he has us chasing down this Linda, some other son of a bitch's wife, so we can find Hank. By the time we figure it out, Barry's gone with Molly, probably out of the country."

"I don't understand why you're determined to pin this on Barry. You should've heard this Hank guy, Phil. He's creepy."

"Or a good actor. Why wouldn't he give Renee his wife's last name so she could contact her?"

She sighed. "I *told* you. He's playing games."

"Maybe." Phil nodded. "Or maybe there *is* no wife, so he has no name to give. Listen, it's possible Barry's not involved with the kidnapping, but something's going on. He's way too defensive. About the garage key, about the remote, about the tape."

"All circumstantial."

"And the gate? How did Hank get Molly outside the property if the gate was locked?"

Jessie groaned. "We went over this. Molly knew the code."

"According to Barry, which of course he'd say. Otherwise the finger points at him."

She was so tired of all this. "Maybe you're right."

He scowled. "Don't say that just to get me off your back."

"You made valid points, but I want to think about this."

"You're resisting 'cause you know him."

She bristled. "I'm not ready to strap him into the chair, *okay*?" She glared at him. "I said I want to *think* about it. Okay?"

"*Okay*." Glaring right back.

She turned her back to him and continued writing but found she couldn't concentrate. She slammed her pen onto the desk and massaged her temples.

"What did the lawyer say?" he asked, calm again.

"Not much. She didn't know about Molly, so I tried to find out if she was concerned about the custody case. She said something about the judge not going to be taken in by Renee's desperate actions. I blew it. I asked if she was referring to Renee's going public on air about the divorce. That's when the attorney asked me why I was there."

He nodded. "Why'd she *think* you were there?"

"I don't know." Jessie frowned. "She asked if Renee was charging Barry with extortion. To tell you the truth, I'm still trying to figure that out."

"So what did she mean by Renee's desperate actions?"

She lifted the teacup, remembered that it was empty, and set it down. "The night I went to see him, he had a beer, and there were more empties on the kitchen counter. Apparently Barry's been hitting the sauce lately. Maybe Renee told her own attorney, who told the judge."

Phil was scowling again. "What makes you think that?"

"Barry's attorney said something about Renee casting aspersions on Barry's ability to be a good father."

Phil waited.

Damn. She should have told him. "When I spoke to the dead housekeeper's friend, she told me a man from social services questioned Blanca about the Altmans and asked whether Barry had a drinking or drug problem."

"Maybe he was fishing."

"Blanca told him he did have a drinking problem. She was afraid not to, because the guy intimidated her, talked about turning her in to Immigration." She flushed under Phil's intense gaze. "I didn't tell you because I thought this was Hank, posing as social services to get at Molly."

"Hey, you don't have to explain," he said, his voice too quiet. "I'm only your partner."

Her face was flushed. "Come on, Phil."

"I'm the one who's picking up the slack here, running down Silo and the Iranian rug thugs while you're out there trying to cover Barry's butt—why, I don't know."

She didn't answer. What could she say? He was right.

"I'm the one who's going to take the heat for this if Espes finds out."

"I don't think Barry set this up, Phil."

"You don't *think* so?" He grunted. "The lawyer practically told you Renee was pulling something. Barry was anxious he wouldn't get custody. In my book, that gives him a motive for snatching his kid."

"You're right. I *was* resisting. And I agree that there's something going on with Barry. I'm sorry."

"Sorry doesn't cut it. You held out on me, Jess. That's not what partners do." He shoved himself away from his desk and lumbered across the room.

She watched him for a moment. He had stopped at Harris's desk, and the two were talking. She opened a "blue book" but couldn't stop thinking. About Phil, about Barry. About loyalties to colleagues and friends and lovers. She picked up the phone receiver to call Gary, then put it back down.

She was doodling on a sheet of paper, something that often cleared her mind and allowed her thoughts greater freedom, when Phil returned.

"About the gate," she said.

"What?" He practically barked the word.

"You're right, Phil. Something doesn't work."

He pursed his lips. "Throwing me a bone?"

"Just thinking it through. Even if Molly had the combination to the lock, how did the *kidnapper* know she did?"

He nodded. "There you go."

((30))

Dr. Emanuel Freiberg shut off the tape recorder. Leaning against his armchair, the LAPD psychologist removed his tortoiseshell-framed glasses and massaged the bridge of his thin nose.

Jessie waited.

"I think of myself as a civilized man," he said. "I find myself arguing against capital punishment, because I like playing devil's advocate and I like pissing off my brother-in-law, who's an opinionated jerk." He made a face. "The truth is, I don't see how capital punishment is a deterrent to other would-be killers when the appeals process after a conviction can drag events out for over a decade. And I worry about the possibility, however slim, that an innocent man may be executed. But I would have no problem pulling the plug on any person who kidnapped a child. No problem at all," he repeated softly.

"What can you tell me about him, Manny?"

He grunted. "You want his name and address?"

She smiled. "That would be great." She hadn't seen Manny in almost five months and had missed their talks. She was surprised by the gray in his curly brown hair, mostly at the sideburns and the temples, which had begun to recede, but decided she liked it.

He put his glasses back on. "I'd guess he's in his mid to late thirties. Caucasian, upper-lower or lower-middle class. Some education, but not polished, judging by his diction, so I don't think he's a college grad."

She wrote that down.

"What comes through all the tapes is anger." He sounded troubled. "This is a guy who's used to getting his way and likes to play games. In the first tape he tells Dr. Renee he's done

154

something wrong and wants to make amends, but what he's doing is setting her up for the last tape, where he springs the trap."

"What about the second and third tapes, Manny? The ones where he talks about his wife leaving him?"

He checked his notes. "In the second tape he sounds like a clueless male out of touch with his wife's needs. I hear petulance, a regressive childishness because he can't get what he wants."

"I thought all men were like that." She smiled.

"You spoke to my wife, huh?" Manny smiled back, then quickly assumed a serious expression. Another look at his notes. "In the third tape he's more manipulative, and when Dr. Renee doesn't buy it, the gloves are off. Unlike in the first tape, where his anger has a brooding quality, now he's seething."

"He doesn't sound so angry in the last tape."

"Oh, he's *angry*, Jessie." Manny frowned. "But he's *enjoying* himself. He's getting off on baiting his victim, showing he's in control. He's baiting the police, too. 'Catch me if you can.' "

Jessie nodded. She'd noticed that, too.

"And the whole world is listening," Manny continued. "He *loves* that. Here's this popular radio shrink who solves people's problems, and he strips her of her authority in front of all her fans. He tells her he'll hang up if she takes him off the air, and she has to do what he says. So all of a sudden she's not infallible. She's not a comfort-giver. She's as vulnerable and scared as the rest of us." He smiled sadly. "Ten to one he'll get to hear the replay on the evening news."

"The other talk shows are discussing it, playing segments of the call." Driving downtown to Parker Center, she'd listened in on several shows, had been appalled by the spectaclelike atmosphere.

"So what's new?" Manny sighed.

Jessie wasn't surprised, either. People had listened again and again to Nicole Simpson's terrified call to 911. They'd watched on a national network the last moments of a man helped to his death by Dr. Kevorkian. They'd witnessed the live television coverage, played over and over, of a man who had set himself on fire in the middle of a freeway and burned to death with the cameras rolling and millions of people watching, including young children whose regular programming had been interrupted to bring them this up-close, important event.

"My partner, Phil Okum, doesn't think this guy is for real."

Manny frowned. "What's to think? You have the tapes. You know he has the little girl."

"Phil thinks Renee Altman's estranged husband, Barry,

snatched the daughter and paid this guy to make the calls, et cetera, to throw us off." She told him about Barry's possible motive, about his defensiveness, about the niggling facts that made Phil suspect him.

Manny listened intently. When Jessie finished talking, he tilted his head and narrowed his eyes. Rubbed his chin. "What can I say? It wouldn't be the first time a dad kidnapped his own child. Happens all the time. But this seems like a pretty elaborate setup. Why not just grab her and run?"

"Phil says Barry wanted to divert suspicion from himself, so we wouldn't go looking for him."

"Then why is he still here?"

"Because the housekeeper's dead."

Manny shrugged. "It's possible. I don't know the husband, how desperate he was, how calculating."

"He's a writer." Jessie smiled.

Manny laughed. "Well, that answers it. Go cuff him."

"His career is going nowhere, according to Renee."

"So you're thinking maybe he's killing two birds with one stone? Taking the daughter and getting at his wife at the same time?"

She hadn't thought about that, but considered it now. "If Barry's behind all this, how does that change what you hear on the tapes?"

More chin rubbing. "I don't think this guy's anger is fake, if that's what you're asking."

"Phil says maybe he's a good actor."

"Then it's an Oscar-winning performance." Manny shook his head. "What I hear is genuine. The only other possibility I see is that this is a scam, but Hank has his own reason to be angry at women, at the police, at society. So he's tapping into that when he's calling Dr. Renee."

She nodded. "Assuming he's real, and Barry's not involved. Do you have a term to describe him?"

"Is a label going to make you feel better?" Manny paused. "He doesn't strike me as a typical batterer. That kind of guy would be violent only toward the wife or child or girlfriend, but not to society in general. From what I heard on the tapes—and this is just a preliminary, rough assessment—your man displays signs of anti-social behavior, what we used to call sociopathic. He's incapable of caring about others—the fact that the girl may be in medical danger doesn't matter to him."

"What else?"

"He's in major denial about his relationship with his wife,

which is typical of abusive personalities. He enjoys the cat-and-mouse game, the sense of danger. And it's always the other guy's fault. It's his wife's *friends'* fault that the wife left him. It's the *talk show host's* fault that the wife didn't come back, the *housekeeper's* fault that she's dead. He never accepts responsibility for the consequences of his actions."

Typical of most perpetrators she interrogated, Jessie had found. *He made me do it. I had no choice.* "Does he honestly believe she'll come back to him after he's kidnapped a child and killed someone?"

Manny grunted. "You heard what he said—she'll know he did it because he loves her and their child, because he wants to restore the family unit. He's constructed a world view to accommodate his behavior, and he can't let go of it."

"So what happens when she won't come back? Will he leave Molly somewhere and disappear?" She'd been agonizing about this.

Manny sighed. "I can't answer that. Depends how angry he is, and at whom his anger is directed. Right now he's focusing his anger on the talk show shrink." He grimaced.

"You don't like her." A comment, not a question.

He shrugged. "It's not Dr. Renee specifically. It's all of them and the quickie format they follow. Microwave psychology."

"Renee tells people she's not doing therapy, Manny. She's helping them make moral choices. More than half the time she gives sound advice. Sure, it's fast. But sometimes she helps people cut through the crap and figure out what's important."

She wished she had quick answers to her own questions: *Dr. Renee, I don't know if I should remarry my ex-husband with whom I'm really pissed off right now. Dr. Renee, I don't know how to deal with my envy over my sister's pregnancy. Dr. Renee, how do I rebuild my relationship with my mother and connect with my father?*

Manny nodded. "I'm not saying no. I've listened to her show a few times, Jessie. I wanted to hear what she's like, to try to figure out why people are drawn to her."

"Jealous?" She smiled.

Manny laughed. "I wouldn't mind having her income. We have three kids in private Jewish schools. Do you have any idea how much tuition is?" He sighed. "Sometimes her advice is on the money. Other times she's shooting from the hip, making assumptions about the callers or ignoring what they're saying, or she steps on her moralizing soapbox." He paused. "And a lot of times she's downright nasty."

"The callers know exactly what they're going to get. Maybe they like it."

"A verbal spanking, you mean?" He shook his head. "I don't think so."

"Then why *do* they call?"

"My assessment?" He ran his hand across his Adam's apple. "A, every caller thinks that he's a little better than the other callers, that his question's a little smarter, so he doesn't expect to be slammed. B, the caller genuinely trusts the talk show shrink and is willing to accept whatever she dishes out. C, and this isn't so far removed from the cult syndrome, Jessie, the caller is so taken with the grandiose persona of the host that he craves getting close to her, no matter what she does. By connecting to her, the caller feels honored and special. At the same time he's feeding her narcissism."

Jessie frowned. "Renee isn't narcissistic, Manny."

"She may not have full-blown NPD. Narcissistic personality disorder," he explained when he saw Jessie's puzzled expression. "But she fits the pattern. She has a grandiose sense of self-importance. She thinks she's smarter than others and expects people to recognize that. When they don't, she's irritated. She's impatient with her callers and often shows an emotional coldness toward their problems."

"Not always. I've heard her on the verge of tears when she's talking to a caller."

"And I've heard her tear a caller to shreds. Look, everybody has some narcissistic qualities. Maybe Dr. Renee's were exacerbated by her radio show success."

Barry's theory. "She wasn't always like this, you know," Jessie said, feeling the need to defend. "When she began her show, she was much less abrasive. She started out in private practice. I don't know why she turned to radio."

"More adulation, a large base of devoted supporters. This is not a happy woman, Jessie. This is someone who craves attention to compensate for her underlying insecurities."

Jessie shook her head. "That's not Renee. She really loves helping people, Manny."

His eyes showed surprise. "You know her well?"

"Actually, we used to be close. When I was in high school, I don't how I would've survived without her. She was the only one I could talk to about my mom, the only one who made me feel I wasn't a terrible person." Manny knew all her secrets.

"You told me a friend helped you out." He nodded. "So what

was she like in high school? Charming? Center of attention? Lots of boyfriends?"

"She was popular. She was very smart, too, and ambitious. In her yearbook she was described as Most Likely to Succeed."

"At any cost."

Jessie shook her head. "She's not an opportunist, Manny."

"So what happened to your relationship?"

She shrugged. "We drifted apart."

"Just like that, huh?" He smiled knowingly.

Jessie hesitated. "She resented my criticizing the way she talked to her callers. And I disagreed with some of her views."

"So that ended the friendship?"

"It put a definite crimp in it. Then we had a major disagreement." She shifted on the seat, uncomfortable with the direction the conversation was taking. "I told her Gary blamed me for losing the baby, even though the doctors didn't think I miscarried because I fell." She'd been chasing a suspect and had tripped and fallen to the ground. A few hours later the bleeding had started. "Renee sided with Gary."

"You felt hurt?"

She nodded. "More like betrayed, which wasn't fair. She was entitled to her opinion. But it wasn't just that. She said that I had no clue as to the responsibilities of being a parent and the single-minded commitment it involved. That I obviously had ambivalent feelings about having a baby or I would never have put myself in a situation where I could risk losing it." The memory still rankled. Jessie found herself flushing.

"That is *so much crap*." Manny was scowling. "But you, of course, believed it because it corroborated your own feelings of guilt."

"I guess." She'd been thrilled with the pregnancy, terrified at the prospect that she would continue the cycle of abuse she'd learned at her mother's expertly brutal hands. "But I was angry. I told her there were mothers who successfully combined parenting with a career, that I wasn't one of her three-minute callers and didn't appreciate her instant analysis." Jessie paused. "She accused me of being jealous of her success and stormed out of my house." She felt drained, as if she'd relived the argument.

"So that was it?"

"Pretty much. I called her a few days later to patch things up. We spoke awhile. I've been trying to remember whether there was another call after that, and who made it." She shrugged.

"Everything you're describing says NPD. The inability to tolerate criticism, the lack of empathy for others, the patronizing attitude."

"No one likes criticism, Manny."

"But they don't break off relationships because of it."

I can't afford to surround myself with negativity. She decided not to mention that Renee wasn't speaking with her parents, wondered again why she felt the need to defend her. Loyalty for past acts of kindness, when she'd been Jessie's emotional savior? "I didn't try very hard to rekindle the friendship, Manny."

"Does she have a lot of friends?"

"Not as far as I know. Then again, neither do I." Until recently she'd been reluctant to form intimate relationships and trust someone with her painful past.

She mentioned this to Manny now. "It's ironic, isn't it? I didn't even tell Gary the truth about my mom until after the divorce. People call Renee and the other talk shows and reveal the most sordid details to thousands of listeners."

"*Anonymous* listeners. We live in a society that encourages public confession and spectacle. Look at the television talk shows, at the proliferation of memoirs and books where the writer reveals a life of alcoholism or incest or adultery or bondage. Whatever happened to personal dignity, to the preservation of privacy?"

"Ask Kenneth Starr." She smiled.

"Point taken." He smiled, too, and pushed his glasses back against his nose. "Here's another question. Why are we *listening*? Are we voyeurs, hooked because we're fascinated by the kinky, titillating details we overhear? Do we listen so that we can provide sympathy with an unseen nod, so that we can become better parents, daughters, sons, lovers? Or so that we can reassure ourselves that our lives aren't as screwed up as the callers'?"

"All of the above, I guess." She'd have to give this more thought. "Thanks for your time, Manny. I'll call if I have any more questions."

"How's everything with you?"

"Progress on all fronts." She smiled. "I'll fill you in another time."

"How are your Hebrew classes coming along?"

"*Metzuyan,*" she said, showing off her slowly developing Hebrew vocabulary. Excellent. Not so *metzuyan* with Gary, though she'd calmed down and was prepared to listen to an explanation, if there was one.

"Come for a Shabbos. Aliza and I would love to have you, anytime."

"I'd like that, but I'm not sure when I can." Sidestepping

again. Sooner or later, she'd have to accept someone's Sabbath invitation, to see what community observance was like. Ezra kept telling her that.

Manny smiled. "No pressure. Whenever it's good for you." He stood. "I hope you find the little girl, Jessie."

She took the tapes and slipped them into her purse. "Renee's a devoted mother, Manny. She's *terrified* for Molly."

"I'm sure she is."

"What would you have told this man's wife if she'd called and told you she was afraid of her husband?"

"Get the hell out of there and don't look back." He sighed. "Sometimes, Jessie, there's no one to blame. Makes it that much harder."

"My problem is, Dr. Renee, that my fiancé's eleven-year-old son doesn't respect my authority."

"You mean he's not listening to you?"

"Yes."

"Well, just say so, Denise. This isn't a court of law." Renee laughed. "What's he doing?"

"He won't clear his plate from the table when he's at my apartment. He leaves his clothes and stuff all over the place."

"You don't have kids from a previous relationship, do you?"

"No."

"Didn't think so. This is typical behavior for an eleven year old. Sounds pretty mild, actually. It'll get worse when he's a teenager, and that would happen even if you were his mom."

"Maybe, but it makes me very uncomfortable."

"If you marry the dad, the kid is part of the picture, Denise. So figure out what you want to do before you sign up. Did his mom die, or did his parents divorce?"

"They divorced. His mom has custody, but he's with his dad every Wednesday and every other weekend, and alternate holidays. It isn't just that he's sloppy, Dr. Renee. He won't do anything I ask and basically ignores me. He's rude to me. He's sarcastic and mean. He told me he hates me."

Renee sighed. "I can understand how that would be very painful, Denise. Unfortunately, that kind of resentment is pretty common when a new woman takes mom's place. You can't dictate feelings, but you can set rules for behavior."

"That's why I'm calling. I want my fiancé to set down the rules, but he says to give it time, not to make a fuss now or we'll make things worse."

"He's right in the sense that you want to pick your battles, Denise. Don't throw a fit if the kid leaves a mess. But you don't have to tolerate rudeness or meanness, and you shouldn't. You'd be teaching the boy the wrong values and he wouldn't like you better anyway. You also need to know whether your fiancé is going to be supportive. How long have the two of you been engaged?"

"Two months."

"And before that you dated for how long?"

A pause. "About a year."

"Uh-huh. So this eleven year old has had about a year to get used to the idea that his mommy and daddy have split. Not very long from his point of view. And then you came along."

No response.

"Is there something you're not telling me, Denise?"

"Actually, they were divorced four months ago."

Silence. "I see. So what you're telling me is, you were dating this boy's father when he was still married to his mother?"

"There were problems in the marriage before he met me, Dr. Renee."

"Oh, goodness, Denise. Do you know how tired *that is? Listen, sweetheart, I don't care how miserable he was with his wife. He had no business getting involved with you. I just love this. Here you are, complaining because a child is misbehaving and saying he hates you? You want him to obey your rules when he knows you broke the big one?*

"I don't think *so!"*

She said good-bye to Manny and waited in the hallway for the elevator. Ever since she'd been on the task force, she always felt a little odd coming downtown to Parker Center—the Glass House, convicted criminals called it because of its construction. As an LAPD detective, she belonged, but she was an outsider.

That's probably how Willie Williams, who had taken over for Police Chief Daryl Gates, had felt. Williams had been imported from Philadelphia and had never really been accepted by the department. And now they had Bernard Parks, homegrown talent, a department veteran who was a stickler for rules and order and big on disciplining officers. Not everyone at West L.A. was happy with Parks. Marty Simms bitched about him all the time. So did Lou Harris.

The elevator doors opened and she found herself face-to-face with Detective Frank Pruitt.

He smiled. "How are you, Jessie?"

"Fine, thanks."

She managed to smile back, though she felt acutely uncomfortable. This was the first time she'd seen him after she'd broken off their affair. Since then, every time she'd come to Parker Center, she'd prepared herself for the probability that she'd run into him—he was with Robbery-Homicide, right in this building. But she realized now she hadn't been prepared at all.

"And you? How's it going?"

"Couldn't be better. I made Detective III."

"That's wonderful. Congratulations, Frank." She found it easy to sound genuine. Though she'd found him lacking in soul, he was a terrific cop.

"I'm pretty pleased," he said, his smile wider. "You're looking great, as always."

"Thanks. You, too."

He was running his eyes over her appreciatively, and she sensed he was trying to make her blush. She still found him good-looking—he was well built and handsome in a cragged, rough way—but the intense physical attraction was no longer there.

"How's your sister and nephew?" he asked.

"Great. She's expecting a baby, as a matter of fact."

He nodded. "Nice news."

God, she wanted this conversation to end. "And your boys?"

"Terrific." A real smile. "What brings you down here?"

"I had to talk to Manny Freiberg about a case."

"You used to talk to Freiberg a lot, when you were on the task force. That was a good time, wasn't it? We worked well together, Jessie." His tone was more than a little familiar and rich with innuendo.

She smiled. "After you stopped making my life hell." He'd made it clear he resented her presence when she'd first arrived. Because she was a woman, an outsider. Not everyone was like Phil.

Frank grinned. "Yeah. How about a cup of coffee sometime? Maybe I'll take you dancing."

She smiled again, but now she was blushing. Dancing together had always been a prelude to sex. "Thanks, but I'm seeing someone."

He raised a knowing brow. "Your ex? He's a reporter, right?"

"Uh-huh." She wondered how he'd heard.

"For a while, Rona and I thought about giving it another try, for the boys' sake. Didn't work out." He shrugged. "You change your mind, you know where to reach me. Reporters and cops?"

He made an iffy gesture with his hand. Another smile, and he walked away.

She wondered if he knew about the case and Gary's byline or was just trying to get her goat. In which case, he'd succeeded.

She was on the 10 Freeway nearing West L.A., wondering why the hell Gary still hadn't called, when her beeper sounded. She looked at the screen.

Phil. She punched the station number she'd stored on her cell phone.

"Good news," he told her when he came on the line. "The subpoena for the cell phone company came through early, and they got the name of the guy who belongs to the cell phone. Howard Orzo."

"Howard" could be Hank. She felt a surge of excitement. "Where does he live?"

Phil gave her an address in Venice. "We have a telephonic warrant to search his place. Exigent circumstances."

"I'll be at the station in ten minutes. We'll take my car."

He was waiting in front of the Pizza-Hut-orange-tiled entrance when she pulled up six minutes later.

"No traffic," she said when he was in the car, buckling up. He was always criticizing her for speeding—so was Gary—and she couldn't blame them. She loved driving fast, especially on open stretches of highway. That's probably why you became a cop, Gary had joked more than once.

"Don't kill us getting there now that I lost another pound." Phil leaned against the headrest and shut his eyes. "I have two units in an unmarked waiting for us."

"Good." She pulled away from the curb.

"What did Freiberg say?" he asked, eyes still closed.

Jessie repeated the conversation. "He thinks this Hank is real."

"Hmnn."

They rode in silence. Nothing unusual, but today she was uncomfortable, like the first days she'd been partnered with him, when she'd felt the need to make conversation.

"Anything happening with Silo or the Iranian?" she asked, turning right on Venice.

"Nada. The wife wasn't in. So what else is new?" He grunted.

"I'm sorry about not telling you what the lawyer and the other housekeeper said."

"Forget about it."

Another mile and a half to go. "Gary broke the news in the *Times* this morning," she said.

"I know."

She glanced at him quickly, then returned her eyes to the road. "You didn't say anything."

"I figured you'd seen the byline or heard about it and didn't want to talk about it. Why rub salt?"

"He should've told me about it before he ran the story."

"What for? So you could give him a hard time and try to talk him out of it?"

"Since when are you so forgiving about the press?" she asked, irritated. "Or is it because he's your poker buddy?"

"I don't like it when they make my job harder. But that's the system, Jess. What am I gonna do about it, cry?"

"We're in a *relationship,* Phil. If it's going to work, there has to be trust."

"Did he report something you told him in confidence?"

"No. Then again, I didn't *tell* him anything in confidence."

"So don't crucify the guy for doing his job."

"Maybe cops and reporters don't mix," she said after a moment. She could see Frank Pruitt's gesture, his smile.

"You're looking for easy?" Phil shook his head. "It doesn't exist. Maureen and I have been together fourteen years, and it takes work, compromise. You're not sure about Gary, that's one thing, Jess. But don't blame it on this, 'cause you'd just be lying to yourself."

Abbott Kinney was up ahead. They were almost there. She felt her stomach muscles becoming tighter and tighter, almost cramping, as they neared the street. She turned right on Grand, then slowed when they were a block away and cruised at five miles an hour, looking for the address.

"There it is."

Phil pointed to a neat-looking small house with blue clapboard trim and a gabled roof. An old white Mazda sat in the driveway.

She parked a hundred feet up and turned off the ignition. The block was empty with the exception of two young boys who Rollerbladed past them and two plainclothes police sitting in an unmarked car across the street. The air was filled with the scent of brine from the ocean only blocks away. She looked around while Phil spoke to the officers.

A minute later he was at her side. "Someone's inside," he told her. "They heard crying."

She waited with Phil while the officers moved stealthily to the back of the house to secure the exits. Then she followed Phil up a cracked cement walkway and stepped onto a porch where a tricycle, its red rusted brown, lay on its side. They drew their weapons, stood on either side of the door.

Phil knocked on the door, softly. Not loud enough to be heard by whoever was in the house, but enough to satisfy the law, if he had to testify.

No answer.

They nodded at each other. He turned sideways and, moving back, shoved his shoulder against the door. Wood splintered.

Reaching inside, he twisted the knob to open the door and stepped cautiously inside. Jessie followed.

There was no one in the living room, dusty and littered with newspapers and used paper plates and cups. Jessie noted a formal portrait of a bride and groom on the mantel ledge. Next to it was a smaller framed photo of a little boy.

No one in the dining room.

No one in the kitchen, which reeked with the stench of days-old garbage. Dishes caked with dried food lay stacked in the sink.

Sounds coming from the back of the house. A television. Someone whimpering.

They moved quietly until they were standing in front of a closed door. They braced themselves against the wall. The sound was louder.

She twisted the knob and, both hands on her gun, kicked the door open and entered the room, Phil behind her.

"Police!"

Her heart beating rapidly, she assumed the half-sideways stance and aimed her gun at the T-shirt-and-shorts-clad man lying on an unmade bed. The cat he'd been stroking had leaped off his chest and split the air with an unearthly screech.

The man scrambled off the bed, knocking several beer bottles to the carpeted floor. "Hey!" He stared at Jessie and Phil, backing away.

"Stay right there," she ordered. "Raise your hands real slow and put them on top of your head."

He obeyed and stood stiffly, muscular arms raised high above his head. He was over six feet tall and solidly built, with massive shoulders and a thick neck. A big man, Lupita had said.

"Hank Orzo?" she asked.

"Yeah. Who the hell are you?" He moved his hand to his mouth.

"Hand back on your head! I'm Detective Jessie Drake."

"I'll check the other rooms," Phil told her, and left.

"What the hell's going on? You can't just come in here like you own the place."

She heard fear beneath the bluster, but there were many reasons for fear. She couldn't tell if it was the voice from the tapes. She kept the gun on him and waited for Phil, who returned a moment later, shaking his head.

"No sign of her."

"I wanna see a badge," Orzo said, his speech a little slurred.

With her gun in one hand, she removed her badge from her pants and flipped it open. "Where's Molly?" she asked Orzo.

"Who's Molly?"

"Cut the crap, Hank." Phil glowered. "We know you have her. Tell us where she is."

"I don't know what you're talking about. How'd you get in here? You break the door down?"

"You called the station and said you had her," Phil said.

He stared at them for a few seconds. "You have the wrong guy. I don't know this kid Molly. I never called that station."

"How'd you know Molly is a kid?" Jessie asked, very quietly.

"I heard about it on the news. The kid that was kidnapped, that's who you're talkin' about, right?" His eyes were darting from Jessie to Phil and back again.

Phil said, "We know you're lying, Hank. We traced the call to your cell phone."

"I don't *have* a cell phone." He sneered at Phil, triumphant.

"The subscriber company says you do."

"It's my brother's phone. Howard. I'm Henry. Can you believe those names?" He turned to Jessie. "Someone stole the phone this morning from my car, right in my driveway. Shoulda locked the doors."

"Did you report it stolen?" she asked.

"I was going to, soon as I heard from my brother. I don't know what company he deals with." He took a deep breath, then belched. "Jesus! You come in here like that, you almost gave me a heart attack!"

"Whose tricycle is that on the porch?" Jessie asked, even though she knew in her gut he wasn't their man.

"My brother's kid. Sammy."

"Where is he?" Phil asked, still glowering.

"With his folks." Orzo scratched his chest. "They're visiting his wife's parents, in Frisco. I'm house sitting." Another belch. "You can't come barging in here, you know! I have my rights."

"You watch too much TV, Henry. Get your brother on the phone so he can confirm what you told us."

"They may not be at the house right now."

Phil said, "There's a little girl who's been kidnapped, Henry, and the man who kidnapped her used your brother's phone. So you'd better hope he's where we can talk to him."

Orzo blinked rapidly, then picked up the receiver on the nightstand. He punched numbers and waited, then turned to Jessie.

"The line's busy."

"Try it again."

Ten minutes later Orzo reached his brother, Howard, who verified that he was vacationing with his wife and son at her parents' home.

They spoke to the wife, too.

They checked every room in the house, searched through drawers and cabinets, looked in the garage, and found nothing to indicate that either of the Orzo brothers wasn't telling the truth.

It was hard to admit defeat.

(("32"))

"So my point is, Ray, sure, this guy's a creep," Stuart Logan said. "A major sicko. That *is* the point. What the hell was Dr. Renee thinking, telling his wife to cut out with his kid? I mean, all you have to do is listen to this guy, and you know he's off the wall. Am I right or am I right?"

"You're right, Stuart."

"You're just a butt-kissing yes man, Ray." He snickered and took a sip of soda. "You're afraid you'll lose this cushy job if you disagree."

"You got *that* right!" Ray laughed.

"Let's take some calls." He scanned the screen. "Moshe from West L.A., you're on with Stuart Logan. What's with the name? You're a Hebrew, is that right?"

"I'm Jewish, yes. I wanted to—"

"You've got the earlocks and the yarmulke, and the whole number, huh?"

"No earlocks, Stuart. No horns, either."

Logan grinned. "Good one, Moshe. Chalk one up for the Jew. So what's with the ethnic name? Why not Morris or Mo?"

"About Dr. Renee—"

"Changing the subject, huh?" Logan laughed. "Okay, Mo. Make your point. You've got two minutes." He swiveled in his chair and reached for a large bag of unshelled peanuts.

"I think it's easy in hindsight to say that Dr. Renee should've worried about this guy. We don't know what he said when he called the show the first few times. And if his wife told Dr. Renee that she was being abused, or the child was being abused, what else could Dr. Renee advise her to do?"

"That's it? That's your Talmudic reasoning?" He'd shelled a pile of peanuts and crunched a few.

"You're faulting her for the fact that her daughter was kidnapped. I don't think that's fair. Actually, it's heartless and cruel, considering the anguish she must be going through."

"Good point, Moses. I hear your pain, as President Bill would say." He cracked another shell. "Take two tablets and don't call me in the morning, okay? Better yet, make that *ten* tablets." He disconnected the line. "What a bleeding-heart jerk. You know what, Ray? All of a sudden everyone feels sorry for the doctor. Am I the only one who sees that she brought this on herself?" He pressed a line. "Rita from Agoura. What's up, sweetheart?"

"I'm with you, Stuart. I think she had no business advising this guy's wife what to do, considering she never met the woman."

"You are one smart lady, Rita. Are you single, sweetheart? How about dinner sometime?"

"I'm not your type."

"You sound hot. Are you hot, Rita?"

She laughed. "Good-bye, Stuart."

"What a shame. You could tell from her voice that she was hot, right, Ray? Blond, all legs." He sighed and pressed another line. "Chris from Simi Valley. How's by you?"

"I'm great, Stuart. You know what I think?"

"You gonna tell me or make me guess?"

"I say this is a hoax, Stu. There is no kidnapping. This is a gimmick to boost the ratings."

"You're a pretty sick dude, Chris. I like your style." He chuckled. "So where's the kid?"

"With some family or friends. Then a couple of days from now, the police get a clue, and they find her. And that's it. The ratings are up, the kid's home. Dr. Renee's a star, and the station gets big ad revenue."

"Chris, one problem. There's a housekeeper dead. Is that part of the gimmick, too?"

"Who says she's dead?"

"The police, dude."

"Maybe they're in on it. Wouldn't surprise me. They get kickbacks, you know."

"Chris, what'd you have for breakfast? Conspiracy nuggets? Take some time off, man, and rest your brain." He disconnected the call and blew through his teeth. "Can you believe this nut?" He fluttered his hands over the buttons, pressed a line. "Janine from North Hollywood. What's the word?"

"Stuart, I think you've hit rock bottom here. You're always

sleazy and nasty, but a little girl's been kidnapped. Why can't you leave the family alone?"

"So what're you saying? That I don't discuss this anymore? It's the subject of almost every talk show in the city."

"It went national," Ray said. "Plus I heard a couple of chat rooms will be open tomorrow, when the kidnapper calls again."

"No shit. Did you hear that, Janine?"

"You don't have to play the tape over and over," she said. "It's horrible."

"Like the networks aren't playing it?" He snorted. "It's news, it's theater. A year from now you can watch the story on TV. 'Ripped from the headlines.' I'm not making it up, honey."

"You're exploiting this tragedy."

"And KMST isn't? Sure, it's a tragedy. Sure, it's sick that the kidnapper's calling in live, and everybody's listening. KMST could've said no. They didn't, did they? Hey, Janine. Did you hear him when he called Dr. Renee today?"

"No. I don't usually listen to her show."

"Are you gonna listen *tomorrow?*"

A pause. "I don't know."

"Yes, you are. Admit it, sweetheart. Everybody's gonna be listening, and then they're all gonna be crying about how awful it is."

Logan crunched a peanut. "Welcome to the human race."

((**33**))

Barry looked through the peephole and yanked the door open. His face was ashen. "Is Molly—?"

"There's nothing new," Jessie said quickly. "Can we come in? We need to talk to you."

He shut his eyes briefly. "When I saw it was you, I thought for a moment you were here with bad news." He ran his fingers through already disheveled hair. "What about the phone trap?"

"He used a cell phone he stole from someone's car." She'd phoned the subscriber company and had them cancel the number. "We'd like to talk to you, Barry," she said again.

"I've told you everything I know."

"We have a few more questions."

His face hardened. "Picking up another soda can, are you?"

She smiled in answer.

"Look, I just came back from Renee's. I didn't sleep all night, so I'm punchy and tired as hell, and to tell you the truth, I see no reason to talk to you, considering that you went to my lawyer and tried to pump her for information." He paused to take a breath. "So, no, you can't come in."

"I'm afraid we're going to have to insist, Barry."

"I don't have to talk to you!"

She wondered how much of the belligerence was a product of anger or fear, or the beer she smelled on his breath. She was sure Phil smelled it, too.

"We can do it here," Phil said. "Or we can take you down to the station and question you there. Make it official."

"Do you ever get tired of that line? It's so old, Detective." He sighed, then stepped aside to let them enter. "What the hell. Let's get this over with. The sooner you leave, the sooner I can catch a few hours' sleep."

The room looked lonelier than it had last time, Jessie thought. Different, too, though she couldn't figure out why. A suitcase stood against the far wall. She looked at Phil. He was eyeing it, too.

"Going somewhere?" Phil asked, nodding toward the suitcase.

Barry followed his gaze. "I packed a few things when I planned to stay at the house with Renee, in case this guy would call in the middle of the night."

Jessie and Phil sat on the folding chairs at the card table and waited while Barry rolled over the chair from the computer desk.

"You'll forgive me if I don't offer you refreshments," Barry said, sitting down. "If this is about the goblets, I already told Jessie I sent them, and why. I assume she told you."

Phil nodded. "A few things don't add up, Mr. Altman."

"You know what doesn't add up?" He glared at Phil. "That you're wasting time harassing me instead of looking for the son of a bitch who kidnapped my daughter."

"Here's what we have," Phil continued as though Barry hadn't spoken. "One, the message the kidnapper left has been erased. You say you didn't hear the message, but your wife says you played it when you arrived at the house."

"She's mistaken. She was agitated, confused."

"Two, your remote to the gate and garage are missing."

"I have the key. It was in a different pair of slacks." His face reddened with embarrassment.

"Can we see it?" Jessie asked.

He gave her an ironic look, then went into the kitchenette, opened a cabinet, and returned with a small key. "Here." He held it dangling from a red tag.

"Okay if we take this to make sure it's the right one?" Phil asked.

"Sure." He dropped the key into Phil's waiting hand.

"We checked the entire house, Barry," Jessie said. "We couldn't find the remote."

"I know I returned it," he said doggedly. "Renee ordered me to, so I did. Either Blanca forgot to tell her about it or Renee doesn't remember."

"Your wife *ordered* you to return it?" Phil said. "When was this?"

"One day last week."

"Why did she *order* you to return it?"

"You'd have to ask her. I guess her attorney advised her to do it." The heightened color in his face showed that he regretted having used the word.

"This was right after you called the station and pretended to be a caller, wasn't it?" Jessie said, her tone friendly. "She was angry because you implied you'd tell the station manager about the separation unless she gave up custody of Molly."

He scowled. "I didn't threaten her."

"We can listen to the tape, Barry."

"Maybe you just didn't get around to dropping off the remote right away," Phil said. "It happens. Maybe it's here."

"I dropped it off," he said through clenched teeth.

"What day was that?" Jessie asked.

"After she told me to. The same day I took over the bike." He ran a hand through his hair. "I told you all this."

"Renee said you gave Molly the bike on Wednesday."

"Right. Wednesday. I guess I was wrong about the day."

"You called the station on Thursday," Jessie said.

He frowned, then chewed on his upper lip.

"What I can't figure out," she said, "is why you just can't admit you have the remote. What are you afraid of?"

"I don't have it."

"Then where is it?" Phil asked softly.

"I don't know."

"Your wife was putting the screws to you, Mr. Altman, cutting off access to your daughter, threatening to keep you from seeing her."

He shook his head. "That's just talk. I know I'll get custody."

"That's ñot what your attorney implied," Jessie said. "She's plenty worried. You probably were, too, Barry. It's understandable. You love Molly. You were afraid of losing her."

He was staring now. "What are you saying?"

"I think you paid someone to kidnap Molly. You didn't plan for Blanca to get hurt, but—"

"You're insane!" He stood abruptly and rattled the table. "Get the hell out of here, both of you!"

"Sit down, Barry," Jessie said.

"You have no right to come here and make these horrible accusations! I want you to leave, right now! My God, don't you have any shame?"

"What's in the suitcase, Barry? Molly's doll? The Legos I saw here last week?" She'd realized suddenly why the room had seemed different. Too neat.

"I told you. I packed a few things to take to Renee's."

"Why don't we open it up and have a look?" Phil rose. "Settle this whole thing."

"You can't search my property without a warrant!"

"Give me five minutes," Phil said calmly. "I'll get one over the phone."

Jessie said, "If you have nothing to hide, Barry, just open the suitcase."

He crossed his arms over his chest. "I don't have anything to hide. I just resent your bullying me. I want you to leave, or didn't I make myself clear the first two times?"

Phil turned to Jessie. "I say we take him in."

Barry sneered. "On what grounds? That you're trying to pin something on me because you have no clue how to find this guy?"

Jessie stood. "Give me a few minutes with him, Phil?"

"I have nothing to say to you," Barry told Jessie with the hurt of someone betrayed.

"You heard him," Phil said. "Let's get this over with."

"I'm trying to help you, Barry," she said urgently. She turned to Phil. "Two minutes."

Phil snorted. "Waste of time," he muttered under his breath, but he crossed the room and stood in front of the desk.

"Phil wanted to take you in right away," she said. "But I asked, as a favor to me, to give you a chance to explain. If you tell me the truth, Barry, I can try to help you."

He smiled grimly. "So now you're the good cop and your partner's the bad cop?"

"I know you didn't mean to hurt anyone, Barry. They'll take that into account."

"Isn't that what you had Renee tell Hank on the show today?" He grunted. "If this weren't so outrageous, it would be pathetic. How could you think for one minute that I'd kidnap Molly?"

She dropped her voice. "Barry, one of the neighbors spotted your car in front of Renee's house at around two-thirty. Don't play us for idiots." Not the truth, but he didn't know that.

"You're making that up," he said, but the fear in his eyes betrayed him.

"If you cooperate, I'll try my best to make things easier for you. If not . . ." She shrugged.

He licked his lips. "I don't think I should talk to you without my lawyer."

"You can call your lawyer." Jessie nodded. "Maybe you should. As it stands, you could be an accessory to murder."

"That's crazy!" Eyes widened, lips quivering. "I didn't kill anyone!"

"And since the murder was committed during the commission

of a felony," she continued, "you could be looking at a death sentence. Are you aware of that?"

His hands were shaking. "But I didn't do *anything!*"

"It doesn't matter if you did anything yourself. If you're involved in any way, you're an accessory. If you know something about Hank, tell me now before it's too late."

"I don't know a Hank! I'm not involved."

"On the way here I phoned the pharmacy you and Renee use. They confirmed that on Monday morning you renewed and picked up a double prescription for amoxicillin."

She had him now. The color had drained out of his face, leaving it a sickly gray.

"Oh, God!" he sobbed. He sank down onto his chair and cradled his head in his hands.

34

Jessie motioned to Phil to return to the table, then sat down and rested her hand on Barry's shoulder.

"Where is he, Barry?" she asked softly.

"I don't *know!*" he groaned.

"He has your daughter," Phil said. "Don't you want to help us?"

Barry's head jerked up. "Don't you think I *want* to find her? I'm *terrified* I'll never see her, that he'll harm her. And it's all my fault!" He slammed his fist onto the table.

"You paid him and he double-crossed you?" Phil said. "Is that what happened?"

His eyes were wild with fear. "I didn't *pay* him! I had no idea he would do this!" He turned to Jessie. "He came here Friday afternoon, right after I took Molly back to Renee's. He—"

"What's his name?" Phil interrupted.

"I don't know."

"Jesus." Phil rolled his eyes. "I've had enough of this crap. He's just lying to cover his butt. He paid this guy, things went wrong, and now he's scared."

"*I never paid him!*" Barry took a calming breath. "He told me he was a detective," he said quietly. "He said his name was Gerald Riley and showed me his card. But I'm sure he's Hank."

The man from social services who had questioned Blanca about the Altmans? Had he gone first to Renee's to snatch Molly, then to Barry's? "Go on," she said.

"He wanted to talk to Molly. I said she wasn't here and asked him why. He said Renee claimed I had a drinking problem. He wanted to know how often did I drink, how much. Did I drink around Molly. I admitted I'd been drinking ever since things started falling apart with me and Renee, but not to the point that I was ever drunk. I may have a beer or two, but so what?"

He was looking at Phil now—man to man, Jessie figured. But Phil's face was inscrutable.

"What did Riley say?" she prompted.

"He told me the housekeeper corroborated Renee's statement. I said that wasn't possible, because Blanca knew that wasn't true." Barry paused. "Then he said Renee had filed a complaint charging me with molesting Molly several times when I was intoxicated."

Jessie exchanged a surprised look with Phil. So this was what the attorney had meant by Renee's desperate attempt to malign Barry's character.

Barry frowned. "Renee didn't tell you she was doing that?" he asked Jessie.

She shook her head.

"Really? I figured she would." He sounded puzzled.

"You must've been horrified," Jessie said.

"I was stunned, revolted, furious. I told Riley I'd never touched Molly in an inappropriate way. So then Riley told me Renee had talked about getting a restraining order against me." He narrowed his eyes. "She didn't tell you that, either?"

"No."

Barry looked at her a moment, his brow furrowed. "I don't get it." He seemed lost in thought.

"What else did this Riley ask you?" Jessie said.

It took him a moment to focus. "He asked me more questions. 'Do you bathe your daughter? Do you dress her? Where do you tickle her?' Things like that, and worse." Barry swallowed hard. "He wanted to know how often I was with Molly, did we have a specific schedule. Was I alone with her or was the housekeeper around. What kinds of activities I did with Molly."

If Barry was telling the truth, Jessie thought, this Riley had cleverly gleaned information about when to do the kidnapping. Easier than watching the house for days.

"I kept insisting I'd never molested Molly. So then he said even if he believed me, it didn't matter, because now that Renee had set things in motion, chances were I'd never get custody. Especially since the housekeeper would testify against me."

Jessie wondered if he realized he'd just given himself a sound motive for harming Blanca.

"I didn't believe him," Barry said. "I said Molly would tell the court I'd never done anything to her. Riley laughed." Barry tightened his lips. "He said by the time the social workers and psychologists got through planting ideas in her head, they'd have her believing I was a monster. He told me they'd already interviewed her. I think he said at Stuart House?"

On Sixteenth and Santa Monica. A child-friendly environment with one-way mirrors. Jessie had watched several sessions years ago, when she'd been on Sex Crimes. Even one had been too much, and she'd left each session nauseated, horrified by the evil men and women did to children.

"So then you believed him?" Jessie asked.

Barry nodded. "Why wouldn't I? Renee was furious after I called the show. She said that she'd make sure I'd never get Molly, that she was prepared to play nasty."

"So that's when you asked him to help you get Molly," Phil said.

"No! That's not what happened." His face reddened and he stared defiantly at Phil before turning again to Jessie. "Riley said he believed me. He said he felt sorry for me, especially because his brother-in-law just went through the same thing. The wife lied and charged him with molesting their little boy. So now the guy's not allowed near his son, ever. Riley told me the brother-in-law said if he'd known how things would turn out, he would've kidnapped his son and skipped."

"Riley told you this?" Phil sounded skeptical.

Barry nodded. "After he left I phoned my attorney. She was out of town, but I paged her and she called me back. She said she'd be back Tuesday and would check with social services. I asked her if what Riley had told me was true, that my chances of getting custody now were slim. She didn't say yes, but I could tell she was worried."

"Why didn't you call Renee?" Jessie asked.

"My attorney told me not to. Riley called me again later that day. He said they'd probably have to bring me in for more questioning, and that he'd learned that the restraining order would be in effect on Tuesday."

That wasn't how the system worked, she wanted to tell him. But he probably knew that by now.

"He told me again how bad he felt for me. He said I was getting a raw deal, but that there was nothing anyone could do about it. Then I said, 'Unless I kidnap Molly.' 'Right,' he said. Then he laughed, uncomfortable all of a sudden, and said, 'Hey, I hope you're not serious. You didn't hear that from me.' Something like that."

"But you decided to kidnap Molly," Jessie said.

He flushed under her gaze. "I know it sounds crazy, but I

couldn't *bear* the thought of losing Molly. I felt trapped by what Renee had done. I was desperate. I don't think you can understand what I was going through."

"You were ready to disappear and never come back?" She couldn't imagine suddenly uprooting herself; leaving home, family, friends to travel to an unknown destination; always having to look behind her, ready to run. And what of the child forced to do the same?

"People do it," Barry said quietly. "You read about it all the time. They give up careers, homes, family. What did I have to lose? No job, no house. My parents died years ago. All I had was Molly." He ran his fingers through his hair. "I picked up the phone a couple of times to call Renee, to try to reason with her. But I decided my attorney was right."

"So then what did you do?"

"Monday morning I got some maps from the auto club. I wasn't sure where we'd go. I picked up the amoxicillin." A wry glance at Jessie. "In the afternoon I packed some of Molly's things that were at the apartment and some of my stuff. I filled the car with gas, drove to the house around two-thirty, and parked on the street. I took the remote and opened the gate and went inside." He stopped.

"And?" As if she were listening to a story.

"I couldn't go through with it. I just couldn't." He sighed. "That's when he came up to me."

"Riley?"

Barry nodded. "He must have followed me inside the gate, but I didn't hear him. 'What the hell are you doing here?' he said. He scared me to death. I lied. I told him I wanted to see Molly before I was served with the restraining order. He said it was a terrible idea, my coming here like this, that it would look bad to social services and the judge. I pleaded with him not to say anything. He finally agreed, and told me I'd better give him the remote in case I had any other crazy ideas."

"Did you?" Jessie asked, already knowing the answer.

"Yes." His voice was almost inaudible. "I helped him kidnap my daughter. I practically told him what was the best time to do it." His eyes were tearing again. He lowered his head and pressed his open palm against his forehead.

He sounded tortured. She supposed she should feel sympathy, but she was too angry. He'd lied to her and Phil, had withheld vital information. And he'd put Renee in jeopardy. Jessie made a mental note to alert Lambert and the others.

"And then you went home and phoned your wife?" Phil asked.

Barry looked up. "I was shaken by what I'd almost done. I phoned Renee and left a message for her to call me. I wanted to call a truce, to talk about joint custody. Anything to end the ugliness."

"So when your wife phoned the second time and told you the housekeeper was dead, you knew what had happened?" Phil asked.

Barry stiffened. "I didn't *know*, but I suspected."

Phil looked at him with contempt. "Come on, Mr. Altman. You *knew*. Why didn't you tell us about Riley?"

"I was afraid you wouldn't believe me. I was afraid you'd suspect me of kidnapping Molly and killing Blanca and inventing Riley."

"Did you erase the tape?" Jessie asked.

The color in Barry's face deepened. "I wasn't sure what message Riley had left. I thought he might have implicated me."

"How would he do that?" Phil asked.

"I don't know. I guess I panicked. I wasn't thinking clearly."

"You were thinking clearly enough to erase the tape, though." Phil paused. "Where's the card Riley gave you?"

"Here." Barry reached inside his pants pocket and produced a worn card with the LAPD logo and the name Detective Gerald Riley, Culver City. "Don't bother checking it out. I called there yesterday, after I left Renee's, to try to find him. There *is* no Gerald Riley. He died a year ago." He pressed his lips together. "I made it so easy for him. I can't believe how stupid I was."

Or extremely clever. Barry could have made all this up to protect himself from a murder rap. Jessie didn't have to glance at Phil to know he was contemplating the same possibility.

She slipped the card into her purse. "What does he look like?"

"He's a big guy. About six two, muscular. Dark blond hair cut close to the scalp. A small scar next to his right eye."

"The loiterer, right? You made him up."

He flushed. "I wanted the police to know who to look for."

"It would've been nice to have this information twenty-four hours ago when we sent officers door to door, looking for Molly."

"That's why I *told* you about the guy in front of the house. I thought you'd look for him."

"You *thought*," she repeated with heavy sarcasm. "You thought we'd look for a guy you said didn't look suspicious, or you would've told Renee. A guy who was probably just a fan."

"I don't have an excuse," he said quietly.

"So lemme get this straight," Phil said. "You knew that this Gerald, a.k.a. Hank, who killed your housekeeper and kidnapped your daughter, had the remote to the gate. That didn't bother you, the fact that he had access to your wife's property and garage? You didn't think it was important to tell us?"

"I practically *begged* her to have the combination changed. You heard me," he said, addressing Jessie.

She nodded. "I'll call Renee and make sure she does that, if she hasn't already." Uniformed officers would stay with Renee for now, but then what? And what if they never caught the kidnapper? "You'll have to come to the station to give a formal statement."

His chin quivered. "Am I under arrest?"

"Not at this time. But don't try to leave town, Barry."

"How could I possibly think of leaving when he has Molly?"

"I'll also need you to give a sketch artist as detailed a description as you can of this man." She wanted to get the sketch to the media as quickly as possible.

"Can I come in my own car? I'm not exactly a flight risk."

She glanced at Phil. He shrugged almost imperceptibly. "Okay. But you have to come right now."

Barry nodded. "Do you have to tell Renee?" he asked, his voice filled with pleading. "She'll never forgive me."

Probably not, Jessie thought. She wasn't ready to sort out blame, but at the moment found him despicable. "I think she has a right to know, Barry. And it's not something I can keep quiet."

"She should have *told* me someone was stalking her!" he said with an eruption of anger that blotched his face. "She should have told me about Hank. I would've been on the alert. I would've been more suspicious of Riley." He looked at Jessie and Phil.

It was always easier, she knew, to blame someone else.

35

"This is pretty awkward, Dr. Renee. I'm embarrassed to tell you this, because I respect you so much and I don't want you to think badly of me."

"Believe me, Lucy, whatever you're about to tell me, I've heard worse." Renee laughed.

"Okay. Well, years ago, when I was in college, I did a bad thing. I stole a hundred dollars from my roommate."

"Why?"

"I was jealous. She had money and was able to buy whatever she wanted. I was on scholarship, working to help pay my way."

"So you thought that entitled you to steal from her?"

"I'm not proud of what I did, Dr. Renee. It's been haunting me ever since, and I realized a while ago that I need to make amends, to repay what I stole."

"That's terrific, Lucy. So what's your question for me?"

"Is it okay if I send her cash without an apology?"

"Why do that, Lucy? A major part of making amends is fessing up to what you did wrong and asking for forgiveness."

"I know. But my husband is considering running for public office, and if I write an apology to this woman, she may talk to the media when she finds out he's a candidate."

"Out of revenge, you mean?"

"Maybe. Or to show that she has inside information. Some people are like that."

"No kidding!" Renee laughed. "Was this roommate the type who bore a grudge?"

"Not really. But she was a major gossip."

"Sometimes they're worse. This is a tough one, Lucy. If this thing has been nagging at you for years, I don't think you'll get the peace *of mind you're seeking if you just send money. You said this woman is wealthy, so she doesn't need your money."*

"What if she tells people? It could ruin my husband's chances of getting elected."

"Sweetheart, if he's going into politics, he'd better be prepared that people will dig up stuff about him that he doesn't even remember. Nasty stuff, humiliating stuff. Plus they'll make up stuff, and by the time he proves them wrong, it's too late. So if he has a thin skin, he should give up running right now."

"I guess you're right. I'm just so worried."

"Did this woman suspect that you stole from her?"

"I don't think so. I told her I thought it was the maid who cleaned our room."

"Lucy, Lucy." Renee sighed.

"I know. That was a terrible thing to do."

"No argument here. Did she get fired?"

"No. My roommate didn't pursue it."

"Write the note, Lucy. Send your roommate a check for the hundred plus interest. If she's decent, she'll accept the money and the apology and let it go. If not, well, you'll be temporarily embarrassed until the media find someone else who has a juicier secret, but you'll have done the right thing. Does your husband know about this?"

"No. I'm ashamed to tell him."

"Better do it now, before your past bites him in the butt."

"Do you believe him?" Jessie asked Phil when they were in her car.

"Reserving judgment. You?"

"I think Hank tried to snatch Molly at Renee's, went to Barry's to do it 'cause he thought she was there. But she wasn't. So he used Barry to find out Molly's schedule and help him get her. Probably got a kick knowing how horrible Barry would feel."

Phil didn't answer.

She checked the rearview mirror. Barry's black Maxima was right behind them. "No comment?"

"Altman admitted he planned to kidnap his kid."

"Then he changed his mind."

"So he says. If he admits he went through with it, he's an accessory to. If he says he chickened out, he's not."

She couldn't argue with that. "Then why didn't you push to arrest him?"

" 'Cause you're probably right. I just don't like him much."

It was after four-thirty when she entered the station lot, empty except for a few regular cars and four black-and-whites. No surprise. Most of the detectives had already gone for the day—as much as two hours ago, for those who started their eight-hour shifts at six-thirty.

She dropped Phil at his Cutlass, then parked and waited for Barry in front of the station entrance. She led him upstairs to the detectives' room, where she took down his statement and typed it up while he met with a sketch artist.

Barry was done before she was. He approached her desk and tried to start a conversation. She silenced him with a frown and handed him the statement to sign ten minutes later, when she was ready. After he left, she studied the sketch and sighed. Could be anyone.

She'd had several messages while she was out. Three from Renee, one from her sister. Nothing from Gary.

Renee answered on the first ring and sounded relieved to hear Jessie's voice. "I'm sure you'll call if you know anything, but I just needed to talk to you. I'm feeling stir crazy, on top of everything else. Even if I wanted to go out, which I don't, I don't feel like being bombarded by the press."

"Are they hounding you?"

"They're camped around the house. Officer Lambert and the others are making sure they don't bother me, but if I look out the window, I can see them. Thank God the property is gated."

"By the way, did you have the gate combination changed?"

"No. I don't really believe that the kidnapper has the remote, Jessie. Barry probably lost it."

"You should do it now, Renee. Just in case."

"Is there something you're not telling me?" she asked sharply.

In person was better. "Just take care of it, okay? Humor me. I'll stop by on my way home."

"Home" sounded good, but she had to write up her notes. A brief mention of Henry Orzo, a detailed description of Barry's interrogation and the meeting with his attorney, a synopsis of Hank's phone call to the station and her talk with Manny Freiberg. Pages of notes, and they were no closer to identifying the kidnapper or finding Molly.

Out of the corner of her eye she saw Simms and Boyd approaching their desks. They both looked glum, she thought, and she wondered why they were here so late. She checked her notes a final time, then straightened her desk and walked over to them.

"How's it goin'?" Boyd said in his gentle Arkansas twang.

"I should ask you that. You guys look like the world ended. Something wrong?"

"Remember Dickerson, that creep we nailed six months ago for killing his roommate?" Boyd said. "We just came from downtown. They *accidentally* released him from Twin Towers."

She sighed. "Jesus."

" 'Paperwork problem,' " Simms mimicked, then snorted. "When the hell are they going to get their act straight downtown?"

Good question. This wasn't the first time this year, Jessie knew, that a mistake like this had happened because of clerical error. They kept talking about automating the system, but it still hadn't happened. Errors like this made the entire police force look stupid. Worse, it let another criminal loose on the streets.

"What's happenin' with the little girl?" Boyd asked. "Any good news?"

"I wish." She brought them up to date.

"Stolen cell phone, huh?" Simms grunted. "Clever son of a bitch. What's he gonna do for tomorrow's call? Steal another one?"

"I'm surprised the wife's parents haven't contacted us," Boyd said. "It's all over the news. They must've figured out that's their daughter and grandson everybody's talkin' about."

"Same reason Vicky hasn't called. They're probably too frightened to get involved." Jessie had been wondering the same thing, and that was the only answer she'd come up with.

"Yeah, but there's a little girl's been kidnapped by this guy, and if they know where to find him?" Boyd shook his head.

"They probably *don't* know. He's obviously not staying in his own place, and I doubt that he'd tell them where he is. This isn't the first time the wife's run away," Jessie added.

"Too bad she came back the other time," Boyd said.

"She said she wanted the boy to have a dad. And according to Hank, her family was on his side. Told her to go back to her husband."

Boyd grunted. "Don't that beat all? I hope they're happy."

"Family *is* important," Simms said.

Boyd stared at him. "What're you sayin'? That she should've stayed with him and let him slap her around?"

"Of course I'm not." Simms's face had turned pink. "The guy's a maniac. He probably would've ended up killing her. But sometimes a woman leaves 'cause she's not satisfied or something, and she doesn't think about the effect on the kids. That's all I'm saying. It isn't always the guy's fault."

He sounded angry and more serious than Jessie had ever heard him. She wondered if he was alluding to his own family history—according to Phil, Simms's mother had left to pursue a career. That was probably why he often had an attitude toward women, why he'd never married.

She heard her name called and turned in the direction of Espes's office. The lieutenant was standing in the doorway. He beckoned to her, then disappeared into his office.

"Dum, da dum dum," Simms intoned ominously.

She flashed him a look. "Something I should know?"

"Nope."

He was smiling pleasantly, no sarcasm that she could detect. She couldn't figure him out. Sometimes, like now, he seemed friendly. Other times he had an acerbic edge that she found irritating as hell.

Espes motioned her to a chair as soon as she entered his office.

"Tell me about the kidnapping."

No preamble. She'd brought her notes, a copy of Barry's statement, and the police sketch. She handed them to him and sat down, wondering when she'd stop feeling as though she'd been summoned by the principal, and gave him a concise account of what she and Phil had learned.

The lieutenant had listened attentively while she spoke, his small eyes focused on her. Now he tapped a pencil on his desk. "I heard that your ex broke the story in the *Times* this morning."

"Apparently." She braced herself for a rebuke, wondered who had told. Simms? Was that the reason for the smile? "He didn't learn anything from me, Lieutenant."

More pencil tapping. "You think Altman is trying to save his hide?"

She suppressed a sigh of relief. "I don't know. I think we should get a subpoena to tap his phone and put a tail on him."

The lieutenant cocked his head. "Are you saying that because you suspect him, Drake, or because you want to prove how open-minded you are?"

She tried to figure out what was the right answer. "Because I want to prove how open-minded I am."

"At least you're honest. What's your plan?"

She detected a hint of a smile. "I'm trying to find Vicky, the kidnapper's wife. She may know where we can find her husband, or his friends. I've called several shelters and domestic abuse hot lines, Lieutenant, but no one's admitting they know her. I'm hoping someone will recognize his voice."

"Assuming this someone happened to tune in to this guy's call to Dr. Renee."

"I'm pretty sure there were a lot of listeners. I leaked the news in advance to the media. They gave the story a lot of play."

Espes looked at her with interest. "I like it. Using the media." He chuckled.

"Tomorrow there should be more listeners, sir. And other shows have been playing the tape of the call all afternoon. I'm sure it'll be on the TV evening news tonight." And tomorrow morning and afternoon. Ad nauseum.

"Keep me posted. That would be something, if the media actually ended up helping us."

36

"I was beginning to think you weren't coming." Renee shut the door behind Jessie after darting an angry look toward the street. "I feel like a prisoner in my own home. Vultures." She grimaced. "Did you see them?"

Jessie nodded. Several TV network minivans, some local stations, a few reporters camped out across the street. They'd swarmed around Jessie when she'd rung the bell, but she'd dismissed them with a curt "No comment" and slipped quickly inside the gate, which a uniformed officer had guarded.

At least there were no crime-scene gawkers. The Brentwood police had learned to be strict, after Nicole Simpson's murder and during OJ's trial, about banning thrill-seekers and citing those who violated the rules.

"How about joining me for a light supper? I made sandwiches for the officers."

Jessie was about to refuse, but Renee looked so forlorn. "Thanks. I haven't eaten in hours, and it'll save me from figuring out what to make when I get home."

The house echoed emptiness. She followed Renee into the kitchen and sat on a barstool in front of the tiled ledge while Renee set the counter and brought platters of sliced fruit and triangle sandwiches from the refrigerator. A bottle of Perrier for herself, a diet Coke for Jessie.

"As you can see, I made way too much." Renee smiled wanly and sat down next to Jessie. "But it kept me busy." She unwrapped the platters. "There's cheese, tuna, and deli."

"Tuna sounds good." Jessie put a few of the small sandwiches on her plate and filled a glass with soda. "They traced the cell phone, by the way. Apparently Hank stole it."

Renee pursed her lips. "He isn't stupid. He probably figures you put a trap on the phone. Waste of time."

"Maybe. But sooner or later, Renee, he'll make a mistake. And we'll get him."

Renee nodded listlessly. "Have they reached Blanca's family yet?"

"I haven't heard. I know they contacted her roommate."

"I'm wondering who's going to help support her family, now that she's dead. She was hoping to earn enough to bring her kids here in a year or so. She said it was safer in this country." Renee sighed.

Jessie had no answer. She took a bite of the sandwich.

"I'm sure they'll hold me responsible," Renee said. "She was murdered because she was protecting Molly."

"You couldn't have prevented this, Renee. You had no idea someone was going to kidnap Molly."

"I knew I was being stalked. I thought gates would protect me," she said bitterly.

"Did you change the combination to the remote?"

"Not yet."

"You should do it, Renee."

She cocked her head and looked intently at Jessie. "There *is* something you're not telling me."

"I didn't want to discuss this on the phone." How to begin? "My partner and I just talked to Barry, Renee."

"He lost the remote, didn't he?" She snorted. "I don't know why he couldn't just admit it."

"He didn't lose it, Renee. He says he was conned out of it, by the kidnapper."

Renee frowned. Her lips parted, but she said nothing for a moment. Just stared. "Barry knows the kidnapper?" she finally asked, her voice robot flat.

"He claims that a man impersonating a detective questioned him about his relationship with Molly and told Barry you were charging him with molesting her."

"That's insane!" Renee narrowed her eyes. "Why would Barry believe I'd *do* something like that?"

"To make sure he didn't get custody."

More silence. "Why didn't he *call* me?"

"His lawyer advised him not to."

Renee thought that over. "I don't understand. How did the kidnapper get to Barry? And why did he give him the remote?"

Quietly, Jessie repeated what Barry had told them, feeling

again in the telling the bizarre nature of his story. Which didn't make it less true, or more.

"Barry claims he didn't tell us right away because he was afraid we wouldn't believe him. But he *did* give us a description of the man. We have a police sketch, Renee. It'll be in the papers and on TV."

"The loiterer?"

Jessie nodded. "He urged you to have the combination to the gate lock changed. He didn't want you to be in danger, Renee."

Renee's laugh was like a bark. "God, this is unbelievable, isn't it? My husband helped a deranged man kidnap our daughter!"

"He didn't plan to, Renee." *If* Barry was telling the truth.

"Maybe not. But he planned to kidnap her himself."

"He wasn't thinking logically, Renee. He was desperate. He thought you were going to keep him from seeing Molly. And in the end, he didn't go through with it."

"How do you *know* that? Maybe he *did* kidnap her, with this guy's help. And now that Blanca's dead, he's scared, so he's making up this story about being conned."

Phil's theory. "You can be sure we're checking out everything Barry told us." Tapping his phone, following him. Jessie had put everything in motion before she'd left the station. She took another bite of the sandwich.

"I almost wish Barry *were* involved," Renee said. "I'd feel that Molly was safer, you know?" She stared at the food in front of her, then looked at Jessie. "You think this man is giving her enough to eat, don't you?"

Jessie put down the sandwich, her appetite gone. "I'm sure he is. He doesn't want a sick child on his hands."

"She's a little picky. She doesn't like cheese, and she won't eat bread if you don't cut the crust off or drink milk without a cookie or some chocolate." Renee bit her lips. "I hope she doesn't make him angry." Her eyes brimmed with tears.

Jessie took Renee's hand. "Molly's a smart girl, Renee." Not really an answer.

"I keep going into her room, touching her things, wondering if I'll ever see her again."

"Don't do this to yourself." She stroked Renee's hand. "You'll make yourself crazy if you think like that."

"I can't *stop* thinking, Jessie. I'm exhausted, but I'm afraid to sleep. Every time I close my eyes, I see Molly." Her lips quivered.

"Maybe you should take a pill tonight, to help you sleep. The officer on duty will wake you if anything happens."

"I don't *want* to take pills. I want to be alert, in case he calls, in case . . ." Her voice trailed off.

"Do you want me to spend the night with you, Renee? I'd be happy to."

Renee shook her head. "Thanks, but I have to get used to this. It isn't just tonight. It's tonight, and tomorrow night, and who knows how many nights until I get Molly back."

"You don't have to prove you're strong, Renee. It's okay to accept help."

"I know." Renee smiled lightly. "My parents offered to come down and stay with me, but I'm not interested in being interrogated. 'Who was watching Molly? How could this have happened?' As if I'm not asking myself the same questions all day."

"Maybe they just want to give you comfort."

She withdrew her hand. "You know what gives me comfort? Reading all the faxes that have been coming in to the station from people who support me and believe in me. Knowing that I'm helping callers with their problems."

Jessie hesitated. "You're surrounding yourself with people who make you feel good, Renee. That's fine. But don't shut your parents out. You might regret it later."

Renee raised a brow. "As I recall, I'm the shrink. Why don't you stick to being a detective and find Molly."

Jessie looked at her steadily, then slid off the barstool. "You're tired. We'll talk in the morning."

"I'm sorry," Renee said in a low voice. "That was nasty. I know you're doing everything you can to find Molly. I don't know why I'm snapping at you."

"Don't worry about it. I know you're under stress."

"You're angry, and I don't blame you."

"I'm not angry, Renee." She measured her words. "Actually, I'm sad more than anything. Sometimes, like a second ago, I don't know who you are anymore. The Renee I loved and respected didn't lash out at everyone who didn't agree with her."

She stiffened. "You sound like Barry."

Jessie shrugged.

"You think I'm arrogant, but I'm not," Renee said. "I'm just more secure about who I am than most people, more confident, more trusting of my judgment. And yes, I'm impatient with those bent on criticizing me. Why shouldn't I be?"

"People like your parents?" Jessie asked gently. "People like me? Seems to me that if you were so secure about yourself, you wouldn't react so violently to criticism. But you're right—I'm a detective, not a shrink."

"Thanks for your input." Renee was a study in contrasts: cool tone, flushed face.

"For what it's worth, I hope you give what I said some thought. I'm not the enemy, Renee. I'm your friend."

"Anything else?"

"Uh-huh. Change the combination to the remote, Renee. Do it now. That's my professional advice."

"You really think he could come back?" Renee was somber now.

"Let's not take any chances." *Again,* Jessie added silently. Probably what Renee was thinking, too.

((**37**))

"*My dilemma, Dr. Renee, is that I'm attracted to my wife's sister, and I don't know what to do.*"

"*Is the sister-in-law coming on to you, Jerry?*"

"*No. She doesn't know how I feel.*"

"*Thank goodness. You have a problem, Jerry, not a dilemma. If you were talking about your girlfriend's sister, you could dump the girlfriend and hook up with the sister, assuming she was interested. That would make you a jerk and a cad. But you're married. You made a commitment. How is this a dilemma?*"

"*My dilemma is, should I tell my wife how I feel about her sister? Or should I tell the sister?*"

"*Absolutely not! You'd be devastating your wife if you told her, and ruining a family relationship. You need to get help, Jerry. In the meantime, take cold showers and stay away from the sister-in-law.*"

"*That's pretty near impossible, Dr. Renee. She and my wife are real close. She's at our apartment all the time.*"

"*Let me repeat. Get immediate professional help for your problem, Jerry, but don't make it your wife's problem.*"

"*She knows something's wrong. She keeps asking me what.*"

"*Tell her that you're having some problems, that you're going to get help. But don't mention the sister. Once you do, there's no taking it back.*"

"*I listen to your show all the time, Dr. Renee. You're always saying how important honesty is in a marriage.*"

"*Honesty is crucial in a marriage, Jerry. But this isn't about honesty. This is about selfishness and immaturity.*"

"*Believe me, I feel terrible about this. I love my wife, Dr. Renee. I want to be faithful to her, but it's getting harder and harder. I'm thinking about my sister-in-law all the time, fantasizing about her when I make love to my wife.*"

"You are a prince, aren't you?" Renee sighed. "How long are you married?"

"Almost two years."

"Any children? Please, please *say no."*

"We had a miscarriage five months ago, and we're trying again."

Renee was silent a moment. "Let me get this straight," she said, her voice frosty. "You're fantasizing about your sister-in-law while you're trying to make a baby with your wife? Jerry, you're not selfish and immature. You're depraved. Do your wife a favor. Keep your pants zipped until you get your head straight."

"She really wants a baby, Dr. Renee. How will I explain that to her?"

"You're into fantasy, Jerry. Make something up."

"I don't want to hurt her, Dr. Renee."

"Then don't get her pregnant. 'Cause if you do, Jerry, ten to one she'll be calling me a year or two or three from now, wondering whether she should leave her cheating husband."

Her answering machine was blinking furiously. Jessie pressed the play button and walked to her bedroom, listening to her messages as she kicked off her shoes and changed into shorts and a tank top.

Helen, Frances, a chimney company, Ezra, Gary. Helen again.

"Call me when you get in, Jess," Gary had said.

She flipped through her mail—mostly bills—and saw the letterhead of the Jewish agency she'd contacted. Holding her breath, she slit open the envelope and removed the slim sheet of paper that conveyed, with official regret, that as of yet, no success had been made in finding evidence that any of her mother's family had survived the war.

She told herself she hadn't really expected anything, but was disheartened anyway.

She was listless and still hungry, and her refrigerator was practically empty—she'd been too tired to stop at the market on the way home. There were steaks and hamburger patties in the freezer, but she wasn't in the mood to cook.

She phoned Ezra, curious as to why he'd called, and was disappointed to learn that he was out. She left a message on his machine and phoned her parents.

Her mother answered. "I can't believe that just this past Saturday we were talking about that poor Moran girl! How absolutely *heartbreaking* about her little girl. But of course, that's the price a woman pays for having a career instead of staying home with her children."

"Mom, Molly wasn't kidnapped because Renee has a career. The kidnapper took Molly because he wants Renee to persuade his wife to come back to him. Haven't you been listening to the news?"

"I listen to the news all the time, Jessica. There's no need to be snide."

"I'm sorry."

"And I'm entitled to my opinion. Anyway, I didn't call about that. Your father and I are coming up for the weekend, dear, and I wanted to take you and Helen out for lunch on Friday. I had such a lovely afternoon the last time, didn't you?"

"I really did, Mom. I can't make Friday, though. How about Saturday?"

"Saturday your father and I are attending an engagement party for the Kramers' youngest daughter. She's marrying that cardiologist I wanted to set you up with months ago." Frances sighed. "Is it your work that's the problem? Surely you can take an hour off to have lunch with your mother."

"Actually, I'm having lunch with some friends Friday."

"Do I know them?"

Jessie hesitated. "It's my Judaic studies teacher's sister. She invited me for Rosh Hashanah, Thursday and Friday."

Silence.

"I thought it'd be interesting to see what it's like, Mom."

"As you wish. It'll be just Helen and me, then."

"I'm sorry you're upset."

"I'm not upset, Jessica. I'm simply worried about this infatuation of yours. Where is it leading?"

"I don't know where it's leading, Mom. That's the whole point. I'm exploring, studying."

"This is ridiculous. One minute you're perfectly happy with who you are, the next you're lighting Sabbath candles and doing Rosh Hashanah. Six months from now you'll probably be married to a Hassid with earlocks and a beard."

Jessie gritted her teeth. "You didn't seem to have a problem with the fact that I lit Sabbath candles when you were over a few weeks ago. You said how lovely it was."

"What did you expect me to say? If I'd told you the truth, you would have been upset and angry."

"Well, you're upsetting me now. I'm all grown up, Mom. I have to make my own choices."

"You were always headstrong, Jessica, always set on spiting me."

"God, Mom!" Jessie groaned. "This isn't about you."

"Whatever you say, Jessica. Forget that I called. Have a lovely time with your new Jewish friends."

Jessie heard a click, then a dial tone. She felt as though a giant foot had trampled on the delicate filaments of closeness they'd begun to weave on Saturday. So much for small steps, she thought sadly. With Frances, it was more like one step forward, a dozen steps backward.

She opened the refrigerator, frowned at the limp vegetables, and settled for a glass of milk. She was searching through the refrigerator again, more dissatisfied than hungry, when the phone rang.

It was Helen.

"Finally!" her sister exclaimed. "I've been calling you all day! Didn't your partner tell you?"

At this moment, her sister sounded so much like Frances at her slighted best. "Phil told me. I just got home, Helen. And I have to tell you, it's not a good idea to phone me at the station unless it's important."

"Phil didn't seem to mind. He was very friendly."

"Phil is *always* friendly, Helen. But he doesn't have time to spend on taking my personal messages."

"*Somebody's* grumpy."

Jessie clenched her jaw. "I assume you've been calling about Renee. I don't have anything to tell you."

"That poor woman! That's all they've been discussing today on all the talk shows. I was listening to Dr. Renee and cried when I heard her little girl on the air. My heart goes out to Renee, Jessie. How is she holding up?"

"How do you *think* she's holding up? She's terrified."

"You don't have to snap at me, Jessie."

"Two days ago you made a point of saying how nasty Renee is, so forgive me if I'm not overwhelmed with this sudden sympathy."

"That doesn't mean I wanted anything bad to happen to her." Helen's voice quivered with hurt. "I feel *terrible* about what I said, but you don't believe me, do you? You're always ready to think the worst of me. You think I'm just being nosy."

"That's not true, Helen. And I *do* believe you." It occurred to her that she was taking out her irritation with Gary and with Frances on her sister. Hardly fair.

"I'm a mother, too, Jessie," Helen said, still wounded. "I *know* how Renee's feeling. I'd *die* if anything happened to Matthew."

"I'm sorry I snapped at you. I've spent the last two days thinking and talking about nothing else but Molly's kidnapping. To be honest, I'm all talked out." God, she was tired. Maybe a hot shower would help ease her muscles. Better yet, a bath.

"Why don't you come for a swim, or sit in the Jacuzzi? I can give you a massage if you want."

Helen *did* give good massages—surprising, since she had such small hands. Frances had small hands, too. Small, but powerful. . . . She brushed the image away. "I'm too tired. Another time."

"Whenever you want. Do you have any leads as to who this Hank is?"

Count to ten, Jessie told herself. "Helen, I can't discuss an ongoing case, even with family."

"I wouldn't tell anyone."

"I know. But those are the rules. Listen, I'm going to eat a light supper and go to sleep. Talk to you tomorrow?"

"Sure. I *do* care about Renee. Please tell her I'm thinking of her."

After Frances and Helen, she decided she deserved a treat. She took out a pint of Cookies 'N Cream ice cream from the freezer and ran a bath. So much for dieting, she thought ruefully as she savored a few spoonfuls before stepping into the too-hot water and parting the mountains of foam.

She was soaking in the tub, the pint finished, when the doorbell rang. She knew it was Gary. She was reluctant to leave the lethargy of the bath, tempted to give in to childish spite and ignore the bell. It would serve him right.

Minutes later she was standing in the entry in a cotton robe, peering through the privacy window before opening the door, mindful of the fact that the media had been full of reports about a rapist targeting West L.A. No one was there. She felt a mix of relief and disappointment, but then Gary's face appeared. She opened the door and he stepped inside.

"Hey." His usual casual greeting, his usual sexy smile, as if nothing had happened. Too damn handsome in a deep blue shirt that brought out the blue of his eyes and made her stomach tighten with longing.

"Hi," she said, very cool.

"You're all flushed. Are you okay?" He moved closer and reached out a hand to touch her face.

She stepped back. "I was in the bath when I heard the bell."

He dropped his hand to his side and looked at her, puzzled. "Sorry I interrupted."

"That's all right."

"You sound upset, Jess. How's Renee? This must be hell for her. And Barry."

Was he totally clueless? "You tell me. You seem to know everything."

"You're *mad* at me." He sounded surprised. "This is about my story, huh?"

She rolled her eyes impatiently.

He scratched his head, then sighed. "I guess we need to talk."

They sat at opposite ends of the den sofa, both staring at the blank television screen. The awkward silence, broken only by the cracking of his knuckles, was making her uncomfortable, and she was about to say something when he turned to face her.

"I don't get it," he said quietly. "I'm a crime reporter. I wrote about a kidnapping and a murder involving a radio celebrity. That makes it news, Jessie, and—"

"That's *gossip,* not news," she said, her anger flaring.

"To *my* eyes, it's news." His words were measured, calm. "And the fact that the kidnapped child is your friend's daughter is terribly sad and unfortunate, but it's also irrelevant."

She raised a brow in sarcasm. "*Is* it?"

"Yeah, it is." He nodded. "It may make things uncomfortable for you, Jessie, and that makes me unhappy, because I care about you. And believe me, I wish to God I didn't know the people involved. But I can't let any of that affect how I do my job. I wouldn't expect you not to investigate a crime just because it involved a friend of mine, or a relative."

"It's not the same thing, Gary."

He cocked his head. "Why not? 'Cause I'm just a reporter, and you're a cop? I'm a little tired of your constantly telling me how insignificant my job is."

She flushed at the accusation and the edge in his voice. "I never said that, Gary. I'm very proud of the investigative pieces you've done."

"As long as I'm not stepping on your toes, right? As long as I'm writing something you consider newsworthy." He was scowling now, his eyes darker. "You're always making comments about the media in general—they have no scruples, they're immoral, intrusive, irresponsible."

"Sometimes they are."

"And sometimes cops beat the shit out of innocent civilians

or shoot them or stop drivers because they're black. But you don't hear me trashing the LAPD."

"I've never defended bad cops, Gary. I've never said the department doesn't have problems." She sighed. "Why did I have to read your byline in the morning *Times* along with the rest of the world? Why didn't you let me know before you broke the story?"

He snorted. "Like *you* called to tell me when it all happened, right?"

Her chest tightened. "*Forgive* me for not interrupting a homicide investigation to call you so you could scoop the other papers."

"You could've called me when you got home." He took a breath. "You want me to apologize for breaking the story? No way. I'm damn proud I scooped the others, no thanks to you."

"You could've called," she repeated.

"Why, so you could try to talk me out of running the story? That's what you would've done, isn't it?"

"Probably," she admitted. "And you would've run it anyway."

"Right. So what would've been the point?"

"I would've been prepared, Gary. I would've felt better when Lieutenant Espes mentioned it."

"*Nothing* in my story came from you, Jess." He stabbed the air with his finger. "Not one word. Hell, you didn't *tell* me anything, and you know what? I was relieved. I didn't want anything pointing to you. That's *another* reason I didn't call you until after the piece ran, by the way."

"That was thoughtful of you," she said, meaning it.

He glanced at her quickly to see if she was being sarcastic. "Yeah, it was. *Damn* thoughtful." He raked his fingers through his hair. "I'll phone Espes, take a lie detector test if he wants."

"I already told him, Gary. I'm pretty sure he believes me. This isn't just about my feelings, you know. If you'd called, I might've convinced you not to print that the housekeeper was dead. The kidnapper is less likely to turn himself in now that he knows he's wanted for murder. You didn't think about that, did you?" she asked softly.

"He would've found out anyway," Gary said stubbornly, but something flickered in his eyes.

"Maybe, maybe not. Now we'll never know, will we?"

He folded his arms across his chest. "I'm not going to apologize for the story, Jess. I did what I thought was right. Did I screw up about the housekeeper? I don't know."

She contemplated what he'd said, wondered what he was thinking; wondered, too, whether Phil was right, and she was being unreasonable. And then he was next to her, turning her face toward his.

"I love what I do, Jess. I believe in it. If this is going to work between us, you have to trust that I'll never compromise you. And you have to accept that you and I see things differently sometimes, that we have different views about the jurisdiction and purpose of the press."

"It's hard," she said, looking into his eyes.

"It's hard for me to accept that you put yourself in danger all the time, because the thought that you could get hurt drives me crazy." He stroked her cheek. "But I'm working on it, because I know how much your job means to you."

"You've been great about it." He had. No comments, no digs.

"So where are we, Jess?"

His face was inches from hers, and she wanted badly to kiss him. "What if we're turning to each other because it's easier than looking for someone else?"

He stared at her. "Is that how *you* feel?" Very quiet.

She realized she'd hurt him, wished she could retract her words. "No. But what if we're fooling ourselves?"

"There hasn't been anyone for me since we split, Jessie. Not that I didn't try." A half smile. "But you were always there, in my head, in my heart." He paused. "I know you were involved with Frank Pruitt. And now there's Ezra."

"He's just a friend. Really."

"Then what are we talking about?"

She didn't answer.

He sighed. "Sometimes I think you're looking for problems so you won't have to decide about us. *Your* job, *my* job, when to have a family, your interest in Judaism. Now this."

He knew her so well. "I guess I just need time."

"A month? Three months? A year? You won't know anything then that you don't know now. What's *really* bothering you?"

He sounded annoyed, and she couldn't blame him. "I couldn't bear it if we failed again."

He picked up her hand, played with her fingers. "There are no guarantees, Jess. But I don't think we'll fail. Not as long as we're open with each other, as long as we're willing to work on our relationship, to compromise."

That's what Phil had said. She wished she had someone to guide her. Not her mother, whose opinions and values she'd always found suspect. Not Helen, whose views she didn't really respect (maybe unjustly, she thought guiltily, because she was the younger, dependent sister). And now not even Renee, who had been her rock, her confidante. You're almost thirty-five, she told herself. You have to find the answers yourself.

"If you're not sure, you're not sure." Gary released her hand. "How *is* Renee?" he asked after a moment. "You didn't say." He sounded so hurt.

"Trying to hold up. It's not easy."

"I don't even want to imagine what she's going through. This guy's wife, Vicky, may be in a shelter. I can give you the names of the directors of the shelters I checked out when I was researching my story on domestic violence."

"Thanks. That would help." There were twenty-five shelters in L.A. County, some of which, including the ones Alicia had mentioned, Jessie had already contacted. Having directors' names might open up some avenues. And maybe there were private ones she didn't know about.

"I'll fax you the information at the station in the morning. There's also a woman you may want to talk to—Rosalynn Denby. I'll give you her phone number."

He was all business now, no tenderness, but what did she expect? "Who is she?"

"She helps abused women and their kids disappear."

"How?"

"Talk to her. She isn't shy. You can tell her I gave you her name." He checked his watch and moved to the edge of the sofa. "I'd better go. I didn't have much sleep. You probably didn't, either."

"Stay tonight," she said, suddenly loath to let him go. She had the irrational feeling that if he did leave, it would be over between them.

She saw surprise in his eyes and put her arms around his neck. Pressing against him, she knew he must be aware, as she was, that only a thin layer of cotton separated her body from his.

He leaned back against the sofa cushion and studied her, smiling lightly. "Is this sympathy sex?"

She kissed him. He pulled her close, his mouth still on hers, and lifted the damp tendrils curling against her neck. Kissed her neck, then the hollow of her throat, then her mouth again, while his other hand undid the belt of her robe.

She felt her heart pounding.

Suddenly he pulled away. He was breathing hard, his face flushed. "I'll probably shoot myself later, but I don't think this will give you the answer you're looking for."

She drew the edges of her robe together and turned her head.

"I want you to be sure, Jess," he said quietly. "I don't want you to be sorry."

She stayed in the den while he let himself out.

((·38·))

Someone had recognized his voice.

"A woman just phoned the station," Renee told Jessie Wednesday morning, her voice shrill with excitement. "Pollin gave her my number, and I just talked with her. She's *certain* it's him, Jessie, but she said his name is Stan, not Hank. That's the name he used on the very first call!"

"Stan what?"

"She wouldn't give his last name. She wouldn't give her *own* name, either, or her address or phone number, but she's willing to talk to you, but only in person. I gave her the West L.A. number, but she said she wouldn't call there. So I gave her your cell phone number. I hope that's okay."

"That's fine."

"I told her to try you at the police station in ten minutes."

"I'll be here." Obviously, the woman was concerned that a leak from the radio station would lead to the exposure of her identity. She probably didn't want her name and photo plastered all over the media.

"You'll phone me after you meet with her?"

"Absolutely. But don't get your hopes up, Renee. This woman may be wrong."

She took her cell phone from her purse and, turning on the power, noted that the battery was low. She hoped the woman would phone soon.

"What's that about?" Phil asked, nodding his head at her cell phone.

She told him. She walked to the hot water unit at the far end of the room, fixed herself a cup of instant soup, then returned to her desk and continued contacting shelters, including those whose names Gary had faxed her this morning.

So far, no luck.

Earlier Jessie had phoned Rosalynn Denby and left a message on her answering machine. She phoned her again now and listened once more to the woman's identifying message, delivered in a smooth, low southern drawl that reminded Jessie of Boyd.

She was on hold, waiting to talk to the director of a shelter in North Hollywood, when her cell phone rang. She lifted it and pressed SEND.

"West L.A., Detective Drake," she said automatically.

"Is this the police department line?" The woman demanded anxiously.

Jessie had forgotten that the woman was skittish. "No. You've reached my private cell phone number. Are you calling about Hank?"

"Yes." One word, but she invested it with tension.

"Dr. Altman told me you'd be contacting me because you recognized the kidnapper's voice," Jessie said, careful to sound calm. "I'm glad you called, Ms. . . . ?"

"His real name is Stan. I *know* it's him. It's his voice, for sure, and I know that Vicky disappeared a few weeks ago with their boy." She said all this in a rush, as if she were eager to be done and get off the phone.

Maybe she was worried that Jessie was tracing the call. "What's Stan's last name?"

"I'm not comfortable talking on phones. If you want, I'll meet you and tell you what I know. But just you. No one else. And not at the police station."

"Do you want me to come to your home?"

"No! Somewhere public."

Talk about cautious. "Fine. Name the place."

She was silent a moment. "The Beverly Center, seventh floor, in front of Express. I'll meet you there in fifteen minutes."

"It might take me a little longer with traffic." Jessie checked her watch. 9:40. "I'll be there at ten-fifteen."

"Okay. What are you wearing, so I'll know it's you?"

"Taupe slacks, a cream-colored silk blouse under a tan blazer." A gun and holster underneath. "I have shoulder-length brown hair. What about you?"

"I'll find you. Keep your cell phone on, okay?"

"Okay."

"If anyone else is with you, I'll know. And I won't contact you again. I mean it."

"No one else," Jessie promised. "What's your name?" she asked, but the woman had hung up.

*   *   *

At 10:25 the woman still hadn't shown. Jessie had given up studying every female who exited the elevators directly across from the
store. She was studying the window display when she heard the
muffled ringing of her cell phone.

It was the woman. "Go to Macy's, sixth floor," she told Jessie.
"Stay near the on-sale shoe racks."

This was beginning to look like a runaround, Jessie thought,
annoyed. She glanced quickly to her left, then to her right, trying
to spot a woman with a cell phone in her hand.

Too many women, their footsteps echoing in the wide, high-
ceiling corridor. Too many of them hurrying along with cell
phones to their ears.

Welcome to L.A.

If the woman had wanted anonymity, she'd chosen well. The
department store was having a shoe sale, and the place was noisy
as hell, mobbed with impatient customers and whining, unhappy
children and frenzied-looking salespeople, darting as if in a
strange race, many of them staggering under stacks of boxes that
threatened to topple over.

Jessie was examining a black silk dress shoe when she heard
her name called. Turning to her right, she saw a slight, blond-
haired woman in jeans and a beige cotton sweater. A thin, bony
face, with faint lines around her lips. Probably in her thirties,
although it was hard to tell without seeing her eyes, which were
hidden behind dark sunglasses.

"Sorry I made you run around," the woman said, leaning
closer to Jessie to make herself heard above the din. "I had to be
sure you were alone."

She didn't sound all that sorry. "No problem. What's your
name?"

She hesitated. "You can call me Dee."

Obviously not her name. "I appreciate your help, Dee."

"I heard about the kidnapping, and I was listening to a tape
of Dr. Renee's show on the news yesterday? I *knew* it was Stan,
and I knew I had to do something."

"You didn't call until this morning." Jessie had tried not to
sound critical, but the woman flushed anyway.

"It isn't that I don't care. I feel *terrible* about the little girl,
and her parents." Her voice rang with sincerity. "I couldn't sleep,
thinking about that little girl, hearing her voice. So I called, even
though I was afraid to get involved."

"By telling us his last name?"

A salesman approached. "Can I get you the mate to that?" he asked Jessie, who was still holding the shoe.

"No, thanks." She slipped the shoe back onto the rack.

"Everything's forty percent off." He glanced at Dee.

She shook her head.

"Let me know if you need anything," he announced with the resignation of someone who expected nothing.

Dee waited until he'd disappeared into the throng of shoppers. "You don't want to mess with Stan," she told Jessie with quiet intensity.

"How will he know you told us?"

"Oh, he'll find out. I'm probably crazy for being here." Her smile was grim. "I almost didn't show up, but I couldn't live with myself if something happened to that girl and I could've done something to stop it."

"I'm glad you came," Jessie said. The woman had a bristly quality and obviously needed stroking. "How do you know him?"

"Me and Vicky, we're good friends. In spite of Stan," she added bitterly. "The son of a bitch wouldn't let me in the house for months. Not her other friends, either. I'd have to make sure to call her when he was at work, and if we were talking and she hung up suddenly, I'd know he came home." Her lips tightened, deepening the fine lines around her mouth.

A prince of a fellow, Stan. "What's his last name?"

"Weigund." She said the name with contempt and watched Jessie carefully, as if she were waiting for a reaction.

Was the name supposed to mean something to her? It rang no bells. "Do you know where he lives?"

"He and Vicky have a house in Santa Monica, not far from mine. But I doubt he's there now."

So did Jessie, but she wrote down the address Dee gave her. Maybe one of Weigund's neighbors would provide a lead. "What about his family?"

"His parents died when he was a kid, and there's an aunt somewhere, I think. Vicky doesn't talk much about her."

"Maybe Stan is staying with a friend. Do you know who he hangs around with?"

"Not really."

Something in her voice and the sudden stiffness of her manner told Jessie she was lying. She decided to let it go for the moment. "What about Vicky's family?"

"Her parents live in Downey." She was more comfortable now. "There's no brothers or sisters. Well, there *was*—a brother, but he died of leukemia a long time ago. Vicky's little boy, Andy? He's named for the brother that died."

"Do you know her parents' names and address?"

She didn't answer immediately. "Their name is Reston." Clearly reluctant.

"First names?" Jessie prompted.

"Mildred and Walter. I don't know their address, though."

Jessie didn't believe this, either. "Anybody else you can think of who might know where Stan hangs out?"

The woman shook her head. "No, sorry."

"Vicky might know."

"I don't know where Vicky is, but I'm glad she finally got away from that animal!" Her nostrils flared.

"She might call you. If she does—"

"I won't do your work for you! I won't put her in danger."

"The last thing we want is to put Vicky in danger," Jessie said quietly. "We want to rescue Molly, but we won't jeopardize Vicky or her son." No response from Dee. "You could give her a message. You could tell her we just want to talk to her. She might be able to help us find her husband."

Dee looked pensive. "I might be able to do that," she finally said, her tone grudging. "If she calls."

"She never said where she might go if she left her husband?"

"The first time he beat her bad, she went to her parents, but they sent her back home. They said if she'd been a better wife, this wouldn't have happened, that little Andy needed his daddy." Dee's face contorted with anger. "Vicky talked a lot about leaving Stan, but I didn't think she'd ever do it. She'd be walking on eggshells for a while. Then he'd beat her, then romance her, then beat her again."

Jessie sighed. A typical abuse pattern. "So you have no idea where she could have gone for help?"

Dee looked suddenly pensive. "There was this lady she read about in a magazine, who helps women like Vicky? Vicky talked about getting in touch with her, but like I said, she talked a lot, then always changed her mind."

The woman Gary had mentioned? "Rosalynn Denby?" Jessie asked, trying not to get her hopes up.

Dee frowned. "I don't remember the name."

At least that wasn't a no. "Dee, do Vicky's parents know that Stan kidnapped Molly Altman?"

"I don't know. I called them this morning, before I called the station. The mother answered, but the father made her hang up before I could say anything."

"So you have their phone number," Jessie said.

The woman licked her lips. "I don't want them to know I gave you their name and number. They might tell Stan."

"Dee, I know you're afraid of Stan, with good reason. And you obviously don't want to get his in-laws involved. But you said you want to help this little girl."

"I *do*," she cried softly. "This whole thing is making me sick! It's just—" She stopped. "You don't know Stan. If he finds out I tried to help you, there's no telling what he'll do to me."

"If we find him, no one has to worry about him anymore, Dee," Jessie said patiently. "He'll be behind bars for the rest of his life."

"And if you *don't* find him? What then? He'll know you've been asking around because of something I told you." She was trembling, her hands clenched at her sides.

"He can't know that, Dee."

"Oh, really?" Contemptuous again. "When Vicky disappeared without saying a word, I thought, maybe he killed them. Her and Andy. I went by the house, and he wouldn't let me in. 'She's gone for a trip,' he told me. I said I wanted to call her, drop her a line. He slammed the door in my face. So I went to the police."

"You reported her missing?"

She nodded. "They said they'd look into it. I called them back the next day and they told me they'd spoken to Stan, that everything was all right." She sneered and shook her head.

"He came by my apartment that night. I didn't want to let him in—I knew he was mad that I'd talked to the police. But he didn't sound mad at all. He said he was crazy with worry, wanted to know did I have any idea where Vicky might have gone. He was standing at my door, crying like a baby, begging me to help him. So I let him in."

Jessie had a sinking sensation.

"I should've known better. As soon as he was inside he got this cold look in his eyes. He was yelling at me, saying he knew I was in on it, knew I'd convinced her to take Andy and leave. 'Why would I go to the police if I knew she'd left you?' I asked."

"He laughed. He said that was part of Vicky's plan, that I would go to the police and make it look like he'd done something, just to get him in trouble. Just to throw them off from asking me where she was." Dee paused. "He got real quiet. 'You know you shouldn't have done that, don't you?' he said. He was smiling, wagging his finger. Then he punched me with his fist."

Jessie flinched.

"He put me in a choke hold. 'Don't mess with me and my

family,' he said. Then he punched me again and again—I don't know how many times. He trashed the apartment. Then he took out his gun, real casual, and said if I reported it to the police he'd come back and finish the job."

"Did you?"

"I knew he meant it," she said softly. "He knows where I live, where I work. He can wait till he's ready, then come for me anytime he wants. And nothing will happen to him."

"You didn't think the police would protect you?"

Dee snorted. "Yeah, right. If they did, they'd have to deal with the whole mess, drag up all the stuff about Vicky. They didn't want to do that."

Jessie frowned. "All which stuff?"

"The reports she made." She sounded impatient. "The first time, she called the cops, but changed her mind when they showed up at the house. The second time, she filed a report."

"And what happened?"

"They questioned her, questioned him. Vicky had to tell her story to some other guy, over and over again. The whole thing dragged on forever. In the end he said she was partly responsible, because she'd been drinking. Anyway, he *determined* that there wasn't any evidence to show Stan had done anything wrong. It went on her record." She was glaring at Jessie.

None of this made sense. "So she didn't report the other incidents?"

Dee looked at her as though she were an idiot. "What for? Vicky knew there was no point. They take care of their own."

Jessie stared at her. "Their own?"

"Stan's a cop." Dee had a smug look on her face. "I thought you'd figure that out." She paused. "Vicky was a cop, too, before they forced her to quit."

39

"From what I gathered, Vicky reported the second incidence of abuse to the Santa Monica police," Jessie told Espes in his office. "Someone in CAPS probably investigated, plus someone in IA." Internal Affairs, downtown at Parker Center.

Espes had listened without comment, rolling his pencil between his fingers as if he were warming dice. "So Vicky Weigund never filed a second report?"

"Would *you*, in her place? She's beaten up, and she's rewarded with a reprimand from the LAPD for calling in the local police." Probably a CUBO, though Dee hadn't said. Conduct unbecoming an officer.

Espes's beady eyes showed surprise at her tone. She knew she'd come across a little snide, maybe impertinent—different from her usual demure, yes-sir demeanor, but she was seething. No wonder Dee had behaved paranoid, had insisted on Jessie coming alone. Jessie gave her major points for showing up at all, for trusting *any* cop, even a female one.

"When did she file that report?" Espes asked.

"Dee thinks it was about two and a half years ago. So much for progress."

After a Domestic Violence Task Force report, based on its review of 227 cases handled by Internal Affairs over a seven-year period, found the LAPD more likely to sustain allegations against female officers and prone to wearing down female complainants by dragging them through lengthy investigations. *After* the LAPD had promised to clean up its act, to start prosecuting abusive male cops the same way they did civilians. Jessie had been horrified by the report, outraged. But not really surprised.

"Things *are* better," Espes said. "Not perfect, but better."

"How do we *know* that?" She ignored his frown. "We have no clue how many cops are abusing their wives or girlfriends. And getting away with it."

"Not everyone is a Stan Weigund, Drake. Cops like him give all of us a bad name, and that's not fair. And not every case is open and shut."

"You're right. They're mostly shut, as far as women cops are concerned, so why should any woman cop bother filing a report?"

Espes was scowling now. "Are you finished, Drake?" He slapped his pencil on his desk and hunched forward. "You can't change the system overnight. You want to make a start, find Stan Weigund and put him away instead of sitting here bitching." He leaned back. "If, in fact, what this Dee woman told you is true."

"Stan Weigund's a Detective II. He's been at Robbery-Homicide for the past five years. His wife, Victoria Jean Weigund, was with Hollywood for ten years before she quit the force eight months ago. They live in Santa Monica."

As soon as she'd returned to the station, Jessie had run Weigund's name through the LAPD e-mail address book, then had obtained the rest of the information from TEAMS. Obtained it with Phil's help. You could only use the computerized program to access information about someone on the LAPD whom you outranked. Phil was Detective II, Jessie a Detective I.

The room was silent, except for the tapping of Espes's pencil. "Did you talk to anyone at Robbery-Homicide?" he finally asked.

"Not his captain, if that's what you mean. I asked to talk to Weigund and was told he took vacation as of Monday." The day Molly had been kidnapped.

"Checking out the rides at Disneyland." Espes grunted. "This still could be a coincidence. We have to verify that he's the one. You'll have to take this to IA, Drake."

"I know. But first I want to get a warrant to search Weigund's house, in case he's there with the Altman girl." Which was unlikely.

"We don't need word getting out that he's a cop."

"I plan to walk the warrant through myself, sir." If she found a cooperative judge, she could get it in an hour or so. "I want to talk to the Santa Monica PD and IA and find out who let Weigund off without so much as a slap on the wrist. And who his cronies are. One of them may know where to find him."

"And if his pals don't know where to find him? Did you call all the shelters?"

"Just about. One of the directors I spoke to said she'd mention to the other shelter directors that we need to talk to Vicky." She paused. "But I doubt that Vicky Weigund went to a shelter, Lieutenant. Weigund's a cop. He either knows the locations of all the shelters or how to find them. His wife knows that, too."

"Good point." He nodded perfunctorily but looked annoyed.

Probably because she'd reminded him of something he should have known. Sometimes, you couldn't win. "Also, he's got to figure we put a trap on Dr. Altman's home phone and the station's lines. But as far as the station or Dr. Altman goes, sir, I'd like them to think we're still working the trap."

"So you don't have to explain that the kidnapper is a cop." Another, more generous nod. "So where the hell is Vicky Weigund? And how do you plan to find her?"

"Dee said Vicky talked about getting in touch with a woman who helps abused women disappear. She doesn't remember her name, but I heard about a woman like that, too, and I put in a few calls to her and left messages. I'll try her again."

"Rosalynn Denby."

Jessie looked at him, surprised. "You know her, sir?"

"When I was with Foothill, she and I crossed paths. A husband wanted us to arrest her for helping his wife and two kids skip on him."

"Did you?"

Espes smiled. "She made bail before the ink dried on the papers."

The woman must have made some impression. Jessie had never seen Espes look so human. "What's she like?"

"Very smart, very rich. She inherited a bundle from her late husband. Husband number two. Number one beat her one time too many. She smashed him in the face with an iron, told him she'd kill him if he ever came near her again. So she doesn't scare easy. Who told you about Rosalynn?"

She debated, then said, "My ex-husband."

"Jimmy Olsen." He was studying her, his eyes curious. "Does he expect a favor in return? Professional, I mean?"

He had her blushing. "No. He's doing a story on domestic violence and offered to help. He hasn't asked me about the case and knows I wouldn't discuss it if he did."

She'd phoned Gary at the *Times* to thank him for faxing the information, but he'd been away from his desk. Just as well, she supposed. She was still embarrassed by last night.

"What about Vicky Weigund's parents?" Espes asked. "Maybe they know where their son-in-law is."

She was relieved that Espes was apparently satisfied. "I'll talk to them, but Dee doesn't think they do. Or if they do, they're probably too afraid to say anything." She rose from her chair. "Dee is terrified of Weigund. That's why she wouldn't give me her name. She says if he knows we're on to him, he'll figure she fingered him. And he'll kill her. I offered police protection, and she laughed in my face."

Espes sighed. "The FBI contacted me. They want to know whether we have any indication that the Altman child has been taken out of the state. In which case, and maybe even if not, they want to 'participate.' " He grimaced.

That's all she needed, interference from the Feds. "What did you tell them?"

"I thanked them for their interest and concern and told them we were handling things just fine." He paused. "Weigund should be calling Dr. Renee's show again soon, right?"

She glanced at her watch. Eleven forty-five. "Dr. Altman's program begins in fifteen minutes. He said he'd call the same time as yesterday, about ten to one."

"That doesn't give you time to do anything else if you want to be at the station when he calls."

"I can't afford to spend the time at the station, Lieutenant. What if Weigund doesn't call until later in the day? Or not at all? Dr. Altman can handle him. She did fine yesterday. And the show's being taped."

"And if he pushes her buttons?"

"She's a professional, sir."

"She's a mother, and this is the third day her daughter's been gone. But I guess you know her better than I do." He cocked his head. "This lets Altman off the hook, doesn't it? Weigund duped him, just like he said."

"Looks like it."

"Okum must be disappointed. You filled him in before you came to me, right?"

She thought she detected criticism in his tone, but wasn't sure. "I needed his help to access TEAMS."

"You'll need to tell the others at your table—after you verify that Weigund is our man. Talk to CRASH and Fugitives so they can be on the lookout. But make sure no one spreads the news. We don't want word to get out that Weigund is a cop," he said again. "Especially to him."

As if she needed the reminder.

★   ★   ★

Rosalynn Denby phoned just as Jessie was about to leave for the courthouse to get a search warrant for Weigund's house.

"Where'd y'all get my number?" the woman asked, the twang more pronounced than on her recorded message.

"Gary Drake. He's—"

"The stud reporter. I sure remember him, honey. They don't make them much cuter where I come from." She sighed. "Didn't you say your last name is Drake? Are you his sister?"

"Ex-wife."

"Well, any ex-wife of Mr. Drake's is a friend of mine." She had a deep, throaty laugh, rich with innuendo. "What can I do for you, Detective?"

"You've probably heard about the recent kidnapping of Molly Altman, the daughter of the radio talk show psychologist."

"Yes, I have. A terrible tragedy, terrible."

"I'm trying to locate the kidnapper's wife, Ms. Denby, and I thought you might be able to help me."

"I don't see how. What on earth could I possibly tell you, Detective? I don't have a crystal ball, I'm sorry to say."

Jessie detected a guarded note in her voice. "The wife's name is Vicky Weigund," she said, keeping her voice low.

"I'm afraid that doesn't mean anything to me."

Definitely guarded. "Maybe if you thought about it, you might remember something."

"I *beg* your pardon? Where I come from, Detective, it isn't polite to call someone a liar."

"Ms. Denby, I just spoke to Vicky's best friend. She said Vicky told her she'd met with you, and that you were going to help Vicky and her son disappear."

"Well, that *is* strange. This Vicky couldn't have told this other woman any such thing, because it never happened."

Jessie had detected a hesitation in her voice. "I can bring you in for questioning as a material witness, Ms. Denby," she said pleasantly. "Or you can cooperate. It's up to you."

Silence on the line. "Even if I *did* know this Vicky—and I'm not saying I do—there is no way on earth that I would reveal where she is."

"Why don't we meet at your place and talk about it."

Rosalynn Denby sighed. "Very well, Detective, although I should warn you you're wasting your time. Four o'clock? I have appointments till then."

"Four is fine. If I see I'm going to be delayed, I'll phone you. Where do you live?"

She gave Jessie an address in Beverly Hills. "I can tell that *you* must've been the one who decided to end your marriage, Detective Drake. You don't let go easily, do you?"

". . . no news yet as to the identity of the man who kidnapped little Molly Altman, daughter of popular talk show psychologist Dr. Renee Altman."

A photo of Molly appeared above the full-haired anchorwoman. Then a photo of Renee, followed by a sketch of a male, a question mark above his face.

Stan Weigund grunted. "Not even close." He flipped over a jack of spades and set it on the queen, then thumbed to the next three cards.

"We're going to take you now, live, to KMST's studio, and Patricia Alizondo. Patricia, any news?"

The screen showed a slim brunette gripping a microphone, trying not to squint in the glare of the noon sun.

"Diane, it's very tense here, as you can imagine, while we're waiting for the kidnapper to call. Security is tight, and you can see the people behind me, showing support for Dr. Renee."

Zoom to the crowd, mostly women and children, a few men. One woman was cradling an infant against her chest, a poster in her free hand. WE LOVE YOU, DR. RENEE!

"Love don't cut it," Weigund muttered. He turned over a three of clubs. Nothing.

"We don't know when he's going to call," the reporter continued. "We assume it will be around the same time as yesterday's call, ten to one."

The anchor was back. "And we'll be bringing you that radio broadcast live, as soon as it happens. We have in the studio a family therapist, Dr. Gerald Kanton, who works with victims of domestic violence." She turned to a balding man sitting to her right. "Thank you for joining us, Dr. Kanton."

The man nodded briskly. "A pleasure."

"Dr. Kanton will stay with us during the radio broadcast. Afterwards, he'll give us a clearer idea of what is going on in the mind of this angry, violent man. Doctor, you've heard the tape of yesterday's call. What can you tell us about the kidnapper's thoughts right now?"

"Ask *me*," Weigund said. "I'll tell you."

"Well, without talking to him, this is only speculation." A thin smile. "But I can safely say, Diane, that he's enjoying this horrific drama that he's created and the fact that he's controlling it. He has a starring role, if you will."

"He likes attention?"

"Oh, yes. Most batterers—and from what I heard, I think we can assume he is one—have narcissistic qualities. No doubt he's watching this program right now, listening to us talk about him, enjoying being the center of attention."

"Shrinks," Weigund muttered in disgust.

"What a creepy thought." The anchor shuddered for the camera. "Dr. Kanton, if you were Dr. Renee Altman, what would you say during the phone call? And what *wouldn't* you say?"

"Well, Diane . . ."

"You know what *I'd* say, *Diane?*" Weigund sneered. "I'd say that you're full of bullshit. You and the doc and Dr. Renee."

With a jab at the remote, he shut off the TV and tossed the cards onto the coffee table. In the kitchen he made a peanut butter and jelly sandwich and filled a cup with milk. Placing the cup on a plate with the sandwich, he walked to the small bedroom, unlocked the door with his free hand, and pocketed the key.

The room was darkened by miniblinds. The little girl was huddled on the bed on her side, her thumb in her mouth.

He set the plate with the sandwich and the cup on a nightstand. "I brought you lunch."

She shut her eyes.

"Answer me when I talk to you, Molly," he said, annoyed.

She opened her eyes. "I'm not hungry."

"I made you a peanut butter and jelly sandwich. Grape jelly. That's my boy's favorite." He put the plate under her nose.

"I don't like grape jelly."

"This isn't a restaurant," he said, losing patience. "Eat it or don't eat it. I don't give a crap." He dropped the plate onto the nightstand.

"I want to go home," she whimpered.

"Cut it out," he snapped. "I told you, no crying."

She gulped back a sob. "When can I go home?"

"When it's time. I'm not going to hurt you, Molly. I told you that. But you have to cooperate."

"Why can't I go home *now?* I miss my mommy and my daddy."

"Well, you know what, kiddo? I miss my kid. So I guess we're in the same boat."

"Where is he?"

"With his mom. When your mom talks to them, and they come back, I'll take you home."

"What if they don't want to come back? Will I have to stay here forever?"

He set his jaw. "Here. Sit up and drink some milk. Sit up, I said," he repeated when she didn't move.

She took a few sips, then put down the cup.

"What now?"

"I don't feel good."

"That's because you're not eating."

"Everything hurts. Please, can I go home?"

"Don't play games, Molly. I'm not stupid."

"I really don't feel good."

He narrowed his eyes and studied her. She *did* look flushed. Shit. That was all he needed, a sick kid. "Lemme see."

He put out his hand. She pulled away and cowered on the bed.

"Don't piss me off." He gritted his teeth. "C'mere."

She flinched when he moved his hand toward her again, but sat still as he touched her forehead.

"You're okay," he said. "Nothing's wrong."

The kid felt hot to his touch.

41

A multicar accident on the 10 Freeway near Crenshaw heading east had tied up three lanes for over two miles.

Damn, Jessie thought, sighing. A few minutes later she exited at Fairfax and drove to Olympic. Traffic was light, and she made faster progress than she'd expected.

One of the officers in the studio with Renee would page Jessie when Stan called, and Weigund wasn't due to call in for another half hour. Just in case, she'd kept her car radio tuned to KMST since she'd left the station lot.

So far, nothing from Stan, but she'd listened to the end of Ted Harkham's program (not bad, from the little she'd heard) and a fifteen-minute oddball news segment.

Renee came on. She sounded in control but very subdued, and Jessie detected a tiredness in her voice that worried her and made her wonder whether Espes hadn't been right. How long before Renee cracked under the pressure of doing a show and forcing herself to be civil to the man who had kidnapped her child?

Jessie passed Western, then Vermont, and was in the heart of Korea Town. She thought again with some nostalgia how different the neighborhood had been not so many years ago. The lettering on the stores' display windows and posters was all indecipherable to her—mostly in Korean, some in Thai.

Many of the establishments had been rebuilt after being irreparably vandalized or torched during the Rodney King riots, despite the valiant efforts of Korean shop owners, some of them armed, to stop the madness. Rebuilding had been easier than restoring normalcy to the neighborhood, which seemed always to be on the qui vive for another flare-up of the tension that had remained, like ash that falls silently, again and again, and clings after the fire and smoke are long gone.

One thing hadn't changed: The tall Union 76 building, with its bright orange ball, was still there as she neared downtown. It rose, undaunted, to greet her like a fiery sun.

At the Temple Street courthouse Jessie waited impatiently while the search warrant was prepared. She'd brought along a portable radio she'd borrowed from a detective in Sex Crimes, but she needn't have bothered. Someone had turned on the radio in the waiting area.

". . . so I don't think you should punish your daughter for lying to you about what your son did," Renee said. "He really put her in a difficult situation."

"I know, Dr. Renee. But if she'd come to me and told me, maybe we could have avoided this whole mess."

"Angie, what's done is done. Deal with your son and his actions, but don't take your frustration out on your daughter. Good luck.

"Darlene, welcome to the program. . . ."

With the warrant filled out, Jessie went to find a judge who would sign it. She wasn't worried—she had probable cause—but was dismayed to learn that two of the judges whom she knew fairly well were tied up for the day.

Another judge she knew had a full docket but would be taking a half hour recess in forty-five minutes, his clerk told Jessie.

"It's urgent," Jessie said.

"It always is," the man said, not unkindly, and agreed to page Jessie as soon as the judge was in his chambers. He had his radio on, too, the volume discreetly low, and was listening to KMST.

He followed Jessie's glance. "It's after one, and he hasn't called in yet. What a nightmare."

He didn't know the half of it.

From the courthouse she drove to Parker Center. She took the elevator to the fifth floor, identified herself to a courteous black woman in Personnel, and asked her to pull Weigund's package.

"Why do you want it?" the clerk asked.

A routine question. "Weigund may be involved in a case I'm investigating," she said, reluctant to give out more information.

The clerk frowned. Too vague, Jessie thought, but the woman nodded, and a few minutes later Jessie was looking at a black-and-white, head-and-shoulders shot of Stan Weigund.

A friendly, rugged young face; blond hair cropped very short; a scar at the corner of one of his candid dark eyes, eyes that shone with optimism and held no hint of the menace of which he would be capable. She wondered what had happened to dim the light in those eyes.

Weigund had enrolled in the academy right after high school, had earned high marks and approval from his instructors, commendations from his supervisors when he was a patrol officer working Hollywood. A golden boy. He'd made detective eight years after he joined the force, then five years ago had transferred to Robbery-Homicide, where he'd received additional commendations.

Then a complaint, four years ago, from a woman who accused him of using brute force when he arrested her for a jewelry heist. Internal Affairs investigated and determined that the charges were unfounded. Two and a half years ago, Jessie read, Officer Victoria Weigund had filed a complaint with the Santa Monica PD against her husband. Internal Affairs had taken over and after almost a year had deemed the charges "unresolved." For Weigund, that wasn't as good as "unfounded."

But it hadn't stopped him from being promoted to Detective II last year, Jessie read, feeling a surge of resentment. She'd made detective eight years ago after acing her civil service exams, written and oral. A year and a half later, knowing it was too soon, she'd applied for a Detective II opening, advertised on the monthly employment opportunity sheet. She'd applied again, twice, but each time the position had gone to someone else. Both males. She'd suspected then that it was a gender bias, but maybe not. It wasn't the case now. White males had a tough time getting promoted these days, at least according to Phil. And she felt confident about going before the three-person oral board. She had the knowledge. She had the experience. She had glowing recommendations, including one for capturing a serial killer who had terrorized the city. She was waiting for an opening.

"Waiting for someone to leave or die," Phil said.

There were no details about Vicky Weigund's complaint or the Internal Affairs investigation. Jessie was friendly with someone in IA; she would talk to him to find out what had happened.

She returned Weigund's package to the clerk and asked for a photocopy of his picture. She was about to ask the woman to pull Victoria Weigund's package when her pager sounded.

She checked the screen. It was the judge's clerk.

* * *

The Weigunds' house, a small white two-bedroom stucco about a mile from the Santa Monica pier, was vacant.

"Only a couple of miles from here to Orzo's place," Phil commented, shutting the refrigerator, empty except for a few bottles of salad dressing, some eggs, and a jar of mayonnaise. "He probably cruised around till he found someone dumb enough to leave a cell phone in a car."

"Probably." She rummaged through the last of the kitchen drawers with gloved hands, then shut it. "Nothing here."

Nothing anywhere that revealed anything about Weigund's intentions or possible whereabouts. He'd cleaned up before he'd left: no dishes in the sink, no newspapers or magazines lying around, no clothes on the floor of either bedroom, or in the hamper. Only a fine layer of dust marred his efforts.

They had found almost no clothing, his or hers, in the closet or chest of drawers in the master bedroom. Very little in the second bedroom, either—just some little boy's shorts and T-shirts and an old pair of athletic shoes, so small they'd made Jessie's heart ache.

There were no personal papers in the house—no bills, letters, or correspondence of any kind. No photos, either, loose or in albums, but one beige living room wall had a lighter beige rectangular area that suggested something had been hanging there. A family portrait?

"At least we know what he looks like," Phil said.

"*Looked* like. The photo I got is fourteen years old." That was when Stanley Weigund had joined the LAPD, a year after she had. How odd, she thought, if we'd been in the same class.

The medicine cabinet held no clues, just a half-used box of bandages, some pink liquid antacid, an almost empty can of spray deodorant. No prescription vials.

There was no luggage in the closets or in the garage at the back of the tiny, well-kept yard. They sifted through the contents of the trash bins, wrinkling their noses at the putrid smells emanating from the plastic bags, but found nothing. If Weigund had disposed of personal papers, he'd done it elsewhere.

"He definitely wasn't planning on coming back," Phil said when they were back in the house. "No way he could, once he took Molly, even if he hadn't killed the housekeeper. He knows we would've been on to him sooner or later."

"He told Renee he plans to take Vicky and their son and start over somewhere else. Mexico, maybe. South America, Europe."

Phil grunted. "Like she's really going to go with him."

"Manny said he's living in his own world."

"How's he planning to disappear with a woman and a kid, with their faces plastered all over the media and the FBI on their tail?"

"He probably hasn't thought it all through."

"I don't know." Phil glanced at his watch. "It's two forty. He hasn't called in to the show yet."

"Maybe he won't call today." Jessie had phoned the station several times from her car and had spoken to one of the officers waiting with Renee. "For Renee's sake, I hope he does."

"You have kids, you never stop worrying," Phil said quietly. "You check their breathing when you bring 'em home from the hospital. They sniffle, you're calling the doctor in the middle of the night. The school phoned me one time at the station when they couldn't reach Maureen. Told me Brian stabbed his palate with a pencil and was bleeding bad. I died a thousand deaths till I got there and saw he was okay." Phil sighed. "But you never think something like this is going to happen. Not to your kid."

They left the house the way they'd entered, through the back door Phil had broken.

"Weigund's careful," he said when they were walking to Jessie's car. "He made sure not to leave anything for us."

"So?"

"He's a cop. He knows it'll be hard enough for him to disappear alone, almost impossible with a wife and kid."

Jessie darted a look at Phil. "You're thinking he's planning to kill Vicky if she meets with him?"

"Maybe the boy, too. She betrayed him, didn't she? She left, took his son with her. She betrayed him before that, too, when she reported him to the police."

Jessie thought for a moment. "Manny listened to the tapes, Phil. He said he's probably telling the truth when he says he loves her."

Phil grimaced. "Loves her to death."

(("**42**"))

"Jenny, I know it's hard to deal with a cranky older loved one," Renee said. "They don't seem all that lovable. Try to remember that not too long from now, you'll be just as cranky, and you'll want caretakers who will love you in spite of that."

The woman sighed. "Thank you, Dr. Renee. You're so wise. Just hearing you say that gives me heart."

"Hang in there, Jenny. I know you'll do fine. Until tomorrow, this is Dr. Renee Altman, telling you to—"

"He's on Line Four," Alicia announced with breathless urgency on the IN STUDIO line. "He *just* called, damn him."

At 2:55, with minutes left to the program, Renee had told herself he wasn't going to call, that he was punishing her with silence. So it took her a few seconds to adjust to the knowledge that he'd called after all, to form intelligible words and speak them when what she wanted to do was rest her head on the smooth table and cry.

"Hank, you're on the air." She pressed Line Four and signaled to the officer to trace the call.

"I thought you wanted to get your kid back, Dr. Renee."

"Of course I do, Hank."

"You could've fooled me. I listened to your entire show, yesterday and today, and Vicky hasn't phoned in."

"I don't know where Vicky is, Hank. I asked her on air to call the show, but she hasn't." She'd done that repeatedly yesterday after his call, and today, hoping the woman would call and provide the police with a lead. "If you were listening to the program, you would have heard that."

"I heard it, but I figured Vicky called you off the air."

"She hasn't contacted me at all, Hank. That's the truth. I'd like to speak to Molly now." She glanced at the officer. He held up a finger. Not yet.

"After I talk to Vicky and my boy. That's fair, don't you think? It's not a moral dilemma, is it?"

He was playing games with her again. She wanted to scream, to pummel his chest with her fists. "I want to know that she's all right, Hank. Put her on the phone," she said firmly.

"No 'please'? Getting a little attitude, are we?" His voice toughened. "Make nice, Doc, or I'll hang up and never call back. And you'll never see Molly again."

She glanced again at the officer. He raised his thumb in the air and smiled.

"Hank, I want to help you, but if you don't put Molly on the phone right now, I'm hanging up."

"Don't try to bluff, Dr. Renee. I have the winning hand."

"Good-bye, Hank. If you decide to cooperate, call back." She disconnected the line and started trembling, appalled by what she had done.

The silence in the room was deafening. She turned to Alicia, saw the screener's openmouthed stare, then faced the officer.

"Do you think they can find him?" she asked.

"We traced the call, but whether he'll still be there when the units arrive?" He shrugged.

The buttons on the console were lit like a Christmas tree. Renee licked her lips and held her hand over Line Three.

"He's back!" Alicia announced with quiet urgency on the IN STUDIO line. "Line One."

Renee's heart pounded madly in her chest. She pressed the line. "Are you going to put Molly on, Hank?" she asked with a calm that amazed her.

"Don't you *ever, ever* hang up on me again!" he roared.

His voice reverberated through the headset, hurting her ears. "Or what, Hank? Or you'll kidnap my daughter?"

"Don't go there, Doc."

She could tell from the intensity in his voice that he was losing a measure of control. The thought pleased her and terrified her.

"I could kill her if I wanted to, you know that."

An image flashed in front of her eyes. Big hands lowering a pillow over Molly's sweet face. "And then what, Hank? Where would that leave you?" She paused. "Or maybe Molly's already dead," she said, choking on the words, "but you don't want me to know, because then Vicky would never come back to you."

No answer.

"Hank?"

"I'm sorry, Doc," he said, his voice low. "It isn't what I wanted. I hope you believe me."

"What are you saying?" Bands of dread tightened across her chest, and she couldn't breathe.

"Your little girl must have taken real sick in the middle of the night. By the time I saw her in the morning, it was all over. She looks peaceful, though."

She opened her mouth, but no sound emerged.

"If you want her body, you'll have to cooperate, same as before. If not . . ."

She shut her eyes. "Please," she whispered. "Please."

"Gotcha." He laughed. "I was just kidding, Doc. Your precious darling is okay, for now. I had you going, though, didn't I?"

She was filled with rage so intense, her whole body shook. "How could you be so cruel?"

"Don't mess with me, Doc. Don't ever, *ever* play games, 'cause you'll lose."

Her face was tingling now, the blood pulsing against her temples. "Let me talk to her, Hank. You have nothing to lose."

"I want to talk to Vicky."

"I can't make her call."

"Vicky, I know you're listening, baby. You know how much I love you, don't you? You know things could be so fine between us, the way they were before, if you'll just come back."

"Hank—"

"We'll start over, just you and me and Andy. I know things have been rough. I know I haven't always been the best husband, but as God is my witness, I'll do it right this time. Just give me a chance, baby. Give *us* a chance. You won't be sorry."

"Can I talk to Molly now, Hank?" she asked, her tone reasonable, patient.

He sighed. "Yeah. You can talk to her."

Renee braced herself, chewing her lips, and waited what seemed like an eternity before she heard Molly's voice.

"Mommy?"

She let out her breath. "Hi, angel. Are you okay?"

"I want to come *home*, Mommy."

"Soon, sweetheart. Very soon. Are you eating enough?"

"Uh-huh. But I don't feel good, Mommy."

"What's wrong, angel?"

"My head hurts."

Her heart froze. "Does anything else hurt?"

"She feels a little warm," Hank said, back on the line. "But I could be wrong. I don't have a thermometer."

Renee forced herself to stay calm. "Hank, I explained to you last time that Molly needs to be on antibiotics."

"I can get her some aspirin."

"She doesn't need aspirin. She needs amoxicillin, right away."

"I'm sorry, Doc. I really am," he said, sounding sincere. "But I can't do that, and you know it."

"She could get seriously ill, Hank." She could die, Renee wanted to add, feeling the panic rising in her throat, choking her, but Hank probably had the radio on, and Molly would hear. She lifted the receiver to the off-air line. "She could die, Hank. I'm not exaggerating."

"Put me back on air, Doc." The anger was back in his voice.

"Please—"

"Put me back on air!"

She obeyed. "You're a father, Hank. I'm sure you're a good one. Wouldn't you want someone to help your son if he needed medical attention?"

"Get Vicky to call, Doc. Get her to agree to meet me. That's all I'm asking. You heard what I told her. I meant every word."

"What about Molly?"

"You'd better hope Vicky calls, soon."

Jessie and Phil were in her car, on the way to the Santa Monica PD, when she heard Weigund's voice on the radio.

"That's him," she said, feeling prickly.

She pulled over to a curb and listened to the exchange between Renee and Weigund, waited impatiently until 3:07, when she received word that GTE security had traced the phone where the call originated to an address in Culver City.

She attached her siren to the roof, made a U-turn, and sped the six miles even though she knew with reasonable certainty that Stan Weigund wouldn't be there when the police units arrived. Phil must have had the same thoughts, she assumed, but he didn't say anything, didn't even tell her to slow down.

The address was just north of Venice Boulevard. Two black-and-whites were in front of a small, windowless structure that looked like a warehouse. One car was half up the sidewalk. The second, parked diagonally across the street to block traffic, was shielding the two uniformed police who were crouching, weapons drawn, at either side of the vehicle.

"Is he in there?" Phil asked, drawing his gun as he approached one of the officers.

"No sign of him."

Even when you're certain, Jessie thought, you're hoping you're wrong. She walked with Phil to the structure and entered after they identified themselves to the two officers inside.

There was no phone, just a six-by-six square blue box on the concrete floor, one phone connection going into the box, another going out. The kind of box the phone company leaves in places like abandoned homes that no longer have phone service.

The kind a cop like Weigund would know about.

* * *

"I used to come here with my folks, when it was still Helmes Bakery," Phil said, pointing to a large building, now housing the Antique Guild, as they drove along Venice toward the National freeway entrance. "God, the smell!" He sighed.

"They should package it." She smiled, but she was thinking about the time they'd wasted, about the fact that Weigund was too smart to be caught by the phone trap they'd set.

They passed Plummers, a furniture store where she and Gary had bought a leather sofa. She realized she'd barely had time to think about him since this morning, when he'd faxed her the information about shelters.

And Rosalynn Denby. She checked the car clock, always a minute fast. Five after four. Using her free hand, she found the Post-It with Rosalynn's phone number and called. The woman answered on the second ring.

"I was wondering where you were, Detective," Rosalynn said after Jessie identified herself.

"Sorry I'm late, Ms. Denby. My partner and I were involved in something unexpected, and it'll be a while before we can get to you." She wanted to talk with the Santa Monica PD officers who had handled Vicky Weigund's complaint. "Is six-thirty okay?"

Out of the corner of her eye, she saw Phil grimace.

"*Dinner* time?" There was mild reproof in the woman's drawl.

"Again, I'm sorry for any inconvenience."

"All right." She sighed, clearly annoyed, then hung up.

"You don't have to come along," Jessie told Phil. "I'll drop you back at the station after we talk to the Santa Monica PD. I know you want to get home to Maureen and the boys."

"You sure?"

She nodded. "It might be better if I meet with Denby alone. If she helps women run away from abusive husbands, and abusive cops, she may not take too kindly to you."

"Okay." He sounded relieved. "I'll tell Simms and Boyd, talk to CRASH and Fugitives."

They drove awhile in silence.

"The truth is," Phil said after a few minutes, "I want to spend some time helping Brian with his homework. He's having some problems with his reading."

"Is this recent?"

"It's been going on awhile. Last year, too. Maureen spoke

to the teacher. He suggested having Brian tested for learning disabilities." Phil grunted.

She glanced at him, then back at the road. "You don't want to?"

"He just needs a little more help. I wasn't an ace at school, either."

He sounded defensive, so she let the matter drop. She took the Lincoln exit, then drove to the police station on Fourth Street and parked in the lot. A much larger lot than the one West L.A. had, but it served the courthouse as well. A much prettier view, too—tall palm trees, their fronds flapping like umbrellas in the mild breeze against the robin's-egg-blue sky.

She was familiar with the courthouse, where she'd testified numerous times, but she hadn't had much occasion to spend time at the police department.

Phil spoke to a detective he knew in Vice, who took them over to Gerald Rondell, a tall, barrel-chested detective in CAPS. Crimes Against Persons.

Rondell brought two extra chairs to his desk, which was littered with papers, a coffee mug, and three packets of Reeses's Pieces that Phil eyed longingly.

Phil began. "About two and a half years ago, a Victoria Weigund called the Santa Monica PD because her husband, Stan Weigund, beat her up. The husband's a cop."

Rondell nodded. "I know Weigund. He introduced himself when he moved into the area, said he was LAPD. Robbery-Homicide, I think. Seemed like a real nice guy."

"Did you handle the case?"

"Me and Chuck Stroker. He's not here anymore. Moved to some small town in Idaho."

Along with tons of other Angelinos, looking for a simpler life. Jessie wondered if it existed anywhere. "Can we take a look at the file?"

"What's this about?"

She exchanged a quick look with Phil. "We'd rather not go into details right now."

Rondell linked his hands behind his head. "He beat her up again?"

"Look, we don't want to mislead you," she said. "He probably *did* beat her up again, but that's not why we're interested in him."

"Then why do you need to see the file?" His brown eyes had narrowed with curiosity.

"Background. We're looking for him—that's just between us

for now, okay? Maybe something in the file will tell us where to find him."

Rondell nodded. "IA took it over, did you know that? Shut us out like we were rubes with turnips growing out of our ears." He stood up. "Be right back."

A few minutes later he returned with a thick folder and sat at his desk. He opened the folder, thumbed through the pages, then handed a sheet of paper to Phil. "That's the report on the first time she called us, over two years ago."

"We appreciate this." Phil scanned the sheet, then passed it to Jessie.

"She told the officers who responded to her call that she'd bumped into a wall and called them because she was mad at her husband," Rondell said.

". . . bruise on her cheek," Jessie read to herself. "Right eye swollen shut . . ." She returned the paper to Rondell.

" 'Course, they didn't believe her, but she swore he hadn't touched her. So there was nothing they could do. She didn't say he was a cop, or that she was." The detective shrugged. "A couple of months later, she calls again, hysterical, afraid for her life. Here's what she looked like when we brought them in."

He handed a color photo to Jessie. She was nauseated, imagining the blows that had purpled Vicky Weigund's once-pretty face. Blood had seeped out of the corners of her swollen mouth and streaked her blond hair pink. One eye was shut and looked like two lids with a slit.

Jessie passed the photo to Phil. He tightened his lips when he looked at it, then handed it back to Rondell.

"He slammed her against the wall, turned her around, punched her in the mouth. Then he threw her on the floor and yanked her by the hair so hard, some of it came out. The kid was there the whole time, watching."

"You arrested him?" Phil asked.

"Arrested him, booked him. Kept him two nights. All the time he's saying, 'Hey, you guys know me. I'm a cop, my wife's a cop. This is all a mistake, a lover's quarrel, you know how that is.' Next thing I know, a suit from IA is here, telling us Weigund is their problem, thank you very much for your trouble." Rondell scowled.

"Do you have his name?" Jessie asked.

He checked the file. "Mike Newell."

That would save time. She wrote down the name. "So that was it?"

"Pretty much. Mrs. Weigund didn't want it to go to IA.

'They'll bury it,' she kept telling me. But there was nothing we could do." He sounded tired. "Three weeks ago his name comes up again. But I guess you know that."

Jessie didn't answer. Neither did Phil.

"This woman comes by, says she's a friend of Mrs. Weigund. She's worried 'cause she hasn't seen or talked to Mrs. Weigund in days. She thought he might have killed her, the boy, too."

"You talked to him?" Phil asked.

Rondell nodded. "I went out there that night with my partner. Weigund was friendly, offered us beer. Cop to cop. Told us his wife had taken their little boy to visit family in Virginia."

"Did you check it out?"

Rondell sat up straighter. "I asked him if he minded if we looked around. He said no problem. The place looked fine— neater than my place, if you want to know the truth." A tight smile. "There was no sign of foul play, no indication anything violent happened to her or the boy." He sounded defensive now, nervous.

"So you believed him?" Jessie asked.

"Nope. I figured she skipped on him, and he was too proud to admit it. That's what happened, is it? She left, took the boy?" Hopeful, now.

"That's right."

His shoulders relaxed. "So why are you here?"

"The friend that came to talk to you," Jessie said. "What's her name?"

"Hold on." He opened the folder again and flipped through the pages. "Trudy Brookhurst."

Dee. "He went to her apartment the next evening and beat her up, ransacked her place."

Rondell frowned. He said nothing for a moment, and sounded defensive again when he finally spoke. "She didn't file a complaint."

"He said he'd come back and kill her if she reported him to the police."

More silence. "So *that's* why you're here? This Trudy changed her mind? She wants us to go after him?" He frowned. "But why go to you? This isn't your jurisdiction."

"Do you have any idea where Weigund hangs out?" Phil said. "Who his friends are?"

Rondell shook his head. "Aside from that time when he first introduced himself, I never talked to him casually. Hey, I've answered a lot of questions. What the hell is going on?"

"Have you been listening to the news, Rondell?"

"I'm not much into news," he said, aiming for easy but sounding wary. "Too depressing, and I get enough depressing on the job. I get home—I shoot hoops with my kid, watch a video." He looked at Jessie, then at Phil.

"We think Weigund kidnapped a little girl," Jessie said.

Rondell's eyes widened with shock. "The talk show host's kid."

Phil said, "So you *do* listen to the news."

"My wife's a fan." He chewed on his upper lip. "You're sure it's him?"

"Trudy Brookhurst recognized his voice from the tapes the media replayed. Did you hear them?"

"Once, maybe. Like I said, I'm not into the news."

"I'm surprised you didn't recognize his voice. You talked to him three weeks ago."

Rondell shook his head. "Maybe this Trudy is wrong. She's mad at him, wants to get him in deep."

"He told Dr. Altman on the show that his wife's name is Vicky. That they have a little boy."

"There's lots of women named Vicky," Rondell said, unhappy. "Lots of couples with a little boy."

"Where is she, then?"

No answer from Rondell. He massaged the back of his neck.

"We checked out Weigund's house," Jessie said. "It's empty, cleaned out. He's not coming back. Robbery-Homicide says he's on vacation, as of this past Monday. That's when Molly Altman was snatched."

"*Jesus.*" Rondell sighed deeply. "I didn't hear an APB."

"We don't want this broadcast all over," Phil said. "We want to keep it tight."

Rondell nodded. "How can I help?"

"Stop by his place a couple of times. Talk to the neighbors. Keep an eye out for Weigund's ride. A black Mustang." He gave the detective the license plate number and year. "Call us if you hear anything, and make sure this doesn't get out to the media. We don't want Weigund to know he's been made."

Easier said than done, Jessie knew. The media paid their LAPD sources well. "If Weigund does find out," she said, "Trudy Brookhurst will need protection."

She hadn't asked Gary who had leaked the word to him about the kidnapping, knew he wouldn't have told her.

(("44"))

"What I want to know, Stuart, is how do we teach our young people accountability for their actions if they see their leaders getting away with lying and cheating and adultery?"

"The Final Jeopardy answer is: 'Nobody with half a brain.' "

"What are you saying?"

"Sorry, babe. Wrong answer. Ding-ding-ding. The correct question is, 'Who cares?' "

"Come on, Stuart. It's a legitimate question."

"Monica Lewinsky got a book deal and a great makeup job for her heart-to-heart with Barbara Walters. Paula Jones got a bundle of cash and a new nose. Where's the harm?"

"So you want to send a message to the women in this country that they can be humiliated and treated like objects as long as they get reimbursed? They were taken advantage of, Stuart, by someone in power. That's sexual harassment."

"You know what it is, Cynthia? It's *old*. Get over it."

"What if you had a daughter, Stuart, and some senator was groping her? I bet you'd feel different then."

"You don't like sex, do you, Cynthia?"

"This has nothing to do with my personal life, Stuart."

"What are you, divorced? Your husband left you for a younger model? Uh-oh, Ray. Cynthia hung up." Logan pressed another line. "Kevin, my man. Were you listening to Cynthia? Am I right or am I right?"

"Actually, I wanted to talk about the pit bull thing."

"The one that mauled the kid to death? What about it?"

"You said the dog should be put to death, and I'm saying it's not the dog's fault."

"So whose fault is it, Kev?"

"The parents'. They should of known better than to leave their kid alone with the dog."

"So you want to put *them* to death?"

"Maybe not that, but they should be punished."

"*Maybe* not that? You're scaring me, man."

"You can't blame the dog, Stuart. It doesn't know better."

"Hey, man, I'm with you. Makes a lot of sense. Do me a favor? Shake your head side to side a couple of times."

"Okay. Done."

"You hear that sound?"

"I don't hear anything, Stuart."

"Guess that's because there's nothing there, Kev. *Comprende?* Stay off the Alpo." Logan ended the call. "Is it me, Ray, or does everyone today sound like they've got a couple of loose wires? What do you bet we see this guy's face on a Wanted poster some day?"

"No bet, Stuart."

"Speaking of which, did you hear today's Hank and Dr. Renee segment? I listened to a tape. If this goes on much longer, KMST oughtta do a spinoff. She has moxy, though, doesn't she? Hanging up on him."

"She took a risk. What if he didn't call back?"

"Like he's got something *better* to do? The guy's a loser." Logan dropped his voice to a low rumble. " 'Look at me, I'm so mean and scary, I could kill your kid.' "

"He's psycho, Stu."

"The guy's pathetic. His wife skips, so he terrorizes a *kid?* Hey, Hank, you're a *real* macho man."

"Come on, Stuart. Don't mess with him."

"What, I'm afraid of him? Hey, Hank, are you listening? We're talking about *you*, man. You're pathetic, and you're a moron. You really think your wife's coming back to you?"

"We have Delilah on Line Five, Stu."

" 'I love you, Vicky,' " Logan said in the same low rumble. " 'Come back to me, baby, so we can be happy and I can beat the crap out of you again.' Yeah, Miss Vicky's really gonna buy what he's selling." Logan pressed a line. "Hello, Delilah. That's a foxy name. Are you foxy, sweetheart?"

"I called about the pit bull, but I heard what you just said about this Hank. I listened to him on the air with Dr. Renee, and he sounded like he really loves his wife, Stuart. How do you know he's not feeling remorse for what he did?"

"How do we know the Menendez brothers aren't writing Mother and Father's Day ditties for Hallmark? This is a bully who picks on women and kids. He's got the brain of a carp. What do you think his IQ is, Ray, five? Delilah, how about you?"

"Obviously what he's done is terrible. The kidnapping and murder, I mean. Maybe he snapped. But we don't know that he abused his wife. You shouldn't judge him without giving him a chance to explain."

"What are you, his defense attorney?"

"I'm not defending him. I'm just saying he may be sincere."

"If he's sincere, I'm the Pope. Vicky, if you're out there listening, we're with you. Call Uncle Stuart before you do anything stupid like going back to that poor excuse of a man. He's a coward, darlin'. He doesn't even have the *cojones* to admit what he did."

"Come on, Stu. What if he's listening? You'll piss him off."

"Oooh, I'm shaking, Ray. He's probably too stupid to find the station. Vicky, honey, call in. Tell you what. You give me an exclusive, on-air interview, I'll get the station to pay you fifty thousand bucks. Not a windfall, but it's a start for a new life."

"Stu, are you crazy?"

"If the station won't do it, I'll pay it myself. I'm putting my money where my mouth is, Ray. Guys, what's your take on this bozo? We're gonna break for a commercial, and we'll be right back."

Logan ended the call and removed his headset. He swiveled his chair to his left. "How'd I do, Delilah?"

Jessie nodded. "Great."

"You weren't bad yourself, for a first-time caller." He ran his hand across his mouth. "I'm sweating like a pig. God, I can't believe how nervous I was. My hand's still shaking."

"We really appreciate this, Mr. Logan."

"Stu."

He was wearing a white Polo knit shirt and jeans and looked like a squeaky clean college student—not at all what Jessie had expected. She'd pictured him George Hamilton tanned with slicked-back, gelled hair, too-tight pants and a silk shirt unbuttoned to reveal a gold chain against curly chest hair. A link bracelet, too much cologne. Shaking his hand during a news break, she'd tried not to stare at the dimples in his full-cheeked baby face.

He'd caught her look, leaned back against his chair, and laughed. "That's why I don't let them put my face in the ads. Good-bye, credibility." He'd gestured to the empty chair to his left. "So to what do I owe the pleasure of this visit, Detective?

Did I violate some new decency law? You have about two minutes."

She had told him why she was here: The man who had kidnapped Molly Altman was obviously aware that the police had put a trap on KMST's lines and on Dr. Altman's home phone. But he wouldn't expect Logan's station's lines to have a trap. If the station allowed phone security to set a trap, and Logan managed to goad Hank into calling his show, maybe the police could catch him.

Logan had been frowning while she was talking. "I don't know," he'd said when she was done.

Jessie had barely contained her impatience. "A little girl's life is at stake, Mr. Logan."

"Hell, *I* have no problem doing it. I hope you fillet the bastard. It's management. I don't think they'll go for it. But I'm happy to talk to the station director after I finish the show, try to get her to listen."

Jessie shook her head. "That's too late. I need you to bait this guy *today,* so that maybe he'll call your program tomorrow. We have to find him as soon as possible. The girl has a medical condition that may need immediate attention."

"Thirty seconds, Stu," the producer called from his booth.

Logan exhaled loudly. "I want to help, Detective. I really do. But as you can see, I have to go back on the air. What should I do? Play the Best of Stuart Logan?"

She waited.

He massaged his chin. "Even if the program director goes for it, I don't think she can give you an answer on the spot. She'll have to check with the station owners."

Jessie waited some more.

"We have another news break coming up at five-thirty," he said. "I'll take you in to the program director, tell her I'm for it. That's the best I can do."

Twenty-five minutes later Logan had introduced Jessie to the program director, a tall blonde with no hips and no curves and a hard face that made her look like she could chew bullets. He'd made a serious, heartfelt pitch, then returned to the recording room. Jessie had been prepared for First Amendment arguments, for "I'll get back to you." But the woman had agreed on the spot.

"Get the bastard," she'd practically snarled.

"What if he doesn't hear my show?" Logan asked now.

Jessie had given this thought. "He may not be a regular listener, but I'm sure he's watching television news. I'm pretty sure at least one station is going to pick up on this. And after that, the others will, too."

"And if they don't know about it?"

"Can you leak word of the segment? I'm sure they'll give it play. The money offer will hook them." The program director had agreed to pay Vicky the $50,000, too, in the unlikely event the woman actually called in.

"I can have someone leak the segment, no problem." Logan nodded. "But what if no one bites?"

"I'll make sure someone does." Gary had media connections. If necessary, she'd ask for his help.

Logan chewed on his lip. "Let's say he *does* call tomorrow. What if I mess up? What if he figures out it's a setup?"

(("45"))

"My dilemma, Dr. Renee, is that my brother always manages to get out of paying for his share of things."

"What kinds of things, Cathy?"

"Anniversary gifts for our parents, for example. Birthday gifts for a family member. My niece had a sweet sixteen party a month ago, and he wanted to get a joint gift. He said price was no object. I found two beautiful pearl necklaces, one for a hundred and fifty dollars, one with larger pearls for two fifty. He said to get the larger one. Now he's putting me off every time I ask him for his half."

"Does he have the money?"

"He lives in a very nice house, larger than mine, actually. He drives a BMW."

"I didn't ask you where he lives, Cathy, or what he drives. Do I hear jealousy here?"

"I'm not jealous, Dr. Renee. I'm annoyed. I'm sure he has the money. If he didn't, why did he tell me to get the larger necklace? He did the same thing when we made a party for my parents' silver wedding anniversary. I wanted to host it in my home. He insisted on having it catered in a hall. He had me order flowers, hire a band and a professional photographer. He still hasn't paid me his half."

"I guess you should have learned your lesson, Cathy. You were pretty stupid to buy the necklace."

"You're probably right. What really bothers me is that he insisted on presenting the necklace to my niece. And at the anniversary party, he was the one who made the toast to my parents. It may sound petty, but it's annoying when my sister-in-law keeps talking about the necklace Bob picked out for Nancy, or my parents talk about the wonderful party Bob arranged. He didn't arrange anything."

"This isn't about the money, is it, Cathy? You feel inferior to *your brother, less valued. My guess is that this has been going on for a long time."*

"No, it's not that, Dr. Renee. I know my parents love me, and so do my sister and her family. I just don't think it's honest of my brother to accept credit for something he hasn't done. And my question is, should I confront him about the money or let it go?"

"Cathy, you're obviously not in touch with your feelings. I think you must have deeper, underlying issues with your brother. Maybe he's always been more popular. Maybe you're trying to show him up by spending more than he can afford."

"He's the one who tells me how much he wants to spend."

"Because you make him feel too embarrassed to be honest. He sounds like someone who thinks with his heart, not his head, and you're enabling him. The question is, why? Maybe you like putting him in a position where he'll feel inadequate."

"That isn't true, Dr. Renee. I don't think you're hearing what I'm saying."

"Well, if you're not honest with yourself, Cathy, I can't help you. And neither can anyone else."

Rosalynn Denby poured tea into a beautiful porcelain cup with the practiced grace of a geisha. "One or two, Detective Drake?" She held small silver tongs over a matching porcelain bowl filled with sugar cubes.

"One is fine, thanks."

Jessie preferred artificial sweetener—why waste calories?—but didn't see any on the silver gallery tray which Rosalynn had centered on the carved-leg, reddish-brown-wood coffee table. Country French, Jessie guessed. Frances and Helen would have known for certain.

"Lemon?"

"No, thanks."

Rosalynn carefully dropped in a sugar cube and handed the cup and saucer to Jessie.

"Please help yourself," she offered, pointing to the slices of chocolate and mocha torte prettily arranged on a doily-covered platter. She poured tea for herself—two cubes, a wedge of lemon—and filled a small porcelain plate with two slices of pastry. "I have a terrible sweet tooth," she said, taking a bite.

You couldn't tell, Jessie thought enviously. The woman was no more than five feet tall, with a teeny frame. That, and her straight, short black hair and blue eyes, gave her a china-doll quality. Jessie tried, but couldn't picture her bashing her ex-husband's face with an iron.

"I was beginning to think y'all weren't going to show, Detective," she drawled, pronouncing the "I" as "ah." "Not that I would have minded."

"I'm sorry for the inconvenience." Jessie had apologized earlier, when she'd phoned from Stuart Logan's studio to postpone the meeting, again, this time until seven o'clock. She'd apologized again as soon as she'd arrived at the house, a Spanish one-story that thumbed its antiquated nose at the rest of the houses on Palm near Burton Way, most of them relatively new or the recipients of major face-lifts.

"Well," Rosalynn said, in a tone that indicated she wasn't altogether mollified. She settled back against the overstuffed cushions of the chintz-covered sofas, one of two in the large, airy room. Matching drapes, pulled back by corded tassels, spilled onto the hardwood floor.

"It's urgent that we speak to Vicky Weigund, Ms. Denby."

The woman brought the teacup to her lips and sipped. "I do like tea, Detective. It's so civilized, don't you think?"

"Ms. Denby, I don't have time to waste."

"Well, then you're in for disappointment. I spoke with my attorney. You fibbed. I'm not a material witness in any way, and neither is Vicky Weigund."

"So you admit that you know her."

"I suppose denying it is pointless. But that's all I plan to tell you. And you can't force me to do anything more."

"My lieutenant said he knows you. Karl Espes?"

Rosalynn Denby looked puzzled, then broke into a smile. "That *charming* man!" She sighed. "Too bad he's married. He has quite a way with women."

Was she talking about the same person? "Lieutenant Espes was hoping you'd help us out."

The woman's laugh tinkled. "You really ought to learn to lie better, honey. Lieutenant Espes and I took a shining to each other, but we're on different sides. I'm not going to put Vicky in danger."

"She wouldn't be in danger. We just want to talk to her, to find out if she knows where her husband might be hiding out, who his friends are."

"If you know Vicky's last name, I assume you also know that her husband is a cop. Cops hang out with cops, Detective. They protect each other, lie for each other, cover up for each other."

"Not all cops are like Stan Weigund, Ms. Denby."

"I don't know which ones are and which ones aren't. Neither do you. So you'll forgive me if I'm not ready to trust Vicky's safety to the people who abandoned her and betrayed her."

"I know what happened, Mrs. Denby. I'm sick about it."

Rosalynn put down her cup. "Do you, now?"

"I talked to the Santa Monica police. I read the report she filed. I saw the pictures." They popped up in her mind's eye again. She blinked them away.

"*One* report, Detective." Rosalynn held up a ringed finger. "One report, and countless beatings. It took her a long time to get the courage to file that report. She kept excusing what he was doing. 'He has such a stressful job. He sees so much violence.' And she kept telling herself things would get better, because he'd apologize every time, swear on his mother's grave that he'd never hit her again. Like this afternoon, on Dr. Renee's show. The loving contrition phase, therapists call it."

Jessie nodded. She was familiar with the terminology. Loving contrition, followed by tension building, followed by acute battery. *"Mommy loves you, Jessica,"* Frances would whisper, stroking her forehead. *"Why do you make Mommy so angry? Why can't you be good?"*

"Do you know why she didn't file a *second* report, Detective?"

"I know Internal Affairs took over. I haven't read their report, but Vicky's friend told me they didn't find anything to support her charges."

Rosalynn nodded. "If Stan had been a civilian, he would have been imprisoned for what he did to her. Did you know that they branded Vicky a troublemaker? She was charged administratively for reporting the incident to the local police. They tried to take away her gun and gave her menial work. She was shunned by her fellow officers. Then they suspended her, without pay. After a while she couldn't take it anymore. That's why she quit the force, Detective, but that's only part of the reason she didn't file a second time, or a third, or a fourth." Rosalynn took a sip of tea. "I'm sure you're familiar with Title 18 USC 922."

"A federal law." A law that made it a crime for anyone convicted of domestic violence to hold a gun. Including a cop.

"Stan wasn't about to risk being taken off the force. First he told Vicky no one would believe her. She knew he'd already been talking about her to his colleagues, telling them she was nuts. He said he'd get her committed, get custody of Andy."

The "sluts or nuts" defense. The phrase, Manny had once told Jessie, that domestic violence experts had coined because victims were so often presented as promiscuous or crazy.

244

"But that wasn't enough for Stan," Rosalynn said. "The next time, he told Vicky he'd kill her if she ever reported him again. He'd kill her and cut her up and hide little pieces of her body where no one would ever find them. And no one would even care. She believed him," Rosalynn said softly. "Wouldn't you?"

Another gruesome image to add to the catalog of those that took turns haunting her. Jessie wondered if she would ever be tough enough to look at horror and not flinch. Probably not. "So she came to you."

"Not right away. She thought about taking Andy and moving someplace he wouldn't find her. But where? Stan's a cop. He's an expert at finding people and watching them without being seen. She decided she couldn't live her life in constant fear for herself and for Andy."

"How did she hear about you?"

"That's not important." A quick smile. "She came to me, told me her story, and I agreed to help her."

"You've helped other women, I understand."

"Someone has to, Detective," she said with feeling. "These women have no other place to turn. Sometimes they're afraid for themselves. Sometimes, for their children. A wealthy husband trumps up evidence that his wife is an incompetent or neglectful or abusive mother. The court believes him. I try to help her keep her child." Rosalynn shrugged.

"What if the husband's telling the truth?"

"I check out each case thoroughly, Detective Drake. I'm not easily fooled."

"Where do you send them?"

"There's a lovely four-star hotel in the city that graciously helps by putting up our women for a day or so, free of charge, if they have vacancies." She smiled. "And of course, we have a network of safe houses," she said, very serious now. "After that, they relocate. It's difficult, pulling up roots, changing identities, always looking over your shoulder. But it's better than being dead, or having your children stolen from you, or battered."

"Where is Vicky Weigund now?"

Rosalynn smiled.

"Is she in the city? In another state? In another country?" Still no answer. "Ms. Denby, don't you want to help us find Stan and put him away?"

"More than anything. But I won't risk Vicky's life to do it. He'll kill her if he finds her, you know. He has nothing to lose, now that he's kidnapped that child and murdered the house-keeper. He talks about loving her, but that's just a pack of lies."

"The little girl has a medical condition that could need immediate attention."

The woman frowned. "I thought they were saying that to convince him to bring the child back."

Jessie shook her head. "Molly's spleen was removed, and she's susceptible to infections. You heard what he said on the show today. Molly might be running a fever. If she doesn't get an antibiotic right away, she could die."

Rosalynn sighed and held her hand at her throat. "The poor thing. I don't know what to tell you." She looked anguished.

"If we could talk to her—"

"She doesn't know *where* Stan could be hiding," Rosalynn interrupted. "I asked her. She'd tell me if she knew. She wants to help, Detective, but there's nothing she can do."

"What if she called the show?"

Rosalynn tightened her lips. "Never."

"She could tell Dr. Renee she'd be willing to talk to Stan if he allows someone to deliver the antibiotic to the child."

"You've got to be kidding, Detective. If she phones the show, you'll trace the call, and she'll be dead. He'll find her."

"He won't know."

"Can you assure me of that? Can you promise me with total certainty that someone in your police department won't find out her whereabouts and leak the news to his good buddy Stan?"

What the woman was suggesting was terrible—that someone could be abetting Weigund. "Vicky can go to a pay phone. Even if you're right, by the time this person, if there is one, would tell Stan where the call originated, Vicky would be long gone."

"I'm sorry. I can't let her take that chance."

Jessie thought a moment, her brow furrowed in concentration. "She can tape the message, and Dr. Altman can play it on the air."

Rosalynn frowned, then shook her head. "How would she get the tape to the station without coming out of hiding?"

"You tape the message, then, when you're talking to her. I'll pick up the cassette from you and take it to the radio station."

"This is so complicated. I'll have to think about it."

"We don't have much time." Jessie leaned forward. "If Molly Altman dies, Ms. Denby, how will you feel, knowing that you could have saved her life? How will Vicky Weigund feel?"

(("46"))

The house in Downey was a small beige stucco with a Spanish tile roof. An old Chevy, its brown vinyl upholstery peeling, sat in the driveway.

She rang the bell several times before she heard footsteps approaching, then the sound of the privacy window being opened.

"Yes?" A man's voice, cautious.

"I'm Detective Jessica Drake, with the LAPD. I'd like to speak to Mr. or Mrs. Reston."

"I'm Walter Reston." He sounded reluctant to admit the fact.

"May I come in, sir?"

"Can you tell me what this is about?"

"It's about your daughter, Vicky."

"Did something happen to her?"

"Actually, I was hoping you could tell me. We're trying to find her."

"She's not here, Detective. If you'll excuse me?"

"I'd like to talk to you and your wife. Is she home?"

"Yes, she is. But this isn't a good time, Detective."

"I won't take long, Mr. Reston."

"I don't have anything to tell you. Neither does Mildred."

"Just a few minutes of your time, Mr. Reston. It's very important."

"Oh, all right," he muttered, and a few seconds later the door opened with a sigh.

Jessie stepped into a small, tidy living room furnished with two brown love seats facing each other across a wood coffee table. Plants filled the room. Tall, thriving ficus benjamina occupied two corners; a palm, the other. Wandering Jews and ferns hung from the ceiling. Several Chinese evergreens lined the hearth, and on the fireplace mantel were smaller potted plants.

Way too much chlorophyll, Jessie thought, wondering why with all that greenery the room seemed so devoid of life.

Reston was back a few minutes later with his wife, who was blinking nervously. They looked like a matched set. Short torsos with thickening middles, graying hair, identical silver-tone-framed glasses. They sat on one sofa, Jessie on the other.

"I appreciate your seeing me," Jessie said. "I know this is difficult for you, talking about your daughter, but I need your cooperation."

"We don't know where she is," Reston said. "I told you."

"We don't," his wife chimed. Her hands lay on her lap, gripped together.

Jessie nodded. "I'm sure you've heard about a little girl who's been kidnapped, the daughter of Dr. Renee Altman, the radio talk show host."

"A terrible thing," the woman said in a hushed voice. "Terrible, terrible."

"We have reason to believe that your son-on-law, Stan Weigund, kidnapped her and killed the housekeeper."

"We don't know where Stan is," Reston said firmly. "No idea."

"None." Mildred's eyes were riveted on Jessie's face.

"So this isn't a surprise to you," Jessie said.

They exchanged glances.

Reston cleared his throat. "Mildred recognized his voice on the radio."

"But you didn't call the police," Jessie said, keeping her tone conversational.

"We considered calling," he said. "But there's nothing to tell. We don't know where Vicky is. We don't know where Stan is. We called their house several times and drove by. They're gone."

"I understand," Jessie said, not understanding at all. "I'm hoping you'll be able to tell me something about Stan."

"We haven't heard from him," Reston said.

"He didn't call you after Vicky left him?" Jessie asked the mother. Some softness there, she'd sensed. "I understand she came here the last time."

"Well, yes." The woman's face had turned pink. "He called a few weeks ago and wanted to know if Vicky was here. We told him we hadn't seen her."

"She knew better than to come here," Reston said. "We

would have told her to go on back home, same's we did last time." He pursed his lips in disapproval.

"He didn't call again, to find out if your daughter had contacted you?"

Mildred cast a furtive glance at her husband.

"I don't blame you for being afraid to get involved, Mr. and Mrs. Reston," Jessie said. "I would be, too, in your situation. But if he *did* call, we need to know."

"He asked us to call him if we heard from her," Reston said. "But we didn't."

Jessie sensed some hesitation. "He never phoned again?"

"He phoned on Sunday," the man said, clearly unhappy. "He said he was going away for a couple of days and wanted to know if we'd heard from her."

The day before the kidnapping. "Did he leave you a number where you could reach him in case your daughter called you?"

Reston shook his head.

"*Have* you heard from her?"

"Once." Mildred sighed the word. "That was right when she left. She phoned to tell us she was all right, but she wouldn't say where she was. I told her to go back home to Stan, with little Andy, but she said she couldn't." Her eyes sidled toward her husband, then back to Jessie.

Reston said, "If she *had* gone back, none of this would have happened, that's certain."

He was blaming his daughter for the kidnapping and murder? "Can you think of anyplace your son-in-law might have taken the Altmans' child? Another house somewhere? A cabin?"

They both shook their heads.

"Can you think of anyone he's especially friendly with?"

More head-shaking.

"What about his parents?"

"They died when he was a little boy," Mildred volunteered. "In a car accident. He was ten at the time, and his aunt took him in for a year or so, but it was too much for her, because she had five children of her own. So he ended up in a foster home. First one, then another. He was lucky, though, Vicky said, because he got friendly with the Big Brothers. They do good work."

"Where does the aunt live?"

"Iowa, I think." The woman frowned. "Or maybe it's Nebraska. I don't think he's been in touch with her for years, though."

"That's why he was so upset when Vicky left and took Andy,"

Reston said. "Because he didn't want to lose his family again. I explained that to Vicky."

"You have to work at a marriage," Mildred said. "I told her that, more than once. And there's the boy to consider. A boy needs his father. I told her that, too." She sighed again.

"He beat your daughter," Jessie said, unsure whether she was more dumbfounded or revolted. "You knew that, didn't you?"

Reston frowned. "Stan may have put her in her place, but he didn't beat her. A man has to set rules, or there's no order in the family."

"Vicky can be headstrong sometimes," Mildred said sadly.

"It wasn't just Vicky," Reston said. "It was her friends. Putting ideas in her head, making her unhappy with Stan. And being a police officer didn't help. That's not a job for a woman," he said, looking pointedly at Jessie.

"She was going to be a teacher," Mildred said. "She was always so good with children."

Jessie wrote her pager number on her business card and handed it to Reston. "If you hear from Stan, no matter what time of the day or night, please call me right away. And make sure you don't tell him we know who he is."

"All right." He accepted the card gingerly and slipped it into his shirt pocket.

"I don't think he means to harm that little girl," Mildred said. "I *know* he didn't intend to kill that woman. He's not like that, you know. He's just . . ." Her voice trailed off.

"It didn't have to happen," Reston said. "He just couldn't bear the thought of losing Andy."

It occurred to Jessie that they were defending Weigund because to do otherwise, they would have to admit that they'd betrayed their own daughter.

She debated, then took an envelope from her purse in which she'd placed a copy of the photo of Vicky's battered face. She removed the photo and handed it to Mildred Reston.

"Who . . ." The woman's eyes widened. Her hand flew to her mouth and she gagged.

"That's what Vicky looked like the night they arrested Stan," Jessie said, feeling no satisfaction.

Reston turned his head aside and stared at the wall.

((**47**))

"Our thirty-two-year-old son moved back into the house a few months ago, Dr. Renee, with his three-year-old son. He invested all his money in a business venture that went bad, and lost the house and almost everything else."

"He's divorced?"

"His wife died of pancreatic cancer. It was a terrible tragedy—six months, and she was gone."

Renee sighed. "One thing on top of the next. I'm sorry for your pain, Charles."

"Well, we're healing. The problem is, my son is taking advantage. He just assumes my wife will take care of all his needs: his laundry, and the boy's. His meals. He expects her to take care of Luke all day—that's our grandson. He says he's going out on business meetings, but still. He never asks is it okay, and she never says no."

"Why not? Does she enjoy being a slave?"

"She's hurting for him. She says we need to be extra kind after everything he's been through, to give him time."

"And you obviously disagree."

"I feel bad for him, but I don't think coddling him is the right way to go. I think he ought to toughen up, for his sake and for Luke's. And the truth is, I'm suffering for it, Dr. Renee. My wife isn't happy about all this. She's not used to running after a little one. It wears her out."

"She's told you this?"

"She doesn't have to tell me. She's a different person since they moved in. Cranky, fussy. Always snapping at me. But if I bring up the subject, she tells me I have no heart, that families have to pitch in during hard times."

"That's true, Charles. Families do have to pitch in and make

251

sacrifices for each other, but in this case I think you're right. As much as your wife may feel sorry for your son, he can't abdicate his parental responsibilities, and he can't just go back home to Mommy, which is what he's doing. Back to the womb, where it's safe and warm."

"Thank *you, Dr. Renee. My wife really respects your opinion. I almost didn't call, 'cause I thought you'd tell me I was being uncaring and selfish." He laughed nervously.*

"Well, for all I know, you are selfish and uncaring." She chuckled. "You and your wife have put in the years, Charles. Now it's your son's turn. He can ask your wife to watch your grandson once in a while, but he has to have a backup plan. And he has to do his own damn laundry and do some designated chores around the house until he gets it together to move out. There are no free rides, Charles. You either pay up front or later."

"I'll tell my wife. I hope this makes her feel better about saying no."

"What was your son like in your home before he married?"

"Well, he didn't do chores, if that's what you mean, or clean up after himself. My wife was always kind of soft on him."

Renee sighed. "Charles, if I were you, I'd get used to cranky and fussy and snappy. They're going to be your companions for a long, long time."

Driving home from Downey, Jessie turned on the radio and switched from station to station every few minutes, nursing the slim hope that she'd hear someone discuss "what that awful Stuart Logan has done now." But of course it was too early. Logan had barely had time to leak the segment to any of the radio or TV stations.

It was after eight-thirty when she pulled into her driveway, but the porch fixture and the bank of outdoor lights lining the walkway, all on automatic timers, dispelled the cloudy darkness and the emptiness. The gardener had mowed the lawn and actually planted pansies and snapdragons. She hoped the neighborhood dogs wouldn't dig them up before they had a chance to bloom.

She kicked off her shoes, poured herself a glass of milk, and listened to her messages.

Barry had phoned, sounding agitated, almost belligerent: No one was telling him what was going on, he had a right to know, he wanted to do something "to catch the bastard."

Gary had called, ". . . just to say hi."

Frances was peeved: "I know you're busy with this terrible kidnapping, Jessica, but you can take out five minutes to return a call to your mother." You had to laugh, Jessie thought.

Ezra had returned her call. He was sorry Jessie hadn't been able to attend classes. He wanted to know if there was anything he could do to help the Altmans, and hoped to see Jessie tomorrow morning at Rosh Hashanah services and at Dafna's for lunch.

Rosh Hashanah. The New Year. She'd forgotten all about the two-day holiday, although just a week ago she'd been engrossed in studying its customs, its significance.

She couldn't phone Ezra or Dafna—they wouldn't be answering their phones. The holiday had begun over an hour ago, while Jessie was questioning Rosalynn Denby. Right now Ezra was probably returning from synagogue, immersed in the spirituality of this special day. She didn't feel all that spiritual. She was depressed and disheartened, wished she'd never met Vicky Weigund's parents. Talking with them had stirred up anger at her father, and it wasn't something she wanted to deal with.

She had no challah, no wine, no honey or pomegranates or any of the special foods she'd planned to buy to celebrate the sweet promise of the new year. Still, she lit the candles and recited in transliterated Hebrew the blessings she'd been practicing for over a month, and thought fervently about Molly Altman as she thanked God "for keeping us alive."

She'd planned on broiling the steak she'd defrosted this morning and relaxing with a book. But she was worn out from the long day and felt battered by the despair and ugliness of Vicky Weigund's life. She didn't want to eat in the solitude of her home, didn't want to return any phone calls.

She drove to an upscale restaurant on Wilshire, where she sat at a small table and ordered a glass of wine and oysters and a delicious cut of steak with a butter-based cream sauce, sticking it simultaneously, she thought, to her diet and to God, who wasn't doing much to make the world a better place, not if He allowed people like Stan Weigund to exist. Or maybe she was deliberately flouting Him and Ezra, poor guy, distancing herself so that she and Gary had one less area of dissonance.

That wasn't the answer, either.

"I decided to take you up on your offer," Jessie said, walking with Helen toward the breakfast room. "The Jacuzzi?" she prompted when she saw Helen's puzzled expression.

Helen smiled. "Right. You look exhausted, actually. Are you hungry? I have leftover London broil and mashed potatoes."

"Thanks, I already ate."

"Did you bring a swimsuit?" Helen asked.

"No. I came straight from the restaurant. I figure I'd use one of yours."

"No problem. I won't be wearing them for a while, not with this." She smiled and massaged her belly. "Take whichever one you like. They're in the armoire, bottom drawer."

"Aren't you going to join me?"

"I'm not supposed to use a Jacuzzi now."

"Right. I forgot." She'd read that in one of the many books she'd bought when she was pregnant, books she'd stored at the back of a closet.

"You look upset. I'm talking about my pregnancy too much, aren't I? I'm sorry."

"No, of course not." She smiled to show she meant it. "I just don't feel like sitting in the Jacuzzi alone."

"I'll keep you company," Helen said.

Jessie followed her sister up the wide, cream-carpeted staircase and stopped to get a fierce hug and kiss from Matthew, who was doing homework in his room.

"Where's Neil?" Jessie asked when she was in Helen's bedroom, slipping off her clothes. "Still at the office?"

"He's in San Francisco, just overnight." She rummaged in a drawer and handed Jessie several bathing suits. "He's flying to Singapore next month for ten days. He wants me to come with him, but I'm not sure what to do about Matthew."

"I wish I could have him stay with me, but my hours are unpredictable." She looked at the suits, chose a two-piece that was more likely to fit, since Helen was shorter and slimmer.

"Oh, I know. You were his first choice, though." Helen smiled. "Actually, Mom offered to stay here with Matthew. I almost fainted."

Jessie was surprised, too. "What about Dad?"

"He would come down Wednesday and stay over the weekend. I didn't know how to say no, but I'm worried. Mom's not used to being around kids." She had removed her skirt and slipped on a pair of shorts.

"She'll be fine, Helen. She loves Matthew, and he's such a good kid."

"We were good kids, too."

Jessie sighed. "If you're nervous, Helen, make up some excuse."

"She'll be hurt. What if you stayed here, too, Jess?"

"She'd see right through that. She'd be insulted. I could stop by every day, though. That would be a natural thing to do."

"Why does everything have to be so hard?"

A good question.

They took towels and walked down the stairs and out the family room's French doors into the spacious, well-lit back yard.

"You could do laps first," Helen suggested when they neared the oval swimming pool, but Jessie was too tired.

She eased herself into the hot, bubbling waters of the Jacuzzi and, sitting on the bottom step, rested her head against the tiled wall. Helen sat near her on the top step, her feet submerged up to her ankles.

"You didn't call today," Jessie said after a moment.

"I learned my lesson."

"I meant at home." She turned her head and looked up at Helen. "I'm sorry I snapped at you yesterday."

"I'm sorry, too. I *was* being nosy."

"Yeah, you were."

Helen kicked water in Jessie's face, and they both laughed.

Jessie shut her eyes and sighed.

"A lot on your mind?" Helen asked.

"Yeah."

"I'm not prying."

"I know. It's my relationship with Gary. It's religion, which I know you don't want to talk about, so I won't go there." She gave her sister another look and smiled. "Mostly it's not knowing how to find Molly Altman."

"You're doing the best you can, Jess."

"That won't be much comfort if she dies. She could, you know." Jessie explained about the splenectomy.

"Maybe he'll reconsider. He won't want a dead child on his hands."

"He's a brute. I spoke to people who know him."

Helen gasped. "You know who he is?"

"But not *where* he is." Jessie paused. "He beat his wife badly, several times. He threatened to kill her. I listened to people describing what he did to her, and I thought, how does someone turn into an animal like this? And then I thought, I don't really care, you know? I don't want to hear that he was abused or victimized or molested as a kid, because it doesn't really excuse the fact that he used his wife as a punching bag."

Helen swirled the water with her toes. "You're right," she said quietly.

Jessie looked up and saw her sister's flushed face. She pulled herself out of the water and sat next to her. "I'm sorry, Helen. I didn't mean . . ."

"No, that's okay." She averted her head. "Dr. Rothman tells me all the time that I'm entitled to be angry at Mom for hitting me, but that while abuse creates a cycle, ultimately, I'm responsible for my behavior. *I'm* the one who hit Matthew, not Mom."

"Mom thinks you blame her for what happened with Matthew."

"I did. I still do, sometimes. It's easier than accepting responsibility." She smiled wryly.

Jessie leaned closer and put her arm around Helen's shoulder. "I'm so proud of you, Helen. You've come a long way."

"I have, haven't I?" She nodded somberly. "But I worry about Matthew, what all this has done to him. He doesn't seem angry, and his teachers tell me he gets along fine with other kids. But so did I when I was his age."

"He's much happier than he was a year ago, Helen. It's so obvious. He's relaxed, he's more open."

Helen's foot played with the water again. "I almost hit him the other day," she said, her voice barely audible over the churning waters. "He knocked a glass off the counter. There was milk all over the floor, and broken glass, and I got so angry."

She bit her upper lip. "He knew I was going to hit him. I could see it in his eyes. He was terrified, absolutely terrified. That made me feel like a monster, and I wanted to hit him even more, to get that look off his face. And I knew if I hit him, I wouldn't stop. And Neil would take Matthew away and I'd never see him again."

Jessie's heart ached. "But you didn't hit him, Helen," she said softly.

"No." She sighed. "No, I didn't."

They stayed outside awhile longer, then returned to Helen's bedroom.

"I promised you a massage," Helen said as Jessie removed her bathing suit. She left the room and returned a moment later with a white lace-bordered sheet.

Jessie hung the suit in Helen's bathroom. Wrapped in the sheet, she watched Helen, who was flitting around the room like Tinkerbell, lighting the thick, scented candles that sat on her nightstand and dresser and the ledge of the uncurtained bay window that looked out on the pool.

They had both always loved candles, had secretly lit them in Jessie's room and shut the lights and read aloud from the books they devoured. Ghoulish tales when they were younger; heady, erotic romances when they were in their teens.

"You are both pyromaniacs!" Frances would shriek, dousing the flames and distributing rapid-fire smacks that left angry red brands and sent both girls into gales of laughter after their mother slammed out of the room, and didn't stop them from lighting the candles the next time.

Helen shut the light, then slipped a CD in the player. Soft instrumental music filled the air, then a woman sang in Celtic.

"Ready?"

Jessie lay, face down, on the high, platform-based king-size bed and shut her eyes. Cool ointment drizzled onto her shoulders, quickly warmed by Helen's sure fingers.

"Oh, God, that feels good!" Jessie moaned.

"You're so tight," Helen said reprovingly. "You're a mass of knots."

She worked Jessie's arms and legs first, then her neck and shoulders and back. A delicious languor stole over Jessie, from the tingling massage and the musky fragrance of the candles and the music, all of it so wonderful. She drifted off to sleep.

When she awoke, Helen was next to her on the bed, knees to her chest, watching her.

"You slept for over an hour," she said tenderly.

"I don't feel like ever leaving this bed."

"Why don't you stay the night?"

"Maybe I will. I'd forgotten how wonderful your massages are, Helen. You have a gift."

Her face shone with pleasure. "Thanks. It isn't often that I can do something for you. I don't mean that critically," she added quickly. "It's just that I've always felt that you're the caretaker, and I'm the one who needs taking care of, that you're always in the wings, not only waiting to pick me up when I fall, but expecting me to."

Not entirely untrue, Jessie admitted to herself. "You're very capable, Helen. You don't give yourself enough credit."

"I'm working hard to believe that."

Jessie shut her eyes again.

"You mentioned your relationship with Gary," Helen said. "Maybe it would help if you talked about it."

Jessie sighed.

Helen pouted. "I'm a good listener, Jess, but if you'd rather not . . ."

"I don't think talking will help, Helen." She wished her sister weren't so quick to take hurt, and wondered uncomfortably if she herself was to blame in part for Helen's insecurity. She rolled over onto her back.

"Gary wants us to get married, but something's keeping me from saying yes." She told Helen about the other night's conversation. "I think I hurt him a lot, Helen. I don't know why it has to be so complicated."

"You have a tendency to *make* things complicated, Jessie. You overanalyze."

"That's what Gary said. I do, don't I?" She smiled ruefully.

"That may make you a good detective, Jess, but it doesn't always work in relationships. Do you love him?"

She'd been thinking about this all day. "I think so," she said, suddenly shy.

"You love him. He loves you. You've learned from your mistakes, you're both eager to make this work. So what's the problem?"

She thought about all the answers she could give—their conflicting careers, their views on family, on religion. Then she tried to imagine not having him in her life and felt hollow.

"I guess there really isn't any," she said.

"So tell him how you feel."

"Maybe I will," she said, feeling lighter than she had in ages.

She was sleeping soundly when the chirping of her pager woke her. Moving to the edge of the bed, she groped in her purse and found the pager.

She rubbed her eyes and read the illuminated numbers.

Phil.

Using the phone on the nightstand, she called his home. He answered on the first ring.

"It's Jessie," she said, yawning. "I'm at Helen's."

"Silo's ex just called. She heard that the big man is going to be partying at his favorite hangout with a group of friends."

Jessie checked her watch and groaned. "It's one-thirty."

"The night is young, baby."

48

"Foxy lady." Phil whistled as Jessie sashayed toward his car. "How do you walk in those things? What do you call them anyway?"

"Open-toed platforms. Actually, they're comfortable." Comfortable enough to run in, if she had to, and secure, because of the ankle straps.

"How do I look?" He was wearing black chinos and a black silk shirt, with the top two buttons open to show a gold chain-link necklace.

"Not too shabby, Zoro."

He opened the door for her. The miniskirt was so damn tight she was afraid it would split. She sat down sideways on the edge of the bench seat and swiveled to face the windshield.

"Where is this place?" she asked when he was in the driver's seat.

"Ronny's. A bar on Hollywood near Cahuenga. If this doesn't pan out, we can always catch a late-late flick." He backed out of Jessie's driveway and headed north.

"Lou is going to be upset you didn't take him along."

"Yeah, well, he kind of screams 'cop,' you know what I mean?" Phil shrugged.

"What will you tell him?"

"That I needed a woman for cover. I got me a fine one, too." He flashed Jessie a smile, then frowned. "A little more lipstick, maybe," he suggested, and massaged his chest.

"I don't want to look like a 'ho." She pulled down the visor, checked herself critically in the small illuminated mirror, then applied more lip gloss and blush.

"What did the Denby woman say?"

"She gave me a rundown of life with Stan Weigund." Jessie repeated what she'd learned and saw Phil's face tighten. "So maybe she'll get us a tape from Vicky, maybe not."

"What's your guess?"

"I don't have one. Have you heard anything on the news about Stuart Logan? The talk show host?" She'd slept through all the evening newscasts, and she doubted that the segment had made CNN.

"I know who he is. A major jerk. No, nothing. Why?"

"He's going to help us bait Weigund by goading him into calling the show."

Phil darted a look at her. "No shit. He called you and offered his services?"

"I went to him. He was eager to help. So was the program director. She okayed a phone trap. I'll have phone security take care of it in the morning."

Phil smiled. "Nice."

"Only if the TV news stations play the segment. Otherwise, Weigund won't know Logan is dissing him."

"It's too soon. I'll bet we hear something in the morning."

He took Santa Monica to Highland, then Highland to Hollywood Boulevard. The street was still filled with foot traffic and cars and hookers standing on corners. A few years ago the LAPD had tried to eliminate the hookers by making a real presence. That had worked for a while. Then the police had left, and it had been business as usual.

Phil parked his Cutlass on a side street in the red and placed his pass prominently in the windshield. He walked around to Jessie's side, opened the door, and helped her out.

She smoothed her skirt and the clingy red halter top, loosened the curls in her hair with her fingers, and adjusted the strap of her small purse, inside of which was her gun. "I'm ready."

Ronny's was overcrowded and filled with a haze of cigarette smoke and noisy laughter. They walked in, Phil's arm around her waist, and found a small table at the back of the long, narrow, L-shaped room. He sat facing the entrance, nibbling on mini pretzels and peanuts while he scanned the place.

"Is he here?" Jessie.

"I don't see him." He winced.

"What's the matter?"

"Heartburn." He reached into his pants pocket and took out two pastel tablets. "He'll show. I feel it."

A waitress came over, took their orders, and left.

Phil crunched on the tablets, drummed his fingers on the table, then scooped another handful of peanuts into his palm.

"Why don't you lay off those until you feel better?" she said.

"I'm okay." He tossed the peanuts into his mouth. "Why were you at Helen's? Everything okay?"

"No particular reason. She's fine, Matthew's fine." She wasn't about to tell him she hadn't wanted to go home to an empty house. That sounded pathetic. She realized suddenly that she hadn't returned any of the calls. Frances was definitely furious by now, and Gary was probably worried. Jessie sighed.

Phil frowned. "What?"

"Nothing. Barry phoned me at home and left a message. He wants to be in on everything, wants to help 'catch the bastard,' as he put it."

Phil grunted.

"He's not a bad guy, Phil."

"Save it for someone who cares."

They talked about Weigund, about the fact that they had no leads about the dead rug dealer. Phil was telling her a story about Lou when he leaned over suddenly and cupped her chin in his hand.

"He's here, darlin', with a couple of ladies. Checking out the place, looking our way."

She felt an adrenaline rush. "You're too cute," she said, and laughed. "Where is he now?"

"At the bar. He's wearing a white jacket, white pants. He could be packing."

"Let's do it."

Phil moved his chair back and stood, swaying a little, then walked around and helped her out of her seat. He put his arm around her shoulder and nuzzled her neck, then steered her toward the bar.

It was impossible to miss the man. He looked like an igloo.

"Hey, Silo," Phil called above the noise.

The man turned around and scowled at Phil, then at Jessie. "Do I know you?"

"You do now. LAPD. We want to talk to you."

The women standing on either side of Silo backed away. Several others at the bar did the same, but most of the people in the room were oblivious to what was happening.

"What's this about?" the large man demanded. "Can't a guy have a drink without being hassled by the police?" His hand moved toward his jacket.

"Don't do it," Phil warned quietly, his hand inside his jacket.

"Do what? I was going for my wallet. They don't give you drinks for free, last I heard."

"No wallet, no drink. Party's over. Put your hands on the bar, Silo."

Jessie had slipped her hand into her purse and locked her fingers around the grip of her gun. There was an electric moment when she wasn't sure what Silo was going to do.

Silo placed both hands on the bar ledge. "Whatever it is you think I did, you got the wrong guy."

Phil said, "Let's talk about it at the station."

"You arresting me?"

"Right now we're having a conversation about some stolen goods you pawned."

The man nodded. "So I talk to you, tell you what I know, and that's it?"

Phil smiled. "That's it. Let's go."

Silo slid off the barstool and stood, shaking his head. Suddenly he lunged at Phil and Jessie, growling as he shoved each with a huge hand with such force that he knocked them both down.

Someone screamed.

He ran toward the exit, and the crowd parted for him like sheaves of wheat.

Phil was first to get to his feet. Jessie was right behind him, still gulping air and feeling as though she'd run into a wall as they ran out of the bar.

She strained to see through the crowd of people.

"There!" She pointed to her left at the large white figure across the street, thankful that Silo had made himself so easy to spot.

She crossed the wide boulevard with Phil and ran, her feet cushioned by the rubberized three-inch soles. Too many pedestrians around to try for a shot. Some of them gaped and moved quickly out of their way. A green-haired man planted himself in the middle of the sidewalk and bellowed, "Police brutality!" Phil elbowed him roughly aside.

They were gaining on Silo. Jessie was feeling a little winded, but she concentrated on the steady, rapid thumping of her heart that kept time with the pounding of her footsteps, and Phil's heavier ones, on the sidewalk.

Silo was fifty feet ahead. Too far to get a clear shot. Phil's breathing was labored and he was losing ground. She sprinted ahead, narrowing the distance until she was almost on top of Silo. Then she tackled the huge man, clasping her hands around his beefy neck as he dropped to the sidewalk with a loud thud, felled not by her weight, she knew, but by his own momentum. Landed right in front of Mann's Chinese Theater, on the Walk of Fame.

Silo attempted to rise, then flailed his arms and legs, like a fish trying to dislodge a harpoon, but he soon gave up. She held her gun to the back of his head and waited for Phil, who was there a few seconds later, huffing, his face a dangerous shade of red.

Silo's palms were pressed on the pavement, next to the cemented handprints of the diminutive Mickey Rooney. Some irony there, Jessie thought, catching her breath and tasting remnants of the steak and cream sauce she'd enjoyed earlier.

Phil yanked Silo's arms behind him and cuffed his hands.

"*Now* I'm arresting you," he wheezed, then clutched his chest and sank to the ground.

49

He was conscious and breathing.

Jessie radioed 911, frantic, then ran her finger around the inside of Phil's mouth to make sure his air passage wasn't obstructed. His pulse seemed normal, and she took some comfort in the fact that his color looked less red and his breathing sounded more even.

Silo had stopped moaning and had turned his head at an impossible angle to gawk at Phil. Several pedestrians stopped to gawk, too. Jessie shooed them away.

The paramedics arrived, sirens blaring, while she was calling for a black-and-white to transport Silo to the station. They placed Phil on a stretcher, and she gripped his hand while they slipped the stretcher inside the van.

"Another cowboy hits the dust," he said, smiling wanly.

"You're going to be *fine*."

"Hell, yeah," he said, sounding scared. "Call Maureen?"

She nodded.

"You gonna keep me lying on the sidewalk forever?" Silo called. "I'm hurt, too, you know."

"Shut up," Jessie told him tiredly, and watched the van pull away and tear down the street.

Silo muttered something, but she ignored him. She took her cell phone from her purse, punched Phil's home number, and braced herself.

Maureen sounded half asleep when she answered.

"It's Jessie," she said, and told her what had happened. "He doesn't look bad, Maureen," she added, praying that she wasn't offering false hope.

"Where did they take him?" Maureen asked, eerily calm.

"Cedars-Sinai."

Silo was still muttering minutes later when two police officers showed up. They hoisted him to his feet—no small accomplishment—and maneuvered him into the back seat of their vehicle.

Jessie had remembered to take Phil's car keys. She drove his Cutlass to Cedars-Sinai and sat anxiously in the waiting room. Maureen was inside the examining room with Phil, a receptionist had told Jessie, looking at her curiously after Jessie had identified herself as a detective.

The last time she'd been here had been a year and a half ago, with Matthew. The time before that, when she'd had the miscarriage. Almost three years ago, she realized with a fresh pang of loss.

Please, she thought, please be all right.

She fidgeted with her purse, watched the wiry, tense young woman sitting across from her who kept sniffling and wiping her nose with her fingers. Druggie, Jessie guessed.

She glanced at the clock on the wall and was surprised to learn that only fifteen minutes had passed.

Paramedics wheeled in a man with a pasty white face who was groaning and thrashing on the stretcher. A cheerful volunteer rushed over to direct them.

She heard her name and turned quickly. There was Maureen, looking tiny and fragile. But she was smiling. Jessie jumped up and half ran toward her.

"They said it's acute indigestion and probably an anxiety attack," Maureen said, wiping her eyes. "He admitted he ate too many peanuts too quickly, and didn't really chew them well. I could kill him."

She started laughing and crying, and hugging Jessie, who was laughing and crying, too.

After seeing Phil, she drove to West L.A. and parked his car in the lot. Silo had been booked and was in a holding cell but hadn't asked for a lawyer. He was grumbling about "Constitutional rights" when they brought him to the interrogation cubicle.

He was full of bluster at first, pretending not to recognize the watch Jessie held up in front of him, the one he'd pawned. "I seen lots of watches," he told her.

She told him that his prints were on the watch, that the pawnshop owner would ID him. Told him the watch connected him with the murder of its owner, Noreen Gelbart.

He pouted. "I didn't kill no one. You can't pin this on me."

Based on his rap sheet, she was inclined to believe him. "Then give me a name, Silo."

"I got no name, 'cause I don't know nothing about a murder."

"Where'd you get the watch?"

"Found it on the street."

She smiled. "A fifteen-thousand-dollar watch?"

He shrugged. "My lucky day. What can I tell you?"

"You want to fry for this, go ahead." Jessie nodded. "It doesn't matter to me who goes down as long as we clear the case."

Still mute.

"You're in big trouble," she said. "Detective Okum is in critical condition. They're saying he may not make it."

He snorted. "What's that got to do with me? He had a heart attack."

"You assaulted him, Silo. You punched him, over and over, before you went down. You're a lethal machine. A jury takes one look at you and it's over."

He was staring at her, his mouth wide open. "You're crazy! I shoved him, once."

She frowned. "Funny. That's not how I remember it."

"Uh-huh. Well, I got people in the bar who saw what happened." He sneered at her, but his eyes were blinking rapidly.

"I'm not talking about the bar, Silo. I'm talking after, when he caught up with you."

"You're the one got me, not him."

She shook her head. "Not me. Detective Okum brought you down."

"You can't do this," he said.

She checked her nails.

He was silent for a while, his mouth working. "Suppose I give you some information about the watch?"

"That would depend on the information."

"I can tell you who killed the woman."

"Then my memory might get a little clearer."

Another silence.

"A friend of mine offered me a cut if I unloaded the watch," Silo finally said. "That plus some other stuff."

"Who's the friend?"

"Joey Montrose," he said, sounding unhappy. "The dead woman's son hired him to do the hit and make it look like a follow-home. The guy wanted to collect his mom's life insurance."

"So that makes you an accessory after."

Silo shook his head violently. "No, it don't. I didn't even *know* the woman was offed until I tried to unload another piece, and the dude tells me cops were there, looking for some guy who killed this rich lady. So I called Joey, and he said, yeah, stay low."

He expelled a big breath. "That's all I know."

A patrol officer dropped her in front of her house at five-thirty in the morning. Still dark outside, except for the pale yellow light from the street lamp. Jessie flashed the kitchen light on and off to signal that she was inside, and heard him drive off.

It hardly paid to sleep, she thought, pulling down the comforter and crawling into her bed, still dressed. She shut her eyes.

God, what a night. And the morning would be no better. She had to type the report about Silo, and someone had to pick up Joey Montrose and Wayne Gelbart, the dead woman's son. Maybe Espes would send Simms and Boyd, or Lou. And she had to talk to IA, Robbery-Homicide.

She had just fallen asleep when the doorbell rang. Her eyes were bleary, and she checked the clock radio twice to make sure she was seeing right. 6:10.

Yawning, she padded barefoot to the front door, looked through the privacy window, and opened the door.

"Hi." Gary handed her the paper, a little damp from the sprinklers, and stepped inside.

"I heard the *Times* was cutting back, but I didn't know they had reporters doing deliveries," she said, and yawned again.

"I know it's early, Jess. I have to talk to you."

He sounded solemn. No smile, no kiss. She shut the door behind him and saw that he was staring at her quizzically.

"Big party last night?"

She'd forgotten about her clothes. She looked down at her halter top and miniskirt, then back at Gary. She laughed. "You don't want to know. I need something to wake me up. How about a cup of coffee?"

He followed her into the kitchen and waited while she put up the kettle, then sat with her at the breakfast room table.

"I left several messages on your home phone, Jessie. Didn't you get them?"

"Just one, and I didn't have a chance to call you back. I slept at Helen's last night. If you can call it sleep." She yawned again, then told him about Silo and Phil. "The doctor said Phil can probably come home tomorrow or the next day."

Gary nodded. "Thank God he's okay. I love that guy." He paused. "Jessie, the reason I'm here—"

The kettle whistled. She went into the kitchen, shut the flame, and prepared a cup of unflavored instant coffee for Gary, French vanilla for herself. She wondered suddenly if he'd come over to end their relationship. But why at six in the morning?

"I've been thinking about the other night," she said when she returned to the table. "You were right, you know. Sleeping together would have been a mistake."

"Yeah, but a *great* mistake." He smiled. "Funny, isn't it? It's usually the guy who has commitment problems."

He sounded so nervous.

"I know this hasn't been fair to you, Gary."

"Pressuring you isn't fair, either, Jess." He stirred his coffee. "Actually, I've been thinking about what you said."

"Me, too. Gary—"

"I know I've been trying to convince you that we could make a go of it, but maybe you're right, Jessie. Maybe I'm just ignoring the truth. Our jobs have put us in conflict before, and they will again. We have different views about raising kids. And then there's religion."

She wanted to tell him that he was wrong, that while sitting in the waiting area to find out whether Phil would die, she'd realized that she wanted to spend her life with Gary, that life was too short, too precious, to fritter away on doubt.

Instead, she nodded. "So what are you saying?"

"I think we should go back to being friends, Jess."

"If that's what you want." A lump formed in her throat, and her eyes burned. She told herself she was just tired.

"I think it's what we both want. You were just smarter, Jess. You knew it all along."

She lifted her mug with both hands and took a long sip until she had her face under control. "That's what you came over to tell me at six in the morning?"

"No. I came to tell you that I know who the kidnapper is. Stan Weigund." He paused. "An LAPD cop."

So fast! she thought, her mind in turmoil. She put down her mug with an abrupt gesture, sloshing coffee over the rim. Who was the source? Someone from Santa Monica? From Fugitives? From CRASH? "So you're running the story?" she asked, struggling to sound matter-of-fact.

"I haven't, yet. I don't know if I will."

"It's vital that Weigund doesn't know we're on to him, Gary. I'm sure you can understand that. Also, the woman who identified him is a friend of his wife's. Her life will be in danger once he finds out that we know."

He nodded. "I hear you. Like I said, I haven't decided yet."

"I'm not asking you not to run this story because of our relationship, Gary."

"I know." He rose from his seat, reached into his pants pocket, and handed her a plastic bag with a cassette. "Rosalynn Denby asked me to give this to you. She phoned me last night after you met with her, wanted to know if she could trust you. I told her absolutely."

"Thanks." She put the cassette on the table, her satisfaction that Vicky Weigund had come through significantly dampened.

"I should thank *you*. You gave me my headline."

He removed the string from the newspaper she'd tossed onto the breakfast room table and placed the open paper in front of her.

WIFE OF KIDNAPPER PLEADS:
LET MOLLY ALTMAN GO.

In a tape to be aired on *Talking With Dr. Renee* this afternoon, the wife of the man who kidnapped Molly Altman has finally come forward to plead with her husband for the immediate release of the six-year-old. The tape cassette was delivered anonymously this morning to KMST . . .

"I promised Rosalynn I'd keep her name out of this," Gary said.

"She told you about Weigund?" Jessie supposed that was better than having someone from the department leak the information, but the effects could be just as damning.

"She thought I knew. I didn't tell her otherwise," he said, with no hint of apology.

Jessie could hardly blame him—at least he'd done *his* job well. She was angry with herself for assuming that Rosalynn wouldn't tell anyone about Weigund, for not specifically telling her not to say anything to Gary. If Gary revealed Weigund's identity, Espes would have her head. And he'd be right.

At least Frances would be happy, Jessie thought glumly. She was always nagging at Jessie to choose another line of work.

She walked Gary to the door, feeling awkward and miserable. He leaned over and grazed his lips against her cheek, and she resisted an urge to wrap her arms around him and ask him not to go.

After he had left, she returned to the kitchen and read the rest of the article about the tape, then glanced at the index on the newspaper's second page. More related articles on the kidnapper in the Metro section, nothing about Stuart Logan.

((«**50**»))

"My ex-husband's mother died, Dr. Renee, and I don't know if I should go to the funeral."

"How long are you divorced, Laurie?"

"Eight years."

"And are you on civil terms with your ex?"

"Better than when we were married." She laughed lightly.

"Do you find divorce funny, Laurie?" Renee said coldly. "Because I don't."

"No, not at all. I'm just a little nervous. The thing is, I loved my mother-in-law, Dr. Renee. She was always good to me, even after the divorce, and she never talked badly about me, like some of my ex's family."

"Unfortunately, Laurie, divorce doesn't always bring out the kindest behavior in people, and family inevitably has to choose sides. So why are you thinking about not attending the funeral? Does your ex not want you there?"

"Not so much my ex, but his wife. My daughter told me this, so I don't even know if it's completely true."

"Uh-huh."

"I feel terrible, Dr. Renee. I'd like to pay my last respects, but I don't want this woman to create a scene."

"Is that likely?"

"She's very insecure, and she's jealous of me. She told a mutual friend that she thinks I want to get him back."

"Have you remarried, Laurie?"

"No. I haven't met the right person."

"Is it possible that you are hoping your ex will come back to you?"

"No, not at all."

"Are you sure? Sometimes we're awfully good at fooling ourselves, Laurie."

"I'm positive. So what do you think I should do, Dr. Renee?"

"I think you need to discuss this with your ex, Laurie."

"I could. But I hate bothering him at a time like this."

"You don't really have a choice. As much as you loved this woman and want to pay your respects, your ex's feelings come first. Either get his okay or stay home and pay your respects privately some other time. You can visit the cemetery and put some flowers on the grave. You can send your ex a card."

"My father-in-law would want me there, Dr. Renee. And what about my girls? This is their grandmother. I should be there for them."

"It sounds to me, Laurie, like you're having a harder time letting go of your ex and his family than you're willing to admit. You have to bury your past, not your mother-in-law."

"This is Detective Drake from West L.A.," Timothy Groton said from behind his desk. "Detective Drake, Mike Newell."

Two men and a lady, Jessie thought. She'd developed a friendly relationship with Groton, a Detective III, long before he'd transferred to IA, where he'd been for more than a year. He was in his mid-forties: short; receding, wavy reddish brown hair; a hawklike nose; and the beginnings of a paunch.

Newell was at least ten years younger. Tall and lanky, he had thick black hair and keen blue eyes behind small, metal-framed round glasses. Both of them wore dark suits and white shirts with conservative ties.

"Detective Drake has some questions to ask you about a case you handled," Groton began. "Stan Weigund. I told her you'd be happy to help."

She almost missed the flicker of irritation in Newell's eyes. Groton was sitting too straight in his chair, looking unhappy. He'd been shocked when Jessie had explained why she was here, uncomfortable when she'd asked him not to tell Newell the truth. But he'd reluctantly agreed.

"Stan Weigund," Newell said, narrowing his eyes. "Sorry. Doesn't ring a bell. What's this about, Tim?" he asked, pointedly ignoring Jessie.

"This was two and a half years ago," Jessie said pleasantly. "Victoria Weigund filed a complaint against her husband, Detective Stan Weigund, for spousal abuse."

"We conduct a lot of investigations, Detective."

"Victoria Weigund was a cop, too."

"We conduct a lot of investigations into altercations between cops." Newell smiled. "That's our soup du jour."

"The original charges were filed with the Santa Monica PD," Jessie said. "Does that help?"

"Are we playing twenty questions, Detective? I don't have all day."

"Mike," Groton chided quietly.

Newell darted a look at Groton, then adjusted his glasses. "Yeah, I remember Weigund. Why are you interested in him?"

"He may be involved in a case we're handling. I was hoping, since you probably got to know him pretty well, that you could tell me about him."

"Not much to tell. He's a great guy, from what I recall. But I don't remember the particulars."

Real great. "We're trying to find him. Would you know where he goes to relax? Who he hangs out with?"

"Not with his wife, that's for sure." Another, smug smile. "Sorry, Detective. Wish I could help, but I have nothing to tell you."

She'd come here disliking Newell for letting Weigund off; now he was beginning to grate on her nerves. "Maybe you could take a look at Weigund's file and see if anything in it refreshes your memory."

Newell looked again at Groton. "You know what case she's talking about, right?"

Groton nodded. "Relax, Mike. It's nothing personal."

"No problem." Newell stood and left the room.

"You're pissing him off," Groton said. "Tell him why you want Weigund, maybe he'll help."

"Want to place a bet? You heard what he said—'Weigund's a great guy.' "

"That was different. You're talking murder now and kidnapping. You want to get information that can help you find Weigund, or you want your pound of flesh?"

"The truth? Newell's not interested in helping me, even if he could. So I'm going for the pound of flesh."

Groton sighed. "You're putting me in a tough spot. I work with him, Jessie."

"So that means you cover his butt? It doesn't bother you that he let Weigund get away with this?"

"It bothers the hell out of me, but there's no changing what happened. That was over two years ago. The division's better. Newell's better. He's going to know anyway, once we're involved."

Newell returned with a thick folder. He sat down, flipped through the pages, then shook his head and tossed the folder onto Groton's desk. "Like I said, nothing."

"Okay if I take a look?" Without waiting for an answer, she opened the folder and scanned through the pages.

She looked at Newell. "Interesting. According to your evaluation, you determined that Victoria Weigund was mostly responsible for the events of that night."

He gazed at her with interest for a long moment. "That's right. We found she'd been drinking that night, and she'd instigated the incident."

"She criticized him for coming home late. That, in your professional opinion, gave him the right to beat the crap out of her?" Jessie said casually, as if she were discussing a parking citation.

Newell scowled. "Listen—"

"Let's keep this on track," Groton said.

"No, I'll answer that," Newell snapped. "The fact is, *Detective,* the evidence pointed to fault on both parts. She assaulted him first. He was merely trying to defend himself."

"By slamming her against the wall and punching her in the mouth? By throwing her on the floor and ripping out her hair? That's according to the Santa Monica PD report she filed. This is what she looked like."

Jessie had the copy of the photo of a battered Vicky Weigund. She took it out of her purse and extended it to Newell. He pushed it away.

"This isn't getting us anywhere," Groton said.

"She was drunk." Newell's face was red, his voice flat. "She was volatile. He had to use some force, but according to his statement, she inflicted most of those injuries on herself to get him in trouble. There's no evidence that he was lying."

"There's no evidence that she was drunk, either," Jessie said. "Not according to the Santa Monica PD officers who went to the house. They arrested him, but not her. Funny, don't you think? If she assaulted him?"

"She hit him where it wouldn't show, including below the belt. She bit him, too."

"Because she was trying to get away."

"Because she wanted to inflict pain." Newell's lips tightened. "She knew what she was doing, Detective, and I'm not going to apologize for that report. The other time she called the Santa Monica PD, she recanted. Same thing before that, when she came to us another time and accused her husband of assault. What does that tell you?"

"That she was terrified of her husband and she figured IA wasn't going to be much help."

"That's your spin. It tells me maybe she's out for revenge, maybe she's lying." He sat straight and glared at her. "If she's planning on suing the department, she's wasting her time. There were major inconsistencies in Vicky Weiguind's initial and subsequent statements."

"I'm not surprised. You wore her down." Jessie held up a page and read aloud. " 'Officer Weigund demonstrated poor judgment by reporting what was basically a civil matter to the local authorities.' " She glanced at Newell.

"That's right. Sneer if you want, Detective, but everybody would have been better off if she hadn't blown this out of proportion."

"She *certainly* would have. She'd still have her job with the LAPD."

"If you can't take the heat, stay out of the kitchen."

Jessie continued to read. " 'Officer Weigund instigated the incident and has shown herself to be immature by her unwillingness to take steps to further harmony in the home. She has recognized that her consumption of alcohol may have contributed to the problems in her relationship with her husband.' "

"Correct." Newell nodded.

" 'Detective Stan Weigund is hardworking, mature, and well liked by his peers. He is an excellent officer with tremendous potential. It is regrettable that he chose a spouse who may prove to be difficult and temperamental. A bitch on wheels.' " Jessie looked up. "Nice phrasing."

No response from Newell.

"So Weigund is the poster boy for the LAPD, huh?"

"Weigund's a good man," Newell said firmly. "I checked him out thoroughly. Everybody knew she was giving him a rough time. It was no secret."

"All the *guys* knew, you mean. I'll bet he complained about her all the time so they'd feel sorry for him in case she reported him."

"I'm done." Newell's chair made a screeching sound as he shoved it backward. He started to rise.

"Mike," Groton said, in a somber voice that stopped him. "West L.A. has reason to believe Stan Weigund killed a woman and kidnapped a little girl."

Newell's jaw dropped. He sank against his chair. "The guy who phoned the radio show?" he said after a moment. "But his name is Hank."

"You didn't recognize his voice?" Jessie said, not really surprised that he hadn't. Rondell from Santa Monica hadn't recognized him, either.

"No. Why would I? I haven't talked to the guy in a year and a half." He fell silent. "You're sure it's him?" he asked Jessie a few seconds later, sounding nervous for the first time since he'd entered Groton's office.

"Positive."

"IA will be handling this," Groton said. "Together with West L.A. We don't want word to get out to the media, and we don't want Weigund to find out he's been made."

Newell nodded.

"You investigated him before," Groton said. "You know who his friends are. Hopefully, that'll save us time."

"Like I said, I don't know where to find him. But I'll be happy to help." He chewed his lip, then turned to Jessie. "I still stand by my report."

She'd almost felt sorry for him.

The kid was still sleeping, or pretending to. He'd forced her to take two nonaspirin tablets that he'd found in the medicine cabinet, but her fever was climbing. He knew that even without a thermometer, just from touching her head. This time she'd been too listless to cringe when he reached toward her.

Weigund locked the door and walked into the kitchen. Taking a bottle of chilled beer from the refrigerator, he went to the family room and turned on the television.

". . . interrupt your regularly scheduled program to bring you this special bulletin live from our studios."

Network music, then a shot of an anchorwoman sitting at a large semicircular desk.

"Good morning. I'm Diane Lopez. The wife of the man who allegedly murdered Blanca Gutierrez and kidnapped the six-year-old daughter of popular talk show host Dr. Renee Altman has apparently broken her silence, at least on tape."

Weigund caught his breath and stared at the screen.

"We've received word that Dr. Renee Altman will play a tape, anonymously delivered to KMST this morning, on which the woman whom the world knows only as Vicky pleads with her husband to release young Molly Altman."

"Come to Papa, baby," Weigund whispered. He tilted his head back and drank in long, noisy gulps.

". . . don't know exactly what Vicky will tell her husband, but it's certain to be an emotional moment. Back with us in the studio this morning is renowned family therapist Dr. Gerald Kanton."

The camera panned to the therapist.

"Dr. Kanton, thank you for joining us again."

" 'A pleasure to be here,' " Weigund mimed with the doctor.

"Doctor, this is certainly a climactic development."

"A very dramatic development indeed, Diane."

"Sometime this afternoon, we will hear, for the very first time, from the woman who is so centrally involved in this terrible, terrible tragedy. Can you tell us why she's come forward now?"

" 'Cause she loves me, you dimwit." Weigund laughed.

"Well, Diane, I would guess that like the rest of us, she's aware that Molly Altman may need medical attention. This must weigh heavily on her, since her husband kidnapped the child to persuade his wife to return to him with their son."

"Oh, that is *so* observant, Doctor," Weigund said in a mincing falsetto. "You are *so* smart."

The camera stayed on the anchor.

"In a related story, the always controversial talk show host Stuart Logan has once again pushed the envelope of outrageousness by offering fifty thousand dollars to the kidnapper's wife for an exclusive live interview."

"Now you're talking." Weigund grinned. "You're the man, Logan."

"Logan, not known for his gentility, took potshots yesterday at the kidnapper, calling him, among other choice things, 'pathetic.' He promises to do more of the same on today's program. We have a tape of yesterday's program."

"Go ahead, Logan," Weigund said. "Give it your best shot."

". . . guy's a loser. 'Look at me, I'm so mean and scary, I could kill your kid.' "

"Sticks and stones, baby," Weigund said, but his grin had faded. A muscle twitched in his cheek.

". . . Hey, Hank, are you listening? We're talking about you, man. You're pathetic, and you're a moron."

"Asshole," Weigund muttered. He pointed the remote at the screen, jabbed the button, and switched to another channel.

" 'I love you, Vicky. Come back to me, baby, so we can be happy and I can beat the crap out of you again.' "

Another jab of the button.

". . . a bully who picks on women and kids. He's got the brain of a carp . . ."

". . . brain of a carp . . ."

He threw the remote at the television. It bounced off the screen and fell soundlessly onto the carpeted floor.

". . . pathetic and a moron . . ."

((•**52**•))

Frank Pruitt glanced up at Jessie, then pushed back his chair and stood. "Changed your mind, I see," he drawled. "I guess you couldn't stay away from the Pruitt charm."

He was grinning suggestively, and she smiled in spite of herself. "I need to talk to you, Frank. It's important."

"Business, huh? You're breaking my heart, Jess." He pretended to clutch his chest, then saw her wince. "What's wrong?"

"My partner, Phil Okum, collapsed early this morning right in the middle of a bust. The good news is, he'll be okay." Stopping at the hospital before coming downtown, she'd been encouraged by the color in Phil's face and by his spirits. "The bad news is, I'm overworked and I'm without a partner." Unless she wanted Lou, which she didn't.

"As long as he's going to be okay," Pruitt said, solemn.

Jessie looked around the room, filled with detectives, most of whom she didn't know. "Can we talk somewhere private? This is a little delicate."

He raised a brow, looked at her quizzically for a moment. "No problem." He steered her out of the large detectives' room and down the hall into a small interrogation room.

"So what's this about?" he asked when they were both seated.

"You have a detective here at Robbery-Homicide by the name of Stan Weigund."

Pruitt nodded. "A good cop. Bright, ambitious, friendly. He's going places."

"I think he's already gone somewhere, Frank."

He narrowed his eyes. "Meaning?"

"He kidnapped the Altman girl and killed the housekeeper."

Pruitt was staring now. Suddenly he laughed. "You're pulling my leg, right?"

279

She shook her head.

"Weigund?" He was silent a moment. "You're sure about this?"

"I'm sure."

He ran a hand through his hair, then sighed. "I can't believe it. That's *your* case?"

"You must have known he was investigated by IA for spousal abuse."

"He wouldn't be the first," Pruitt said, wary now. "But he was cleared of the charges."

"He shouldn't have been." With a fresh surge of anger, Jessie repeated what she'd learned from Trudy Brookhurst and Rondell. "Anyway, he's the one. I need you to introduce me to his partner."

"Bill Saunders." Pruitt nodded. "A good cop."

"Going places, ambitious, friendly?" she said quietly.

Pruitt tightened his lips. "Don't tar all of us with the same brush, okay?" he snapped.

"You're right. Sorry." She would get nowhere antagonizing him, or anyone else, but she was so damn angry. "I had almost no sleep last night, and it's been a rough few days. I really have to talk to Saunders, Frank. He may know where we can find Weigund. By the way, this doesn't get out, okay?"

"Tell your boyfriend, not me." Pruitt was scowling. He stood and left the room.

He's not my boyfriend anymore, Jessie thought, and was overcome again by sadness. She was thinking about Gary when Pruitt returned with a short, dark blond, thirty-something man sporting a goatee.

Pruitt performed the introductions.

"Detective Pruitt says you're a friend of his from West L.A.," Saunders said pleasantly. He was sitting next to Pruitt, across the table from Jessie. "So what's this about?"

"I wanted to ask you a few questions about your partner, Stan Weigund."

Saunders threw Pruitt an irritated look, then faced Jessie again. "If you want to know something about Stan, you'll have to ask him. I'm not his mouthpiece."

"I would, but I understand he's on vacation. I was hoping you might know where he went."

Saunders leaned back and rested his arm on the top of his chair. "Stan didn't tell me where he was going, and I didn't ask."

"It's important that we talk to him."

The detective smiled. "That's the whole idea of a vacation,

Detective Drake. Getting away from your job and everyone connected with it." The friendliness was entirely gone from his voice.

"Where does he hang out?"

Saunders lifted his hands, palms up. "Beats me." He laced his hands behind his head.

"You're his partner. Are you telling me you don't know where he goes to relax? Who his noncop friends are? Where he goes for a beer when he's off duty?"

"Wish I could help, Detective Drake, but Stan's a private kind of guy."

She found it hard to believe him. She didn't know Phil's darkest secrets, and he didn't know hers, but she knew he played poker, and with whom. Knew where he liked to take Maureen, where he took the boys. Knew that he often had a beer after hours at the bar on Olympic near Barrington that many of the West L.A. police officers frequented.

She glanced at Pruitt. His face was impassive. No help there. She turned back to Saunders. "Do you know his wife, Vicky?"

"I've met her," he said, his tone curt.

"I take it you don't like her."

Saunders shrugged.

"I guess that's because she filed a report that your partner physically abused her. He probably wasn't thrilled being investigated by IA."

Saunders sat up and leaned toward her. "IA cleared him, and you know why?" He pointed his finger at Jessie. " 'Cause Stan didn't abuse her. She made that up to get him in trouble. She's crazy. Ask around, Detective. Everyone'll tell you the same thing."

Everyone who had been prepped by Weigund. She wished she knew whether Saunders had believed his partner or was covering his butt. She'd heard that the International Association of Chiefs of Police was planning to recommend holding police officers liable for criminal prosecution if they withheld information about their partners' acts of domestic violence.

"Did Weigund tell you his wife left him a few weeks ago?" she asked.

Saunders lifted his brows. "No shit." He smiled, then nodded. "Good for him. He's better off without her. Maybe that's why he took vacation, to celebrate. Did he say anything to you?" he asked, turning to Pruitt.

Pruitt shook his head.

"I told you he was private," he said, sounding pleased with himself.

Jessie decided he was lying. She was frustrated, angry, then wondered uneasily how she would react if police came and questioned her about Phil.

"I'm going to level with you," she said, watching Saunders's face carefully. "We believe that your partner kidnapped the six-year-old daughter of a radio talk show psychologist and killed the housekeeper."

She saw surprise in his brown eyes, a stiffening of his body. Both of which could have been feigned.

"The one on the news," he said, his voice noncommittal.

"That's right."

He ran his hand across his bearded chin. "How do you know it's him?" he finally asked.

"Someone recognized his voice on the radio." Jessie paused. "I'm surprised you didn't. It was on the television news, too. Local and national."

"I don't listen much to the news." Very calm. "I heard about it, though."

He sounded pensive, troubled. She found it interesting that he hadn't protested Weigund's innocence. Maybe he'd seen danger signs and was thinking about them now, and the fact that he'd ignored them. Weigund using excessive force during arrests or when questioning suspects. Drinking more. She wondered whether Saunders was rethinking his partner's "crazy wife."

"The little girl needs medical attention. That's why we have to find her right away."

Saunders sighed deeply. "I wish I could help."

She believed him. "I know this puts you in a tight spot. You want to be loyal to your partner. I understand that."

"If I knew anything, I'd tell you. Believe me."

"She lost her spleen, and she's running a fever. She could die if she doesn't get an antibiotic."

"I don't know where he is." He sounded impatient now.

"Are you married, Detective Saunders? Do you have kids?"

"I was married. It didn't take." He pushed himself away from the table and rose. "No children. Even if I had kids, I wouldn't know where Weigund is. If that's it?"

"He may call you," she said. "You may feel obligated to tell him we're on to him, because he's your partner. If he does, I hope you'll remember that little girl."

"A cop." Manny Freiberg sighed. "Jesus. That's all we needed. What's his name?"

"Stan Weigund. Do you know him?" She handed him the glossy photo Frank Pruitt had found for her—Weigund, with some other cops, including Saunders, at a Christmas party—and pointed to Weigund. At least she knew what he looked like now. Same blond hair, same face, but harder, older, especially around the eyes.

The police psychologist shook his head and handed back the photo. "Nope."

"Too bad. I thought maybe you'd talked to him when he was investigated by IA."

"Which would make our conversations privileged, Jessie. You know that." Manny smiled lightly. "You're sure he's your guy?"

Jessie nodded. She repeated what she'd learned from Weigund's wife's girlfriend, from Rosalynn Denby, from the Santa Monica PD, from IA.

"And nobody, including the partner, knows where to find him?" Manny rubbed his chin.

"I think his partner's holding out, but that doesn't mean he knows where Weigund is. Frank Pruitt promised to talk to Saunders again, but thinks the partner really may not know anything. And if he did, I don't think he'd tell. The code of silence." What would she do, she wondered again, if Phil were being hunted by the police?

"I heard they're going to play a tape the wife made, asking him to release the little girl," Manny said. "I don't think he will."

"I don't, either. I'm hoping he'll allow someone to deliver the antibiotics."

"Your idea?" Manny thought for a moment. "He'll probably see it as a trap."

"I know. We'll promise to send the stuff with one person, unarmed. He can name the place and the time and the conditions."

"Maybe he'll do it. If you make him feel secure. Depends on his mood, though, which I don't think is great right now."

Jessie frowned. "Why not? He doesn't know we're on to him." She hoped. She crossed her fingers.

"You didn't hear? Apparently Stuart Logan laid into this guy on his show yesterday. Called him all sorts of choice names. They've been playing the tape of the segment all morning. I'm not in Weigund's head, Jessie, but if he's heard the tape, he's probably one pissed-off guy."

"I hope so, Manny. The Logan segment was my idea."

He stared at her. "May I ask why?" he asked quietly.

"I thought if I goaded Weigund into calling Logan's show, we could track him. He knows we put a trap on KMST's lines. He won't expect a trap on Logan's station's lines."

"I see."

His tone, and his frown, made her uneasy. She shifted on her chair. "You don't think it could work?"

"It could work." He nodded. "Or it could set him off in another, more violent direction."

She had a prickling of fear. "Like what?"

"How the hell do I know? We're not talking about someone who's acting or thinking rationally, Jessie. He actually believes that his wife will come back to him."

"Phil thinks he wants her back so he can kill her."

"Phil may be right." Manny paused. "The fact that this guy is an abusive cop just underscores his need to be in control. He's used to being in authority, to calling the shots. You push him, he pushes back. Hard."

What had she done? She licked her lips. "Do you think he'd take it out on Molly? *Do* you?" she repeated urgently when he didn't answer.

"I don't know. What I do know is, you're playing with fire. I wish to God you'd talked to me before you did this." He sounded more sad than angry.

"I had to do something, Manny. We have to get to Molly."

"I know that, too. At least he doesn't know you're on to him."

Not yet. Again, she crossed her fingers. "We've tried limiting the number of people who know about Weigund, but we can't hunt him down without help, and that means telling people. The

Santa Monica detective who handled his arrest knows. IA knows. So does Weigund's partner. And we briefed the CRASH unit at West L.A., and Fugitives."

Manny shook his head. "Too many people. Let's hope they keep their mouths shut so Weigund doesn't hear his name on the four o'clock news."

"Gary knows," Jessie said. "He found out from someone else. As of this morning, he hadn't decided yet whether to go public with this."

"You'd better do everything you can to convince him not to."

"I told him it would be that much harder for us to get Weigund if he knows we're on to him."

Manny grunted. "That's not the worst possibility, Jessie. If Weigund finds out, he'll feel cornered. And if he feels cornered, there's no telling what he'll do. Kill himself, kill Molly."

"Why?" she whispered, realizing, even as she asked, the pointlessness of her question.

"Why not? He has nothing to lose, Jessie. He may as well go out with a bang."

She phoned the *Times* from Manny's office, but Gary wasn't in. She left an urgent message for him to page her.

She said good-bye to Manny, then walked from Parker Center to her car. It was after ten o'clock. Almost two hours before Renee's show, before they played the tape, at least two hours before Weigund—maybe, maybe—would call the show and agree to have someone drop off the antibiotic.

If he called at all.

Leaving downtown and its skyscrapers, she used her cell phone and learned that she had several messages. Three from Barry, one from Helen. And she still hadn't returned calls to her mother, who was probably wondering if she'd fallen off the face of the earth.

Barry answered on the first ring. "I've been calling and calling," he complained when he heard her voice. "I don't know what's going on!"

"You know as much as I do, Barry." Hardly the truth. "I assume you heard that Vicky sent a tape to KMST?"

"Big deal. He's not going to release Molly just because his wife sent a tape."

"Probably not." She turned left onto the ramp leading to the

Harbor Freeway. "But I'm hoping he'll allow someone to drop off the amoxicillin."

"Let me do it."

"Absolutely not."

"I'm the one who helped him kidnap Molly. Please, Jessie. I need to do this."

"No way. I understand how you feel, but even if I agreed, my lieutenant would never go for it. It has to be a cop." She merged with the traffic, then sped up.

"I'm the perfect person, Jessie. He'll be suspicious of a cop. He'll think maybe it's a setup. He won't be afraid of me."

"I'm sorry, Barry."

"Think about it, at least."

"I'll think about it," she lied. She could imagine Espes's face if she suggested the idea.

She promised him she'd keep him informed of any developments, then hung up. Turning on the radio, she settled back against the seat cushion.

" '. . . so mean and scary, I could kill your kid.' "

She shut the radio and drove.

(((**54**)))

The synagogue was on Pico, just east of Beverwil. Jessie parked several blocks away and walked quickly to the small building, tucked between a dry cleaner's and a children's clothing boutique.

She opened the wide door and stepped into a narrow hall, not sure where to find the women's section Ezra had told her about. A little girl was standing on tiptoe and leaning over a water fountain, trying to capture the jet of water that arced and spluttered and dribbled down her chin onto the lacy front of her dress.

Jessie waited for her to finish, then followed her, through another door to her left, into a long, narrow area. To her right was a short wall made up of series of wood panels, topped with latticework. The *mechitzah*, Ezra had said. The partition that divided the sanctuary.

The women's section was elevated, and Jessie could see the burgundy-velvet-draped ark where she knew the Torah scrolls were housed. In the center of the men's section was a velvet-draped, raised platform. Around it were several tallit-wrapped men, one of whom was reading in Hebrew from what she assumed was the Torah portion. The tune was mournful. Or maybe it was her mood.

The upholstered seats—only a few were unoccupied—were filled with children and young girls and, mostly, with women wearing hats. So many hats. She'd locked her purse in the trunk of her car, and her gun was hidden by the taupe jacket of her suit, but she felt conspicuous as she stood in the doorway and searched for Dafna, wondering how she would recognize her in this multicolored sea of straw and felt. And then Dafna was looking right at her, a small-brimmed navy hat framing her thin, lovely face, her eyes bright with welcome.

287

Dafna smiled and waved. A moment later she was at Jessie's side. "I'm glad you made it," she said. "Ezra wasn't sure you were coming. There aren't any seats next to me, but—"

"I can't stay long," Jessie whispered. "I'm so sorry I didn't call, Dafna. I'm investigating a case, and to be honest, I forgot all about the holiday."

"The Altman kidnapping." Dafna sighed. "Ezra told me. He also said you're close friends with the family. This must be especially hard for you, Jessie."

It was all hard, wearying. It was Molly's kidnapping, and Vicky Weigund's story. It was Silo's stupidity and greed that had led them to Noreen Gelbart's killers. Simms and Boyd had picked up Wayne Gelbart and Joey Montrose this morning.

It was the wife of the slain rug dealer who had sat, huddled in fear as Jessie had talked to her, again, just before coming here. It was the cases she'd already solved, the ones she never would, the ones that hadn't yet come across her desk.

It was why she'd come here, Jessie realized, not just to apologize to Dafna and Ezra, but to find some solace, some renewal of her spirit. Maybe that was asking too much.

The reader had stopped, and Jessie heard the expanding hum of conversation. She looked around the room. "I guess I'd better go."

"Can you stay awhile? They're finishing the haftorah reading, from Prophets. After that they'll blow the shofar."

There were more cousins of the Iranian to question, and in about an hour or so, KMST would be playing Vicky's taped conversation. "I'd like that," she said.

Dafna found her a seat between two older women, both of whom smiled genially at Jessie, then returned their attention to their Rosh Hashanah prayer books. Jessie held the book Dafna had given her, opened to the Torah reading.

Another male—not the reader—recited a blessing. Jessie was pleased that she understood some of the words, but when the room quieted and the reader resumed, she was lost and felt suddenly isolated.

The woman to her right was running her finger, right to left, below a line of Hebrew words that her lips formed easily. Jessie watched her a moment, curious, envious, then looked at her own prayer book and read in English the story of Hannah, the barren wife of Elkanah, who vowed that if God would bless her with a child, she would dedicate his life to the service of God.

Another pause, another blessing. The reader continued. Could you make a bargain with God? she wondered. And if so, what bargain could Renee make to save her child? She sat, thinking about Molly, then about Helen and her unborn child, about her own miscarriage, and was taken by surprise when the congregation rose as one. She stood, too, and saw through the lattice that someone had lifted the Torah scroll high above his head.

She followed the lead of the people around her. Sitting, rising again. Hoping she was blending in. Dafna turned around and smiled at her encouragingly from time to time.

Someone—the rabbi, she assumed—spoke about the redemptive power of the shofar, then instructed the congregation that there was to be no talking from the first blast until the hundredth one, after the completion of the Mussaf, or additional, service.

Ezra had brought a shofar to class two weeks ago. She had touched the smooth, yellowed gray and white surface of the long, twisted ram's horn. The women, and the men, on the other side of the partition, were saying a prayer. She listened to the soft murmur of voices and waited with rising expectancy, hoping she wouldn't be disappointed, though she didn't exactly know what she expected.

The rabbi recited several blessings, then a voice called out in the absolute silence. Ezra's voice, surer and stronger than she'd ever heard it in class.

"*Tekiah.*"

The long, single blast pierced the stillness of the room. She shut her eyes.

"*Shevarim.*"

Three shorter, firm clarion calls.

"*Teruah.*"

A staccato of nine sounds.

The pattern was repeated, then varied, with different permutations of the three types of shofar sounds, and she wanted the sounds to continue. The "*teruah*" with its rapid, machine-gun insistence. The "*shevarim,*" stark, unadorned, bold. And the "*tekiah,*" for her the most moving: mournful and proud, sharp in its clarity, primitive, profound. She heard in it the panicked wail of the ram, snared by its horns in a bush; the exquisite relief and joy of Abraham, who had been spared at this last minute from sacrificing his beloved son and could now serve his God by offering up the ram in Isaac's place; the awesome, unfathomable nature of God and His creations. Her heart was pounding harder, and she felt a connection to everyone around her that transcended language and experience.

"*Tekiah gedolah.*"

The grand *tekiah.*

She heard another sound, and realized it was her pager. She shut it off quickly and, her face crimson, murmured an apology and slipped out of the row.

It was Gary. She hurried to her car and retrieved her cell phone from her purse in the trunk.

"You said it was urgent," he said when he came on the line.

"I'm asking you not to go with the story, Gary."

"Jessie—"

"Hear me out. Manny Freiberg thinks if Weigund knows we're on to him, it could set him over the edge, and there's no telling what he'll do to Molly."

"I'm sorry, Jess. It's too late."

She bit her lip, frustrated, angry, disappointed in him. "You printed it?"

"It'll be all over the media within the hour. We got an anonymous call at the *Times*, apparently right after the networks got the same call. It's out of my hands, Jessie. I had no choice but to go with the full story."

Who had told? Newell from IA? Saunders? There were too many possibilities.

"I'm sorry," he repeated. He sounded upset.

"I believe you. Thanks, Gary."

She said good-bye and flipped the cell phone shut, then sat in her car, trying to comprehend why someone would identify Weigund to the media. Gary hadn't heard this from one of his usual sources, and all the media had been informed almost simultaneously. No scoop, no quid pro quo.

Unless, she thought, the person's goal hadn't been to notify the media. Suppose Weigund had disappeared without telling anyone where he could be reached, not even his partner or close friends. Suppose someone wanted to warn him he'd been made.

What better way to make certain he found out?

((**55**))

At ten after twelve he turned on the radio and raised the volume on the television, which he'd had on all day. Earlier the anchorwoman had promised a live feed into KMST, and there it was, right on TV, the end of the fifteen-minute daily segment that began at noon.

"We're standing by," the anchor said.

And there was Dr. Renee's voice, on the radio and on the TV, welcoming her dumb audience and sounding twice as cool, he had to hand it to her. As though nothing was going on, as though her kid wasn't burning up with fever, not his fault, not his problem.

". . . play a tape of a conversation recorded by your wife, Hank."

On the television screen the large photo of Dr. Renee was replaced by a graphic of a woman holding a child's hand.

"The tape should start any second now," the invisible anchor stated to fill the momentary silence, and Weigund wanted to yell at her to shut the hell up, this wasn't some effing Olympics where they needed her stupid commentary, for Christ's sake.

"Honey, this is Vicky," the soft voice began shakily.

He froze, clenched his jaw. That was her, all right.

"I feel so terrible about all this," she said. "I know you're hurting, that you didn't mean for all this to happen."

"Damn right," he muttered. Not his fault, not his problem.

"I know you don't want that little girl to die, Stan, just like you wouldn't want anything bad to happen to Andy."

"*My* son," he hissed, glaring at the screen. His hands tightened into fists. "You took away *my son,* you bitch. What made you think you could get away with that, huh?"

"Andy loves you, Stan. He wants so badly to be proud of you, and you can do that, honey. You can let someone drop off the medicine that little girl needs. That's all you have to do, Stan. And if you do that, I promise I'll talk to you. I promise, Stan."

He hadn't really paid attention to the rest of her words, because it dawned on him that she'd called him Stan. So now they knew his name wasn't Hank, like he'd said.

Not that it mattered. They still didn't know who he was, they were still running like rats in a goddamned maze.

"You have goodness in you, Stan. You have decency. I know you're feeling trapped, but I also know you want to do the right thing. I'll talk to you, Stan, I'll listen to whatever you have to say. Please let them give you the medicine, honey. Please, please, help that little girl."

He heard static through the radio and the TV, then Dr. Renee's voice.

". . . nothing to lose," she said. "The police have agreed to deliver the amoxicillin. All you have to do is name the time and the place, Hank. But please, for Molly's sake, do it soon. I'm waiting for your call, Hank. I know you want to do the right thing."

He switched off the radio and turned his attention to the anchor, whose face once again filled the screen.

". . . take you once again to Patricia Alizondo, reporting live from the studios of KMST, where this tape was just played on air for the very first time. Patricia?"

The screen showed the reporter against a background of hundreds of people, most of them holding candles.

"As you can see, Diane, hundreds and hundreds of people here and around the world are showing their support for little Molly Altman and her family. Yesterday they stayed through the night, holding a candlelight vigil. Tonight they plan to do the same and join in prayer for Molly Altman's safe return."

"Any word from the police, Patricia?"

"They are hopeful that the kidnapper will hear and heed his wife's plea, Diane. Standing with me now is Detective Jessica Drake of the West L.A. Division, who is heading this investigation."

The camera showed a shot of the reporter and a dark-haired, pretty woman wearing a suit.

"Detective Drake, what message do you want to give the kidnapper?"

"Hey, Detective Jessica Drake, what message do you want to give *me*, sweetheart?" Weigund smirked.

"I want to assure him that we will make no attempt to apprehend him," Jessie said. "Our goal is to ensure that Molly Altman receives the medicine she needs. He can call the station, or call KMST, and advise us where and when we should deliver the antibiotic. And we will do it. We are ready and eager to cooperate with him."

"Thank you, Detective Drake," the reporter said. "So there you have it . . ."

"Damn right, you're eager," Weigund muttered.

". . . a poignant moment none of us will ever forget," the reporter said somberly. "And now the question remains, will the kidnapper respond to his wife's heartfelt plea and accept the medicine that can save little Molly Altman's life? That's what Dr. Renee Altman and her husband are hoping. That's what we're all hoping. Back to you, Diane."

"Thank you, Patricia. This just in: We've received news that the kidnapper has been identified. His name is Stan Weigund . . ."

He stared at the screen. "Son of a bitch!" he whispered.

". . . with the elite Robbery-Homicide division of the Los Angeles Police Department. A shocking development, in an already shocking case."

Weigund frowned. So what if they knew who he was? He was smarter than most of the cops he'd ever worked with. Faster thinking, too.

". . . tuned to this channel for developments. We have with us again renowned family therapist Dr. Gerald Kanton. Dr. Kanton, how does this information impact on what we already know?"

"Well, Diane, as you said, this is a shocking development, one . . ."

Weigund jabbed the power button on the remote, and the screen sizzled to blackness. He sat on the sofa for a moment, then went into the kitchen, picked up the wall phone receiver, and punched numbers. A woman answered.

He told her whom he wanted.

A few minutes later a man came on the line and identified himself.

"It's me," Weigund said. "Can you talk?"

Silence. "You okay?"

"I've been better. When did they make me?"

"Yesterday. I leaked it to the media, so you'd know."

Weigund grunted his thanks. "How'd they make me?"

"Some woman. A friend of your wife's. You shouldn't call

here," he said anxiously, his voice almost inaudible. "I told you that last time."

Trudy. Weigund's jaw tightened. "Do they know where Vicky is?"

"Not so far as I know."

"Who delivered the tape?"

"I don't know."

"Find out."

"Leave it be," the man urged. "You're never going to win this one. You know that."

"I need your help, man. I have to see my kid. You can understand that."

"The best help I can give you is to tell you to get away before they catch you. Get the hell out of this country while you still can."

"They're never going to catch me."

"This detective, Jessica Drake. She's determined to bring you down."

He laughed. "I'm shaking, I'm so scared. I saw her on TV. She looks hot, doesn't she?"

"She's smart."

"I'm smarter. Is this a trap they're setting with the medicine?"

"I don't think so. Why don't you disappear, then call in and tell them where you left the kid? Why don't you do that?"

"Find out about the tape. I'll call you in two hours."

"Don't call here."

"I'm counting on you, man. I don't want to hurt Vicky. I just want to see my kid. Don't let me down."

((56))

"I'm getting married in two weeks, Dr. Renee, and I have a real problem with the person my fiancé asked to be his best man."

"And what is that, Amanda?"

"Basically, he's a sleaze."

"Define 'sleaze.' "

"He's gross. He makes off-color remarks to me and my friends when he drinks, which is most of the time. Last week, a few of us were in a restaurant together, and he simulated a sex act. It was disgusting."

"How did your fiancé react?"

"He laughed. When I told him later how upset I was, he said Jack—that's the friend—is just a clown, that he doesn't mean any harm. He said he'd talk to him and tell him to behave better around me. The thing is, when we're alone, my fiancé is so different. He's sensitive and sophisticated. When he gets together with Jack, he turns into an immature kid."

"Are you having a religious wedding, Amanda, or a ceremony in front of a justice of the peace?"

"We're having a church wedding."

"Well, then, you're perfectly entitled to want a best man who respects and demonstrates the values and morals and spiritual refinement you're celebrating on this holy occasion. So yes, I think you should tell your fiancé that you're not happy with his choice of best man. But I have to be honest, Amanda. Even if he goes along with what you want, you may have a bigger problem."

"I don't understand."

"Yes, you do. You just don't want to face it. Pigs don't flock to swans, honey. Think about that before you walk down the aisle."

★   ★   ★

Harris was sitting on a chair next to Phil's bed when Jessie entered the hospital room.

"Hey," Phil said. "About time you got here."

"Hey, yourself." She still couldn't get used to seeing Phil in a hospital bed.

Harris had craned his neck toward the doorway. "He was just askin' about you, Jessie." He stood and hiked up his jeans, almost in slow motion. "Chair's all set for you."

"Don't leave on my account," Jessie felt compelled to say.

"Got to get back to the station." He faced Phil and gave him a high five. "Take care now, pardner."

Jessie rolled her eyes and caught Phil's frown. Suppressing a smile, she waited until Harris left the room, then approached the bed.

"I brought you these." She held a bouquet of sunflowers in front of her, then laid them on the adjustable swing table, next to a pitcher of water.

"I was hoping for chocolate," he grumbled.

She studied his face, decided he looked a little drawn, a little pale. "Hospitals can kill you," her father's mother, Louise, had once told her and Helen. Jessie dismissed the thought.

"You sound tired. Maybe you're having too much company."

"Not that much. Simms and Boyd stopped by right after you left this morning. Espes phoned, said he'd stop by tonight. Oh, and your ex-boyfriend called a while ago."

"Gary?"

"Frank Pruitt." He looked at her with interest. "Gary was here in the morning."

She knew her face was flushed, but she didn't want to talk about Gary right now. Too painful. "What did Pruitt want?"

"He was looking for you. He'd called the station, and they told him you might be here." He smiled.

She found this puzzling. "Did he say what he wanted?"

"Something about Weigund. He said it wasn't a big deal, he'd talk to you later. A big talker, Pruitt. He'd probably still be jabbering if the nurses hadn't come in and taken me down for a test. They wear you out."

"The nurses or the tests?" she asked, and was rewarded with a smile. She wondered what Pruitt had for her. "How's Maureen?"

"In her element. She's been here all morning, fussing over me like a turkey. She stepped out to grab something to eat when

Lou showed up. She brought the boys here on the way to school. I could tell they felt better after they saw me. Pretty scary all around," he said lightly, belying the seriousness in his eyes.

"Pretty scary," she echoed.

He yawned and covered his mouth.

"I'm going." She stood. "I'll come back tonight."

"First tell me what's happening. I'm bored out of my mind."

"Five minutes, and I'm out of here." She sat down again. "Okay. Simms and Boyd picked up Joey Montrose and Wayne Gelbart. Joey caved in all of two minutes and copped a plea. Espes is happy as a pig in mud."

"What about the Iranian?"

"I questioned the wife. She's scared but won't talk. I just talked to a cousin, who said he'd heard that the victim was smuggling contraband into the country and paying off some gang. But the cousin doesn't have any names, just hearsay."

Phil nodded. "And Dr. Renee's kid? Lou said KMST played a tape the kidnapper's mom made."

"Along with all the networks. Probably got higher ratings than Princess Di's wedding and funeral combined. We're waiting to hear from Weigund, see if he'll go for it."

"Think he will?"

She shrugged. "Did Lou also tell you the media revealed Weigund's identity and informed the world that he's a cop?"

"Uh-huh. What about the wife's friend, the one who fingered Weigund? Think she's in danger?"

"She skipped, according to Rondell. He sent two units to her house yesterday to make sure she was okay. The place was empty. A neighbor told them Trudy said she was leaving town for a while."

Phil grunted. "Smart woman. So how are you getting along with Lou?"

"Fine."

"You're sure?"

"Why? Did he say something? Come on, Phil. Give."

"Lou is kind of hurt, Jessie. He figured he'd go along with you, now that I'm stuck here, but he says every time he offers, you brush him off."

"It isn't personal," she lied. "It just takes longer to explain everything than do it myself."

"He's lonely, Jess. He feels unwanted."

"Maybe if he'd stop calling everybody 'pardner' he'd have one."

Phil sighed.

"Okay, you're right," she said. "I'm being mean. But do me a favor, will you? Get the hell out of this hospital bed and back where you belong."

"She likes me, she really likes me." Phil grinned and yawned again.

She left to get a makeshift vase for the flowers. When she returned, he was fast asleep.

Jessie was in her car, halfway back to the station, when she heard the voice she'd come to recognize and loathe.

"Dr. Renee, it's LAPD'S finest," Weigund said. "Doesn't that make you feel all secure?"

"I'm glad you called, Stan," Renee said. "You're doing the right thing."

How could she be so calm? Jessie marveled.

"Short and sweet, Doc. Two-fifteen, near the Santa Monica pier. I want the very fine Detective Drake to be waiting in her car with the pills in a clear plastic bag. Radio on, listening to KMST for further instructions. How are the ratings these days, Doc? Jumping right out of the stratosphere, I'll bet. And you haven't even said thank you."

Jessie was startled at hearing her name, but nodded. He'd probably seen her on television. Now he had a face for his "enemy." She checked her watch. An hour or so to pick up amoxicillin from Renee's house and get to the pier. Plenty of time, if there was no traffic. But if he announced the drop site on the radio, they'd have an impossible situation on their hands, trying to control the lookers and the media.

"That's just an hour from now, Stan," Renee said. "Someone has to get the antibiotic, and I have to locate Detective Drake."

"I'd make it earlier, but I have another appointment to keep. Hey, you're the one who keeps saying how urgent this is, Doc. And it is, I'm sorry to tell you. Your little girl's burning up. Eyes kind of glassy, skin way too pink."

He wasn't even human, Jessie decided, gripping the steering wheel. She wondered if he was exaggerating the urgency of Molly's condition.

"I want the detective in shorts and a tank top, or a bathing suit, if she wants to grab a tan. No purse, no bag, no hat, no visor. No boots. Nothing that can remotely conceal a weapon. Not that any of my colleagues would ever double-cross me."

Pruitt had said Weigund was smart.

One of the officers in Renee's home could drop off the amoxicillin at Jessie's. That would save time while she changed clothes. Whoever provided backup would need the right clothes, too.

"What if I don't find her in time?" Renee asked.

"I'm sure she's listening right now and heading over to the nearest pharmacy. And Doc, this is your one chance. I know there's going to be twenty cops covering Detective Drake, and that's cool. But somebody takes me down, dead or alive, you'll never find your little girl in time to save her. Same if somebody follows me. Somebody does that, I'll know it. I'm a very, very good police officer, Dr. Renee. You'd better believe that."

"I believe you, Stan."

"Yo, security guys. I'm using another cell phone, so take your time running down the call. I lifted the unit right out of an unlocked Jeep Cherokee. People are so careless these days, don't you think, Dr. Renee?"

Harris rode with Jessie in her Honda, back-seat driving all the way until she thought she'd scream. Simms and Boyd followed, along with six other units from West L.A.

She arrived at the pier at 2:09 and parked on the east side of Pacific Coast Highway. Her radio was tuned to KMST, and she was grateful that Harris had the sense not to talk.

At 2:17 he still hadn't called. What if it's a game? Jessie wondered, half listening to Renee counsel a young woman undecided about having breast implants to please her boyfriend. Or what if he couldn't get through to KMST?

The thought worried her, and she was about to phone the station to make sure Alicia was keeping a line open when she heard Renee say his name.

"Hey, Doc. Hey, Detective Drake. Great day for the beach, isn't it?" Weigund chuckled. "I hope to hell you're listening, Detective, 'cause I'm not doing reruns. Drive to Venice, no sirens. Park in the corner lot of Ocean Front Walk and Market and go to the boardwalk. I'll find you."

"There's gonna be a mob scene," Harris said. "All the idiots listening to the show who live anywhere near here are gonna show up. Not to mention the media."

She had the same worries. She radioed Rondell at Santa Monica, apprised him of the situation, and asked him to send enough units to Market and Ocean Front Walk to clear the area of media and gawkers. She started the engine and did a quick U-turn in the middle of the palm-lined boulevard. Simms and the others, she saw, pulled behind her but kept their distance.

"Maybe they can trace him now," Lou said quietly.

She shook her head. "He's probably still using the cell

phone." No reason he wouldn't do so until they found out who it belonged to and shut down the account.

She radioed Simms. He and Boyd and two of the West L.A. units would drive ahead and park farther back, then position themselves on the boardwalk. The four other West L.A. officers would help Santa Monica keep the lookers and media away.

She drove slowly, thinking how any other day she'd love to be here at the beach, walking along the shore, swimming. With Gary. The thought crept into her mind and she quickly dismissed it. She took Pacific and made a right turn onto Market and parked in the lot. One of the unmarked cars was already there.

The boardwalk and beach were crowded with tourists and locals, young and not so young. Some were playing volleyball on the sand. Others were searching for souvenirs at the corner kiosk or watching one of the local artists. Still others were bicycling or Rollerblading. Hard to believe it was a workday, Jessie thought with envy as she waited anxiously.

She recognized two officers in cutoff jeans and colorful T-shirts. They jogged over to the sand and began tossing a Frisbee back and forth. Boyd, a bare-chested hunk in cargo shorts, stopped at the kiosk and was trying on sunglasses. Simms was last. Wearing a black T-shirt and jeans and a red bandanna tied around his forehead, he looked swarthy and mean, like Captain Hook. But he fit right in. On the boardwalk, you'd have to be in a suit or an evening gown to draw attention. And even then . . . Simms sat on the sidewalk and played his harmonica.

Amazing that they'd pulled it together in less than an hour. She hoped no one screwed up.

Harris would stay in the car, in radio contact with the station. Jessie waited another minute for good measure, then opened her car door and stepped out, the clear plastic bag with the amoxicillin pills in her hand.

It was hot and sunny. She squinted into the bright light and, making her way slowly to the boardwalk, looked casually around her to see if she could spot Weigund, knowing she probably wouldn't.

She stood on the boardwalk, pretending to watch the volleyball game in progress. She didn't know what direction Weigund would come from, and she felt more vulnerable than usual, dressed in a halter top and shorts and sandals. But Simms and Boyd and the others had her in their sights, ready to bring Weigund down if he became dangerous, which she didn't think would happen. He'd come here to do them a favor.

And just in case, she had her key chain. The keys dangled

from a yawara stick concealed in her clenched fist: a black Lucite four-inch-long round dowel with grooves, used in martial arts.

Three little girls, two black and one white, were taking turns with a hula hoop. A pencil of a woman strolled toward Jessie, an infant strapped to her chest. Around her teenage boys whizzed by on Rollerblades. She and Gary had talked about getting blades, for the exercise and for the recreation. She decided she'd get a pair anyway, maybe this weekend.

A towheaded boy on blades zoomed past her. A moment later he reappeared and, without stopping, snatched the plastic bag from her hand.

"Hey!" she protested, about to go after him, then realized that Weigund had obviously sent him.

She watched the boy speed along the boardwalk and saw him come to a full stop several hundred feet ahead, in front of a tall blond man, to whom he handed the plastic bag.

The man—Weigund, obviously—raised the bag and waved it at Jessie, then saluted her. From a distance, it was hard to read his expression, but she knew he was grinning. She didn't blame him. He was thumbing his nose at her, at all of them, getting off on the fact that they had him within their grasp but couldn't do a damn thing about it.

Catch me if you can.

They'd debated trying to follow him—Simms had pushed hard to do it—but Espes had decided it was too risky. Weigund had said he would know, and Jessie, for one, believed him. She was filled with helplessness and frustration, then reminded herself that although Weigund had won this round, so had Molly. The most important thing right now was to get the medication to her.

Weigund waved again, turned around, and trotted off.

That was it. Jessie took a few steps toward the parking lot, swallowing resignation, and saw a man wearing a baseball cap emerge from under the awning of one of the boardwalk shops and race in Weigund's direction. She'd had only a fleeting glimpse of his face, shadowed by the cap's visor, but there was something familiar about him. She gasped with recognition a second before the man screamed, "Weigund, wait!"

Barry. "You idiot," she hissed in an undertone.

Weigund, still moving, looked over his shoulder, then straight ahead, and continued at the same unhurried pace.

"Take *me*, Weigund!" Barry called.

Simms had jumped up and was at her side. So was Boyd. The two officers playing Frisbee had their hands on their concealed weapons. She motioned them to stay, did the same to Simms and Boyd, and started running after Barry.

"Let him go, Barry!"

"Take *me* instead of Molly!" he yelled. "You don't need a sick child on your hands."

He was gaining on Weigund, and she wondered why Weigund didn't run faster. Barry was about fifty feet away when Weigund suddenly stopped and turned around.

"Please!" Barry pleaded, closing the distance. "Let Molly come home!"

Weigund slipped his hand inside his jacket. A gun, Jessie thought, her heart racing faster than her legs.

"Barry, stay back. Weigund, you don't have to do this!"

Weigund's hand emerged, holding the plastic bag. He spilled the pills into his palm, raised his arm high, and flung them into the stiff breeze toward the sand.

"No!" Barry screamed.

"You're such a loser, Altman. You keep messing up." Weigund turned and resumed his trot.

The man was a monster. "Wait, Weigund!" she yelled. "Don't take this out on the little girl!"

Weigund waved behind him.

Barry was on his knees, scrambling frantically in the sand. A moment later he was up and running again, his hand clenched around the pills he'd salvaged.

"I have the pills, Weigund! You said you'd take them!"

Weigund's gait quickened.

"Take them to Molly, goddamn it!" Barry screamed.

Weigund was far ahead now, his figure becoming smaller with every second.

An absolute monster, she thought as Barry sank onto his knees on the boardwalk and buried his head in his hands.

((·**58**·))

A Venice Beach local had caught everything on videotape.

"Figures," Jessie said aloud in her bedroom.

She switched off the radio with an angry jab and changed back into her street clothes. She was disgusted with the local, who had probably already peddled his historic reel for big bucks to one of the networks.

She was disgusted, too, with the way things had turned out. Part of her was furious with Barry for screwing everything up, but that part fought with the intense pity she felt for the poor son of a bitch. Nothing she or anyone could possibly say was worse than what he was telling himself. She couldn't begin to imagine Renee's reaction, admitted to herself she wasn't up to phoning her friend to find out.

Simms didn't feel an iota of pity for Barry. He'd used some choice words to his face right there on the boardwalk—which, no doubt, would sound great on the video when it was played on network TV sometime this afternoon or evening. He'd wanted to arrest him for interfering in a police investigation, had been that close to punching Barry before Boyd had pulled him away.

Simms was angry at her, too. "I could've stopped the jerk," he'd said, meaning Barry. "And the kid would've had the pills."

Maybe Simms could have run faster than she had, though she had her doubts. She was pretty damn fast; even her academy instructors had told her so. And she had the feeling that from the minute Barry had started running after Weigund and pleading with him, the cop had already decided to toss the pills.

Simms was probably reporting to Espes right now, blaming her. She would have driven straight to the station, but she'd had to come home first to change. The only good part was that Harris had gone back with Simms and Boyd. Another car ride with him next to her, directing her every two minutes, would have been cruel and unusual punishment, no matter what she'd promised Phil.

She thought again about how close they'd come to success, to getting the pills to Molly. She didn't think Weigund was angry about what had happened. Annoyed, if anything, but just for the moment. And then he'd enjoyed the despair to which he'd reduced Barry, reveled in his pain.

That was probably what life had been like, most days, for Vicky Weigund.

Jessie wondered whether Vicky would be willing to make another plea for Molly's release. She could send another tape or, better yet, talk to Weigund on Renee's program.

She picked up the phone to call Rosalynn Denby, then returned the receiver to the cradle. In person was better.

The same car was in the driveway—a white convertible Mercedes. Jessie rang the bell and waited, then rang again. Maybe Rosalynn had gone for a walk.

She was about to return to her car and wait awhile when she heard a crash. She pressed her ear to the wide door. "Ms. Denby?"

Frowning, she tried peering into the front rooms, but the wide plantation shutters were closed. She walked around to the back of the house and looked through the windows of what looked like a den.

Everything seemed in order.

Back in front, she rang the bell again and called Rosalynn Denby's name, and heard what sounded like a faint moan.

She twisted the front doorknob and found the door unlocked. She drew her gun and her breath, pushed the door open, and stepped cautiously inside the house.

"Ms. Denby?" Her voice echoed in the marble-floored entry.

A stronger moan, coming from her right.

Still wary, she crossed the entry and stepped down into the living room where Rosalynn Denby had served her tea late yesterday.

Now she was lying near a white baby grand piano, next to a shattered crystal vase and a fringed lace cloth that Jessie had noticed yesterday on the piano. She'd probably pulled on the cloth to topple the vase and attract Jessie's attention. Loose, wilted flowers were strewn on the hardwood floor in a pool of water too shallow to do them any good.

Jessie knelt at Rosalynn's side and phoned 911. The woman's pulse was strong, but her breathing sounded labored. Jessie had no way of knowing whether there were any internal injuries or bleeding.

"The paramedics will be here within minutes," she told Rosalynn, holding her hand.

Rosalynn rapidly blinked her open eye.

Jessie found it painful to look at her. Her face, so china-doll pretty yesterday, was bruised and bloodied, and one of her eyes was swollen shut. Around her neck were angry welts, visible above the corded drape tassel that she'd managed to loosen. Her light brown hair, underneath the black wig that lay several feet away, was short and thinning and caked with blood. Her left arm was bent at an impossible angle. Jessie assumed it was broken.

"Can you tell me what happened, Rosalynn?"

"Weigund," she whispered, and winced. "Hurts." A tear trickled out of the corner of her less bruised eye.

"When did this happen, Rosalynn?"

"Don't . . . know." She drew in a few shallow breaths. "Blacked out . . ." She touched her hand gingerly to her throat.

Weigund had mentioned having another "appointment." Jessie found it pathologically fascinating, and terrifying, that nothing in his face had indicated he'd come straight from battering Rosalynn Denby to pick up medicine for a little girl.

"I'm so sorry," Jessie said. "I don't know how he got to you." As far as she knew, Rosalynn's name hadn't been mentioned by any of the media. "He tried to force you to tell him where to find Vicky? Is that what happened?"

Rosalynn's nod was an almost imperceptible movement of her chin. A proud smile played around her trembling lips.

"Didn't tell," she mouthed.

((•59•))

"So what are you saying, Stuart? That the government take away all the guns from law-abiding citizens? The gangsters and the crazies will *still* have them, and where will we be? Dead, that's where."

"You have Jell-O for brains, you know that, Don? What do you do, watch *Gunsmoke* reruns all day? Go outside your house looking for a shoot-out?"

"Come on, Stuart. Look at the issue."

"Issue *this*, man. The likelihood of a guy needing a gun to defend himself is zip compared to the probability that he's gonna shoot himself with it. Or that his kid is gonna find the piece and take it to school for a little show and tell, or pop little Tommy 'cause he won't share his yo-yo."

"You're picking on a few tragic but isolated incidents, Stuart. You're being unfair."

"And you're a moron, Don-don. You and Charlton Heston and all the other 'everybody's-entitled-to-an-AK-47' bozos in the Neurotic Robocops of America." Logan ended the call. "Ray, does somebody have an acting role for Charlie? Get his mind back on track."

"Can't think of anything offhand, Stu."

"Maybe Lemon and Matthau need a third for their *Grumpy Old Men* flicks." He pressed another line. "Simone, from Las Vegas. Sexy name. You're on with Stuart Logan. How are you, sweetheart?"

"Great, Stuart. I'm calling about your comment yesterday about the guy with the pit bull."

"First things first, Simone. You're from Vegas, huh? So what are you, an exotic dancer? How do those tassels stay on, anyway?"

307

She laughed. "Actually, I'm a high-school teacher."

"Say it ain't so, Simone." Logan sighed loudly. "A guy's gotta have his fantasies. So what's on the Las Vegas curriculum these days? Roulette? Lap dancing?"

"Lap*tops*. I teach computers. There's more to the city than casinos and showgirls, Stuart."

"Yeah, like people get *Playboy* for the articles. You know, I could use some computer ed. How about it, Simone? Teach me to megabyte?"

"You'd have to enroll in my class, Stuart, and to be honest, I don't know if you'd pass the entrance exam."

"Ouch! Talk about pit bulls. So what's your comment, Miss Grundy? You think these dogs should take a class in anger management, right?"

"I think the dog that mauled the child should be killed, Stuart. But I also think the owners should be held responsible. These aren't average pets."

"I hear you, Simone. Class dismissed." He disconnected the caller. "Ray, no more calls about dogs, okay? No cats, either, or snakes. Speaking of which, what's the latest on our guy, Hank?"

"His name is Stan."

"Right. Stan. Probably short for Stanley. No wonder he changed his name. Stanley, macho man, doesn't cut it. Can you believe he's a cop, Ray? Doesn't that make you feel warm all over? Did they air the video of that beach scene yet?"

"Not as far as I know, Stu."

"They got the whole damn thing on tape. So now we're gonna have all these experts analyzing the tape, frame by frame."

"I feel sorry for the dad."

"That moron? What the hell did he think he was doing, running after Stanley?"

"I heard he offered to take his little girl's place."

"That poor son of a bitch. I wouldn't want to be in his shoes." Logan sighed. "I could've told him Stanley wouldn't go for it. Not that sorry excuse for a man. I'll bet he had no intention of taking those pills. He was just jerking them all off, having fun. Moron." He snorted and pressed a line. "Ebala, in El Monte. What the hell kind of name is that, man?"

"I do not know what it means, Stuart. It has been in my family for generations."

"Well, ditch it, man. It sounds like that virus Dustin Hoffman saved us from."

"I find your comment offensive, to be telling the truth."

"Just trying to help. So Ebe, what about this cop, Stanley? Do you think he intended to take the medicine for the kid?"

"Actually, Stuart, I am calling you to discuss about the gun-control issue."

"Hey, man, this is my show, know what I mean? About the cop. He did or he didn't."

"I am not prepared to give an opinion on this matter."

"Well, I am not prepared to continue this call. Change the name, Ebe, and lose the accent. All this talk about multiculturalism, but the truth is, you have to blend, baby, blend." Logan chose another line. "Olivia in Simi Valley, what's happening?"

"Hi, Stuart. My husband's a police officer, and I just wanted to say that he and all his colleagues are horrified by Stan Weigund."

"So does your husband know this guy?"

"No."

"Any of his friends know him?"

"Not that I know."

"Thanks for the call, Olivia. Ray, you know what I'm thinking? I wanna hear from cops who *do* know big, bad Stanley. Cops, or some fine citizens he's pulverized. Or maybe his high-school sweetheart, or his neighbor. Let's find out all about this guy, see what makes him tick." Logan selected a line. "Felice, you're on with Stuart Logan."

"Hey, Stuart. I've been listening to your show, and I want to say that you'll never know the whole story about this police detective unless you talk to him."

"Well, let him call the show, Felice. I'm open-minded, isn't that right, Ray?"

"Absolutely."

"I'm willing to listen to the guy try to explain why he beat his wife, killed a woman, and kidnapped a little girl. I'm sure he has a good reason. We just don't know it. Is that what you think, Felice?"

"You're being sarcastic, as always, Stuart."

"Come on, sweetheart. I'm willing to listen, but Stan's not going to call. You know why? 'Cause he has nothing to say for himself. Not one damn thing. *Nada.* And he doesn't have the guts to talk one on one with Stuart Logan. No *cojones,* Felice. The guy is full of hot air."

Logan ended the call. He ran his hand through his hair, shrugged his shoulders at the police officer, and pressed another line.

60

Phil was asleep. Jessie stood at his bed, hoping he would sense her presence and wake up on his own. She watched the rise and fall of his chest for a minute or so, then called his name.

He stirred, but his eyes remained shut.

"Phil?" A little louder this time.

His eyes fluttered open, and he gazed at her. He smiled weakly. "Twice in one day?"

"I have to talk to you."

He rubbed his eyes. "You sound upset. Something wrong?"

"Stan Weigund beat up Rosalynn Denby and practically choked her to death."

Phil frowned. "But she's alive?"

"The paramedics took her to UCLA. I just left her now. She's got several broken ribs, a broken arm, a broken cheekbone. And her larynx is swollen."

"Jesus." He sighed deeply.

"I've been trying to figure out how Weigund knew Rosalynn helped Vicky disappear."

Phil pulled himself up to a half-sitting position. "The media didn't mention her name?"

Jessie shook her head. "Gary was the one who told me about her. He's never talked to Weigund." She had checked with Gary on the way here. "Espes knows Rosalynn, but I can't imagine him having any connection with Weigund."

"Me, either. Maybe Weigund heard about her the same way Gary did and went to her on a hunch."

"I don't think so. Rosalynn told me Weigund knew she'd obtained the tape cassette and given it to Gary. How could he know that?"

Phil chewed on his lip.

"You're the only person who knew that, Phil," she said quietly. "I told you this morning, when I stopped by on my way downtown. Espes didn't know. I haven't had a chance to tell him."

Phil was scowling. "So what are you saying?"

"I know you didn't talk to Weigund, Phil, but somebody did."

"There must be another explanation, Jessie."

"Like what? Believe me, I'd be thrilled to hear it."

Again, he didn't answer.

"You said Frank Pruitt phoned this morning, Phil. That he wanted to tell me something about Weigund. You said he talked a lot." Pruitt, who was at Robbery-Homicide with Weigund. Pruitt, who had looked on impassively while she'd questioned Weigund's partner.

"Right. Just chatter, nothing important."

"Did you talk about the case?"

"Yeah, some."

"Did he ask you how we got the tape from Vicky Weigund?"

"No."

Not the answer she'd expected. She frowned. "You didn't mention Rosalynn Denby's name?"

"No. Why would I?"

"You're sure? You were kind of sleepy before."

"I said *no*, all right? I may be in a hospital gown, but my brain's still working."

He sounded defensive. Maybe he *had* told Pruitt—he *had* been sleepy all day, not really at his sharpest. Maybe he was afraid, or embarrassed, to admit it.

"I'm sorry," she said. "I'm just trying to figure this out. Maybe you're right. Maybe there's another explanation. You heard about what happened at the beach?"

He shook his head. "I've been asleep most of the afternoon."

"We almost got Weigund to take the amoxicillin to Molly. We met on the Venice boardwalk, and everything went fine." She described what had happened. "Anyway, Weigund threw the pills in the sand and practically laughed in Barry's face. But you know what I think?"

"What?"

Phil sounded curt, she thought. "I think he was already pissed off when he got there because Rosalynn Denby wouldn't tell him where Vicky is."

"Maybe."

"I'd better go. Get some more rest, okay?" She stood.

"It was Lou," he said, his voice mournful.

She stiffened. "Lou?"

Phil's face reddened. "I told him about the tape, about Rosalynn Denby. He was telling me he felt unneeded, unwanted."

She nodded. "This was earlier, when he was here?"

"Right. I didn't see why not to tell him, you know?"

"Of course not. How does he connect with Weigund?"

Phil shrugged. "No clue. Unless they worked together at another division."

"Where was Lou before he came to West L.A.?"

"Hollywood."

She licked her lips. "Weigund was at Hollywood."

She was lost in her own thoughts for a while, and assumed Phil was, too.

"Did you tell him about my Stuart Logan plan?"

Phil didn't answer right away. "I was half asleep when he was here. We talked a lot about the case." He paused. "The truth? I don't remember."

Damn, she thought. Damn, damn, damn.

Espes signaled to Jessie to shut his office door and waited until she was seated. "So?"

"I spoke to someone I know at Hollywood. Harris was Weigund's mentor when Weigund was a rookie. In fact, it's because of Harris that Weigund became a cop. Harris was with a Big Brothers group that helped foster-home kids. They took a liking to each other." She'd phoned the Restons, but neither Mildred nor Walter had known the name of the Big Brother who had befriended Weigund.

"That's still not proof."

She couldn't decide from Espes's dark look if he was angry or depressed. Probably both. That was how she felt. "Harris didn't mention to me or Phil—or anyone, for that matter—that he knew Weigund. That's suspicious, don't you think?"

"Maybe. Or he was too crushed to talk about it. Here's this young man he fathered and encouraged to follow in his footsteps."

"Maybe."

Espes rifled through the pages of a folder, then slammed the folder on his desk. "What the hell, I'm fooling myself. I guess I don't want to admit one of my detectives would turn."

She couldn't remember ever feeling sorry for the lieutenant before, but she did now.

"Okum doesn't know if he told Harris about the Stuart Logan thing?" Espes asked.

"He's not sure. I'd like to keep the phone trap on, just in case he didn't tell Harris."

"And if he did? What's your plan, Drake?"

Harris was looking her way when she returned to her desk. She caught his eye and smiled, then waved. She pretended to busy herself with a "blue book" and wasn't surprised when he appeared at her side a few minutes later.

"Everything okay?" he asked. "I hope Espes didn't dress you down because of what happened with the medicine. Simms talked to him, but I don't know what he said. He's a hothead."

"Espes was okay, and I don't really blame Simms for being upset. I'll talk to him." She and Simms had exchanged cold looks when she'd arrived at the station, and he'd glared at her as she'd passed his desk after leaving Espes's office.

"Well, that's good, then. I hear they got a videotape of the whole thing."

"They'll be playing it forever, and talking about it. Stuart Logan's already ripping into us for how we botched everything." An opening, if Harris wanted it.

"I don't listen to Logan. Too crude." He grimaced. "You took your time coming back to the station."

"I just came from UCLA. Stan Weigund beat up the woman who helped his wife disappear." She watched him carefully, saw him pale. "Her name is Rosalynn Denby."

Harris clucked. "The guy must be desperate. Is she badly hurt?" Very quiet.

"Pretty bad." Jessie described Rosalynn's injuries. "The good news is, she didn't tell Weigund where his wife is."

"Does she know?"

Jessie smiled. "That's the other good news. She can find out. She couldn't talk much, but she *did* say she could contact Vicky Weigund. I'm going back to the hospital in an hour or so to talk to Rosalynn."

"Want me to come along?"

"That's nice of you to offer, Lou." Snake, she thought. "I'm afraid she'll be gun-shy if she sees another cop, especially after what just happened. I'm surprised she trusts *any* cop, even me. She has police protection, though. I insisted on it."

Harris nodded.

"If you want, I'll call you after I see Rosalynn, and we can go talk to Vicky Weigund together. I'm going to beg her to call Dr. Renee's show and talk to Weigund. I don't know what else to do. I'm out of ideas." Again she waited for him to say something about Stuart Logan.

"Wish I had one to give you." He sighed. "Guess I'll be goin' on home."

"How about joining me for a bite to eat? I don't much feel like being alone."

He cocked his head. "You're sure? I had the feeling sometimes that you didn't much like having me around."

She smiled. "Maybe I was jealous. I know you and Phil are thick. Anyway, how about it?"

"Sounds nice. But just for a bite. I'm tuckered out."

He was probably expecting a call from Weigund. "I want to clear the air with Simms. Meet you downstairs in five, okay?"

She straightened her desk and waited until Harris was out of earshot, then walked over to Simms. He pretended not to know she was standing there. Baby, she thought.

"Talk to you a minute, Marty?"

He looked up and glowered. "I didn't say anything to Espes, if that's what you want to know."

She was about to retort that she hadn't done anything wrong. Another time, she told herself. "Someone here has been feeding Weigund information."

His eyes narrowed. "Who?"

"Lou Harris."

He snorted. "Come on."

She explained about Rosalynn Denby, about what she'd learned from Hollywood about Lou Harris and Weigund, and watched Simms's face darken. She explained about Stuart Logan and the fact that Phil may have told Harris.

"So we're screwed." Simms picked at his lip for a moment. "What's your plan?"

That's what Espes had asked. What was she, General Schwarzkopf? "I told Harris Rosalynn Denby can find out where Vicky is. I'm betting Weigund will contact him again. I just invited Harris to join me for dinner. I want you to get a subpoena and have a trap put on his phone before he gets home."

"It's four o'clock. I hope I can find a judge who'll do it in a hurry. How will phone security know which call to trace?"

She'd considered that. "I guess we'll have to trace each one."

"Lots of running around. Let's hope Harris doesn't have a lot of friends."

61

The kid was shivering, and her eyes were glassy. Weigund pulled the blanket up to her neck and dabbed at her forehead with a wet washcloth.

She whimpered, then started bleating like a lamb.

Shit, he didn't need this.

He threw the washcloth onto the bed and left the room. This was the goddamn father's fault. He, Weigund, had gone out of his way to help the kid. Not his problem that the father had run after him. If the kid died, he had only himself to blame.

Effing moron.

He went to the kitchen and poured himself a beer, then placed a call. One ring, two, three. After eight rings he slammed the receiver onto the wall unit.

Where the hell was he?

He took the beer into the living room and, sitting on the sofa, turned on the TV. They'd showed the videotape about ten minutes ago on NBC. He switched to a local station, and there it was again. A shot of the whole scene, then Detective Jessica Drake, pretty damn hot in shorts and a skimpy top.

There was the dad, running.

"Come on, asshole," Weigund urged, waving the beer bottle toward the screen. "You can do it. Pump those legs."

He smiled as he watched himself, looking pretty damn good himself, no extra ten pounds on him. Lean and mean.

The dad was on the sand now, a puppy sniffing for a bone. Then he was running again. Then he was on his knees, crying.

"Cut," Weigund said. "That's a wrap. The Oscar is yours, baby."

The large-haired anchor, Ms. Diane, appeared. Weigund shut

the TV with the remote before she could ruin the moment with her blather.

The radio was on. Stuart Logan was yakking about some stupid dog thing.

". . . special guest in the studio with us this afternoon, and that's none other than the man of the hour, Stan Weigund."

Weigund started. "What the—"

"I guess I was wrong when I said he didn't have the courage to talk to me, and I think we all want to hear what he has to say. So, Stan, my man, how'd a nice cop like you turn into a shmuck?"

The detective's face turned red.

"Hello, Stuart. Thanks for having me on your show," Logan said in a mincing falsetto. "I'll admit I was upset with you when I heard the nasty, nasty things you said about me, but of course, you didn't know the truth. That's why I'm here, to tell the world the truth."

Go ahead, wise guy, Weigund thought, bringing the beer bottle to his mouth.

"Stan, first off, what's with the voice?"

"Not too many people know this, Stuart. My name was Henrietta before I had a sex change. I'm low on hormones right now because I can't get to a pharmacy, and that's why I sound like this."

Weigund clenched his jaw.

"A sex change, huh? So you literally *didn't* have the balls to talk to me."

A tinklelike laugh. "Naughty, naughty, Stuart. You promised you'd be civil."

"You're right, sweetheart. So what happened? You had a great career, a great life. Why throw it all away?"

"It's a very sad story, Stuart. When I was five years old, I had my heart set on winning a red bicycle, but someone else won it. I've never gotten over that, Stuart. The devastating sense of loss, the grief. I felt a little better after I beat up the little girl who won the bike. But from that day on, I vowed that I would never be hungry again, as God is my witness."

"Sticks and stones, baby," Weigund muttered. He put the beer bottle on the coffee table and picked up his gun.

"You're quoting from *Gone With the Wind,* aren't you, Stan?"

"Yes. That's a beautiful movie, isn't it? I loved Scarlett's gowns. Anyway, that's why I won't lose Vicky and our little boy."

"Stan, why should Vicky come back to you after you beat her, killed a woman, and kidnapped a child?"

"Because she knows I love her, Stuart, with all my heart, and that I'm so sorry. Vicky, darling, if you're listening, this song is for you. 'Cause ai-iyai-iyai will always beat you-uh-ooh-uh-ooh.' "

"You heard it right here, on the Stuart Logan show. Thank you, Stan, for telling America the truth."

"Love hurts, baby. Thank *you*, Stuart."

Weigund had been clenching his teeth so hard, they hurt. He aimed the gun at the radio.

"Bang, bang, you're dead," he whispered.

He caressed the trigger with his finger, then put down the gun. In the kitchen, he phoned again. This time someone answered.

"Where the hell have you been?" Weigund demanded.

"At the station. Stan, you almost killed that woman. You promised me you wouldn't hurt her!"

"She was taunting me, Lou. It wasn't my fault."

Harris sighed. "Stan."

"Logan just did a real number on me. I'll deal with him later, don't you worry."

"I told you, Stan. He's trying to bait you so you'll call."

"Good thing you told me." Weigund grunted.

"How's the little girl?"

"Not good. But it's not my fault. You saw what happened."

"You have to take her to a hospital, Stan. You know that."

"No can do, Lou. Not until I see Vicky and the boy. All I want is to talk to her one time, just once. Then I'm out of here."

"You'll leave the country?"

"Yeah. You're right, Lou. It's too late for me. I can't stay. But you have to find Vicky."

"How do I know you won't kill her, Stan? You practically killed the Denby woman."

"I don't love the Denby woman, do I? But I love Vicky. She's the mother of my son, Lou."

"You hurt her bad before, Stan."

"Not as bad as they say. And I'm sorry for that. Lou, you know how I feel about her. You were at our wedding. You're Andy's godfather. Help me out, man." He waited.

"Drake said the Denby woman knows how to find Vicky."

Weigund nodded. "I thought the bitch was holding out."

"Drake is going to the hospital to talk to the Denby woman and get the info. Then we're going to visit Vicky together."

"When is Drake going to the hospital?"

"She's on the way there now. She said she'd call me when she knows."

"So when do you figure, an hour?"

"Something like that. Give me your number. I'll call you after I talk to her."

"No, I'll call you in about forty minutes or so."

"Could be later."

"I'll call again. Hell, I got nowhere to go."

62

"I thought you were going to call," Harris said.

He was standing in the doorway to his apartment in a T-shirt and jeans, a surprised expression on his face. No weapon, as far as Jessie could see.

"I figured I'd stop by instead. Great news. Rosalynn Denby came through, Lou. I know where Vicky Weigund is." She grinned. "We can go there right now."

Harris shook his head. "I can't leave just yet. I'm expecting an important call from my brother about our dad. He may have had a heart attack."

A call from Weigund. He'd probably phoned Harris earlier, but the trap hadn't been in place until ten minutes ago. Finding a judge had taken Simms a little longer than he'd expected. "Sorry to hear that, Lou. When do you expect him to call?"

"Hard to say. Look, I don't think we can afford to wait. Vicky's probably heard what happened to Rosalynn Denby. She won't feel safe staying where she is."

Jessie frowned. "Good point."

"Much as I want to be in on this, you'd better go yourself. Give me the address, and I'll join you as soon as I can."

"You know what? I'll give it fifteen minutes. Then I'll go on my own." She took a step toward him. "Aren't you going to let me in, Lou?" She smiled.

A brief hesitation. "Sure. No problem." He stepped aside.

Jessie walked in. Harris started to shut the door, but was pushed aside by Simms and Boyd, who had been hugging the wall in the narrow hall.

Boyd slammed the door shut. Simms punched Harris in the mouth, then grabbed his arms and held them behind him while Jessie patted him down.

Harris stared at her. Blood trickled out of the corner of his mouth. "What the hell is going on?"

Jessie stood up. "He's clean."

"Hardly." Simms shoved him down onto a blue vinyl sofa and drew his gun. He sat on the coffee table, inches away from Harris.

"I have his piece," Boyd said. He held up a holster and gun that had been on the kitchen table.

"Are you all crazy, or what?" Harris's eyes were riveted on the gun Simms was pointing at his chest. He wiped his mouth with the back of his hand.

"Cut the act, Harris." Jessie glared at him. "We know you've been talking to Weigund."

"That's a lie!"

"You were his mentor at Hollywood."

"So?"

"So you didn't mention that you even knew him."

"Would *you* have? He's a disgrace, an embarrassment."

"Good try." She sneered.

"You're wrong." He faced Simms. "I'm filing assault charges against you, you son of a bitch. You'll lose your badge."

"You told him about Rosalynn Denby," Jessie said. "He almost killed her, thanks to you."

Harris shook his head.

"You told him about Stuart Logan. You blew the one chance we had to get him. I hope you're proud."

"It wasn't me. Someone else, not me."

"We'll find out soon, when your brother calls. We'll see what he says." She looked around the room and noted a phone on the wall behind the dinette table. "Do you have another phone?" She started walking out of the living room.

"You have no right to go through my apartment!" he called after her.

She found a cordless phone on the nightstand in his bedroom and brought it back to the living room.

"Here's what's going to happen," she said. "Weigund is going to call to find out where Vicky is."

"You're wrong. I haven't talked to Weigund in weeks."

"You're going to tell him she's at a place on Wilcox, south of Hollywood." A vacant house where two units were already positioned. Jessie handed Harris a slip of paper on which she'd written the exact address. "You'll tell him that I and another detective are taking her into protective custody and moving her to a safe house tonight."

"He's not going to call. He's—"

"If he asks, tell him I'm going to talk to Vicky in an hour or so, without you, as soon as I have the address of the safe house, and that you won't be able to find out where she is after that." The idea was to push Weigund to act, so that he would leave the house, and Molly, and they could rescue her as quickly and safely as possible.

Harris's shoulders sagged. He shut his eyes. "You don't understand," he whispered. "Weigund—"

"Shut up," she snapped. "I'll be on the extension, listening to every word you say. Simms is going to be right here, and he is just itching for an excuse to blow you away. If I were you, I wouldn't give him one. If he shoots, he'll shoot to kill."

"I'm unarmed!"

"You won't be when they find you. And I'll swear you tried to take him out first."

"You are all certifiable," Harris said, but his voice lacked conviction.

She handed the cordless phone to Boyd, then walked to the dinette and sat on one of the chairs.

They waited.

Five minutes passed, then ten.

The phone rang. Jessie's heart was pumping madly. "One wrong word, Harris," she warned. "Boyd, answer on my count of three, so there's no double click.

Boyd nodded.

She moved her hand to the receiver. "One, two, three." She lifted the receiver.

Boyd held the cordless phone to Harris's ear.

Simms moved his gun closer to Harris's face, which was sickly white and bathed in sweat.

"Hello?"

"Did you get it?"

Weigund's voice. Jessie's stomach muscles tightened.

"Yeah, I got it." He darted his tongue across his upper lip and looked down.

"Where is she, Lou?"

"In a house on Wilcox." He read the address from the paper in his shaking hand. "But they're taking her into protective custody tonight and moving her to a safe house."

"When are you and Drake going to talk to her?"

"I'm not going. Drake is, in about an hour, as soon as they give her the address of the safe house." He looked at Jessie. "I don't think I'll be able to help you after that, Stan."

"Who's with her now?"

Harris looked at Jessie. She shook her head.

"No one," Harris said. "Just Vicky and Andy. Drake just found out where she is."

"Thanks, man. I owe you. You won't regret this, Lou. I'm not going to hurt Vicky. I just want to see her one more time."

"Be careful, okay?"

Weigund hung up.

"I didn't mean for anyone to get hurt," Harris whined just before Simms slammed his fist into his nose.

63

They had Weigund's location: an address in Palms, near Over-
land. A twenty-five- to thirty-minute drive to Wilcox. A little
closer from Harris's apartment in Los Feliz, not far from the
academy. How rich was that?

It was a hard call, deciding whether she should go to Molly
or to the Wilcox address. In the end she chose Wilcox, not because she didn't want to be at Molly's side—she ached to hold
the little girl, to soothe her. But she needed to see Weigund
brought down, needed to know it was over.

Boyd stayed with Harris in the apartment, in case Weigund
phoned again. Jessie radioed West L.A. from Simms's car and
was put in touch with Espes. He was sending units in unmarked
vehicles to the Palms address. They would make certain Weigund
was gone before they entered the house to rescue Molly. Paramedics were on call.

Jessie was too pumped up to talk and assumed Simms felt the
same. She drummed her fingers nervously on the leather seat and
bit her tongue when he almost sideswiped a Suburban. It seemed
wrong to be sitting next to someone other than Phil.

"Phil's gonna be pissed he's missing this," Simms said, as if
reading her mind.

"Yeah."

He drove west down Franklin, below the HOLLYWOOD sign,
south on Vine, then made a right onto Sunset, a wide but otherwise unspectacular boulevard that took on glitz only west of La
Cienega, and even then needed the seduction of night and
neon lights.

She checked her watch and saw that eight minutes had elapsed
since they'd left Harris's apartment. Almost thirteen from the

time Weigund had hung up the phone. By now he must have left the Palms house, and she wondered anxiously why Dispatch hadn't radioed to tell her Molly Altman was safe.

Simms slowed as they neared the address. Weigund couldn't have arrived here yet, but she checked all the cars anyway, looking for his black Mustang. She didn't recognize any unmarked cars, either. A good thing—if she spotted them, Weigund would, too.

Dusk was falling. Simms parked at the end of the block, and they hurried to the small pink house with the picket fence and neat yard.

There were two male plainclothes officers inside. Simms and Jessie identified themselves and checked out the house. All the blinds were shut, the drapes drawn. There were two entrances— the front door, which was solid oak, and the side door, with a large glass pane, that led into the laundry room.

Earlier, while Harris thought she was at UCLA, talking with Rosalynn Denby, Jessie had tried to make the place look lived in: Stocked the fridge. Rinsed some dishes and cutlery, which she'd left to dry on a drain board. Slung towels over the shower door. Scattered toys around the house—Legos and a Tonka truck that she kept at her house for her nephew, Matthew. Unmade the master bed. Strewed little-boy clothes in the smaller bedroom and fashioned a "sleeping" form tucked under the comforter. Not that it would fool Weigund if he got close enough to look. . . .

Jessie switched on a table lamp in the living room and the overhead fluorescent fixture in the kitchen. She left the living and dining room drapes drawn, but partially opened the miniblinds in the two bedrooms so that Weigund could "sneak" a look and see that the place was occupied. She and Simms decided against turning on the radio, but she turned on the TV in the living room.

She positioned herself in the smaller bedroom, at the end of the outer wall, away from the window and out of sight. She left the door to the room ajar. Simms was in the bathroom connecting the bedroom with the laundry room. One of the officers was in the master bathroom; the other officer, behind a sofa in the living room.

The waiting made her jumpy. She checked her watch too often, unable to stop herself. Thirty-two minutes had passed from the time Weigund had ended the call. He should be here any minute.

If he came. She worried that he'd detected something wrong in Harris's voice. Maybe that was why Dispatch hadn't notified her that Molly was safe.

She had been standing motionless on the carpeted floor. Her

legs felt stiff. She flexed one, then the other, and heard a twig snap.

She tensed. Her weapon was drawn. She unlocked the safety and flattened herself against the wall.

A creaking sound.

He was trying to open the window. She inhaled sharply, felt her ribs against her chest wall.

Silence. Another twig being snapped.

She strained her ears, but heard only the pounding of her heart.

A moment later she heard a tap. The side door?

Then the distinct tinkle of breaking glass.

The door opened almost, but not quite, soundlessly. She heard a soft, rubber-soled footstep, and crossed the room with silent speed to stand behind the partially opened door.

Another footstep, and another. She knew he was in the hall, just feet away from the entrance to the bedroom.

The footsteps stopped.

Maybe he sensed something was wrong. Even with the TV on, the house was too quiet, with no sound of Vicky or Andy.

Jessie inched forward, her weapon at her side, and stole a glance through the half inch opening between the door frame and the door.

He was just standing there, frowning, frozen in place.

She was about to move when he took a step inside the room. She held her breath.

He walked toward the bed and the small mound under the blanket.

"Police! Freeze!" she yelled. Heart pumping madly. Legs apart, both hands gripping the weapon she was aiming at his back.

Weigund whirled around. His hand dove inside his jacket.

"Don't try it!" she warned.

Simms was beside her in an instant, his weapon aimed at Weigund. A moment later the two plain clothes officers arrived.

Weigund grinned. "I figured this was a setup, but hell, I had to try. Got to see my family, right?"

"Move your hand very, very slowly from your jacket, Weigund," Jessie ordered. "Place both hands on your head."

He shook his head. "I don't think so. What I think is, I'm going to walk out of here. Once I'm sure I'm not being followed, I'll call you and let you know where you can find the kid."

"We have the kid, you son of bitch," Simms snarled.

"Do you?" Another smug grin. "I wouldn't bet on that. You

think I'm stupid enough to walk in to this, knowing it could be a setup, without taking some insurance?"

"You're bluffing," Simms said.

"You say that, but you can't be sure." He glanced at her. "Detective Drake isn't sure at all. Are you, sweetheart?"

Dispatch hadn't called. The fact pounded in Jessie's head. She kept her face expressionless.

"You don't have a chance, Weigund," Simms said. "Game's over."

"Well, go ahead." Weigund nodded. "Take me out. Four against one, be a pissant hero. But then you'll *never* find that little girl in time. Did I mention the poor thing's practically unconscious? What kind of hero will you be then, huh?" He faced Jessie again. "Your partner may not care about kids, but you do, don't you?"

"Put your hands on your head," Jessie ordered again, then addressed one of the officers. "Kolakowski, call Dispatch. Find out if they have the Altman girl."

The officer nodded and hurried away.

"Wish I could stick around and find out the ending." Weigund smiled. "But I have places to go, people to meet. I'm counting to three and leaving."

"Make a move and you're dead," Simms warned.

"And so's the little girl. Bye-bye, Miss Molly." He took a step sideways toward the doorway.

"I don't think so." Simms cocked his weapon.

"Wait," Jessie told him.

"Your choice," Weigund said. "I got nothing to lose, but no way am I gonna let you take me in. Let me go, I tell you where the kid is. We both win."

"No choice," Simms said. "Put your hands on your head."

The two men stared at each other.

"All right." Weigund nodded. "All right. I guess you got me. I had you going though, didn't I?" He smiled wryly.

Jessie allowed herself a silent exhalation of relief. Simms looked grimly pleased.

"Women." Weigund shrugged. "Can't live with 'em, can't live without 'em. I'm taking out my hand now, okay?"

"Nice and slow," Simms said.

Weigund's hand whipped out. She saw the glint of metal, then the ugly hole of a gun barrel staring right at her.

By then Simms had fired, and so had she.

(("64"))

Weigund's eyes widened in shock. He staggered, then crumpled to the floor. The room was filled with the acrid scent of gunpowder.

"Call for an ambulance," Jessie instructed the other officer.

Blood was seeping out of a small blackened hole near the center of Weigund's chest and from another wound a few inches higher. Still aiming her gun at him, she bent down and picked up his weapon just as Kolakowski entered the room, breathless.

He stared at Weigund.

"Well?" she demanded.

"They don't have her."

"Jesus!" she whispered. For a moment she couldn't breathe.

Simms clenched his jaw and turned aside.

"The place was cleaned out when they got there," Kolakowski reported. "Closets empty. No sign that he planned to come back."

Especially if he suspected that the police might be on to him, Jessie realized.

Simms was leaning over Weigund, who was groaning.

"Where is she, Weigund?"

Weigund grunted. Beads of sweat had formed on his forehead, and he looked ashen. "Not such a big hero after all, are you?" He smiled thinly.

"Come on, goddamn it!" Simms hissed. "Do one decent thing in your lousy life."

Weigund spit at him.

Simms's face reddened. He wiped the spittle off his face, then grabbed the man's bloodied shirt. "Where the hell is she, you piece of shit!"

"Marty," Jessie said quietly.

Simms jerked his head up and glared at her. He released Weigund's shirt, stood up, and stomped out of the room.

Jessie crouched at Weigund's side and took his hand. His pulse was faint. "Tell us where she is, Stan."

"Too bad you thought I was bluffing, huh?" A spasm of pain twisted his smile into a grotesque leer.

"They'll go easier on you if you tell us. You know that's true."

He winced, then bit down hard on his bottom lip. "What I know is, I'm not . . . gonna make it. So what the hell . . . difference does it make?"

"Do the right thing, Stan. You won't be sorry."

"Right for who?" He took a labored breath. "For Dr. Renee?" Another breath. "Brought . . . this on herself."

"The little girl didn't do anything to hurt you."

Weigund didn't answer. He was breathing in loud, greedy gulps.

"Think about your boy. Andy, right? Think about what Andy would want you to do."

"Andy wanted . . . be with *me*," Weigund whispered, his eyes hard. "She ruined it all. Took him . . . away. *Poisoned* him against me."

Renee, or Vicky? Not that it mattered. Jessie squeezed his hand. "Make Andy proud, Stan. Give him something good to remember his father by."

He smiled.

"Come on, Stan. You have nothing to lose." She looked into his eyes and was chilled by their emptiness.

"Screw . . . all of you." He turned his head aside and shut his eyes. He coughed up blood.

Jessie turned and glanced up at Kolakowski. "Could they tell if the girl had been there?"

"They found a packaged thermometer on the nightstand in one of the bedrooms and some kid's aspirin. A doll, too. No blanket on the bed."

Maybe he'd wrapped her in it. "Any sign of where he might have taken her?"

Kolakowski shook his head.

Weigund hadn't had much time to plan, Jessie thought. He must have left almost immediately after talking to Harris. No time to take Molly anywhere else, but he hadn't left her there, either. He'd needed to take some insurance, he'd said. He'd—

"The car!" she exclaimed, rising quickly. "He took her along with him in his car. Stay with him," she instructed Kolakowski.

She ran out of the room and out the side door toward the street, where Simms was pacing.

"Weigund's black Mustang," she yelled. "Did you spot it?"

Simms turned toward her and shook his head. "Why?"

"I think Molly's in it!" Half hope, half conviction.

She raced up the block while Simms began running in the other direction. Car after car, too many of them black or some other dark shade deepened by the inky pen of falling night.

She found the Mustang a block and a half away. The doors were locked, the windows shut. Nothing on the front seat or back bench, but there was a blanket on the floor in the rear, and Jessie could barely make out, peeking over the satin border, a fringe of blond hair.

Molly!

She took her gun and slammed the barrel hard, again and again, on the front passenger window. Finally, the window shattered. She reached inside carefully and, unlocking the door, yanked it open, aware of the irony that the car alarm was blaring.

Seconds later, with the rear door unlocked, she crawled over the bench and lifted the blanket. The little girl lay frighteningly still, and Jessie couldn't see any movement of her chest.

Her heart lurched. She leaned over Molly carefully, placed her ear to her chest, and groaned with relief when she heard the steady beating. She touched the little girl's forehead. Impossibly hot.

Molly's eyes fluttered open. Glassy, too bright. "Mommy?" she whimpered.

Jessie wanted to cradle her and kiss her fears away, but was afraid to move her. She took Molly's hand. "Mommy's coming soon, angel."

The little girl nodded. She shut her eyes, then opened them again. "Is the monster gone?" she whispered.

"All gone, Molly." Jessie stroked her cheek and smoothed the sweat-dampened tendrils off her forehead. "The monster is all gone."

(("**65**"))

Molly's skin was a worrisome translucent pearly gray. She looked painfully tiny and fragile in the hospital bed, and Jessie felt like crying when she saw her early Friday morning.

But she would be all right, Renee said. Her body had been weakened by a raging infection, but she was responding to the antibiotics being administered with the IV saline solution.

"Another few hours without antibiotics, though . . ." Renee hugged her arms. "I don't want to think about what would have happened if you hadn't found her."

Jessie didn't want to, either. Nor did she want to think about the psychological trauma Molly had suffered, trauma that would leave scars long after her body had healed.

Renee looked so tired, Jessie thought. She and Barry had kept an all-night vigil at Molly's side here in the Cedars-Sinai pediatric intensive care unit. They hadn't slept much in the preceding days, either.

"Has she said anything?" Jessie asked. They were standing outside the door to Molly's room. Barry had gone for a cup of coffee.

"No. She's not unconscious, just sleeping. The doctors said that's normal." She turned to gaze at Molly, visible through the open door to her room, then faced Jessie again. "I can't believe she's here. I keep thinking I'm going to wake up and find out that this is all a dream, that she's still with that monster."

The monster was dead. Jessie wasn't sure which bullet had killed him, hers or Simms's. An autopsy and ballistics would determine that.

"Barry said your parents are driving up. I can imagine their relief."

Renee's face tightened. "That'll last for about an hour. Then they'll let me know this was all my fault. The kidnapping, the divorce."

Wrong subject, Jessie realized.

"The good news is, I'll probably be at the station when they arrive. I wasn't going to. I wanted to be here when Molly wakes up. But the doctors said she'll probably be sleeping all day, and Barry said go. And I think I owe it to my listeners to reassure them, you know?"

Jessie knew what Manny would say: NPD. Maybe, maybe not. "Barry told me you went to his apartment yesterday afternoon to comfort him about what happened at the beach. That was very kind of you, Renee." And surprising. Maybe this was a gentler, softer Renee, one who would be more sensitive with her callers, less ruthless.

"I knew he must've been despondent. I was afraid he might do something desperate, and I wanted to tell him I knew he'd done it to save Molly."

"You seem less angry with each other."

Renee looked thoughtful. "I'm not angry, not anymore. When I heard what he did, I wanted to kill him. But when I saw him on that videotape, my heart went out to him. The anger just seeped away." She shrugged. "I'm a shrink, and I can't figure it out."

"I'm glad for your sake, and Molly's."

She nodded. "Barry and I talked last night. I don't know how we'll work things out, but we will. Whatever's best for her."

Jessie hesitated. "Any chance of a reconciliation?"

"I don't think so. We've drifted too far apart, inflicted too much damage on each other. We want different things."

"Don't you want to try, if just for Molly's sake?"

"I can't believe I'm saying this—it goes against everything I've ever preached." She smiled wryly. "Molly is better off with two happy parents, apart, than two parents living together who hate each other. Not that I hate Barry." She sounded wistful.

"He doesn't hate you, either. He doesn't know who you are."

Renee sighed. "You were always the incurable romantic, Jessie."

She supposed she was. She liked happy endings, would have liked one for herself and Gary. Maybe that was why she'd held on so long. She wondered what he would say if she went to him and said, *Yes, I'll marry you,* and knew she wouldn't do it. Pride, maybe. Or maybe it was just over. Time would tell.

She went to visit Phil. She'd stopped by last night, after visiting Rosalynn, but had stayed only long enough to tell him what had happened. She'd been bone-tired after the adrenaline had worn off, desperate to crawl into her bed.

She found him stuffing toiletries into a small black satchel.

"They're letting you go home?" she asked.

He looked up. "They can't find anything wrong. Maureen's a little disappointed. I think she wanted them to scare the hell out of me so I'd get serious about losing weight."

"Are you? Going to get serious, I mean?"

"Yeah. I figure this was as big a wake-up call as I want." He grimaced. "I'm taking the day off, though. Just me and Maureen, quality time. So how's Molly Altman?"

"Holding her own." She repeated what Renee had told her.

"Thank God they got to her in time. I'm glad everything turned out okay."

He still sounded uncomfortable. She debated bringing up Lou Harris and decided to let it go. Some things, she'd learned, needed time's softening touch, not dissection.

At the station she typed a report on yesterday's events, paying particular attention to the shooting of Weigund. In the world of bad, Weigund was up there, but she and Simms still had to show that he'd posed an imminent lethal threat.

She reviewed her notes and found herself smiling when she read about Stuart Logan. He'd been relieved when she'd explained that Harris had told Weigund about their plan.

"So I didn't blow my first undercover assignment," he'd said.

"You did great," she'd told him, meaning it.

She made a mental note to show her thanks. Lunch, maybe. She imagined lunch with Stuart Logan would be a great deal of fun. She could use a little fun, she decided. She was entitled.

She was on the phone, talking to yet another relative of the slain Iranian rug dealer, when a medium-height, blond-haired woman approached her desk. She looked vaguely familiar, and Jessie tried to figure out where she'd seen her.

"Detective Drake?"

She recognized the voice, though she'd heard it only once. She pushed her chair back and stood. "Mrs. Weigund?"

The woman extended a slim, bony hand. "I just came from Rosalynn. I don't know how to thank you, Detective. I honestly don't." Her lips trembled. "If you hadn't . . ."

Jessie squeezed her hand. "I'm glad you and your son are okay."

"Andy and I are going to be fine. We have a new life. We don't have to run anymore." She took out her wallet and showed

Jessie a snapshot of a towheaded child. "The best, bravest little boy, you can't even imagine."

She wanted to know about Molly, was visibly relieved to learn that she would be fine. "I keep thinking about that poor housekeeper," she said softly. "And her family. It's so hard . . ." Her lips trembled. "It's so very hard to know that so many people have been hurt because of me."

"Don't," Jessie said. "None of this is your fault."

The woman started crying. Jessie stepped closer and put an arm around her tentatively. And then Vicky Weigund was sobbing, her body heaving convulsively, and Jessie was crying, too, hugging tightly this woman she'd never met before and would probably never see again, this woman whose life had filled her thoughts for so many days.

She kissed Jessie on the cheek. "God bless you," she said softly, grasping both of Jessie's hands in hers.

And she was gone.

Jessie had planned to leave the station by ten-thirty, but it was well after twelve when she drove out of the parking lot. She turned on the radio and, curious, pushed the button preset for KMST.

". . . went to his apartment, and I think he must've drugged my drink, because when I woke up, my clothes were off. So I don't know if he raped me, Dr. Renee. And I wanted to know if you thought I should file charges."

"*File charges*, Donna? You're the one who should be charged, with aggravated stupidity. You went to a man's apartment, alone, had drinks, and you want me to feel *sorry* for you? This is the problem with women today who grow up without morals and abdicate all common sense and responsibility. Do you really think . . ."

Jessie sighed, and switched to her oldies station.

Dafna was wearing a taupe hat today. Jessie caught her attention and waited in the entrance to the women's section, which seemed less forbidding, though she'd been here only an hour yesterday.

"I'm glad you came back." Dafna smiled. "I'm so sorry you weren't able to join us for lunch yesterday. Can you make it today?"

"I'd love to."

Frances had phoned last night to ask if Jessie had changed her mind about joining her and Helen for lunch. Sorry, Jessie had said, and Frances hadn't been as difficult.

Frances had heard from Helen that Jessie and Gary were probably getting engaged. "It's about time," Frances had said. And Jessie had to tell her she and Gary had decided to be friends. She dreaded telling Helen, who had been so happy for Jessie, so pleased to have played a part in helping her older sister decide.

"Well, you're not getting any younger, Jessica," Frances said. "I noticed some lines around your eyes, and you could lose at *least* five pounds, dear. I didn't mention it, but now that you'll be looking again, it's something you should take care of."

Jessie tried to remember the affection she'd felt for her mother less than a week ago. She supposed there would be other tender moments. She would have to horde them and let them tide her over during what promised to be a long winter.

She sat in the same seat she'd occupied yesterday, and received smiles of recognition from the women on either side. She'd missed the Torah reading, and the first few rounds of shofar blasts. The cantor was leading the congregation in an acrostic hymn. She followed along in English, then paged back to the day's Torah reading, the one that dealt with Abraham offering his only son as a sacrifice.

Isaac had been spared through God's will. Maybe Molly had been spared through God's will, too. Molly, and Vicky Weigund and her son, Andy. And Rosalynn Denby, that brave, brave woman.

And Weigund was dead. God's will, too? Where did God's will end and her responsibility begin? She wasn't sorry Weigund was dead—for a split second she'd been gratified, she admitted, to see his gun, had *wanted* him dead, not alive, until worry had taken over that he wasn't bluffing, that he'd hidden Molly somewhere, that they wouldn't find her in time. And then she'd had no choice but to shoot, because he'd aimed his gun right at her. But there was something undeniably awesome in the taking of a human life, no matter how worthless, how base, something that shook her to the core, and she supposed her soul had been tarnished by the act, no matter how legal, how just.

She looked through the latticework of the mechitzah and saw Ezra stepping up to the platform where the rabbi would soon blow the final blasts of the shofar. He turned around and saw her, and she was warmed by his broad smile, by the caring in his eyes. She wondered what Frances would make of him if they ever met.

"Tekiah."

She rose with the congregation and, shutting her eyes, waited for the pure sounds of the ram's horn to work their magic.